Senlac was awarded the Book Vi
Award in the category of

Senlac was awarded the Historical Fiction Company's
Bronze Medal for Historical Fiction of England, Scotland
and Ireland.

More Books from
The Sager Group

Chains of Nobility: Brotherhood of the Mamluks (Book 1)

A Lion's Share: Brotherhood of the Mamluks (Book 2)

The Swamp: Deceit and Corruption in the CIA
An Elizabeth Petrov Thriller (Book 1)

The Living and the Dead

Three Days in Gettysburg

Vetville: True Stories of the U.S. Marines

Straight Fish: A Correctional Officer's Story

Miss Havilland: A Novel

The Orphan's Daughter: A Novel

Lifeboat No. 8: Surviving the Titanic

SCOTLAND

Stamford Bridge

York

Fulford Gate

Irish Sea

Humber

ENGLAND

North Sea

Chester

Lincoln

Trent

Nottingham

Norwich

Warwick

Huntingdon

Ely

Cambridge

Worcester

Gloucester

Little Berkhamsted

Colchester

Oxford

Dorchester

Wallingford

London

Thames

Winchester

Canterbury

Dover

Hastings

Lewes

Pevensey

Senlac Hill

Exeter

St Valery-sur-Somme

English Channel

N

Seine

Rouen

Bayeux

Dives

Bec

Coutances

Evreux

Duchy of Normandy

Avranches

Mont-St-Michel

FRANCE

Maine

Senlac

A Novel *of the* Norman Conquest *of* England

BOOK TWO

JULIAN DE LA MOTTE

This is a work of fiction. Many of the details, places, characters, and events were inspired by real life; many have been altered for the purposes of the narrative. Any resemblance to actual living persons is entirely coincidental.

Senlac: A Novel of the Norman Conquest of England (Book Two)
Julian De La Motte

Cover Designed and Illustrated by Siori Kitajima, SF AppWorks LLC

Cataloging-in-Publication data for this book is available from the Library of Congress
ISBN-13:
eBook: 978-1-950154-35-7
Paperback: 978-1-950154-34-0
Published by The Sager Group LLC
TheSagerGroup.net

Senlac

A Novel *of the* Norman Conquest *of* England

BOOK TWO

JULIAN DE LA MOTTE

THE SAGER GROUP

Artifex Te Adiuva

LIST OF CHARACTERS

The English

Adelbert, Companion of Harold

Aeldyth, Sister of Edwin and Morcar and wife of Harold [*]

Aelfwig, Uncle of Harold and Abbot of New Minster Winchester [*]

Aelfwold, Abbot of St Benet

Aesegar, Shire Reeve of Middlesex and Port Reeve of London

Adelbert, Physician to Edward the Confessor [*]

Agatha, Mother of Edgar Aetheling [*]

Alfi, Companion of Harold

Amund, Danish deputy of Tostig in York [*]

Arnaud of Mons, Navigator, pirate and translator

Bjorn, Danish second cousin to Harold and companion

Caedmon, Welsh personal Chaplain to Harold

Ceofwyn, Companion of Harold

Copsig, Chief Deputy of Tostig [*]

Eadmar, Companion of Harold

Eadric, 'Steersman,' Master of the Fleet [*]

Ealdred, Bishop of York [*]

Edgar Aetheling, Blood heir to the English Throne [*]

Edith Godwinsdottir, Wife of Edward and sister of Harold [*]

Edith, 'Swan neck,' Common law wife of Harold [*]

Edward, 'The Confessor,' King of England [*]

Edwin Aelfgarson, Earl of Mercia [*]

Gareth, Welsh hostage and companion of Harold

Godric, Shire Reeve of Berkshire [*]

Godwin, Eldest son of Harold and Edith [*]

Grimketl, Leader of the Danish mercenaries at Hastings

Gyrth Godwinson, Earl of East Anglia and brother of Harold [*]
Gytha, Wife of Godwin and mother of the Godwinsons [*]
Gytha, Daughter of Harold and Edith
Gunhild, Daughter of Harold and Edith
Haakon, Nephew of Harold [*]
Harold, Earl of Wessex and King of England [*]
Harold, Youngest son of Harold and Edith
Judith, Flemish wife of Tostig [*]
Leofgar, Companion of Harold
Leofric, Bishop of Exeter [*]
Leofwyn Godwinson, Earl of Kent and brother of Harold [*]
Magnus, Second son of Harold and Edith [*]
Morcar Aelgarson, Earl of Northumbria and brother of Edwin [*]
Odde, Servant to Edith Godwinsdottir
Oswy, Manservant to Harold
Ravensweart, Danish deputy of Tostig in York
Stigand, Archbishop of Canterbury [*]
Thorri Arnulfson, Anglo Danish merchant of York
Tostig Godwinson, Deposed Earl of Northumbria and brother of Harold [*]
Thurkill of Bedford [*]
Ulf, Son of Harold and Edith
Wulfnoth Godwinson, Brother of Harold [*]
Wulfstan, Bishop of Worcester [*]

The Normans and Their Allies

Agatha, Daughter of William [*]
Aimery, Anglo Norman translator
Drogo FitzPons, Squire to William
Bigod, Norman nobleman [*]
Bohun, Norman nobleman [*]
De Tosny, Norman nobleman [*]
Eustace, Count of Boulogne, Vassal to William [*]
Fulk of Anjou, Norman ally [*]

Geoffrey Malet, Younger brother of William Malet

Gerald Seneschal, Norman nobleman and government official [*]

Gilbert, ArchDeacon of Lisieux [*]

Hugh FitzPons, Squire to William

Hugh de Avranches, Norman nobleman [*]

Hugh de Grandesmil, Norman nobleman [*]

Hugh de Montfort, Norman nobleman [*]

Hugh Margot, Monk of Falaise [*]

Ivo de Claire, Norman nobleman [*]

Lanfranc, Italian born Abbot of Bec and a chief advisor to William [*]

Martin, ship master of the invasion fleet

Matilda, Duchess of Normandy. Flemish wife of William [*]

Maurilius, Bishop of Rouen [*]

Odo, Bishop of Bayeux. Half brother to William of Normandy [*]

Richard de Evreux, Norman nobleman [*]

Riwallon of Dol, Breton nobleman and rebel [*]

Robert FitzWimarch, Anglo Breton landowner and spy to William [*]

Robert of Belleme, Frontier nobleman [*]

Robert. Count of Eu, Leading Norman ally [*]

Robert 'Curthose,' Eldest son of William [*]

Robert of Mortain, Half brother to William of Normandy [*]

Roger of Beaumont, Leading nobleman and supporter of William [*]

Roger of Montgomery, Leading nobleman and supporter of William [*]

Taillefer, Minstrel and freelance Knight [*]

Thibault, Craftsman and engineer

Walter Giffard, Norman nobleman [*]

William, Duke of Normandy [*]

William de Warenne, Norman nobleman {*]

William FitzOsbern, Leading nobleman and friend of

William [*]
William Malet, Anglo Norman landowner and spy to William [*]
William 'Rufus,' Youngest son of William [*]

Other Involved Parties

Baldwin, Count of Flanders [*]
Erlend, Joint Earl of Orkney [*]
Elizabeth of Kiev, One of the two wives of Harald Hardraada [*]
Eyestein Orri, prospective son in law of Harald Hardraada [*]
Godfrey Govan, son of Harald 'The Black' [*]
Guthorn, Companion of Harald Hardraada
Harald Hardraada, King of Norway [*]
Harald 'The Black,' the most powerful Chieftain in Ireland [*]
Konfostre, Norwegian advisor to Tostig
Lachlan Strachan, Port Reeve of Leith
Magnus, Son of Harald Hardraada [*]
Malcolm, King of Alba [*]
Nicholas, Brother of Eyestein Orri [*]
Olaf, Son of Harald Hardraada [*]
Paul, Joint Earl of Orkney [*]
Stryker, Marshal of Harald Hardraada [*]
Stump, Seer and advisor to Harold Hardraada
Sweyn Estrithson, King of Denmark [*]
Thora Thorbergsdottir, One of the two wives of Harald Hardraada [*]
Ulf Ospaksson, Advisor and companion of Harald Hardraada

[*] = historical figure

FOREWORD

Close on to one thousand years ago one of the most significant and far-reaching of all the events of the entire European medieval period occurred within the space of a single year. Although this took some time to evolve and to come about, it occurred in just twelve calendar months. This event was to have consequences that were profound and far-reaching in many ways: political, social, economic and linguistic. They were to affect the English-speaking world for centuries to come and, indeed, are still with us today.

It is the responsibility of the serious historian to attempt to assemble all the facts and information available from a variety of different sources. These are often highly contradictory and often with a heavily weighted bias of views and opinions that are both contemporary and are also coloured by the writings of subsequent individuals and schools of thought. Faced with this often-difficult task it is, then, the historian's task to attempt to arrive at an accurate and objective summary of the event or events in question.

It is also the task of the creator of historical fiction to bear all of the above in mind whilst attempting at the same time to form a creative narrative that the reader will find both compelling and absorbing. The chief problem in creating such a narrative of the event in question is that, whereas much is generally known and thus generally held to be true and much, indeed, has been subsequently written, very few contemporary or near contemporary sources actually exist, throwing the writer back on his or her own imagination. Historical accuracy and a compelling narrative are the twin objectives of historical fiction.

Such is the task facing the writer of a work on the subject of the year 1066, the tumultuous year of the Norman Conquest.

I am deeply indebted to the patience, understanding and forbearance of Anna, my wife, in the research and writing of this work and to the highly motivating encouragement of my old friend Charles McNair and to Mike Sager, who brought all this together and made it possible.

Julian de la Motte

Contents

A Synopsis of Book One

At the end of Volume One of 'Senlac', the story had arrived at the point of the Summer and early Autumn of the year 1066; the scene was set for a final, bloody, and irreversible encounter that would have profound effects on thousands of people for hundreds of years to come.

The years of 1064 and 1065, covered in the first volume of Senlac saw the emergence of a powerful and vibrant military state, the Duchy of Normandy, governed by the determined and single-minded Duke William. Temporarily without immediate outside enemies and conscious of the danger presented by the ambitions of his own volatile subjects, he finds a focus for his considerable energies upon learning of the death of Edward, the old King of England, in the Christmas period of 1065, and also in the coronation of his former guest and supposed ally, Harold, Earl of Wessex.

This was a throne and a Kingdom William believed to be rightfully his, through blood links and the promises person-ally made to him by Harold, Earl of Wessex, himself during an unintended and enforced stay in Normandy the previous year. Determined to revenge and to seek a pressure valve for his own turbulent, and not entirely trustworthy subjects, William sets about the planning of a single throw of the dice; the invasion of the rich, prosperous and much-coveted Kingdom of England, a venture that would either make him or destroy him forever.

In England, Harold, the most powerful man in the Kingdom and the brother in law of the dead Edward, and in the absence of any direct heir, is elected the new King by popular acclaim. Beset with seemingly overwhelming difficulties, haunted by terrifying premonitions, desperate for allies, he is forced to set aside his own beloved common law wife and children in favour of marriage to the sister of two powerful and unreliable men, the new Earl of Northumbria and his brother, the Earl of Mercia. He could feel little confidence in them and their grandiose promises to protect the North for him against the constant threat of invasion from Norway, and the old and half-deranged Viking adventurer, Harald Hardraada.

Meanhwhile, Harold's brother, Tostig, the former Earl of Northumbria, is now in exile and is an implacable and treacherous enemy, seeking the support of four alien states in his search for revenge against his brother the King. Tostig finds support in this in the old King of Norway, the most feared warrior in the whole of Europe, and his own schemes for one last great and glorious Viking adventure.

Knowing from personal experience the power and the threat posed by the growing power across the English Channel, Harold is obliged to balance this against the traditional and undeniable threat from Scandinavia. In a desperate balancing of his resources and manpower, with the harvest lying ungathered and the threat of famine, his finances fast evaporating, Harold must seek a solution to the combined threats of a treacherous brother, a vengeful Duke, and a fearsome and terrifying man from the north.

With the Norman fleet trapped for the time being by a contrary wind, The King of Norway fast gathering support, and his own brother raiding his coastline, this is the prospect facing Harold.

CHAPTER ONE:

Fire from the Sea

England: April to August, 1066

The journey back to Bruges had proved to be no more enjoyable than the outgoing one, a difficult and uncomfortable voyage to the nearest safe German safe port and then a grueling incognito passage overland through the lands of the Empire and then into the lowlands. There was bad food and even worse lodging and weather all the way and the variously recruited guides and interpreters were a disgrace to their profession. When, finally, Tostig made his weary entrance into the presence of Baldwin, who had been expecting him for weeks, once more, accompanied by a seriously disaffected and mutinous Skule Konfostre, he found to his great dismay that the previously genial Count of Flanders no longer appeared to share his enthusiasm for his English adventures. This much was clear as Baldwin curtly indicated them to seat themselves and then did not immediately call for his cup bearer and servants, instead subjecting them to a baleful stare. To Tostig the Count appeared to be much changed. The man was clearly distracted. He had in the interim appeared to have lost a great deal of weight and looked far from well.

In the weeks of Tostig's absence the Count had indeed begun to seriously question the wisdom and the worth of his meddling in the affairs of England. He had a whole variety of reasons for this and the sight of the two men before him, stained and weary and foul smelling, afforded him no pleasure at all. Seated by his hearth side, they gave off emanations that made his fastidious nostrils twitch and wrinkle. To the dismay of his chaplain, who considered such a practice as unchristian, Baldwin bathed regularly, rather than simply dousing himself with expensive scents.

It was now the first week of April and they had been travelling for three weeks. Within the first week Tostig and Konfostre were barely on speaking terms. At Hildersheim the two men had kicked their stools over and squared up for a fist fight in a squalid little hovel of an inn over a misjudged remark and an over sensitive response. It had been, for sure, an especially trying day, involving as it had an incessant downpour, an argument over the route, a drowned pack-horse and an absconding servant. On the very verge of blows, the two men paused and drew back, appalled, while each pondered upon the potentially catastrophic consequences of a falling out. They had shrugged and smiled sheepishly and apologised to each other with an icy and elaborate courtesy. They had striven to maintain that same style of address all the way back here to Bruges and the hall of Baldwin.

Baldwin roasted his back before the fire and contemplated this unlikely pair bleakly and without a trace of fondness in his expression. "So, you are back then," he observed rather redundantly to Tostig, ignoring this Norwegian stranger completely. He spoke in Flemish, thus further distancing himself from the grotesque looking emissary from the Hardraada. These had not been easy weeks for Baldwin. For one thing, a definite clique had emerged amongst certain of the nobility of the Ille de France surrounding the child King at his court in Paris. The legal rights of the Count of Flanders, his integrity and the morality of his guardianship were being put to the question by a fast gathering cabal of influential Frenchmen. These were early days and there was nothing he could specifically pin upon any of his list of suspects, but it was a worry nonetheless, another strand and knot to be teased and worried at and, with the Grace of God, unraveled. The highly intelligent Baldwin, seasoned and consummate weaver of webs that he was, could be forgiven for sensing and suspecting the traps and snares of others.

There was also, worryingly, the issue of the vacant Bishopric of Liege, now promising to turn into a full-blown diplomatic row, and with both Baldwin and the Holy Father at loggerheads over the choice of candidate. Why, at this particular time, God's voice on earth had elected to make an issue out of what in the ordinary course of events should have been a mundane and unremarked election Baldwin simply could not fathom and he feared the worst. Was this perhaps connected in some way with his fast deteriorating relationship with the court of the Emperor Henry of Germany and the Holy Roman Empire? God above, but he sought peace and harmony with the Germans at all times, but frequent reports were now coming in of alleged unpaid border tolls and tariffs, of disputes and disturbances and seized contraband goods.

Only the other day a ponderous and sententious document of complaint had been served upon him by an imperial messenger sent from Goslar. Heavily annotated and dense with footnotes and sub references, it required of Baldwin both an apology and a heavy compensation. God forbid, but were both Pope and Emperor now combining against him? The thought chilled him. One of the inevitable results of Baldwin's fecund imagination was that he could detect conspiracy everywhere. As if this were not bad enough, his troublesome Norman kinsman by marriage was also fanning the flames of the fire seemingly set beneath the County of Flanders. There had been suggestions and demands for this and for that and constant advice that had first been courteous and affable had now turned raucous. Once the Duke had even sent that oily and odious half brother of his, the Bishop of Bayeux, on a visit; an unscrupulous and viperous meddler that Baldwin had never cared for at all.

Worse still, worst of all, he had recently bought for himself the services of a Jew of Spain, a certain Simeon Ben Shimon, physician and practitioner and formerly of Alexandria and Cordoba. The little doctor had come highly recommended and with excellent references and so Baldwin had added him to the household as an additional ornament to his court in the same fashion that he acquired dwarves and fools, talented musicians and inspired cooks.

The solemn and rotund little physician, however, soon began to display an overly keen interest in his sponsor and patron. He began to dog Baldwin's footsteps, coming up unexpectedly upon him in an attempt to smell his breath or grasp his wrist in search of his pulse. Baldwin's incredulous pages had once even reported to him that they had discovered the man going through the Count's night soil, muttering to himself and sniffing his chamber pot.

Made aware of this, and concerned, Baldwin challenged the man and at length reluctantly consented to a full and thorough examination. Ben Shimon was painstaking and, at the end, humane and candid. He noted the Count's weight loss, his lassitude and lack of energy and his much diminished appetite, and with great sensitivity he diagnosed the creeping crab. Baldwin, ever a realist, thanked him, giving him an additional fat purse and also property rights to a derelict estate and some fish weirs. How long? He had asked. Ben Shimon shrugged. Six months? A year? Two years at the very outside. The shadow that Baldwin had felt at his back for some time past touched his shoulder now with a cold and clammy hand. Confiding in no one, he began to set his affairs in order. Not known to be an overly pious man, he now began to make a series of secret endowments, both secular and religious, setting up amongst other things a Chantry where his soul could be prayed for in perpetuity. More temporal matters also had to be dealt with, the safety of his borders, restraints upon actual and possible enemies and future rewards and funds for relatives and friends. It was small wonder, then, that Baldwin now gazed upon this troublesome English relative, returned like a dog to its own vomit, with no fondness at all. He had, moreover, seriously challenged his poor and abused liver yet again the previous evening and was suffering from an annihilating hangover.

***

"Your man Copsig," Baldwin said to Tostig. "I am sorry you missed him. Slipped out like a thief in the night, so he did. Took himself off in one of your boats a week back. Now where on earth has he gone to, do you suppose?" Baldwin positively glared at him. Tostig was shocked. He had expected the usual effusive and insincere welcome, the bear hug and the brimming mug of wine. Instead he was confronted by a suddenly gaunt man, slack-jowled and with dark rings under his eyes, standing before him and jabbing an accusatory finger. Tostig was of course perfectly aware of where his man Copsig had taken himself off to, or rather he hoped he did. All being well, Copsig was now well on his way to the Orkneys and where Norwegian gold had been set aside and with which he could recruit a fleet and an army of mercenaries. Copsig would then, or so the plan went, return south and rendezvous with Tostig somewhere around Thanet off the Kent coast, such were his hopes.

Tostig smiled and bowed from his recumbent position. "My Lord Count, it is good to be back." Baldwin sniffed disdainfully. "Is it? And who is that miserable looking sod you've got there with you? He looks like something the cat's dragged in. One of your new Norwegian friends, I'll be bound." He sniffed disdainfully and seemed then to recall the duties and requirements of hospitality. "Well, then, make yourselves comfortable, the two of you. I can't lie and say that I'm not interested in having your news."

***

Hands on hips, Tostig stood, leaning into the high wind and surveying the men brought before him. The wind came whipping across the Solent, flinging grit and sand into his eyes from the nearby dunes and teasing his hair. Portsmouth was a short way over the water there and he was conscious that such a wind could bring men out in boats to investigate. Just behind him and along the sunken lane the little village of Ryde was still burning. There had, regrettably, been a few deaths and now a thick pall of smoke was rising up that must surely be clearly visible on the mainland.

The people of Ryde and of the isolated hamlets and crofts of the surrounding area had been gathered up into a sullen huddle in the churchyard while the men of Tostig's fleet made free with their sparse possessions. They carried down to the boats what they had been able to find or extort by way of grain, vegetables and pulses. They carried or prodded before them what little livestock there was, scrawny chickens, a few cows and calves and a number of volubly protesting pigs. The people watched in despair as the difference between a difficult winter and an impossible one was thrown into the boats. They were staring actual starvation in the face. There was a dreary wail of children and babies, rising in a counterpoint to the complaints of the animals and the cracking and snapping of burning timber and thatch.

It was coming on for noon, or perhaps just past. The flotilla had reached Sandown at about this time on the previous day. It was a collection of twenty boats and about five hundred men, a mixed collection of dispossessed Northumbrians, paid mercenaries and the sweepings of the gaols of Flanders, offered the choice between a bracing sea voyage and wealth beyond all imagining or the rope. It had been an easy decision to arrive at. That previous day Tostig had divided his force. Half of his command seized a few fishing boats at the nearby village of Toll and then went sailing on to Rye while Tostig and the remainder went overland, picking up along the way a small number of landowners, all technically owing him direct allegiance. Once, of course, Tostig had had the services of a reeve for all of his possessions on Wight. Once he had possessed over one hundred hides of land, each supporting a family and comprised of farms and smallholdings in this rich and rolling arable land. Prudently, that same reeve was now hiding in the woods near Toll in damp bracken and beneath weeping birches, naturally unwilling to assist his former master in a full assessment of his alleged dues. The Abbot of Fishbourne, unfortunate enough to be travelling along the same route in the opposite direction to investigate the rumours, was surprised and taken. Swept up also were fifty or so men, labourers taken from their fields and farms and press ganged into this little army of invasion. They were now corralled under guard on the beach, flicking burning embers from their hair and beards and clothes. It all seemed little enough to show for Tostig's triumphant return to the land of his birth. He consoled himself and prepared a little homily on the duties and responsibilities of leadership to the people there gathered.

It was early days yet and there was after all, or so it would appear, an entire coastline open to him. He might well have the luxury of choice of location, but not the luxury of time. There was a fair wind blowing, fair enough to carry vengeful boats from Portsmouth and Southampton and he needed to be away and off this island and heading east. He could visualise horsemen galloping even now along the cliffs and downs and then through the Weald to London with this news. It would be a race between him and his brother as to who could secure the prize of the port of Sandwich and whatever it might contain. In all events, he had to be off this island by nightfall.

He cleared his throat, spitting out sand. To Tostig's anger, and to the Abbot of Fishbourne, the Churchman had refused to bless the venture and so he proceeded now without the support of Holy Church. "People of Wight," he began. Behind him Konfostre sighed and rolled his eyeballs. Without doubt, these had been the worst weeks of his life, being led like a chained bear around Europe by this maniac Englishman. God alone knew what might be happening back there in Norway in his absence. Nothing good, that was for sure. Without a doubt back in Oslo or wherever Harald happened to be, they would be queuing up to drip poison into his ear about him. He felt marginalised and dispossessed and worthless, trailing after this arrogant windbag in pursuit of a mad scheme he knew to be doomed as each frustrating day followed on from the other. The three weeks he had spent in Flanders had felt like years as he followed Tostig about and while the Englishman had chivvied and cajoled and bullied the men of his growing invasion force. The much vaunted and advertised Count of Flanders had turned out in fact to be a very indifferent host. Baldwin had largely ignored them and the only pleasure the Count had expressed had been at their departure. Far away to the north east, apparently, were those rivers the English called the Tyne and the Humber. There, or so went the story as related by Tostig, a veritable host of enthusiastic Englishmen would be waiting for them, gathered into an enthusiastic and eager bridgehead. There too, Konfostre was assured, he would be reunited with his King once more and he could thus set about doing what he could to salvage his damaged position and doubtless equally damaged reputation, he was gloomy in his expectations.

Tostig completed his passionate peroration to his cowed and sullen audience, as fully aware as his fretting ship master of the need to catch the tide and the wind and to put as much distance between himself and this place as possible. He had already made a mental note of the places he would very much like to pay a visit on his way to Sandwich.

"And so," he concluded, "I bring to you a return to the old ways. I bring you a return to true and proper justice and freedom." Under the circumstances, and as Rye continued to burn and as a body rolled back and forth in the shallows in full view of all, it was an extremely lame and unconvincing conclusion. Tostig himself was fully aware of this. Even so, as he spun on his heel and crunched his way down the shingle to the awaiting boats he still hoped and craved for the roars of support and approval that of course never came.

***

Harold had a favourite room at the Palace of Westminster. The previous incumbent had been Edward's German physician and who had chosen it for its isolation and the view it afforded of Thorney Island, the new Abbey and the river beyond. The unfortunate man had been unnecessarily caught up in the mass exodus following the death of Edward, tarred with the same brush of being foreign, and had fled. Harold, finding the room very much to his liking, had promptly commandeered the room for his own use. He had thrown out the various pots and ointments and scrolls of parchment with their obscure and archaic scribbles, the collection of human skulls, the stuffed birds and all the other obscure impedimenta and installed himself in the little room with its removable framed screen of oiled linen which fitted neatly and snugly into the tiny window. He felt more comfortable here than most places.

At this particular moment the room also contained his brother Leofwyn and the ever dependent Aesegar of London. As far as the tiny space would permit, Leofwyn loped back and forth, fizzing with a nervous energy. Aesegar sat perched upon a stool, holding his peace. Harold cursed to himself. He should have known. He had been warned, of course. He had received frequent reports of his brother's doings by his own people in Flanders and had been informed of his brother's assembly of a mercenary force. He knew now also of Tostig's journey to Denmark and to Norway. Had he not received news of this from Estrithson himself not two weeks back? At the time he had made light of it, not seeing any immediate threat. Sweyn had found himself a scribe from somewhere who was halfway literate.

"Greetings from your loving cousin, Sweyn Estrithson, King of the Danes. Know that, holding him in no love, I have banished your brother from my court in disgrace. Now he travels to Norway doubtless to seek the help of the Hardraada and there also to offer him that which he offered me and which I declined; the Crown of England." The message, written in a relatively fair hand, had concluded with an offer of help and alliance and also, more to the point, twenty warships, fully manned. Gravely and courteously, Harold had thanked the messenger and sent him back to his master with a brace of extremely costly Irish wolfhounds and a torque of Welsh gold.

Surely, despite all of Tostig's posturings, this was just a nuisance raid? A matter of venting a little spleen, the easing of a little spite? He, his father and his brothers had done just the same, acted in just such a manner, against Edward many years back. It had worked then, admirably. Tostig was simply playing the old game as a means of redress, a bid for reinstatement of some shape or form. Well, it would not work!

He would see him in Hell first. Burnings and killings up the coast, followed by the inevitable bloody nose and a slinking retreat back to Baldwin in Flanders, if indeed Baldwin would have him back. Tostig no longer had the power to influence matters anymore. This simply would not be tolerated. A thought struck him. What if Tostig were to be taken alive? What on earth could he then do with him? As if reading his mind, Leofwyn left off his pacing for a moment. "We get him alive and in one piece," he snarled, "and exile is not enough, brother. You know that. Nothing less than a public hanging is what will be required. Elsewise you will have all of the north about you."

Harold nodded. Leofwyn, the least perceptive of all his brothers, was absolutely correct. Tostig must not be taken alive, rather death in battle than the unpardonable sin of Cain. "We must see that it does not come to that," he said distractedly. "Let us just see him off once more with his tail between his legs before any further damage is done. Last heard of, he was in Wight. What next?" Aesegar stirred, he had been having one of his frequent busy mornings." He wants to bring you to the table," he observed. "And he seeks to achieve this by bringing death and destruction to the coast between Wight and the estuary of the Thames. He has misjudged the mood of this country very badly. Such behaviour may have worked in the past," he coughed delicately at this involuntary reference to Harold's own previous career as a pirate," but it will not work now. Besides, we have no firm news of how many he has with him. It can't be that many." Harold nodded, "still," he said, "it would be good to know what he plans next, where he plans to go."

"West," said Leofwyn firmly. "He'll go west. I'd do exactly the same in his shoes. It's getting to be a bit of a tradition in this family. Once beyond Bristol he can hole up with all his little Welsh friends and then next thing you know he'll be raiding across the border. If that goes wrong then he'll be off to Dublin." Aesegar sucked his teeth and scratched his head vigorously, a sign to those who knew him best of doubt and indecision. "Mostly I agree," he said. "But do not forget those visits to Estrithson and Hardraada. It would be as well to call up the men of Kent and Essex. I think we should look east, not west."

All of which left the brothers feeling very foolish and wholly wrong footed when next day there came the news that Tostig and a reportedly large fleet of ships had sailed past the head of Dungeness and had burned the town of Hythe to the ground. At Dover a hastily assembled levy was clearly visible as Tostig's boats arrived off the harbour entrance and so, wisely, the order was given to sail on. There were insufficient ships at Dover to pose any serious threat, but two of the more seaworthy edged cautiously out in their wake and tailed them up the coast whilst messengers rode furiously to call out the men of Kent.

Despite everything, Tostig still managed to catch them all unawares at Sandwich, the first of his major objectives. Exuberantly and in the best of his high spirits he sailed into the harbour and seized eight of Harold's own ships riding at anchor there and pressed their crews into service. Gathered resentfully together in the short time available before sailing once more, he was gleeful as he announced to them their change of master, choosing to ignore their total lack of enthusiasm at this news. The town provided a fine haul of provisions and portable loot and did much to bolster the waning enthusiasm of his mercenaries and pardoned Flemish men. The alarmed citizens put up a spirited but brief fight outside the port reeve's house which resulted in a dozen deaths and the torching of the greater part of the town. By the time the hastily assembled local fyrd of the Canterbury district, led by a vengeful thegn and such housecarls of Stigand as were available, came pounding up the road to Sandwich, Tostig was long gone and heading for Thanet just up the coast, the proud owner of a fighting fleet and close on to eight hundred men.

***

In Westminster Harold was incandescent with fury at the news. Burning with anger, he screamed out commands and counter commands and whipped a horse into a foaming and bloody lather to Chelsea and back before he had calmed down enough to form coherent thought. He felt ashamed of himself as he returned and handed the poor creature over to a groom who looked as reproachful as he thought he could get away with. First Portskewit, thought Harold as he strode back to his room with a cluster of apprehensive servants in his wake. And now Sandwich. Two favourite and highly personal projects now cast into utter bloody ruin by his brother. This was personal. Leofwyn, who was now beginning to get on Harold's nerves rather badly, was despatched to Ipswich in the company of Aesegar, who could at least be relied upon to see that he did nothing unduly rash. The news that Harold had of Tostig's further progress up the east coast was vague. Leofwyn was entrusted to raise the militia of Suffolk and to secure all shipping that he could against any further depredations. Clearly, Tostig's course was definitely fixed on the north. He could hardly hope to return south with impunity. His ultimate succour could lie only with Malcolm of Alba and this made a sort of sense, with exile in Scotland and cross border raids into Northumbria. Time now, then, to warn that pimply little Earl of Mercia and his equally unpleasant brother. Harold cursed and kicked moodily at the fire prepared for him in his room and called for messengers. Men were out on the road already, trying to track down good old reliable Gyrth. They would start looking in Norwich and extend their search from there if necessary. He wished Gyrth were at his side at this moment, Waltheof of Huntingdon too. The boy had his uses, he was loyal and dependable and with an admirable reservoir of energy. Harold was still racking his brains for further inspiration when a servant knocked and, entering cautiously, informed him that the King's mother, who had arrived that previous evening, was wishing for him, for as soon as affairs permitted. Now, in other words.

Harold sighed, deeply and with feeling. He had not seen his mother in months and had not been there to greet her at the time. The thought of this grieved him and caused him shame. His mother most certainly knew how to pick her moments. Gytha was well into her seventies now and defying her age. She was the proud daughter of the oldest and the best of Danish stock, Cnut married her off to a crude and unscrupulous English adventurer by way of services rendered. Gytha had never had an easy time of it married to Godwin. She had been dragged all over England and beyond by her restless and tempestuous husband and had brought little Godwinsons and Godwindottirs into the world with a regular and seasonal monotony. She had followed the tiny coffins of some of these to their graves with a proud and burningly fierce grief. She had worshipped the oldest, Swein. She had worshipped the very ground he stood upon and had watched, her heart broken, as he went to the bad and then, finally, vanished, bare footed and wearing a hair shirt beneath his rough clothing, on a pilgrimage of penitence from which he was never to return.

Gytha had borne all of these vicissitudes, the triumphs and the disasters of the Godwin clan, over the years and at all times had conducted herself with a quiet and a calm dignity. There was little fuss about her, only an old Danish practicality and efficiency upon which she had always prided herself. Since old Godwin's death, Harold and his brothers had seen to it that she lived in peace and comfort and security among her various estates and holdings. Gytha was at her happiest in the fens and flatlands of East Anglia and until recently had the companionship of two loving daughters. Until recently. Now just one daughter remained. Her Tostig too, a charming and clever boy to whom she had taught his first letters at her knee, now also taken from her.

Out of love and guilt and respect, Harold went to her directly, in the midst of all those many things that needed to be done. His mother was lodged in a guest house just across the Tyburn brook with its little wooden bridge that had seen better days. In his highly costly programme of Abbey building Edward had overlooked some of the more basic details and essentials. The guest house was a single storey affair of wood and shingle and, entering it, nodding greetings to her personal guard on his way in, Harold found her there, erect and proud and seated in a chair before the fire with three serving women in attendance upon her. To Harold she looked much the same, tall and angular and with a mane of now silver hair that had always been a source of pride to her. One of her women had been combing through her wet hair and tease drying it with her hands as Harold entered unannounced and without any ceremony. The women squealed, bobbed and curtsied. His mother, on the other hand, viewed him without any surprise and with an overwhelming dignity which unnerved him. She raised her head in a sharp nod and her women, correctly interpreting the gesture, moved respectfully past him and out of the door, closing it behind them.

Harold moved towards his mother. He bent over and embraced her, smelling the cloying scents of an old lady and warm, drying hair. She clutched at him. "Are you well? Eating and sleeping properly? How is that new wife of yours?" The thick Danish accent, as ever, weaved its way through the pattern of her otherwise excellent English. Harold smiled down at her, taking her hands in his. "No, no. It is me who should be asking after you, mother. I fear that I have neglected you of late." He pulled up a stool and sat down beside her. Gytha sniffed."I do well enough," she said. "I sleep little and I ache in my old bones when it is cold and damp. I thank my Saviour that I do not fare worse. Now then," she said briskly, the pleasantries set aside, "I am informed that your brother Tostig is back with us once more. This is why I have come to see you, that and other reasons. Tell me. What do you propose to do about him?"

It was the question he had been anticipating. "In truth, I do not know, mother. I do not even know where he might be at present. I assume you have heard the reports of his most recent activities. Neither do I know how many he has with him. When I do know then I plan to chase him off to Flanders or to Scotland, to whomsoever, wherever, will tolerate his presence. As time goes by he is on the welcome guest list of fewer and fewer people. At this moment, even he must know that he cannot hope to be reinstated. He cannot even be allowed to live in England privately on his own estates. I need the support of the men of the north too much for that."

Gytha patted his hand. "I know, I know," she said wearily. "Harold, I have lost too many of my children in my life, and most recently my own beloved darling Elfgiva. I miss her so much, my favourite daughter. Your favourite sister, I know. It wasn't much of a life, was it? I miss my Wulfnoth, my poor little crippled scrap of a boy that we handed over as surety. I have not seen him in years and he did not come back with you from Normandy. Now I face the prospect of you and my clever, charming Tostig in two opposing shield walls. This is more than I can bear, even for a tough old Dane like me." Her patting of Harold's hand now changed to a grip like a vice. "By all means scare your brother off, teach him a lesson, humiliate him. But do not face him in battle. This is my request of you."

"Mother," said Harold with an absolute sincerity, "this is truly my wish also." Gytha smiled the sweet old smile he remembered so well. "Litigants, applicants, suppliants," she said. "All those seeking the favour of the King should bring something in return." She indicated a table in the corner of the room, which Harold had so far overlooked. "There," she said. "My gift to you, my son, it is on the table."

The gift was a large and tightly rolled length of linen of about eight feet in length and secured by cord. Harold worked at the waxed knots for some moments before finally releasing them and rolling the length of cloth along the table surface, the sides falling down from the much smaller table. Harold gasped at the sight of the image revealed. There, displayed in one of the finest pieces of embroidery work he had ever seen, was the Giant of Cerne Abbas. It was the Fighting Man with club, but with a loincloth stitched tactfully across his private parts. The Red Dragon of Wessex was the banner of his family, but The Fighting Man was Harold's own personal insignia. He felt suddenly cold and he shivered as he contemplated it. This was the very stuff of his dreams, of his recurring nightmare. He had not had that particular doom-laden dream for some time, but now he knew it would come back to him once more in all its chilling particulars. He stared at it in silence for a while. His mother's eyes were upon him. "Well?" she demanded, "what do you think?" Harold collected his thoughts. "It is a magnificent gift, mother. I thank you."

Gytha sniffed, slightly peevishly. "I should think so too. It took some doing, I can tell you. I even got that old toad Stigand to bless it for you, for what that is worth." Harold smiled to himself, picturing the scene as the old Churchman pattered and sprinkled holy water over the uncompromisingly priapic image hinted at in the exquisite needlework. "It is in my heart that this will be a bad year," said Gytha. "I grieve and I fear. Certainly, there will be a big battle when the bastard of Normandy comes. I pray to God, His son and the Virgin and to all the Saints above that this emblem will bring you fortune." Harold took her hands once more. "And that, also, is my wish," he said.

***

After all the elation and excitement of his descent upon the port of Sandwich, Tostig and his fleet finally gained the southern end of the narrow straits which separated the tiny isle of Thanet from the Kent mainland without any further incident, trailed cautiously by the two boats out of Dover. Once more his mercurial side came to the surface and for three nervous and fretful days he bickered and quarreled with Konfostre, Gaiseric and his ship master as his army of invasion took up what seemed to be every last piece of sea room.

The greater part of Harold's fleet lay in the harbours of Sussex and Hampshire and the Thames Estuary. They might well appear at any moment, trapping Tostig and his people without any hope of escape. Clearly discernable and audible on the Kent bank, also, was a growing band of militia. Beyond a shadow of a doubt, more were gathering up and down the coast and every night of their stay here individuals conscripted from Wight and Hythe and Sandwich were attempting, with some successes, to slip away and chance the short swim across to the Kent shore. In the end the arguments of Konfostre and Gaiseric wore Tostig down, as aware as they of the dangers of delay. "We shall give Copsig one more day," he announced.

***

A fighting warship, built and manned by experts, with wind in the sail and twenty fighting fit Orcadians trained since early childhood to man the oars in all weathers was a sleek and fast moving object of dangerous beauty. It was also far faster than even the best of horses floundering along some muddy and rutted bog of a track. They had set out, sixteen boats in all, from Thurso in the far flung north of the Scottish mainland, making excellent progress down the east coast of notionally friendly or at least neutral Alba and stopping occasionally to take on board fresh water and provisions. The men were for the most part young and tough and enthusiastic, guided by experienced older men, experts in navigation and the caprices of wind and tide.

The fifty men of each ship, oarsmen, crew and passengers, were a fighting elite, the best to be found in the lands and islands of the young Earls Paul and Erlend. With such numbers and allied to those of the former Earl of Northumbria, they could trust with confidence that they would see off any local militia. Only the force of the King or an Earl could stop them. With undiminished confidence, they sailed past Berwick and into English waters, hugging the coastline and exciting attention and speculation as they went. They reached the estuary of the Tyne. It was here, they were told, that they would meet up with the Hardraada of Norway later in the season and receive their share of the legendary gold of Byzantium, as well as that of England. Wherever they chose to come ashore they did so with impunity, taking whatever they desired and spoiling and destroying whatever they could not carry off. If, back in Edinburgh, the ever-nervous Malcolm Canmore had known what his putative vassals were up to he would have had a blue screaming fit.

As the Orcadians sailed south the attention of first Morcar and then Gyrth was drawn to their progress and messengers went racing further south with the news through East Anglia and into Kent. Putting all the known facts together, it became clear that this fleet was seeking a rendezvous with the outcast Tostig. Through relays and the use of beacons, Harold was made aware of this new threat just a short time after Tostig had finally put to sea once more and as he and the Orcadians met up near to the shoreline between Thanet and Foulness.

The boats came alongside in comparatively calm waters, the crews screaming out good natured and mutually incomprehensible greetings, taunts and insults. All was well once more in Tostig's world. Grapnels were flung and the boats of Tostig and his faithful man were pulled together and Copsig, his ugly features contorted into a grin of pure delight, clambered heavily aboard. "Copsig, you old bugger!" yelled Tostig delightedly. "I swear you grow more beautiful with each passing day." Gaiseric, who had always hated Copsig, remained silent, as did Konfostre, who was surveying the Orcadian craft with a quiet satisfaction. They were the best thing he had seen in weeks. In truth, they were not Norse, but for all that they looked handy enough. Copsig flushed and scratched, as he always did in moments of high emotion. "My Lord, it is truly good to see you safe and well. We have had us a fine old sail down here and are at your service. What would you have us do now?"

It was a good question and one to which Tostig had already given some considerable thought. "Back we all go," he said. "Back to Alba. Let us gain Berwick and thereafter we can all sponge off Malcolm until the Norwegians show up." He registered the expression of concern on Copsig's face. The man had clearly thought they would all turn south, sail up the Thames and burn London to the ground before heading north one more. Indeed, this is what, with considerable enthusiasm, he had told the Orcadians. Tostig smiled and slapped him on the back, reading his thoughts with accuracy. "I am not the man, though, to deny any other his fun and a chance of riches. By Christ, on our way north we shall be the scourge of England."

***

"From Harold, King of the English by the Grace of God and Earl also of Wessex to his Earls Gyrth of East Anglia, Leofwyn of Kent, Edwin of Mercia, Morcar of Northumbria and Waltheof of Huntingdon. This message goes also to my loyal servants and officials of Essex, Suffolk and Norfolk and to Lincolnshire and Northumbria beyond.

"Greetings.

"Know by this that we have a scourge loosed upon our coast. A wolf's head, a rabid dog whom already we have declared outcast and his properties forfeit. This is the man called Tostig, one-time Earl of Northumbria and is no more and never shall be again. With a stolen fleet and a force of paid mercenaries, the sweepings and the scum of the gutters of Flanders this man, no longer my brother, has burned and killed from Wight to Thanet and in particular has brought death and destruction to Hythe and Romney and Sandwich. We are given to understand that he has now joined with men of the far north, aliens from Alba and the islands beyond. Be advised. These men come in force to burn and kill and steal. Where and when you can and within your means you are to hinder them, But I order you thus. By no means are you to stand against them in full force, save that you are confident of sufficient numbers and power."

There was a postscript to this, added for the benefit of his Earls and shire reeves only. It was not for general consumption.

"As for my brother Tostig. We understand that death in battle or else through subsequent justice through Law is most usually the consequence of rebellion and treason. If God wills this then, with his force destroyed, he is to be chased away. If he is secured by any of you on no account is violence or death to be offered him save that it be so ordered by me directly in writing and bearing this royal stamp. He is to be kept and brought to me."

The missive was unusually long for him, but then again, a great deal needed to be said. "There, then," said Harold to his clerks. "Have copies made in sufficient quantity and sent to those named and by the fastest messengers."

The chief clerk rose from his stool and tucked his little wooden resting pad and writing implements under his arm. He bowed low and ventured a cautious compliment. "It is a most excellently phrased document, my Lord King. If I may so venture to say." Harold bestowed a smile of Royal approval upon him. "You may, you may," said Harold. He smiled a public smile of royal approval upon the man and then made shooing gestures to the clerks, like a man scaring chickens away from his vegetable patch.

"Now, away with you, away. See that this is done." They jostled and crowded at the doorway and Aesegar followed after to arrange for the messengers, Harold sat back and considered, He had still not heard from Gyrth. This disturbed him. Given that he received the message in time then Gyrth could be relied upon to follow the instructions to the letter. Of all people, it would not be Gyrth who would take the law into his own hands or put Tostig to a squalid and secret death in some obscure barn or dark alley. No, even without this letter, Gyrth could be relied upon to do the right and sensible thing.

It was the others that caused Harold concern. Leofwyn, he acted first and considered his acts second. The others, Edwin, Morcar, Waltheof. They were only children, and with all the impetuosity and foolishness and vain ambition that went with their lack of years and experience. Harold had nightmarish visions of them hurling untrained yokels at these seasoned and unprincipled killers, piecemeal and with no concerted plan. With this message now being slapped into the hands of riders in the Westminster stables, he had abrogated command, electing as he had to remain here in the south and await events.

He had surrendered up responsibility to these young and untested men. Worse still, he simply did not trust his Aelfgarson brothers in law. Of one thing there was simply no doubt. If ever either Edwin or Morcar caught up with Tostig and had him at their mercy then they would simply set his head upon a spike, and no amount of humble apologies after the event would ever alter the fact.

***

As any experienced commander of a naval force could have told him, the taking of the communal pulse for morale and motivation of a wholly disparate group of men, volunteers, mercenaries and pressed men, speaking at least four separate languages and with a range of only slightly less unfathomable dialects, was no easy matter. On land, Tostig and his deputies would have found the task that much easier, patrolling around the campfires and listening in and adding the occasional and judicial word of praise and encouragement. Equally, they would have been able to detect the germ, the maggot, the source of dissent, and able to isolate the infection at source.

At sea things were very different and each boat was an island full of unsupervised potential anarchy. At sea and on each boat, men laboured at the oars or lolled and reclined in the central passageway and there was every opportunity for slights and indignities and grievances to take fertile root. If the natural aristocracy of each boat, the master, the bosun and the helmsman, were weak and slow in reacting or, worse still, sympathetic, then major difficulties could arise. This, Tostig was now discovering with his Flemish allies. Thus far, the mercenaries and reprieved men had had a thoroughly enjoyable time of it, exchanging gaol and the threat of the gallows for a brief and entertaining bout of freedom and piracy. Hythe and Sandwich had been particular fun, but now they found themselves, mostly landsmen, embarked upon a long and enigmatic run north across open sea and with the land a distant smudge. They did not like the direction and there appeared to be no immediate prospect of further plunder. They began to mutter to each other in aggrieved undertones. There were boats too with a large complement of seized men. Here too all was far from well, how could it possibly be so? And the few Northumbrian exiles and Flemish mercenaries placed upon them grew increasingly more uneasy.

The men of the Orkneys were at first baffled and then angry. Why was it, they wanted to know, they were returning north once more when they had been promised so much in the south? Orcadian curses rose above their boats as the oarsmen pulled against the wind and as the blisters rose up on the palms of their hands and wept blood and pus and the purifying salt of the sea entered into their open wounds.

So it was that, as Tostig's fleet sailed on, the light-hearted badinage between the boats dwindled and finally ceased altogether and an almost palpable miasma of discontent and incipient mutiny rose up from almost every boat. Tostig, in the lead boat itself untainted by any dissent, could sense this. He knew, as he clutched the taffrail, that he needed to give these people a sense of unified purpose, a meaning to this sea cruise. He knew he needed to provision, that he had to give this fleet of his a reason for being, to indulge them in a spot of rapine and robbery. Most of all, he wished to subject his betraying brother to hurt and humiliation.

Even so, as they approached the two rich settlements of Harwich and Felixstowe lying to either side of the estuaries of the rivers Stour and Orwell, Tostig erred on the side of caution and so gave the order to keep on moving, to sail on past. Who knew what might be lurking further upriver at Ipswich? The answer to this, in fact, was his own brother Leofwyn, fired up with ire and strong spirits and with a strong force, praying that his brother might land.

Two small boats, laden with seasoned Suffolk fighting men of the maritime levy put out to join the weary and fearful men who had been shadowing the invasion fleet ever since Dover. Howls of frustration and protest broke out on Tostig's boats as it became clear that neither town would be given up to them. A short while later, Tostig glanced astern and saw that a boat that he had taken at Sandwich was making a break for it. Having fallen behind, it had now broken away and was making back for Harwich as fast as its oarsmen could pull. He had left four good men on that boat, Northumbrians and Flemings, and he could well imagine their likely fate. To set out after the defecting boat would involve a very real danger of fragmenting the fleet. Now, with the growing dark, they should instead press on and then seek to cast their sea anchors as close to inshore as they felt prudent.

Around Tostig's neck and fastened to a necklace of twine was an old keepsake. It was an uneven lump of crystal the size of an egg that an old woman had pressed into his hand as he had passed through Shipton some years back. The woman, whom all the locals knew to be a proven witch, had told him it was his fortune and to keep it close by him. In his rage at the defecting boat he twisted at the twine and the crystal, worked loose from its fastening, fell first to the deck and then, with a single bounce, over the side. None but he noticed this but, like his brother Harold when faced with the gift of their mother's lovingly crafted banner, Tostig too felt a presentiment of if not doom then at the very least extreme bad luck.

In the morning, after a very trying night at sea bobbing at anchor, a hard few hours of rowing brought them to a small settlement called Aldeburgh. It was a mean little place set in dunes and foul-smelling mud flats and he landed a force off his boats. Most of the villagers fled into the fastness of their familiar marshes and so only a few of the very young and the very old remained to attract the attentions of Tostig's mongrel invasion force. In comparison to what had gone before and to what was to follow after, they were treated with comparative leniency.

It was an altogether different matter with the more prosperous fishing village of Southwold later that day. The village provided a far superior anchorage, allowing all men save skeleton crews to come ashore, and to far better pickings. There followed a number of casual murders and rapes as the village went up in flames. Tostig chose to turn a blind eye to all of this and gave orders instead for the distribution of the casks of fine ale for which the district enjoyed so high a reputation and of which it was so justifiably proud. His men set themselves to enjoying the windfall and all the other pleasures the ravaged settlement might offer up.

Tostig sat now on the sand and shingle beach above the high tide reach at Southwold with his immediate companions, his devoted and worshipping Copsig and the deeply disaffected Konfostre and Gaiseric. It was a beautiful evening, with the stars vivid and glittering in the firmament. Southwold continued to burn and smoulder and from out of the darkness beyond the dunes and coarse grass behind them there arose from time to time shouts and screams of anguish and pain. Campfires had been made all along the beach and men were roasting freshly butchered mutton, pork and beef skewered on daggers and spear points over the flames. At Tostig's side, Copsig stared silently into the flames and the contrasting light and dark gave his lined and scarred face the appearance of a gargoyle off a Norman church roof. At that moment he looked like a child's worst nightmare.

Gaiseric was working with a sailmaker's needle at a splinter lodged deep into his palm. He cursed at the self-inflicted pain, pulled at the open wound with his teeth and then spat out the offending splinter. Ever since the meeting at Thanet he had been quietly calling curses down upon the head of Copsig. Gaiseric had not made that truly awful journey all the way to Oslo and back simply to see this untutored and foul smelling imbecile sitting opposite over the fire replace him. His fertile and imaginative mind seethed with vivid and highly violent thoughts. "We are a good two months too early," he snarled. "We should all of us still be in Flanders and you, Copsig, still with your barbarian friends in the north. This whole thing has gone half arsed."

With food and drink before him and with the triumph of Southwold under his belt, Tostig was at greater peace with the world and inclined to be once more amiable."God's peace upon you, Gaiseric." He leaned across the fire and playfully pushed him, his face alight with good humour. "You saw for yourself old Baldwin back there and how he was. He was fit to bust. We had more than outstayed our welcome. Much longer and he would have simply kicked us out. Besides, the men were getting stale." Tostig hacked at a lump of fat pork with his dagger and chewed at it with vigour. "There were other reasons also. Other things to be taken into consideration." The meat proved too tough and raw and unpalatable and he threw it into the fire where it curled and flared briefly. A brief, uneasy silence fell upon them.

Konfostre had no love at all for this Anglo Danish advisor of Tostig's, but he could not help but agree with him in his analysis of this whole enterprise. It was precipitous, ill planned and premature, lacking in any purpose or direction. "What other things?" he demanded in his poor English. "What other things to be taken into consideration? We are not due to meet up with my Lord Hardraada for nearly a four month yet. He made this very clear to you at Oslo. I remember it, and I remember you agreeing to it. How in the name of God are we to fill in the time? What are you thinking of?" His voice was strident and angry and Tostig looked at him with no affection at all. "Those are three questions, Konfostre, and I am happy to answer each of them in turn. The answers to the first two are easy enough, not so the third." Tostig held up a finger. "Firstly, I made a promise to both Baldwin and the bastard of Normandy some months back. Both men sheltered me, supported me, and to both men I promised that I would be on my way in the spring. Well, it is spring now, and I am on my way." He held up a second finger. "I find no delight in being the supplicant of other men, seeking favours as I warm myself by their fire. I intend to achieve what I wish to achieve through my own efforts and labours. I am sick and tired of appearing cap in hand in the halls of others. I shall bring disharmony to this country which has so dishonoured me and raise the men of the north against my brothers. I will have what is rightly mine, Northumbria, and have it standing behind me when your King arrives." He paused and stared at Konfostre. "Now then, do you have a problem with that?"

"Yes I do," thought Konfostre to himself as he watched the boats rocking and bobbing at their anchors. "And if, in your mighty conceit you fall and fail then you will drag us all down into the shit with you." Aloud, he said, "thank you for that. I am immensely comforted. I do remain very unhappy, however, about the present mood of your Flemings. They clearly desire for more opportunities than presently appear to be on offer."

Copsig leaned forward and nodded. "As to that," he said, "those Orkney boys don't appear too bright at present neither. They'll be needing some jollying up themselves. I was speaking to one just a while back, one as has a bit of the English about him and he was none too pleased. All they've had so far, he says, is blistered hands and a place in a long queue for some wizened old hag of a ploughman's wife. They don't have no problems about going home, but they want something to brag about once they get there again, else there'll be trouble. Mark my words."

"Then," said Tostig softly, "we must see that they get something, mustn't we. There will be opportunities enough between here and Alba." He waved his arm vaguely to the north. "I grant you that up to now there has not been enough. We need bigger prizes and all of the south is now raised up against us. We've all seen the boats behind us and the men on the shoreline. It is my guess that further north they will be less prepared. Cromer shall be next, in Gyrth's own country. It's a fair old town, is Cromer. I remember it from the old days. That'll put a fine old scare into my brother Gyrth. And then, before you know it, Northumbria, and friendly faces." Copsig seemed content with the answer and Tostig smiled contentedly to himself. Across the fire, as unlikely allies as ever there were, Gaiseric and Konfostre exchanged despairing glances.

CHAPTER TWO :

From Anderby Creek to the Sands of Leith

England and Scotland: August, 1066

In Westminster Harold was about to bring yet another crisis meeting to a close. Earlier his child bride Aeldyth had requested him to call upon her when he felt affairs permitted. In itself, this was no reason to call a halt to this particular gathering, but they had been going around in circles for some time now, were getting nowhere and his head was throbbing. Predictably, the talk had been all of Tostig. With Harold in the room was his bellicose old uncle Leofgar, the Abbot of Winchester, attracted to the capital by all of the excitement. Harold's nephew Haakon, whom he had brought back with him from Normandy was also there, accompanied by a man called Breme, a trusted official from Gyrth's household. He and Maerlswyn, the shire reeve of Lincolnshire, had news of Gyrth. He was presently in Norwich and raising the fyrd of East Anglia. Neither man knew for certain, but they rather thought that Edwin was at

Chester and had sent messages on to him there. Godric, the shire reeve of Berkshire, completed the group.

Leofgar rather favoured Leofwyn's offered solution to the problem of Tostig, nephew and blood kin or no. If taken, then Tostig should be executed on the spot without any questions asked. It was, Harold, reflected, a most unchristian view coming as it did from an Abbot of God's Church and a relative to boot. "I think, uncle," said Harold patiently," that this is a decision best made with calm and with a clear head if and when he is actually taken. We must keep all further violence and spilt blood to a minimum." Leofgar subsided back into his seat, muttering imprecations to himself and fiddling with the heavy gold cross on its chain about his neck.

Harold turned to Breme and Maerlswyn, good, honest simple men, and not suited to such high affairs and talk of death and murder. "When you have rested then back you both go. Breme, seek out my brother and assist him in all ways. Maerlswyn, it is for you to track down Edwin of Mercia. Let him be warned but let him also exercise caution. He is not to go seeking trouble where it can be avoided." Maerlswyn nodded back at his King, knuckling his forehead as he did so. He and Harold went back some time into the past, back to the time when Harold was not even Earl of Wessex. Both could tell tales of the other that would do neither any credit in their telling.

Harold turned now to Haakon. "As for you, nephew mine, it is about time that you did something useful for a change, instead of eating me out of house and home. Go with Maerlswyn and be sure to take his counsel. It is always worth listening to." Haakon smiled happily. He had grown bored and stale in Westminster and it would be good to be out on the road again. Besides, he had recently made a very bad new enemy out of a former very good friend over the small matter of a pregnant girl. It was time to let the dust settle and for wounds to heal over. Only Leofgar remained, seeking profitable employment. Harold was very fond of his old uncle and slapped him on the shoulder.

"My Lord Abbot," he said. "Doubtless you have many religious duties to be about. In the meantime, you may continue to sharpen your axe." He moved briskly towards the doorway. "Good day and God's blessings upon you all," he said.

It was a beautiful morning and Harold walked briskly to where he expected to find Aeldyth. He was correct in his assumption. A small and secluded herb garden had been set in the northern precinct of the new Abbey and up against its wall. Other walls and a single wooden gate hid the tiny garden and its covered arbour, seats and stone table from the curious glances of passersby. Harold's sister Edith had always been a keen gardener and gatherer of herbs and now Aeldyth, who shared similar tastes but far less skill, could be found there most days when the weather was fair.

The usual guard was lounging idly against the wall. He stiffened to attention and opened the gate for him. There she was now, busying herself with small terracotta pots containing freshly grafted rosemary, sage and thyme. As the slam of the creaking gate warned her of a visitor, she was busily plucking at the browning leaves of a wind-scorched bay tree, straightened up and turned. Harold, admittedly no expert, could not believe that this was doing the small shrub any good at all. Aeldyth smiled brightly at him, waving her maidservant away and out of earshot. That old Welshwoman, the one with the wall eye and acid tongue that she had brought with her from Northumbria, dozed and snored peaceably in a wicker chair. Aeldyth had a smudge of earth on the left side of her nose and loose strands of hair dangled down in front of her eyes. She looked very young, like a child at play. She curtsied to him, an infuriating blend of respect and mockery, and Harold's heart skipped a beat. This girl, this unlooked-for sprig of Aelfgar, was truly enchanting.

With the events of the past days and weeks he had neglected her and each time he saw her anew he felt an overwhelming delight and a desire to possess her, emotions crowding in along with those of remorse and guilt for Edith and the children down at Bosham. Edith, though, would always be there for him, his rock and his constant support. Edith was his lover and hearth companion and counsellor of so many years and shared experiences. Edith was ever his confidant, the mother of his children, both those yet living and those dead.

And here, in this secluded little garden, was Aeldyth, his political bride. It had been a marriage of cynical expediency, a necessary grafting together of the north and the south in the face of a commonly shared enemy. Thus foisted upon him, he had had no option but to acquiesce. But since then, since their York marriage, she had enslaved and enchanted him, bound him in chains with her young supple body and the intensity and increasing professionalism of her love-making. He was at a total loss as to how best to deal with her bewildering mixture of girlish innocence combined with the sardonic wisdom of someone by far older than her years. She had but to wrinkle her nose or nod her head to empha-sise a remark and he was as unmanned as when he gazed upon the tiny purple birthmark beneath her left breast. The slight Welsh inflection of her Mercian speech, the summer smell of her hair. All these and other things besides, left him tongue tied and helpless in her presence, like some loutish farm hand in the presence of the quality.

He stood there, casting his shadow over her as she beamed up at him. "Very formal, Aeldyth," he said at last." Sit, please sit." She obliged him and he pulled up a stool for himself and sat facing her across the muddy table strewn with the stems of herbs. He plucked awkwardly at a sprig of rosemary. "Well, then. You called for me and now I am here. I apologise that I have not been around much of late, but you will also grant me that there have been many things to see to. These are difficult days we live in." Even as he spoke, he realised how old and pompous and tired he must sound. Aeldyth bestowed upon him one of her more dazzling smiles and he reacted to its warmth and intensity like one caught in a sudden burst of sunshine. Aeldyth, as ever, was gratified by its effect and the way it had seemed to reduce him to the level of a stuttering adolescent.

"In truth, my Lord," she said. "I was beginning to forget what you looked like. Those odious brothers of mine, have you tracked them down yet?"

Harold attacked another stem of rosemary. There were cabbage whites and red admirals in the garden, and the song of a blackbird to its mate in the young trees outside the walls. He was surrounded by aromas and the differing sweet scents of herbs. The sun was warm upon his back and the troubles of the world for a time seemed far away from this enchanted place with its own resident nymph. Harold collected himself and rubbed at his temples and his thinning hair, an unconscious gesture that had been much commented on and imitated of late. "Not as such, no," he said. "I have messengers out on the road. Perhaps I shall soon have news of them."

Aeldyth smiled archly. "Well, they are not to hurry on my account." She rubbed her hands together briskly to free them of the loose soil. "You know as well as I that my brother Morcar is neither use nor ornament. He is as much use as tits on a bull." Harold winced, another way she could throw him off his stride was her occasional and always unexpected descent into the earthy language of men. "No." she continued, "Edwin is the one to mark. As you are looking for him then you could do worse than trying Tamworth. I am given to understand that he is much taken up with the wife of a local thegn there. The thegn himself my brother has sent to Northumbria as an advisor on Mercian affairs." She hooted with amusement and wiped her nose on the back of her sleeve. "At least Edwin has something of my father's sense of humour."

"Thank you, Aeldyth," said Harold gravely, "for the news and the advice. I shall do as you say and send to Tamworth. Now then, as we both know, I am very busy and much preoccupied. I do not wish to sound abrupt, but what is it I can do for you?" Aeldyth regarded him, a half-smile upon her lips. "You bid for and bought me unseen, my Lord," she said. "It was as if I were some prize heifer of which you had heard tell. A prize heifer for which you were prepared to spread your silver on the table and buy. As I say, unseen. What you really wanted was the support of my brothers and the strength of the north and the middle lands they could bring you. And they? What they desired in return was the ear of a King and the prospect of being uncles in time to that same King's son." Aeldyth slapped her knees and leaned forward across the table. "Well then, here is some news for you. They may now have their dearest wish granted them, save that I present you with a girl child. How does that fit then?" Aeldyth concluded with a little triumphant 'hah!' and leaned back, arms folded, to view the effect.

Harold caught his breath. Here, he supposed, was the logical conclusion of his bargain with the Aelfgarsons. A number of different thoughts raced through his mind in swift succession as he snapped the rosemary in his hands again and again. Edwin and Morcar, they now truly had within their grasp what they craved, even a girl child might suffice for the time being. By the same token, surely now he had their support. A child, God send it was a boy, born to a King crowned and anointed and elected. A child of the line of Godwin and born to royalty.

"My Lord King," said Aeldyth levelly. "You do understand what it is that I am telling you? Hurriedly, Harold collected his thoughts. "Yes, yes, of course," he said. "I cannot find the words at this moment to tell you of my happiness. It is just that this is so unexpected. I had no idea. When, I mean, what, that is to say, how long before we may expect the happy event?" Aeldyth, secretly delighting in the moment, cut him short. "With the Grace of God we shall have us a Christmas baby, or thereabouts. Now, think carefully. Tell me what you think."

"I think," said Harold slowly, "that this is news to make all my woes and difficulties at this present time seem like truly small things indeed. I am truly delighted for every possible reason." He leaned across to kiss her, sweeping pots from the table as he did so. The sound of their shattering brought the old Welsh woman awake with a startled snort. "You keep yourself well and safe," Harold urged her, "for the sake of us and of our child. Whatever you need, whatever you lack, you shall have it. Just call upon me. Anything is yours for the asking. For myself, I beg your forgiveness for my neglect. Until this present business is resolved I fear that you will see little of me." Aeldyth grabbed one of his ears and squeezed it hard, another little habit of hers. "I do understand," she whispered into it. "I just thought that you might like to know."

***

On the very same day that Harold was told of the quickening of his child in the belly of his child bride of Mercia, Edwin himself arrived in Lincoln. Fresh from his Tamworth philandering, he too had had his own network of agents and intelligence gatherers out at his behest. En route he had received Harold's open message, a writ, as he interpreted it, to act as he saw fit and best. Even before this, though, he had decided he would take matters into his own hands at the first possible opportunity. Now, flushed with pride and vainglory, he rode through the city gates of Lincoln with his retinue of thegns and housecarls riding respectfully behind him. On the road behind them came a straggle of labouring and plodding militia and hastily conscripted farm hands.

The town of Lincoln was something of an anomaly when it came to the jurisdiction and the rightfully exercised powers of Earls. In law and practice it did indeed lie within the most southern flung possessions of Northumbria, just. In all practical matters, the people of Lincoln judged themselves to be independent and the influence of Mercia to the west and East Anglia was equally strong, causing all manner of litigious difficulties in the local courts. The hard-headed Anglo Danes of Lincoln were a byword throughout the country for stubborn pigheaded independence of thought and action. They were a reminder to all of how much had been left undone in any progress towards unity since the divisive days of Cnut and the Danish wars. As their shire reeve, Maerlswyn had his work cut out for him.

At the hastily gathered assembly of dignitaries and elders Edwin was abrupt and unforgivably dismissive. He billeted himself and his men of rank in the best houses available and left his following to behave like a rabble and impose themselves with the authority of steel and blows upon the rest of the populace. Edwin of Mercia had arrived like the commander of a conquering army and the people of Lincoln noted this for future reference.

Edwin now sat with his muddy boots upon Maerlswyn's table with his hands behind his head. He breathed out exuberantly, he hadn't had so much fun since Northampton. "This whole affair," he announced. "I shall sort out in my own way."

There was a man with him of well over twice Edwin's years. Staffyd was Anglo Welsh, originally a Ludlow man and Edwin's principal advisor and deputy, as in turn he had been to Edwin's own father. Staffyd had gone grey in the service of Mercia. "Should we not perhaps wait?" he asked diplomatically. "After all, we do not know how many Tostig has with him. Why not wait for Gyrth and Waltheof? Your brother, even." Staffyd was a wise and experienced and practical man, but Edwin found him mostly irritating, a cautious old woman. "No," he said. "We can and shall do this on our own. I want no others involved. The victory must be mine and mine alone, a Mercian triumph. I also want Tostig dead. I shall personally rip his liver out and feed it to my dogs." He looked around intently at those present.

Staffyd sighed heavily. "Then I suppose we had better get to planning. We need to rest the men up for a day and get a local man who knows the coast around here to take a group of our boys down there straight away. If they ride fast then they can be there before nightfall. We can all follow on tomorrow." Edwin removed his muddy boots from Maerlswyn's much loved table of Suffolk bog oak and stood. "I have decided," he announced. "We shall send a small force to the coast right away. Choose the best of our men, Staffyd. Do it now and then we shall follow after once we are rested." He beamed out of his handsome young face and Staffyd smiled once more. Old Aelfgar might well have passed his lands and titles and good looks on to his son, but precious little of his brains.

A suitable man was found and hired and within the hour was leading a force of sixty mounted men eastwards to the coast. It was gone nightfall by the time they reined in on a small track running alongside sand dunes and diseased and stunted looking brush and coarse grass. The sound of the sea came to them and the smell of its salt tang, a full moon shone above the immensity of the vast and empty North Sea. They had a miserable night of it there, wrapped in their cloaks and huddled around mean fires of roots and driftwood and dried dung from the fields at their backs. In the morning they divided their forces, half to the south and the other to the north. At regular intervals small groups of men were left to watch the coast all the way between Skegness and Mablethorpe.

By late morning they were all in place along a stretch of fifty miles or so and settled down to wait. The long day passed, but at least the following night was an improvement on the previous one. Local people ventured out to them with timid gifts of food and drink and much needed firewood. It was just past noon on the following day when the southernmost picket placed just above Wainfleet Sands saw sails appearing, apparently sailing directly across the open expanse of the Wash. Two more hours passed before they were able to carry out a count of the number of sails and long before that a horseman was heading north to the next picket and another to pick up the Lincoln road along which Edwin's men must surely now be travelling. At least forty vessels, they had counted, and heading directly for Skegness.

***

Tostig had sailed past Yarmouth and all along the bleak and unwelcoming coastline of mudflats and dunes towards Cromer. At Cromer itself the local militia with a stiffening of local housecarls was lined up on the shoreline, a smaller and less skilled and experienced force than Tostig's, but sufficiently large enough to cause some damage and dangerous delays. Tostig elected to sail on into the open waters of the Wash, his popularity waning with the passing of each sea mile. Even on his own boat, men muttered and cursed and threw dark looks at him up there on the raised deck standing with his companions and the master. Another promised prize had been denied them. The water was now rationed and the bread was sour and mouldy and full of weevils. There was no ale or wine and all of the salt had been used up. This was not what the mercenaries and enthusiasts had signed up for, at least in the Flemish lock ups they had not been seasick. The Orcadians had taken to making sheep sounds and obscene gestures to the men in the other boats, who responded in kind. Tostig no longer presided over a unified force, and he was fully aware of the fact.

"Skegness," said the master, when asked. He knew these waters well. "It's a fair old size and with rich pickings there and inland. I'm thinking that we must have outdistanced the Earl of East Anglia by now, and across the Wash, well, it gets pretty isolated." Tostig stared at the shoreline, aware of the burning angry gaze of men on his back. "Skegness it is, then," he said. "Haul to, so that we can inform the others."

Edwin's tardy and loitering advance guard were now in full view of the coast when the first of the pickets came galloping back with the news. The invaders had come ashore just north of Wainfleet Sands and would by now surely be at Skegness and making free of the place. The messenger had himself stayed just long enough to see a large body of men come roaring exuberantly ashore while the fleet sailed on ahead. Edwin punched one fist into the palm of another in savage joy and yelled exultantly."Now we have them, the bastards." He whooped with glee and forced the pace with those with him who were mounted. He received his second messenger shortly after. Skegness was in flames and men, women and children lay dead in the town and the surrounding fields. What livestock that could not be butchered and carried away had been slaughtered and spoiled and left to rot. The crops in the fields were trampled down and the mills first used and then broken up. This was wanton destruction and the survivors of Skegness would feel the consequences for years to come.

It was coming on for dusk and the men who had landed were giving every indication of settling in for the night. A short while later, a third messenger arrived, his horse covered in foam and blood pouring from its mouth and nostrils. There was a small bay at a place called Anderby Creek about eight miles to the north of Skegness. The fleet had anchored there, obviously waiting for the land force to catch up with them once more. Laden down as they were with stolen goods and chivvying recalcitrant livestock along the treacherous and narrow coastal path between shoreline and marsh, it would take the raiders several hours to regain the safety of their boats. Staffyd was much encouraged by the news. "They have made a very serious mistake," he observed. "Perhaps now we can do this on our own, if we make all the right moves, that is." Edwin feigned a polite interest. "And these right moves, Staffyd. What might they be now?"

In the failing light Staffyd peered back behind him. He sought to hide the scorn in his voice but did not quite succeed. "They cannot have landed much above two hundred men or so. On that track, on the march, they'll not find it easy going. They can move four abreast, perhaps, and very slowly at that. They also seem to be very confident, by all accounts. They do not seem to be anticipating any serious opposition." He sat back in the saddle. "We have here with us some six score men, housecarls and the pick of Mercia. Behind us are the fyrd and local men. We can, I believe, see these people off. Send messages back to hurry them along and leave guides here for them. Nothing for it but a night march, my Lord Earl. Send the fyrd south to Skegness to chase Tostig north in the morning. For ourselves, we need to get ahead of them, between them and their boats. They will make for them as fast as they may."

Given a task such as this Staffyd, an old and seasoned hand in the dark arts of ambush and counter ambush in the Welsh mountains, was in his element and the blood coursed and pounded in his tired old veins. "We must leave immediately and set beacons to let the rest of our men know where we are. God's truth, my Lord. We shall have our main force drive them onto our spear points like lambs to the slaughter."

It was a very long speech for Staffyd, a man who in the ordinary course of events weighed out his words with care, like an apothecary measuring grains of opium. In truth, he admitted to himself, he was getting just a mite too long in the tooth for escapades such as this but, by God, it was a good feeling he had just now. Back home in Ludlow and the surrounding district he had more grandchildren than he could name or number. He should, by rights, be back at home now, fondling the ears of a favoured hound perhaps, or draining a stoop of ale before the fire and teasing the servants. God alone knew that he deserved such an end to his days after all his years of service. But first there was this task to achieve, a fitting end to his busy and loyal career before he could hang his sword up above the fireplace. With a tact acquired over many years he cleared his throat respectfully. "Perhaps, my Lord," he said, "you might care to give the necessary orders?"

***

Tostig roused his men at dawn. Sour mouthed, bleary and jaded, they were cajoled and bullied out of the still smouldering fishing village and off up the coastal path, hampered and harassed by equally foul tempered and obstreperous cattle, independently minded pigs and wilfully stupid sheep. Without armour and with their weapons slung casually about them, they set off, carrying with difficulty such small things as they had been able to retrieve and acquire the previous day, a small sack of already sprouting corn, the charred and half raw haunch of a pig, strings of smoked mackerel, a crock of clarified and now reeking butter. They carried with them the mean little baubles and trinkets of the now defunct village.

An hour or so into the march, their heads began to clear and their spirits to lift. There were all the makings of a fine late spring morning and the rain had held off. Those who had been suffering earlier from the excesses of the previous evening were now sweating out their accumulated ill humours and hangovers and beginning to chaff amongst themselves. They recalled with fondness and poor accuracy their brief and eventful stay in Skegness and it was at this moment that the men in the rear first noticed behind them the presence of a large force of armed men moving purposefully in their wake. Ripples of conjecture and alarm rippled along the column until they reached Tostig and his companions at the front. Together with Konfostre and Gaiseric, he moved back to the rear, urging his men to double up and move faster as he went. Sure enough, separated by a march at swift pace of perhaps half an hour or so, he could see clearly across that flat expanse of fenland. He could not assess numbers, but there looked to be a fair number of them and closing the distance with every stride. As he watched they broke into a trot, the fyrdman's march, fifty paces walking and fifty at the run.

"Oh, shit," said Gaiseric feelingly. "What now? And who the bloody hell might they be?" Tostig stared at him scornfully. "Why," he replied, "they are just the local people come to us in friendship and bearing gifts." Konfostre was staring inland across the arid salt marshes. He pointed. "And those there? who might they be?" The others followed the direction of his finger. About a mile inland and following a raised track that ran parallel to them was a double file of horsemen moving at a speed that threatened soon to bring them ahead to cut them off from the refuge of the boats. Konfostre repeated his question and there was a note of panic in his voice now. Tostig continued to stare about him as he attempted to marshal his thoughts and come up with something decisive. There looked to be about forty or fifty horsemen. "Thegns and their men of the locality," he said, stating the obvious. "And that mob behind us will be the local fyrd. The question is, do they intend to simply see us off into the next district or do they mean to make a fight of it? They have the numbers for it if they do."

"No sense in hanging around to find out," said Gaiseric sensibly. "Let's dump the stuff and make a run for it. What they can do then so can we. Fifty at the run and fifty at the quick walk. We need to close up, armour on and weapons at the ready." Tostig paused before replying, unwilling to give such an order, an admission of failure and defeat." Fair enough," he said finally. "Let's do that. Discretion is the better part of valour." He quoted the tag in Latin, which was totally lost upon his companions. They shouldered and elbowed their way with difficulty back to the head of the column, bawling at the men to shed their livestock and booty and to arm. The cattle and sheep and pigs were let loose to wander among the dunes and the marshes and the men, weapons at the ready, closed up and broke into a run towards the shelter and security of the still unseen boats ahead. The distance between them and their pursuers had lessened and the cries and shouts of the horsemen inland were now clearly audible.

A further hour passed, half walk and half run, with the distance between the two groups lessening. In that time Tostig ran harder and farther than his men, roaming between the head and the tail of his raiders. He encouraged and threatened as he went. An hour or so of this, he urged them, and we shall be back with the boats. An anonymous voice came back to him once from the back of his crowd of men "Let's turn and do for them now. We can take them, those sheep faced whoresons." But Tostig kept them on the move. "No. We shall turn and face them at the boats. Keep moving." After a while the track turned and brought them the welcome view of boats in the far distance undulating gently within the safety of Anderby Creek. A cheer rose up from the exhausted men and they lessened their speed slightly, some stopping, their hands on their knees and their heads down, as they wheezed through their labouring chests and spat into the sand and scrub. "It is not over yet, keep moving." Tostig raged at them as he pushed and shoved them on their way.

Up ahead of them, hidden by dunes and tall bull rushes, Edwin, Staffyd and their men waited impatiently. "Now," Staffyd instructed. A large beacon had been prepared, waiting for the lighting. Oil was poured upon it and a burning brand thrust into its centre. The fire flared up and immediately they threw upon the blaze wet vegetation and green wood. A thick pall of smoke, first black and then a deep and choking grey, rose up into the spring air. At the sight of it the pursuing Mercians howled and broke into a headlong run as the horsemen now came threading their way amongst the ponds and marshes on a direct collision course. Gaiseric was panting with exertion, his breath coming with painful difficulty through his tortured lungs. "This looks bad," he gasped. "Save your breath," Tostig snarled at him, "and run."

The horsemen had now arrived ahead of them to cut them off and were wheeling to meet them. As if conjured up by magic. a further one hundred men or so rose up from cover and screaming like banshees. They formed the shield wall, locking their shields together and blocking the path. They pounded on their shields with their weapons and shouted their defiance. "You wanted a fight?" Tostig yelled at his men. "Well, you have one now. There they stand between us and our boats. Go for them." Snarling and screaming and with their weapons raised, Tostig's men hurled themselves at the Mercians before them, seeking to cut their way through before those behind them fell upon their unprotected backs.

Tostig sought out an enemy, no more than a half-grown boy, in the wall ahead of him. The boy's eyes flickered nervously as he raised his shield and axe. Tostig feinted for the bare head above the shield and then swept his own axe low just below the inexpertly held shield. The boy went down like a felled ox and Tostig followed through with a lethal blow to the exposed neck. There were two others standing directly behind. He barged into them and flailed about with his axe. He knocked one completely off balance and sent him sprawling and stamped his foot hard on the man's face as an Orcadian thrust his spear into the throat of the other.

The two lines merged into a heaving and jostling mob, a riot of men screaming and falling as blows and lunges were exchanged above and below the protection of the round shields of linden wood. The shields locked and clashed, and more men were falling as each side sought to outflank the other, floundering either in the loose sand of the dunes or in the treacherous and shifting ooze of the marsh. The pursuing Mercians at the rear arrived at last, joyous and vengeful, to fall upon the unprotected backs of Tostig's men and the encirclement was complete. It was as finely crafted an ambush as Staffyd could have hoped for. Less experienced, but superior in numbers and with the wrath of men with hearths and homes to avenge, they hurled themselves at their enemy with triumphant shouts.

In a very short time, it seemed, the numbers of Tostig's mixed force had been whittled down by a good quarter. Tostig broke through the line of men facing him, leaping across dead and wounded men. Briefly, Konfostre was beside him, his axe of Swedish steel bloody and begrimed. "You have brought me to this," he screamed at Tostig." You miserable little piece of English shit. I should have stayed in Norway." He swung viciously at an enthusiastic Mercian and caught him in the midriff. As he staggered and sought to pull his blade free, two others sprang at this once darling favourite of the Hardraada. One jabbed his spear into Konfostre's stomach and the other swung a sword. With a discernible thud, the Norwegian's head, eyes wide in outrage, fell at Tostig's feet.

In their fury, Tostig's much reduced command broke at last through the opposing ranks of the Mercians, snatching up discarded shields and weapons and helmets as they ran headlong. Their pursuers were close behind them, hurling spears and axes at their backs. A number of times on that nightmarish retreat they turned to face their tormentors and on that narrowing pathway there was no advantage to be had in any superior numbers and the ambushers came on with more caution.

The men at the boats had long since been aware of the danger, alerted first by the pall of black and grey smoke. Copsig, entrusted to remain with the boats, had recognised all the danger signals and began to make his own contingency plans, Tostig's faith in him had not been misplaced. He landed a shore party of heavily armed men and lined them up on the narrowest point of the track he could find and facing south. The heavy stones that served as sea anchors were hauled aboard and the boats turned about to face the open sea but remaining as close to the shoreline as was prudent. The men at the oars backed water and the ship masters bawled imprecations and orders. If all went well then, this move should allow Tostig and his men to wade out and board as swiftly and as easily as circumstances might permit.

The circumstances, Copsig reflected as he crammed his battered and beloved old helmet on his head, did not appear to be good. His brow furrowed, the slow and ponderous Northumbrian knew that if he could get the land force off the beach and onboard then in all likelihood they would have far too few men and too many boats. Well, they would have to wait and see. They could take the decision to abandon and scuttle when things were clearer. The real danger would come when men panicked and broke and made for the boats.

That was when fights were lost and when retreats became flights and flights became massacres. Laced and secured into his mail shirt, he took up his axe and waded into the shallows to rejoin the thin line of men formed up on the beach. He was just in time to see the first of the fleeing men appear, at first bobbing heads above the dunes, and then men staggering and limping across the shingle of the beach and towards the boats. The sounds of a running battle came to his ears carried over the wind and the sounds of the sea.

At their first sight of the boats and the comparative safety they seemed to offer, the men delegated to carry Gaiseric at first increased their pace but, at the very edge of the sea, they elected to drop him and see to their own salvation, after all, the man was clearly dying. He had taken a number of serious wounds, but the one that was killing him now had been a sword thrust to the lungs. There was a pink foam at his mouth and he could scarcely breathe, each rise and fall of his chest was an agony. He fell heavily onto the wet sand and shingle and into the slap of an incoming wave. There was grit in his mouth and he attempted to yell a protest, realising with a sharp stab of pain and terror that he simply did not have the breath to do so. "What's the use?" he said to himself. It was the last conscious thought he had as he rolled over into the incoming and obliterating tide that came around and over him.

As the fleeing men rushed past Copsig's thin line of defence and plunged into the shallows, the triumphant Mercians coalesced into a solid mass, preparing to rush forward in one last rush. Tostig paused and offered Copsig an appreciative nod. "We have had us a small setback," he said. A Mercian, more audacious than the rest, rushed at him. As Tostig side stepped, Copsig intervened and brought his axe down square on the man's head, there was a loud crack and blood and bones and brain showered over both him and his master. "Tostig," he said."Get your men down to the boats. I'll see to things here."

Tostig nodded and turned, yelling instructions. The battle was now petering out into a brawl and in the confusion Staffyd himself, breathing laboriously, suddenly appeared before Copsig. Recognising each other, they both paused for a moment. They had met once before, in happier times when both old Edward and Aelfgar were still alive. At that time Tostig had only lately been appointed Earl of Northumbria and Copsig had travelled down to Westminster with him. Together, Copsig and Staffyd had compared notes all night long on the caprices of the men set above them, drank heavily and put the world to rights in a lowly little tavern close to the Lambeth ferry. Now they commenced to swing at each other, their blades clashing. It was no even contest. Staffyd, grandfather and reluctant warrior, was struggling for breath. With a ham like fist Copsig shoved him in the chest and toppled him over. Staffyd fell like a sack of meal and Copsig stood over him for an instant as his men began a steady and fighting withdrawal to the boats. "Get out of here," he said, with a certain amount of compassion despite the circumstances. "You are much too old for this kind of thing. Devil a doubt but we shall meet again some other time. Now, just bugger off."

Copsig, pausing only to cut down an unduly confident youngster on the way, turned to gather up the last of his men. He noted briefly a figure in fine and unsoiled clothes upon a large grey horse at the fringe of the fight, recognising him as Edwin of Mercia. Already some of the boats were pulling out to sea, even as men clung to the sides and clambered on or were pulled aboard. About a dozen men remained on the beach, fighting desperately before being overwhelmed. There was no hope left in this world at all for those further inland. Wounded and terrified, they were being brought to bay and killed on the spot, no quarter given, for some two miles back along the track. Copsig laboured towards a boat as jeering Mercians hurled ill aimed spears at his retreating back. He was the last off that beach and it took four men to haul his large and armoured bulk into the boat and drop him to the boards. He lay there, staring up at Tostig, his lungs burning, as the oarsmen heaved away and the wounded and the dying moaned and screamed in the narrow space.

A few more strokes of the oars and they were beyond range of first the spears and then the occasional arrow. All around them, the rest of the boats laboured out to sea. Tostig was staring inland, where a mob of men were hooting and jeering. There were some among them who brandished spears with heads set upon their points. As Copsig gazed up at him, the appearance of the former Earl of Northumbria was far removed from the suave and sophisticated figure with the aloof and sardonic presence he had always so admired. Tostig appeared to have taken no significant wounds, though blood flowed freely from a gash to a forearm and upon the temple. Mud, sand and grit and a great deal of seawater had combined to give him a brown and muddy appearance and his expression was both distracted and manic. Their eyes met and Copsig asked him then the very question he had asked of him when, it seemed so long ago, they had met up at Thanet. "Well, my Lord. And what now?"

***

A week later the survivors of the fleet anchored off Leith, fourteen boat loads of sick and weary and wounded men desperate for fresh water and untainted food. The Orcadians gathered provisions and then sailed on, refusing all commands to the contrary. Ten boats of whole and wounded and dying men full of recrimination, humiliation and anger back to the shelter of their harbours in Caithness and Orkney. On their troublesome way north from their clash with the Mercians,

Tostig's battered and beaten command had scuttled boats and doubled up and each day had dropped the dead over their sides. Once or twice they had risked landfall in search of food and water, quick and anxious visits. Despite all the warnings, the Earl Morcar of Northumbria had failed completely to police and protect his own coast, but neither were the men of Tostig inclined to seek any further damaging confrontations.

Even before they reached Berwick they had lost a further six boats, their mixed crews of Flemings and assorted mercenaries and the forced conscripts electing to cut loose from this damned enterprise and make their own way in the world. Where, with all of England raised up against them, these men thought they might seek to improve upon their fortunes was not clear. Two boats sailed into Hull, calling loudly upon the port reeve for a sanctuary and a reprieve that was, surprisingly, granted to them. They were briefly imprisoned and those Englishmen among them able to persuade the local officials of their innocence and the circumstances of their seizure were released with a wallet of bread and cheese and boiled meats and ten pennies apiece to seek their own way home as best they might to their southern ports and villages. The Flemings and the broken adventurers of the French coast, on the other hand, were sold at a knock down price to a consortium of local landowners and consigned to a future of hard labour in the fields and farms of the north east. The other defecting boats met a variety of fates. Wreckers did for one boat, luring it onto the jagged teeth of the rocks near Jarrow and clubbing the survivors to death in the surf as they came ashore. The other three boats and the men aboard them simply disappeared and were never seen again.

At Leith, and with neither a farewell nor a backward glance, the surviving men of the Orkneys took their leave. Norwegian gold and the promise of more besides had lured them out and their two boy Earls, faced with the anger of the Hardraada, had been powerless to stop them. Bitter and humiliated, the Orcadians now sailed back to face the many widows and orphans, their barren and sterile fields and perilous fishing waters, and left Tostig and his remaining Northumbrian and Fleming exiles to meet a dour faced welcoming committee of royal officials and local notables at the head of a large force of armed men. Tostig was as welcome to them as the bloody flux or cattle murrain. With the hospitality of two Kings, a Duke and a Count under his belt in the space of less than a year, Tostig stepped ashore brightly and with an assumed confidence, as if fully expecting a warm welcome. He advanced towards them, carefree and smiling broadly, and seized their reluctant hands in friendship, happily and, in some cases, remembering names and recounting nostalgic anecdotes.

At his side, Copsig was amazed at the man's resilience and the way he now sought to ingratiate himself into the company and dubious affections of Malcolm Canmore of Alba. With ideas, projects and plans hurtling around inside the shell of his head Tostig, who had contrived to turn an arrest into a form of royal progress, allowed himself, amiably and affably, to be escorted the short distance to Edinburgh and the brooding castle upon its craggy rock.

Apart from Copsig, the remainder of his men were left there on Leith sands, corralled into barns and crofts and under a strict guard. On their reluctantly loaned ponies, the two men ascended the steep slope to the still incomplete residence, past piles of masonry and rubble and workmen who paused at their labours to stare at them. They pulled up before the supposed royal hall, half its roof missing and clad in timber scaffolding. Labourers bustled about them, covered in masonry dust and wood chippings and ankle deep in the quagmire of the courtyard. The latest attempt at laying new cobblestones had clearly not been a success and the not unpleasant mix of smells of turpentine, pitch and resin permeated the air. There was the usual collection of loafers and off duty garrison men and, to Tostig's disappointment, their arrival did not seem to draw any undue comment or interest.

"So then," asked Copsig as they sheltered from an insistent grey drizzle and as their mounts were led away, "how is he likely to receive us? This great and wonderful Malcolm Canmore? This is a right hole, and no mistake." Of late, he was inclining to become less respectful. Tostig smiled and nodded, his bright eyes taking in all around him for possible future use. "I agree," he said. "The place is a midden. It makes Sweyn's place look like Byzantium. As for our Malcolm. Well, he's a long and limping ginger streak of piss. But, he's no fool. He'll listen to reason."

When it had been decided that the visitors had waited long enough in the rain to remind them both of the importance of the King and of their own low status, the new double doors of the hall were hauled open, parting with difficulty and with accompanying squeaks and groans. "They'll need that seeing to," said Copsig, practical as ever. "New leather hinges and a good slap or so of grease. Do you mark how the wood is unseasoned? Personally, I'd hang the carpenter." An ancient looking Chamberlain appeared in a much-patched cloak and clutching his staff of office and beckoned at them irritably. "A good day to you, God's peace upon this house," said Tostig cheerfully, resolved upon a good natured and well humoured approach. Copsig shrugged resignedly. Doubtless, he knew best.

The Chamberlain stood aside with a barely discernable bow as the two men brushed past him and into the dark, austerely lit hall. Clearly, Malcolm had embarked on yet another of his little economy drives. Tostig, with a confidence born from past experience, advanced towards a tall figure seated upon a handsomely carved chair before a very small fire at the far end. The figure gestured the Chamberlain to remove himself and rose from the chair. The man was indeed tall and thin and ginger. As he walked the few steps towards them he moved awkwardly, for one of the legs of Malcolm Canmore, King of Scotland, was markedly shorter than the other.

There was a parody of delight and welcome upon his face. "My good friend, Tostig," he exclaimed. "It has been a long time, so it has." Malcolm spoke good English, though it was clear that it was a second language to him. "Well now, well now. What about you? In all duty, we must do all we can to make your short stay with us as enjoyable as possible before, regrettably, you must leave us once more."

Tostig first knelt in respect and then, upon being urged to rise, seized the King's hand and kissed the ring upon the index finger. "My lord King is as gracious as ever I remember him" Tostig replied. He spoke in a lowland Gaelic that was superior to Malcom's English. Tostig had ever been blessed with the gift of tongues. "But, my Lord, I fear that our stay with you may be a shade longer than your Grace had previously supposed." Malcolm frowned, "how so?" he asked, suspicion quickening in his mind and in his voice. "It is a long and complicated story," said Tostig, "though in it there is much that may well prove of lasting benefit to you." He smiled broadly, one of his most charming smiles, brought out and dusted off for use here. He indicated the stools placed close to Malcolm's regal chair. "May we sit?"

It was a masterful performance from Tostig. Keeping his own council and not being required or indeed able to speak at any point, Copsig marvelled at his master's virtuosity as, in a mixture of Gaelic and English, Tostig played upon the King of the Scots as he might upon a musical instrument, teasing out appropriate notes at appropriate points. Much as Copsig admired and revered him, here was a man who had squandered away the goodwill of some of the most powerful men in Christendom, to say nothing of a sizeable fleet and the lives of scores of men on a preposterous, premature and ill conceived descent upon England. Here he was now also, making free of Malcolm's grudgingly offered whisky, its taste redolent of peat and oak and wood smoke, blandly presenting his latest disastrous escapade as the successful opening phase of a meticulously planned campaign. "So, you can see," said Tostig after a while, "why it is simply imperative that we remain with you here as your guests in Alba for some time." He went even so far as to lean over and pat Malcolm's knee in a comradely fashion. Malcolm flinched and drew away. "You must surely be able to see also the benefits that will accrue to you from your hospitality."

Malcolm stared at him. It was clearly time to get a grip on this conversation, to seize it by the scruff of the neck and get it to go down the paths he desired. "No," he said. "Not altogether, no." He drained his whisky and reached for the flagon at his side. Remind me once more, if you would." His green, feral cat's eyes flickered suspiciously over the exiled and former Earl of Northumbria basking comfortably at his ease before his fire and making free with his whisky. Malcolm had, Copsig noted from the privacy and anonymity of his own stool set in the shadows, a nervous tic to go along with the limp and the unnaturally raised shoulder. The tic which affected his left eye and drew the left side of his mouth into an involuntary grin was increasing in its frequency as the conversation progressed.

Tostig stared meaningfully at the flagon and at his own empty cup. "Once," he said, "I was Earl of Northumbria. So shall I be again, and a true and loving neighbour of the men of the north as I was in previous times. My brother, on the other hand, and that puppet of his called Morcar whom he has set in my place, has no love at all for you and yours whatsoever. As God is my witness, do not have any doubts as to that. Exiled I may be, but I do enjoy the patronage of both the King of Norway and the Duke of Normandy, loving kinsmen to me that they both are."

Tostig ignored Malcolm's derisive snort. If a King could not be permitted to snort in his own hall then what was the price or point of kingship? Tostig ploughed on. "Likewise, the Count of Flanders is also my kinsman and my sponsor. They, all of them, have plans to make things very hot for my brother, and very soon. Do I not have this from their very own lips and in very recent times past?"

Malcolm looked derisively at him. "I don't know, you do? As for me, I have my own pack of loving kinsman and relatives, and I wouldn't trust the one of them as far as I could spit a lead fishing weight." He sneered at Tostig. "Tell me this. Why should I give a rat's arse for either you or your so called loving kinsmen?" It was a foolish remark and he regretted it as soon as he had made it as Tostig pounced. "Come now, come now, my Lord King. Does past experience tell us nothing? Does not the experience of past events inform the wise man as to his most sensible course for the future? What happens in England is very much your concern, as you very well know, and it is within your gift and within your power now to shape events to your liking. If the Duke prospers then he will take the south and the midlands and it will be me who shall be your buffer in the north between he and you. I shall be the one, ever mindful of my love and my debt to you, who shall speak up in defence of your affairs and interests."

"Thank you," said Malcolm, his tone pure acid. Tostig waved his hand graciously. "Do not mention it further, I pray you. But, equally, do not let us, in our pleasure, also overlook the fact that I am also high in the favour of the Hardraada of Norway, whose most immediate servant and emissary I, in fact, am." It was a fine move, arrived at and executed with exquisite precision; the threat of this man most feared by Malcolm and his claim as his direct ambassador.

Dukes and Normans as a threat were all very well, but they were far more remote a threat than a pack of deranged and baby eating Norsemen set about his ears. Malcolm pulled his cloak about him irritably. He was an inveterate fidget and he played with the heavy gold rings upon his fingers. He bridled instinctively at the mere mention of the name of the King of Norway. Separated as he was by a vast expanse of ocean, Malcolm nonetheless feared him more than any Englishman or Norman. The mighty Hardraada, with his men and his swift boats looming up out of the sea mists and his powerful influence so firmly embedded in the north. Malcolm was ever conscious of how thinly his own writ ran north of the lowlands.

In Caithness and the Orkneys, the Hebrides and the Western Isles, on the Isle of Man and in Ireland, the man who mocked the name of the King of Norway or offended him in any other way ran the risk of having the blood eagle carved out upon his back and his hall burnt to the ground in the night and all within it murdered. Directly or indirectly, the man had a long reach. As if reading Malcom's mind, Tostig asked the critical question. "You are famous for your prudence and your wisdom and I know you also for a man who can keep a secret to himself. Tell me now, where do you want the Hardraada to be? Inside your hall, happy and content, or at your gates and in high anger?"

It was a compelling argument and a distressing vision. "More whisky to yourself and your man there?" Malcolm asked, intrigued and suddenly hospitable, for all that he loathed the man before him. A man who in short order had first prostrated himself before him and had then presumed to slap his royal knee. "Don't mind if I do," replied Tostig. He poured himself a measure large enough for the liquid to slop over the rim and then handed the much-denuded flagon to Copsig. "As I said, I take you for a man who knows when and when not to share a confidence. So, this is for your ears only, my Lord King." Malcolm nodded, his eyes wide and solemn. "As the tomb, Godwinson," he said, "as the tomb." He gestured to his unwelcome guest to continue. "Well then," said Tostig. "Whom do you most fear? England or Norway?"

Malcolm stiffened and hissed at him in righteous anger. "Malcolm Canmore fears no man living. I do fear, however, and in equal measure, the designs that both these countries may have upon my own." This was not the answer that Tostig had been hoping for, but he persevered. "Before this year is out," he prophesied, "all of England will be a battlefield. You have my word on this. There will be Normans in the south and Norwegians in the north. Have no doubt of this. Both will require and seek out my aid. Their enemy will be my enemy, their friend will be my friend. I hold the balance of this and my brother will have to fight either one or the other, perhaps both. Whichever of the two prevails, Duke of Normandy or King of Norway, then you will most certainly need me. There now, admit the truth of it."

Tostig could see that the King was still far from convinced of his own supposedly unique value to him. The canny and devious Malcolm Canmore was far from dull witted. Tostig allowed his words to sink in before continuing. "It is my belief that it will in fact be the Hardraada who will be the last man standing. I have taken his measure and seen his power, why else would I now be here and awaiting him? For the man will come, Lord King. He will come and visit you. You do not require from me a lesson in geography. He surrounds you already, in both fact and influence. You need me. With myself established back in Northumbria I can prevent you from being squeezed like an apple in the press. How you propose to deal with him north of here is entirely your concern and beyond my own humble ambitions."

Gratifyingly, Malcolm nodded to himself and reached again for the drink. There was a certain truth to all of this and

Tostig, sensing his advantage, continued. His companion did not have the Gaelic and so he reverted back to that language for the sake of privacy. "In return for your present and future hospitality, in return for men and ships and provision, I pledge you this. My voice shall ever be heard raised in the defence of your interests and when all of these present sad affairs are finally at an end, I shall give up to you Berwick, and Bamburgh and their lands also. The whole of Teviotdale will also be yours once more. Think of all those lovely sheep and their grazing lands and all of that revenue you will thus receive! You shall take up once more your former influence in Carlisle and a return of your lost lands in Cumbria as far south as Allerdale. Gaelic will once more be the language in which affairs are governed there. You have my word and my hand upon it. Let us be frank amongst ourselves. We both fear the power of the Hardraada, but he is no longer young, and his sons are unproven. Who knows what, with my help, you can as well achieve in the north and amongst the islands once he is gone, in Man even, and in Ireland?"

Malcolm Canmore kept his silence. A return of all the lost lands of Alba, no less! His descendants would revere him and preserve his name as the redeemer of the reputation and glory of Scotland. Future halls would ring with words and music in praise of his glory. Copsig stared at the floor, stone faced and nursing his drink. It was true that he did not have the Gaelic, but he could sure enough pick out the names of places, the names of the much fought over Berwick and Bamburgh, of Teviotdale, Carlisle, Alledale. It was clear enough from Tostig's grandiloquent gestures and this Canmore's rapt attention what, exactly, was being discussed. It was not his place to make any comment in this company, but there his master was, sitting there making serious inroads to the grudgingly offered whisky and delivering over to him the lives and the livelihood of thousands of his own people. Tostig was playing a very dangerous game, playing for very high stakes. Surely, he could mean none of this? Deeply unhappy, Copsig, mute, sat there, keeping his place and rightful station in life.

"You see then the need for discretion?" asked Tostig. Malcolm was still in a revery of Teviotdale and Allerdale, of prime grazing for fat sheep and rents and taxes and to the west a bridgehead to the Isle of Man and perhaps Ireland beyond. His thoughts rested also on the customs and dues of Berwick and the impregnable fortress of Bamburgh, an unmoving rock against English aggression. "Tostig," he said at last. "This will make of you a Scotsman. The English will spit upon your memory for all the years to come." Tostig shrugged dismissively. "And if the Norman bastard prevails? What then?" Tostig looked at Canmore and grinned. "In that case then I suppose that the same terms and conditions will apply, and I shall still be your buffer in the north. Duke of Normandy or King of Norway, it is all one and the same to me. Fortune favours the brave and either of them would need me in Northumbria."

There was no more drink in the flagon and Malcolm yelled for more. There was a sound of scurrying and muttering in the small room to the side of the fireplace, as servants roused and busied themselves. Malcolm nodded to himself thoughtfully, nursing his empty beaker, turning it around in his hands. "And what if, as you put it," he asked of Tostig, "your own brother is the last man left standing?" Tostig looked at the King of Scotland for a fraction of time longer than was polite. "Then," he said simply, "I shall be dead, and you will be obliged to seek your own salvation."

CHAPTER THREE:

An Uneasy Autumn

England, Scotland and Norway: July to

September, 1066

As June passed into July and then July into August, Tostig was left to cool his heels in a well-appointed guesthouse in Leith and at a suitably difficult distance from Edinburgh. Publicly shunned but privately courted from time to time by Malcolm Canmore, he made the journey up to the castle rock on a number of occasions when bidden, the quality of his mount much improved. In the meantime, his remaining force of Flemings and Northumbrian diehards were on the beach, nursing their wounds and heavily policed by the men of the King of Alba, shrewdly and circumspectly and sparingly provisioned. For those that remained alive and loyal from those days it was all very reminiscent of Flanders.

Malcolm's outward charm, such as it was, and his control over much of the mainland to the north of him was at best erratic. His northern chiefs of the Highlands were men of wilful and independent spirit and though he was safe enough to throw his weight around in Galloway and Lothian and in the lands to the south of Edinburgh, Malcolm had learned to tread cautiously north of Perth. In all their secret meetings and at his rare occasional public appearances, Tostig took a private pleasure in the spectacle of the increasingly careworn and nervous King of Scots on his best behaviour with his northern noblemen. Malcolm could neither openly defy the English nor refuse to offer aid and assistance to the Hardraada. He came up, therefore, with a classically blurred compromise. He would recruit, finance and equip a small fleet and force of mercenaries.

This would, if God were in his Heaven, be sufficient to appease the Hardraada if he was successful and for his recruited force small enough to disown should Harold of England prevail. He knew in his heart that the compromise would fool no one and he cursed once more the day that brought the Englishman to Leith.

Tostig noted the slow and introspective growth of this new force with a mixture of annoyance at the slowness and the paltry nature of it all and an ill suppressed glee at the inconvenience and grief it was manifestly bringing to his unhappy host. Twice he sent messages to Norway, his second messenger arriving back in excellent time. The King was marshalling at Bergen, he was informed, and waiting for the arrival of the last of his levies. At some time in late August he would take his fleet south to the Shetlands and from there to the Orkneys, to gather to him the men of the Earls Paul and Erlend. Contingents were expected also from the Shetlands and from the Faroes, from Iceland, the Western Isles, Man and Ireland. It promised to be a host of the Northmen such as had never been seen before. And with that, for the time being, Tostig had to be content.

***

Far away to the south, from the Thames Estuary to Wight and the Solent, July arrived in a blaze of glorious summer weather. Midsummer was celebrated in good old pagan fashion, with a thin veneer of the celebration of the nativity of Saint John spread over the top. Larks, plovers and kestrels rose and hovered above the hedgerows and it was an especially spectacular season for butterflies, a riot of colour in the air. In all respects this was an extraordinary year all along the south coast, with so many men away from their farms and fields and the women and the very young and the very old breaking their backs to prepare for the winter and the annually faced difference between going hungry and starving to death.

In a season of blazing heat and exultant bird song the people waited for the September harvest, noting with alarm the near empty granaries, the lean pigs and the cattle and sheep in need of fodder once the tall grass of summer was finished. It was a season when people went foraging in the forests for the supplement of mushrooms and berries and along the hedgerows in search of alternatives to wheat and barley. The spiralling inflation typical of the season put the price of everything but the coarsest and most adulterated of bread beyond the reach of many. Instead they gathered poppies and hemp and ground this with the last of the ergot-tainted barley to bake bread. It was a season, as a consequence, of food poisoning and collective hallucinogenic mass visions and hysteria brought on by the eating of what the people called 'the crazy bread.' It was a season for outbreaks of violence and visions and the prophesying of the deranged. These crazed unfortunates haunted the woods and the fields and the riverbanks. Their screaming and ranting and their foretelling of the direst of happenings yet to come brought fear and dread to the common people.

In the meantime, Harold had half his fyrd of Wessex standing idle along the coast. In Kent, Leofwyn did likewise.

Mixing business with pleasure, Harold moved to Bosham. There, he was within easy reach of the Solent and the eastern coast of Wight, where over three hundred craft of varying shape, size and sea worthiness lay hauled up upon the beach whilst others patrolled the coastline from Lyme all the way to the Thames mouth. The men of the boats lounged in idleness interspersed with occasional violent bursts of horseplay and disorder. Some six thousand men of the special and general fyrds were spread out in encampments along over one hundred and fifty miles of coastline. The military logic of the situation ran thus; not all of the coastline could be defended in strength. Equally, none could foretell where the invaders would land. Everyone there had the memories of the stories of their fathers and grandfathers, of the lightning tip and run raids of the Danes of Sweyn Forkbeard and Cnut. All they could do was to report a landing and wait for Harold's fleet to beat west or east up the channel to get behind the enemy while the English land forces withdrew and consolidated.

So it was that Harold arrived at his beloved Bosham in the first week of June, fifty mounted housecarls following behind in his retinue. Tostig, he knew now, was in exile in Scotland and up to no good at all. Edwin had seemed to have proved himself with a piddling little victory and, with the Grace of God, could be hoped to continue to protect the north and to do nothing rash.

There, once more, was Edith and the younger children gathered together outside the hall to greet him. It had been months since last they had met, months in which much had happened. Most of the housecarls had dispersed to billets arranged by the Bishop of Chichester, but there was still sufficient of a crowd to observe Harold dismount and gather his family up into his arms. His children now truly made bastards through his marriage to Aeldyth, and his common law wife Edith now reduced to the status of a mere kept woman. He swept them all into the hall before him and away from all the curious and prying eyes. In the hall the servants scattered obsequiously before them, offering heart-felt greetings and plates of bread and cheese and cold meat and jugs of ale.

**

They were alone now, for a moment only, slightly awkward in front of an unnecessary fire. "Well, Edith," he began. "I know, I know," Edith interrupted wearily. "You can't stay long. I do hear that you and Aeldyth are expecting a happy event." Harold took breath. Now, just how did she find that out? Edith was as sardonic as ever, and with only a trace of bitterness and rancour. Harold gazed at her. Edith had changed. She was a tall woman, almost matching Harold in height, but there was now an additional gauntness to her. She had lost weight and the planes of her face were now more starkly defined. There were dark rings under her eyes and grey had appeared at last in her hair. "as to that" he said. "I shall stay as long as I want and for as long as it takes, until the bastard arrives. But yes, I shall be out a lot." Edith smiled at him, "I can imagine. But I do suppose that we might have the pleasure of your company for at least the remains of the day and for the night. Is Oswy with you? Perhaps he has gifts for the children?" Harold grinned. "Indeed he is, and indeed he has." One of the loitering servants was summoned and the children were gathered. The boys whooped and rushed outside to where Oswy waited patiently for them, knowing they would be along soon enough. Harold smiled indulgently at the noise."There are, of course, gifts, also for the girls," he said. Outside in the courtyard the noise continued unabated fierce little cries and hoots of pleasure as the man, Oswy, distributed his gifts. They could hear the voices of the servants and the clatter and thumping as they busied themselves with this much expected arrival and the evening meal.

"So then," said Edith, "and don't be telling me how well I'm looking, you old bugger. I can detect a lie in you at a hundred paces." Harold planned his next words carefully. "Edith, I need you to be away from here, you and the children. It is not safe. I cannot give you the day, but before the summer is out the Normans will be here on this coast." Their eyes met and locked before Edith, the Swan neck, moved on to other matters, delaying a decision.

"We shall have have good wine this evening, bucket loads of it, I shall see to it" she said brightly. "Normans, you say?" It was the same flat and ironic fenland accent, "I hadn't heard anything. That's as maybe, but me and the children, we're stopping here until such time as we have to move. Whatever would the neighbours say if we were to creep off like thieves in the night? If we have to move, then we'll move. Ely, perhaps. Or someplace nearer to hand in Suffolk, and how is your dear lady wife?" Edith enquired waspishly. "Well, I trust?" There was hurt there and Harold winced at the sarcasm. He closed his eyes and massaged his temples. He felt her hand pressing gently upon his shoulder. "Well enough, she is well enough Edith. And yes, there shall be a child. In the winter, or in the new year."

"A Christmas baby! How touching! And what then? What of us, Harold? What of our own children?" Harold had been dreading this moment. "That depends largely upon his Grace the Duke of Normandy and his plans," he replied. This was a truly difficult moment, and one that he had been dreading through all the past weeks and months and especially throughout his long ride from Westminster, across the south downs and thus to Bosham. On that journey all other issues of policy had taken second place in his mind as he thought of his true friend and his hand fast wife not recognised by the Church. Edith, and their children waiting for him. He took her hands in his. "I swear this to you, Edith. I swear it by all that is Holy. Me and Aeldyth, this is a marriage of necessity. You know that, you have said it yourself. The girl will, God willing, bear me a son to follow after. Edith, you are the heart of my heart. My true love and companion of my life, now and always, ever since first I set eyes upon you."

"And when you had me hauled before a court and had me fined for wrongful seizure of land, as I recall," Edith said. They laughed together. "And as I recall you never did pay the fine. And no, you are mistaken. It was a matter of fishing rights. Your mind is wandering. Perhaps it is your advancing years. Edith, for as long as I live, and beyond my own death, you and the children will want for nothing. You shall live out your time in safety and in comfort. If the bastard comes and he bests me then I have plans made for you and the children, in Wales or in Ireland."

Edith, her arms folded, was scornful. "Oh yes? That will be nice. I've always wanted to learn a new language." Angered then, Harold snapped at her. "These are difficult and dangerous times, my girl. You have the right of it. I shall be extremely busy over these coming weeks. The day after tomorrow I'm off to Dover to meet with Gyrth. Please instruct the servants accordingly. Now then, I require food and drink and rest, and news of my family."

Over the way in Chichester on the other side of the harbour, Harold's officials gathered, coming and going, on errands and missions as ordered and as circumstances required. The gathering of the fyrd and the maintenance and the provision for bored and hungry men thrown back on their own resources and now seeking diversion and mischief was proving to be a logistical nightmare, as Gyrth confessed when the two brothers met at Dover. Harold was gratified to find his brother as levelheaded and as practical as ever in dealing with the difficulties of the present situation. His business-like approach was a comfort. "We have secured grain from the London traders sufficient to keep the Kent men in the field for six weeks," Gyrth told him. "I didn't like the price and said that it would be a pity if the shire and port reeves were to find any evidence of malpractice in their affairs. We have a fine haul too of dried beans and peas. The stuff is on its way to Canterbury now. Meat and vegetables, we can get locally. Leofwyn has his own ways and means of keeping the price down." Harold laughed; he could imagine. Both brothers were effective in their own separate ways.

"No problem with fresh water, of course," Gyrth continued, "and Leofwyn reckons that Kent has the best ale in the country. If we need more then we can ship it down from Ipswich. Between Thanet and Winchelsea we must have about four thousand men out and East Anglia, Essex and Kent can provide certainly a threescore of boats with their crews. I have the list somewhere. They are either at Wight or else on the way there." Harold nodded his approval. Kent was Leofwyn's land, but it was Gyrth who provided the administrative backbone. "And from Winchelsea to the Solent and beyond, there my responsibility begins," Gyrth said. "I have grain and other things on the road from Winchester. Chichester is the place from where I shall provide for my men. If either of us lacks for anything then we shall each ask the other."

Later in the same day they were joined by others. Leofwyn, recently arrived, fidgeted, fussed and muttered to himself at the end of the table. Aelfwold, the Abbot of St Benet, a man with a peculiar and unpleasant skin complaint, sat bolt upright, clutching a massive sheaf of tally lists. He was a difficult and irascible little man whom most found difficult to like, but the man had at least proved himself to be a commissary of rare talent and ingenuity. Harold's uncle, the Abbot of Winchester, was back once more. So too was young Haakon, entrusted with the task of ensuring the smooth flow of communications all along the coast, the messengers, the spare mounts, the beacons. The task was providing excellent scope for his restless energy. Maerlswyn was also there, still steaming slightly from his long trip to the north and back, aromatic with the tang of the sweat of both himself and his horse. The ever dependable Aesegar had also just arrived from London. Last in this exalted company was a massive, awkward and brooding man named Eadric, known also as 'the Steersman.' On this man's broad shoulders lay the heavy responsibilities of maintaining the fleet presently gathering in the Solent and all along the sheltered northern coast of Wight. It would fall to him, if necessary, to take them all out to sea against the Normans.

Eadric was a master mariner from Southampton, a man who knew the quirks and fancies of the tides and the estuaries and the winds of the Channel as intimately as a man might know the back of his own hand. Looming and laconic, he spoke only when spoken to. At this moment, before the food and drink arrived, Harold was encouraging him into speech, not something he was ever happy to do.

"I shall do as I am bid," Eadric said simply. "Before the month is out we shall have some three hundred boats gathered. I cannot speak for the seaworthiness of each and every one of them, but they will sail, each in their own fashion. They will collect men along the coast as they go and land them at any place of my Lord's choosing. Within reason, that is."

It was a long speech for him and Harold chose not to press him further. "Thank you, Eadric," he said gravely. "And you, Maerlsywn? What is the story up north?" Maerlyswn was an exuberant and cheerful man, a lover of the hunt and the feast. He did possess however, a steel within him, a competence and an ability that one could trust. As shire reeve of Lincoln his immediate duties and responsibilities were to his Earl Morcar. Maerlyswn was a man born and bred in the so called Five Boroughs, however, and his first loyalties to them ran deeper than any owing to the Earl of Mercia.

Young Morcar and his brother Edwin, equally influential in Lincoln, he neither liked nor respected, but he masked this well in his dealings with them and he was Harold's most trusted eyes and ears in the north. "Edwin," he said, "is now presently at Stafford and Morcar is back in York, his eyes directed at Alba and his own coastline. I have messengers on hand, ready day or night. They can get to either of the Aelfgarsons in a matter of two days or so. They are young and keen and eager to prove, those two boys."

At the end of the table Leofwyn, with his memories of Northampton, laughed sardonically. "I would suggest, however," Maerlswyn persisted, "that they could become complacent, too confident perhaps of their abilities, just like their old man. I, of course, have no writ that runs beyond Lincoln and its lands, no authority in either Northumbria or Mercia. I do, however, have a voice in the Five Boroughs. If the need arises then I can raise the fyrd in Lincoln and in Derby, in Nottingham, Leicester and Stamford. My word on it, my Lord. I can raise and hold the midlands. I can take their men either south or north as the need directs. My people have been instructed to gather at Stafford if the word goes out. From there to London it is none too bad a journey, and there is also the direct road to York"

The mobilisation of the men of London and the adjoining shires of Bedford and Hertford and Middlesex was the responsibility of Aesegar, shire reeve of Middlesex and the most prominent man in London. "If the word comes," he said, "then I can bring my men south of the bridging points at London and Kingston. We can hold either the Thames or move south to Guildford, according to your will. With your order, I can have them in Guildford in days. It all depends on where and when they land."

Harold shrugged, "as to that," he said, "we all of us have our own views and opinions. As you all now know, they are gathering at Dives at this very moment. They will either sail directly against us from there or else move east along the coast. It is my thought that the attack will come in late July or early August, but we cannot be complacent. The word I get is that the bastard's force grows stronger by the day and is well provisioned. As to where they will land, well, I agree with Eadric. Most likely it will be at any point between Beachy Head and Dover, either by intention or by force of circumstance. In this event, and hear me most carefully when I say this, the local forces are not to attack. They may harass and raid by all means, but their first duty is to report the landing. We shall then put the fleet to sea and with such land forces as can be placed in it and come at them from the rear, blockade them. Upon my orders the rest of the fyrd is to gather at a given point to their front. Where that place will be we do not know until they actually land, and land they will. Let there be no doubt in our minds as to that. This is why Canterbury and Guildford are good meeting points." The men at the table nodded their agreement. "Time to eat then," said Harold cheerfully. "And while we are all here there are matters other than this disturbance to be discussed."

***

There was indeed much else to discuss and arrange. It was imperative for Harold to see and be seen by as many of his people as possible. Kingship was a highly personal thing and it relied heavily upon his physical presence. In more than two decades of sedentary rule, the placid and largely ineffectual Edward had stirred rarely from Westminster save for his beloved hunting trips. He had remained a remote and enigmatic figure and of little direct relevance to the daily life of the ordinary man. Now, with this looming threat of invasion and with the depredations of Tostig a very recent memory, the people of England were understandably edgy and uneasy, no more so than here on the coast. There had been that comet, the ominous hairy star, and now there was the very real prospect of mailed men on big horses in their midst, a collective folk nightmare of bestial figures descending upon their familiar farms and fields.

In the towns and ports, ordinary people and merchants alike had begun to hoard. Despite the activity of Harold's newly established mints, money was in short supply, It was no longer passing from hand to hand in the market place, as was its purpose, but rather disappearing into secret holes in the ground, under floorboards or into cavities carved into walls. In the countryside, disrupted and dislocated by the absence of so many labouring men now serving their time in the militia, the people feared the times and from there it was a short logical step for them to begin to challenge the suitability and the sanctity of their King of only six short months.

So it was that throughout June Harold made himself as visible and as familiar as possible. He moved among the encampments of the fyrd and mingled with the seamen on the beaches, speaking to them in familiar Wessex argot, sharing their food and drink and bringing his own gifts. He gatecrashed a number of local folkmoots, sitting with the elders and giving his own opinions on local issues.

When called upon for a judgement he prudently mixed justice with compassion and humour. In the village of Hyssal in the rich valley of the Adur close to Lancing, the pigs of the freeman Byrth had been allowed to trample and consume the crops of his neighbour. Harold considered the issue. "Very well then," he said. "For a full season Byrth must collect the dung of his animals and spread it upon the lands of Aellyf." Men nodded their approval and stamped their feet. It was the old common touch that had never left him.

The mood was less easy going in the coastal towns between Southampton and Dover. Harold visited all of them in turn, making his way east and then west again through

Pevensey, Hastings, Winchelsea and Romney. Beneath the deference owing to a chosen, crowned and anointed King, the doffing of caps and the exchanging of gifts, there was a palpable tension. It was easily detectable to a man as sensitive and as attuned to the country's pulse as Harold. He promised and cajoled and on occasion he threatened and punished. Two merchants of Hythe lost their right hands for the illegal exporting of grain to Normandy. A Fleming was flogged and banished for allegedly attempting to compile a head count of the fyrd around Pevensey and Hastings. A pubescent girl from a village near Lewes who was much given to prophesying and soothsaying, none of it good, was despatched to a Convent.

Those thegns, local officials and churchmen that Harold could not fit into his busy schedule were rewarded instead with a visit from a senior deputy, carefully briefed beforehand. By the end of the month Harold and his men had just about visited every man in the south and south east they felt they had a need to. Out of royal and personal funds he bought grain, and had it delivered to local centres to be ground and baked and distributed to the needy of the towns and countryside. As it was doled out there came a constant refrain and litany from his servants. "It is your King who feeds you." This came to be repeated often.

In the first days of July Harold at last dismissed that half of the fyrd that had stood to arms since early May. He dismissed them in batches so that the men of the second fyrd could take up their places smoothly and leaving no section of the coast unguarded. These new men were obliged to come from further afield. They were Aesegar's Londoners and the men of the Home Counties, men from the west, Dorset and Devon, fresh and as of yet, eager. It was, on the whole, a smooth transition. For Harold it was a frenetic and dislocating experience, inured as he was to lengthy periods of travel and hours in the saddle. In all this time it was rare for him to spend two nights in the same place. The condition and the maintenance of the boats was a worry, as was the morale of the men as the initial euphoria and novelty of the experience of being away from home gave way to boredom and fears of a neglected harvest.

The liquidation of all Edward's accumulated assets went on apace at Winchester and at increasingly knock down prices. To accompany the general reluctance to part with coin, reports on the auctions from Harold's zealous Treasury official at Winchester became increasingly gloomier. Holes were appearing in the Royal Treasury and so Harold began to dip into his personal funds of Wessex. The Winchester officials, though scandalised, followed his instructions to the letter, selling for a song a parcel of land here, a flock of sheep there, a string of thoroughbreds or the grazing rights on the hills of the Mendips to flint eyed local stockbreeders. All of which went to Harold's war chest, the provisioning of his army, the repair of his fleet.

***

Late one night in early July Harold and Edith lay in bed in Bosham, planning a fantasy future together. The night was very close, and the shutters were open to let in what little moving air there was. A persistent gnat buzzed irritatingly about the room, evading their combined efforts to track it down. In the still air came the periodic cough of an ailing sheep and, once or twice, the hoot of a questing barn owl. Apart from that the silence of the night was complete.

"There are places I know in Ireland," said Harold, "where the grass is so green that it hurts the eyes to look at it. The sheep and the cattle are so fat that they can scarcely walk. I have in mind a number of places where we could be happy. They have some shires over in the south west with the finest land you can imagine. Rains a lot, but then you can't have everything." Edith nestled cosily in the crook of his shoulder and stroked his chest. "No," she agreed. "You can't have everything."

"A fine old Irish schoolmaster for the children" Harold continued, warming to his theme. "They breed good scholars over there, you know." Edith traced a line down Harold's side, following the grey and puckered line of a Welsh knife wound, long since healed. "And we'd just sneak off some dark night?" she asked, "and leave everyone else in the shit?" The gnat paused, settled and bit. Harold cursed and slapped, sat bolt upright. The moment was broken. "Enough," he said. "This is foolishness, Edith. You are right. I am King of the English and the Earl of Wessex besides. There are thousands who are dependent upon me." Edith sighed and pulled the blankets above her breasts. "I know," she said. "God above, I know." Harold reached for the pitcher of water at the bedside, scratching at the bite. "We are both of us practical people, Edith, you and I. It is time to plan for the future, and to plan for the worst which could happen., to plan against the way that things may fall out."

"Which is?" Edith enquired. Harold was out of bed, standing naked by the open window. "Which is, William of Normandy triumphant and me dead, or in exile and far from you and the children. We need to face these things. Bosham is no place for you and the children in these times. I have enough to worry about as it is without the additional concern for your welfare."

"A compromise then," said Edith. "For I too have made some plans. My manor up at Faldene, near to Norwich. You remember it? I've not visited it for some time. Without a doubt it is run down and the servants are pilfering, but I'll send a man of mine there tomorrow to have it made ready. No more foolish talk of Ireland. I shall send the children there if I need to. As for me, I shall follow after if events prove strictly necessary. In the meantime, I shall stay here. This is my compromise. Now come back to bed."

***

It was a wait of numbing tedium, occasionally enlivened

by jarring false alarms and scares and isolated outbreaks of insurrection among the ranks of the fyrd. The supply lines that Harold and Gyrth and the Abbot of St Benet had set up were working tolerably well, but with occasional disruptions and days of want. Unencumbered by the spirited and high-strung warhorses of his counterparts across the Channel, Eadric practiced at embarking and disembarking men and supplies, sailing as far east as Dover. Men volunteered readily, chancing their lives to the uncertain sea in preference to the stultifying boredom of the watch.

In the first week of August the little Anglo Welsh cleric, Caedmon, fetched up unexpectedly at Bosham, like a piece of bleached and eroded tidal wrack. He came unannounced, limping and haggard, into Harold's hall during the evening meal. Everyone there fell silent, for he was known to many and, anyway, his appearance alone was sufficient to cut off all conversation. Harold's knife fell to the table with a clatter and then to the rushes at his feet as he stared at this apparition, last seen in Normandy and vowing protection to his little brother Wulfnoth. Never a big man, Caedmon had visibly lost weight. His hair was lank and long and greasy and his tonsure overgrown, his tentative smile of greeting showed that he had lost two front teeth.

"Caedmon," Harold exclaimed and rose to meet him. He stepped off the dais and enveloped him in a bear hug that caused both men to wince. Caedmon smelled like the tomb and he was obviously lousy. Harold recoiled and stepped back. Not, he hoped, with an undue haste. "Come, Caedmon," he said. "Without a doubt you have much to tell me. We'll go up to my chambers and also see to your needs." Throwing caution to the winds, he enveloped him in a hug once more and encouraged him up the ladder to the room above. He snapped his fingers at servants as he went, a buzz of speculation following after.

In Harold's room, Caedmon chewed his way with difficulty through a meal of bread and meat washed down with the last of the previous year's cider. Between mouthfuls he began to tell his story. True to his word, William had had him beached unceremoniously at an obscure cove on the Devon and Dorset border. The crapulous little Breton merchant vessel that had conveyed him there then continued on its way to a scheduled and clandestine rendezvous on Lundy island in the Bristol Channel where illicit goods would be exchanged. Caedmon had made his laborious way east, following the coast until pulled up by an especially officious reeve at Lyme. Hearing his story, the reeve provided him with food and a change of clothes, and he was taken speedily to Bosham in far greater style and comfort.

"Very hard to say," he replied in answer to Harold's latest question. "They can certainly be counted in their hundreds, as best as I could guess. But then, I was taken before I could arrive at a full and true reckoning. I was only there two days. Apart from the boats, the whole land for miles around was swarming like an ant hill. Men, materials, more coming in all the time." "Eat, eat," Harold encouraged him. "Did you speak to anyone? Anyone of importance?"

"Some," said Caedmon. "Bretons down at the quayside or men in the sheds mostly, nobody of importance. We got along quite well with their Breton and my Welsh. Interesting, that." He seemed to drift into a private reverie at this interesting linguistic fact. Harold contained his impatience, giving the man space and time. I spoke to the Duke himself, my Lord," Harold started at the news. "High up on his great horse, and in all his iron. They were, they are, waiting for a wind, my Lord. Not a wind to bring them straight here, but further east down the coast." Harold exhaled noisily in his relief, a breathing space, by God! "And why is that, do you suppose?" he asked gently. Caedmon shrugged and Harold watched, fascinated, as the movement caused lice, already active with the warmth of the room, to appear above the top of his jerkin. Both men scratched. He and Edith would have to find somewhere else to sleep tonight. When Caedmon was out of the way, he would have the room thoroughly cleansed. Down over by the kitchen outhouse water was already being heated and in which the cleric would be immersed and boiled and scrubbed, whether he liked it or not. Earlier Harold had called for his leech, a local man well practiced in the doctoring of men and beasts alike and a much sought after setter of bones. He had established already that Caedmon had several cracked ribs and that some more of the teeth in the ruin of his mouth would have to go. Caedmon had suffered greatly on his behalf. He would be well rewarded, a safe and comfortable stipend somewhere, perhaps a job in his Chancellery. Before he keeled over completely, however, there were more questions that had to be asked.

"I was told," said Caedmon, "that they need to get east with the wind behind them because their boats do not have oars. The further east they go the less distance there is between their coast and ours. Also, the land thereabouts around Dives is just about played out, exhausted. They need fresh land to feed that army of theirs." He belched and apologised. Harold paid it no mind. He was busy, his thoughts racing, thinking and planning.

A change of this present and seemingly eternal wind to a different quarter and the Normans would be on the move. He recalled his own time across the water. It would have to be somewhere within the lands of Boulogne or Ponthieu, he would bet a tidy sum on it. With Caedmon seen to, he would then have to seek out and consult Eadric. "And the Duke of Normandy, Caedmon. What of him? You saw him, spoke to him." Caedmon pushed his empty plate aside and stared into space for a while. "Death, misery, dishonour," he whispered dreamily. "No refuge in this life nor the next. An army of God. Excommunication." Harold went cold.

Excommunication! To be cast out of the loving protection of the Holy Church and into the outer darkness, with no hope of salvation in the life to come. Damnation and the flames of the pit of Hell everlasting. His people denied the sacraments, denied all the rites of passage, of baptism and marriage and a sanctified death, his people. An overbearing Norman bastard and a fearful weakling Pope had brought bring him to this.

Caedmon was still muttering away to himself. "A sacred enterprise blessed by God." Suddenly, embarrassingly, he burst into tears, making whooping noises of grief as he attempted to catch his breath. Mucus and phlegm streamed from his nose and gathered at the corners of his mouth. Never mind the smell and the lice, Harold gathered him up once more in his arms to console him, calling out for the servants. "Rouen," Caedmon wailed. "I went there first, to Rouen. That is where the Duke took him. He took him away from Bec, which was his life. Took him away and threw him in the dungeon and then threw away the key." Harold patted the man's back awkwardly. Wulfnoth, his brother and already a stranger, was lost to him. He had already been lost to him, he knew, back there in Normandy the last time he had seen him.

"Lord?" Men had appeared, their heads sticking into the room as they crowded upon the ladder. "See here now, Caedmon," said Harold. "Look, it is your old friends Willi and Alfi come to see you and make you comfortable." He nodded his thanks to the two men. "Well then, you Welsh bugger, let's be having you," said Willi cheerily. Caedmon descended the ladder like a prisoner under escort and Harold was left alone to his thoughts.

***

The iron hand of the Hardraada had come down in a resounding and crushing blow on the unruly and barely

Christian men of the Trondheim and the uplands. Now their troublesome Jarls were vanquished and gone, dead or else pensioners of the King of Sweden or huddled miserably in tents of felt amongst the deerskin clad Lapp pagans of the far north. To all intents and purposes, and in his own Kingdom, the infant settlement of Nidaros was a garrison fort in enemy territory. Oslo was a dangerous seven-hundred-mile sea journey to the south and east. In excess of three hundred of Norway's sleekest war craft lay either beached or at anchor to the south of the Sognefjord near Bergen. There were still, however, enough ships and men with him here at Nidaros to more than intimidate the fractious locals. In a few days, it was said amongst them, the King would take them and the ships of Bergen away from here and across the sea to the Orkneys. It could not come soon enough for the intimidated people of Nidaros. They were counting the moments.

The island of Selja lay just a short way off, dominated by the largest building for miles around and an object of much local pride. The church of Saint Clement was a handsome structure of timber and stone and with a steep shingled roof crowded with noisy gulls. It was as fine a building as anything to be found in the south, at Stavanger, Bergen or Oslo. The church was served by a small number of consecrated men and lay brothers and had evolved over the years into a community rather resembling an Abbey in its administration and routines.

Local tradesmen from the mainland ferried goods and supplies daily and attended highly individual masses of a type that would have more than raised eyebrows in Rome. The sons and daughters of pagans that the locals were, they were justifiably proud of the honour that the church brought to them. Like the town that it was served by, the church was just over fifty years old. What marked it out as special was that it now housed the bones of a saint, and no ordinary saint at that, in their view. Here there rested the poor abused bones of the warrior king now a saint, Olaf, scourge of the pagan and kinsman to Harald. Over the past few decades, miracles had come to be wrought in his name on the island. The lame walked, the dumb spoke and demons were cast out. In his turn, Harald now came, seeking support and favour from on high from a man he had last seen mutilated and dying at the battle of Stikklestadt so many years before. He had crawled away from that battle, himself half dead with wounds, and away to Russian exile and the true beginning of his meteoric career.

Harald stood at the prow for the short ten-minute row across to the island, relishing the spray and the smells, and accompanied by his two sons and various of the currently favoured of his court. He was in anticipation of a face to face meeting with his illustrious kinsman. He could see the welcoming party gathered nervously on the jetty ahead of him, a knot of shaven and tonsured priestlings cowering behind a giant crucifix of crudely carved wood, taller than a man. Battling to keep it upright against the wind, they held it aloft like a talisman before them against their volatile and demonic lord. Harald smiled to himself at their obvious discomfort.

The previous day, in anticipation of the King's visit, the oldest and most senior of the churchmen had decided to give Olaf an airing. The man was not actually graced with a title and in fact was not even fully ordained. He held his position by seniority and by the greyness of his beard. Only slightly more than his companions and his parishioners did he understand the Latin that he pattered at the services, a Latin that he had learned by rote. The full power and authority of neither the Archbishop of Bremen nor the Holy Father in Rome, both still squabbling over ownership of the souls of the far north, had yet to reach Nidaros and so, in splendid isolation, they were inclined to make up the Liturgy as they went along in a happy stew of both pagan and half understood Christian practice. Of this the chief man was a devoted, enthusiastic and inventive practitioner and it was with a great degree of relish that he ordered men with crowbars and jemmies to prise the heavy stone lid off the saint's coffin.

Leaning over the straining men, he peered in eagerly at its contents, sniffing with appreciation the musty smell of death and sanctity. Olaf did indeed make a most satisfactory corpse, even after all these years. The winding sheet carefully and successfully removed, his shrivelled hands were folded over his dried and desiccated chest and protruding ribs, like an old man resting in the sunshine. The skin, resembling darkened, treated leather, had pulled back on his skull and his fine teeth smiled up at them. His hair, fine and silver, flowed down to his shoulders and the nails of his hands were long and curling inwards.

The head man now greeted Harald at the jetty and led him with a deference mixed with glee up the narrow pathway and into the church and where the tomb of Olaf, surrounded by foul smelling and smoking rush lights, awaited him. Harald approached with all due solemnity and reverence. The chief of the priests was most gratified. He would have been less so had he known what his King had been up to the night before.

In the dark hours Harald had gone with just one attendant to a lonely outcrop of exposed rock outside the town. There he had cut the throats of two black cockerels. He poured their blood carefully into a golden chalice and pledged the old Gods of the Norse, calling upon their aid in this his greatest adventure. He had drunk the blood and poured a respectful libation upon the ground. Now, in the Church. Harald leaned into the open tomb and gazed down at the mortal remains of the former King and now Saint Olaf. He took his knife and cut a lock of hair away from the skull and a paring of a nail. The old man next to him gasped involuntarily at this sacrilege and tomb robbing, but prudently did not speak. Harald tucked the hair and nail into his wallet for safekeeping. In turn, he then hacked at a lock of his own hair and placed it gently upon the saint's chest. "There you go, Olaf," he said. "You're looking good, better than the last time I saw you. Wish me luck."

That August it seemed that that the isles of the Orkneys and the northern coast of Caithness were attracting every man out of the far north who was spoiling for a fight, including many who were the putative subjects of Malcolm Canmore. Over the past month, both news and men had filtered up from Leith. Barely a third of those Orcadians who had travelled south that spring had made it north again all in one piece. There was grieving in the settlements of the mainland, in Duncansby and Freswick and Thurso, and in the islands, the Ronaldseys, Hoy and Hrossey and all the others. They too, however, turned out once more in response to the summons and the burning cross, sending as many as they were able.

And then, from a variety of different directions, there began to arrive, in single boats or small flotillas, more exuberant warriors, both young and untested and aged and experienced, bearing old and whitened scars. The young Earls of the Orkneys, Paul and Erlend, had been left in no doubt whatsoever by Harald's messengers of how bitterly disappointed the King of Norway would be if in any way they fell short in their hospitality to these visitors. As the boats arrived, they were diverted to the sheltered harbour at Kirkwell on the island of Hrossey and where, comparatively speaking, they were out of harm's way.

First to arrive were two boats of fighting men from the Shetlands and another packed with barbarous enthusiasts from the enigmatic Faeroes islands far out to sea, whom everyone feared and shunned. To the locals, themselves deprived and barely scratching a living at the edge of civilisation, these newly arrived men seemed barely human. The highly unstable Godfrey Grovan, the son of Harald the Black, arrived next, having put together a fleet of ten ships from Reykjavik, the far off 'ultima thule' and the other scattered settlements of Iceland. Even in a society well accustomed to the antics of wild and boisterous men, people soon learned to steer well clear of Godfrey Grovan and his sudden and violent passions. Four burly men, especially selected for the task by his father, accompanied him everywhere, ready at any moment to restrain and bind him if necessary whenever the dangerous fits overtook him.

The displaced and broken men of the Western Isles had clubbed together and pooled their resources, sailing in with three boat loads of proud and touchy men. As with many others gathering there, they owed no especial allegiance or loyalty to the Hardraada. They came, purely and simply, as mercenaries in the truest sense of the word, men in search of wealth and land. The Irish Norse communities and men from Dublin and the Isle of Man arrived in another ten boats and immediately sparked off a riot in Thurso. They were dangerous men, red haired and pale skinned, though perhaps no less dangerous than the others. Poor Paul and Erlend had to gather up their still smarting Orcadians as a police force and keep the separate factions as far apart as possible. Despite themselves, they prayed for the arrival of the Hardraada so that he could at least take over the problem of knitting these disparate men together. There was no doubt but that he would be more than equal to the challenge. They too had their own quota to fulfil, twenty boats each with fifty fighting men.

In the light of recent events this would not be easy and the Orcadians were already proving to be fractious. Both Earls were still boys in their teens and not in possession of the mettle of their illustrious father, an adventurous and utterly fearless man with the blood of both Gael and Norse mixed in his veins. Erlend, the younger of the two, was inclined to matters spiritual and sought solutions in contemplation and prayer, leaving many of the more onerous and practical responsibilities to his brother.

***

In the far south a most unseasonable storm erupted off the English coast, a storm that brought disaster and broke the heart of Eadric the Steersman, a man who prided himself on the foretelling of the elements. On Eadric's advice, Harold had taken the decision to move some of his ships down from the estuary of the Thames, Sandwich and Dover. At this season, so Eadric's reasoning went, they would be safe enough. Later, with the arrival of the autumn equinox, there would be problems. "Saving a gale, that is," he added. Harold gave the order and, sure enough, a gale was promptly served up to him. His instincts troubling him, Eadric had sniffed the wind and spat, gazing thoughtfully at the greying sky and the fast, scudding clouds, as did the various masters on shipboard as they sailed into Wessex waters. No person could blame Eadric or hold him in any way responsible, for this was truly an unseasonal act of God. The storm struck and scattered that proportion of the fleet which was on its way west. Some sought shelter along the coast whilst others ran before it, arriving crippled and battered into safe havens amongst the creeks and estuaries of the Solent. Some twenty ships had been lost between there and Dover, foundering at sea or else smashed to pieces on the rocks. The fatalities were correspondingly high.

Harold received the reports in grim silence at Bosham as the inconsolable Eadric raved and fretted. Harold was embarrassed at the spectacle of this dependable old mariner behaving so, despite the gravity of the situation. "Eadric," he said to him, "no person here is blaming you. We are none of us the masters of the weather and of how ever and in what manner it will comport itself. So then, please compose yourself, the blame is not yours. We shall, of course, discuss what is to do later. This evening will be soon enough." The ship master knuckled his forehead and subsided into silence, leaving Harold to stare blankly into space. He had just received disturbing news from Westminster regarding Stigand, and, once more, the blinding headaches had returned. Edith had a remedy for these, but she was no longer there. Had God set his face against him? The hall was crowded with men brought by the news. He turned to address them. "That will be all for now. Thank you for your attendance. We can all talk again at dinner." Taking the hint, they variously nodded and bowed, shuffling and muttering and awkwardly crowding the doorway as they left.

Harold was left alone in the hall, but noise surrounded him. He could hear the steady and rhythmic clang and ting from the blacksmith's forge and the muted and bass tones of the men recently dismissed as they talked in the yard. Somewhere an unfastened door was creaking and banging in the high wind. Was that his son he could hear, a high treble voice in counterpoint screaming out at some companion. He smiled to himself. Perhaps it was the fowler's oldest boy and they were friends again, at least for the moment. There was a regular And steady 'ting,ting' from the blacksmith's hut and a sudden squeal of laughter that seemed to come from the dairy and a background murmur of sounds and voices that came from all over the manor of Bosham. There was the high-pitched squeal of metal clad cart wheels and the stamping and snorting of a horse on the cobbles, probably the arrival of the fresh firewood and kindling. Whatever was that old man's name who did the daily delivery? Harold remembered he had been quite ill recently; he must really speak to the reeve about him. The voice of his cook, a talented man and on loan from the Bishop of Chichester. He must remember to return him, a gift also to the Bishop. Rats scuttled in the thatch above him and that annoying wood pigeon was back and calling out from the roof. Harold, though, was entirely alone. Dear God in Heaven! All those ships. All those men. He sat down and cradled his head in his hands.

***

In Westminster, Stigand reached the shelter and sanctuary of the Vestry after the Mass and where acolytes were waiting to remove from him the impedimenta and robes of office. He sighed deeply, wearily, and gestured for his stool. He seated himself and a Canon of the Minster brought him a mug of red wine. He drained it with a single swallow and then held it out for more. These days he felt very old, positively ancient. His bones ached dreadfully in the wet weather, he slept little and his chest and nose when he lay down filled with phlegm and bitter fluids. His cough and poor appetite was in fact a great cause for concern for his personal physician. The man had no love at all for the Archbishop, but where else in these troubled times could he hope to find such a comfortable living?

Remaining on his feet to carry out the full ceremonial of the Mass from start to finish was, Stigand admitted to himself, now truly a test of endurance. The servitors at his Masses were always conscious of the fact that the old man might keel over at any moment and had made contingency plans accordingly. This one to lift by the shoulders, those two to pick up by the feet, others to assure the congregation that there was no cause for alarm and that the good Archbishop was simply a little fatigued. In quiet moments they had practiced the procedure. As with his personal physician and most others, the wizened and irascible old prelate inspired little affection within their breasts, it was simply that they did not desire the embarrassment of a death at the High Altar during the Mass.

Divested now of the heavy cope and the more formal paraphernalia of the Mass, clad instead in a thick cloak above his surplice, Stigand left through the Vestry door to where his horse and his assembled retinue awaited to accompany him on the short journey to Horseferry and across the river to Lambeth and the home of the Bishop of London, whose most unwelcome and unwanted guest he was. Outside a rabble of louse ridden and foul smelling supplicants and petitioners lay in wait. His attendants thrust them aside and formed an empty space between him and his horse, a fine grey of sixteen hands. He began to make his way through the cleared space, arm raised to sign the cross over them and mumbling benedictions as he went. It was the usual crowd of the lame, the sick and the halt and with a typical sprinkling of tonsured clerks waving scraps of parchment; a request for this, a demand for that.

One of these now broke through the cordon and knelt before him. Stigand halted and the young man smiled up at him engagingly. The Archbishop took the roll of parchment that had been thrust at him and handed it to a servant. "Your Grace, my Lord Archbishop," the young man cried urgently. He reached out to seize the Archbishop's bony wrist and Stigand recoiled at this appalling lack of reverence and respect. "Of your courtesy," Stigand raised his eyebrows in alarm at the strong foreign accent in the man's English. "Read this message. I have carried it from Rome and from our Holy Father himself. It is from his Holiness to you." The young man's natural born English carried a foreign inflection, as well it might, seeing as he had spent the last ten years of his life in the English College in Rome. As attendants hurried forward, the young man switched swiftly to Latin and raised his voice for the unlikely event of any there being able to understand a single word.

"I adjure you and charge you, in the name of God and the Holy Father. You are charged henceforth to leave off the celebration of the Holy Mass. You are divorced from the Church of Christ and from the communion of all Christian men." The young man reverted back to his heavily accented English once more. "You hold the document. It is delivered." His voice was of a man relieved and triumphant and released from a heavy task.

It was, in fact, the second such document Stigand had received in his chequered career. He had been issued with the very same writ many years before, when the then Pope had finally been made aware of the fact that Stigand had been enjoying the livings and earnings of two Bishoprics. As it turned out, his first excommunication had passed almost unremarked in all but the rarified circles within the Vatican itself. Life went on. But this, at this time, was very different. Men bore down upon the young messenger, but he ducked and weaved into the crowd and was swallowed up by it. The thin blood in Stigand's veins seemed to freeze. He felt faint and men gripped him firmly by the elbows to prevent him from falling. "Take me back inside," he hissed, indicating the Vestry. "And find me that man. Find him and bring him to me."

Seated once more upon his stool, Stigand, whose poor eyesight had prevented him from reading for nearly twenty years, had the document read out to him in its full and awesome Latin majesty. Outside enough of the crowd had heard the exchange to realise the full import of it. Safely over the wooden bridge spanning the Tyburn as it flowed into the Thames, the young messenger paused once more and looked back at the approaching church officials struggling through the crowd to get at him. "All of you hear this," he bellowed. "The Archbishop of Canterbury is excommunicated and anathematized. All you good Christian people, I urge you. If you pray for salvation and for the life to come, then cast him out from you." He took to his heels once more and was gone, never to be found.

Inside the Vestry, apologetically and fearfully, one of the more literate Canons was working his way painfully through the text. His Latin was not all that it should have been, and he was intimidated by the magnificence of the rhetoric and the very appearance of the document itself, with its Papal seal and what appeared to be the signature of Pope Alexander himself. As he read the Latin aloud another man, a fraction behind him, provided an English gloss for the benefit of their less gifted colleagues.

"Wherefore, in the name of God the Father, Son and Holy Ghost, of the blessed Peter and all the saints, in virtue of the power which has been given us of binding and losing in Heaven and upon earth...." Stigand groaned, he knew what was coming next. He was undone and the game would be up when word of this got out. He could not necessarily even rely upon a further night of hospitality in Lambeth. He was ruined, finished. *"Thus do we deprive Stigand of Canterbury,"* the Canon continued. *"We deprive him and all his accomplices and abettors of the Communion of the Body and Blood of our Lord. We separate him from the society of all Christians."* There was a muttering and murmuring and some men, having heard enough, were already edging through the Vestry door, as if away from the contagion of leprosy. *"We exclude him from the bosom of our holy mother Church, in Heaven and on earth. We declare him excommunicated and anathematised."*

The sonorous Latin of the document rolled on.

"Enough, enough," Stigand waved his arms in his frustration and anger, but the Canon could not now be stopped. *"We judge him condemned to eternal fire with Satan and his angels and all the reprobate, so long as he will not do penance and satisfy the Church; and we deliver him to Satan, to mortify his body that his soul may be saved on the day of judgement."*

As the Canon came to an end there was a loud clicking sound. It was a priest of the Abbey shutting the lid on the box containing the remains of the sacramental host. He exited into the main body of the building, picking up two flagons of the blood of Christ as he left. Another, more circumspectly, was extinguishing those candles out of reach of the Archbishop's poor vision. They were men of the Bishop of London, no men of his. He was left alone with his own horrified servitors, those selfsame accomplices referred to by the Pope. "Find me that man," Stigand raged at them, "and kill him."

***

September, the month for killing the pigs, for the last of the harvest and the gathering of the fruits of the orchards and forest. So many of the men of the south were missing from their farms and homesteads, away and staring out to sea. The fruit gathering was made into a game, a competition for the children. Rounding up and slaughtering the free ranging and half savage pigs fattened on beech mast, acorns and chestnuts was another matter altogether. The men of the common fyrd of Kent and Sussex and Hampshire were anxious and homesick. They had more than served their term, more than fulfilled the statutory duties and responsibilities required of them in return for the land that they held. Time, now, to go home and prepare for the lean times of winter. Surely the bastard would not come now, not so late in the season. The men of the fleet with their superior knowledge of weather, were equally fractious. The autumn equinox, they argued, was all but upon them. They too had their own personal worries and responsibilities. There was the salting and smoking and curing of fish, the repair of nets and boat sheds, the beaching and repair of the boats themselves. An increasing number of desertions from both the fyrd and the fleet were now reported daily.

These continued to be extremely difficult times for Harold. He had a few trusted men in Scotland who sent him occasional reports of the activities of his brother. Tostig was apparently in ill favour, but nonetheless reported to be meeting with Malcolm Canmore often enough and was about the busy task of reconstructing a small fleet and army. There came a second message from Sweyn in Denmark, a repeated offer of alliance and many thanks for the splendid wolfhounds. All appeared quiet on Sweyn's northern border and he certainly was not going to stir things up. Nonetheless, he thought that his cousin should know that the Hardraada had taken himself to Bergen and great activity was reported there. The man was busy, clearly working away like a rooting pig, he was up to something, devil a doubt of it.

Stigand had retreated to Canterbury, far too close for comfort, and where he now lived like a recluse. From there he sent Harold regular outraged missives and calls for action. Harold had an excommunicant Archbishop on his hands. Would he be next? Perhaps even now some anonymous looking cleric armed with a Papal writ was already pacing the quayside in some French or Flemish port and waiting for a ship. As for the Duke of Normandy, the most recent report had him still at Dives. At that time Harold was not to know that that same fatal wind that had savaged his fleet had carried William's army to St Valery.

Bosham was a hive of activity around the empty shell of the hall, for Edith and the children were gone now. A week before, and after a blazing row, Edith had finally capitulated, leaving under great protest. They had stood facing each other in the courtyard as the children were prepared for the journey. He had said goodbye to each in turn, ruffling the boys' hair and promising them extravagant bribes for good behaviour. He hugged and kissed the girls through a mist haze of ill suppressed tears. He told them all to be good and to watch out for their mother. Edith observed all of this little domestic scene in a stony silence.

Harold at last took her in his arms. "Edith, my love," he said. "We must not quarrel. We have very little time. He may still come this year. If he doesn't, then he will be here in the spring. At least we'll have more time together in the winter. I swear this to you but promise me this. If he does come, then make for Bristol or Chester. Whatever is easiest and quickest. In both places a boat will await you there, it is arranged. If the news is bad then the boat will take you to Ireland, to friends of mine who will shelter and protect you." He grasped her shoulders. "Edith, promise me this."

Edith, unexpectedly, was crying. "Harold," she said, "we shared harsh words with each other last night and I leave against my will. You have a great weight placed upon you, and with even greater challenges and danger ahead. I pray to God to keep you safe. You have all my prayers and all my thoughts. If and when you find the time, then come and visit us. No big farewells now." With that she simply turned and walked away. An attendant helped her mount her horse and the cavalcade turned and rode out of the courtyard, the farewells of the children ringing in Harold's ears. Edith did not look back. He watched for a while as they wound their way along the track that would take them over the downs and first to the relative safety of Guildford.

Harold arose from his prayers, his decision made, and called for a council. The necessary members of it, drawn by the news of the gale, were already on hand. The council convened within the hour to hear and discuss the decisions he had arrived at. The initial reaction was deeply divided. "I'm not saying it won't, I'm not saying it will," announced Eadric, referring, of course, to the wind that was apparently still pinning William to his coast. It was not a helpful comment. "It's late in the season, very late. But it could still happen."

Stocks and supplies along the coast were all but exhausted, reported Gyrth and the Abbot of St Benet. They could not guarantee supplies in sufficient quantity for a further week. "We'll face them out," said Leofwyn defiantly, "God will provide." Harold's uncle and nephew added their agreement. "These," said Gyrth firmly, "are the facts of the matter. Desertions grow by the day. This is not good. If these men are not now released, having served well beyond their term, then we can no longer rely upon their support when they are truly needed. Already we face a serious shortage upon the land. If these men do not return then we face a famine."

The days were turning rainy and the last of the wheat and the corn was rotting in the fields. Children splashed through the mud in search of the last of the spoiling windfalls. "Release the Fyrd now," argued Gyrth. "Let them go so that they will return to us willingly in the spring. That is when the Normans will come." Harold was at last convinced and gave the command. With immediate effect and with the deep thanks of their King the men of the common fyrd were free to return to their homes. At key places along the coast, selected thegns and their followers and the housecarls of the King and the Earls of Kent and East Anglia would maintain the watch on the coast. Not needing to be told twice, the men of the fyrd streamed gratefully away to their homes across the downs or through the Weald, rejoicing and singing as they went. The bulk of the boats were decommissioned, free to attempt the safety of their home ports or to remain beached for the winter. Small flotillas remained on standby in the Solent and at ports and coves all the way east to Sandwich.

"Well, that's that then," said Harold once the orders had been sent. "I shall leave for Westminster at the end of the week. This is a postponement only. Sooner or later they will come, and then may God help us all."

***

Far to the north, that same wind that kept William at St Valery and Harold guessing, sped Harald Hardraada's fleet, joyous and exuberant, out of Bergen and across the long haul of open sea to the Orkneys. The fleet paused briefly in the Shetlands and then came sailing into Scapa Flow in the very best of spirits. It was a proud moment for the Hardraada as he stood on the raised deck of his flagship and as they swept into the narrowing reaches. In the journey there he seemed to have shed years. With him were his son Olaf and his immediate intimates and advisors. Old, blind Stump, no longer huddled at his feet, muttering to himself and casting knucklebones. He was left behind, in distant Norway, few mourned the fact. No man there wished to have him there, to ask him what the bones foretold.

Sailing behind the flagship, and in excellent order, came a fleet of three hundred warships, the greatest Viking force ever assembled and stretching as far as the eye could see. He had achieved all of this himself. He, Harald the Hardraada. The memory of his name at the feast and by the fire was assured for all time to come. He breathed in the fine air. It was just like the old days, when his Viking world was young or, at least, far younger than now. A greater Norway was within his reach. By the time he had finished he would make Cnut look like no more than an especially prosperous local farmer. The Faroes and the Shetlands, Iceland, he'd bring them all back to him and make them eat dirt. There would be regencies and governorships for his sons and all those that he trusted and favoured. He would, he had decided, keep and maintain the young Earls of Orkney. Through them he could lean on Alba. He would take the Western Isles and the island of Man, good stopping off places for trade and adventure. He would sort out all those irksome distant kinsmen of his in Dublin, a reckoning was long overdue. Then, of course, there was the greatest prize of all, England with all its bounteous land and unfathomable wealth. By God, he would squeeze Denmark like a ripe fruit. He would take it and make it his own. He would personally carve out the spreadeagle on Sweyn's old, wrinkly back. He laughed aloud at the sheer fun of it all, the burden of his years stripped away from him, he gripped the rail as firmly as ever he had done along the long, dark rivers of the Rus or across the sparkling waters of the Bosporus.

At Shetland they had chosen a boat, giving it a head start of three days. It was a trim little craft with fine lines to it and a crack crew. Away it had gone, speeding south and coursing through the high white caps of the waves like a sleek greyhound to bring the news to Orkney. Thus it was that there was a crowd of cheering men to meet them at the head of the Sound and an impressive number of boats already at anchor there. The representatives of all the contingents had gathered, many of them relatively sober. Godfrey Govan of Iceland, his eyes mad and bulging, was foaming slightly at the mouth under the watchful stare of his keepers. At the head of them stood the nervous and alarmed Earls of Orkney.

Hardraada's boat came alongside the jetty, the men pulling the oars in and catching at flung ropes. The King of Norway had dressed for the occasion; his usual half naked ensemble of bare chest, cloak of imperial purple crimson and kidskin trousers and knee boots. He held his axe and upon his head was a magnificent helmet of iron with inlaid patterns of gold and silver. All about him, torque, necklace, pendants, arm rings, was a profusion of Byzantine and pagan jewellery and ornamentation. Standing nearly seven feet high, he was a truly picturesque and unforgettable figure. He bared his yellow teeth at the crowd as he leaped nimbly ashore. At this range and owing to his failing eyesight, he could make the figures out only as an indistinct blur. He stood erect, arms folded across his massive and scarred chest, and favoured them all with an intimidating stare. One last throw of the dice. This done, who knew? He might even hand it all over to his sons and retire to his feasting hall to spend the rest of his days carousing and begetting bastards. Gratifyingly, the men there to meet him all knelt as one. He was still laughing as he advanced upon them to raise them up and greet them. One last throw of the dice, double or quits.

CHAPTER FOUR:

Fulford Gate

Yorkshire: September, 1066

Never a robust nor a relaxed man, Malcolm Canmore, King of Scotland, fretted and chewed his nails up there on his bleak rocky eyrie high above Edinburgh. From the moment his messengers had brought him news of the arrival of the Hardraada and a huge fleet of invasion in the Firth of Forth he became an introspective, indecisive and brooding shadow, occasionally lashing out in heedless and vicious anger against both people and objects. Malcolm had only just bidden a less than fond farewell to Tostig and his battered, mongrel little fleet, now on its way south, and now here was the news he had been expecting and dreading. An uncountable host of bestial Norse had dropped anchor in the Leith roads. This was a man who could, and well he remembered Tostig's phrase, squeeze him like an apple in a press. Now he was expected at any moment, arriving in Leith and not a half morning's ride from where he now sat nervously fiddling with a scrap of sheepskin. This scrap, until it was worn out and replaced by another, would accompany him everywhere. Malcolm derived great solace and a form of inner peace in playing with it.

Should he hurry to meet his unwanted guest with hastily gathered gifts, or should he, in his own Kingdom, wait to be summoned? Should, and God forbid that any insult be taken, he summons the Hardraada to his presence? God damn it all. This was his own country! There appeared to be no protocol available to deal with this fearsome and uncivilised creature straight out of a nightmare dream of a child and with ten thousand of the Norse world's finest at his back. If so inclined or else provoked, they could tear Edinburgh apart beam by beam and make a wilderness of the country without even breaking into a sweat.

The baggage and all portable wealth was already in the courtyard, ready for a swift flight, if necessary, to Scone or Stirling or Falkirk. Anywhere, if things turned ugly. Malcolm ordered and then postponed, then cancelled and then ordered again a banquet of welcome. Throwing caution to the winds, he told the steward to skimp on nothing. "No cheese paring, mind," he yelled. "I cannot abide cheese paring." As the hapless steward was dismissed for the fourth time, Malcolm was of a mind to order him back and rescind the order once more. What did he have laid by and to hand that the Hardraada might possibly covet or appreciate? Somewhere about the place, he recalled, he had a spare fourteen-year-old Lothian heiress under his wardship. She was pretty enough, would she do? Could he get away with it? The English had called it 'Wergild,' money to pay their own brand of troublesome Danes to go away, only they never really did, always coming back for more. How much did he have? How little could he get away with parting with?

He fretted and visibly lost weight.

These less than happy thoughts were interrupted by the arrival of another messenger from Leith. The Norse fleet had arrived and had dropped anchor in the shallows. The estuary was black with ships. The people of Leith, their belongings bundled together, had fled at first sight of the ships. Thus far, only five ships had come in close, beaching on the sands of Leith before the jetty. There the men aboard them had been met and greeted by the newly appointed port reeve of Leith, a man called Lachlan Strachan. This had been at the hour of noon. "Strachan," screamed Malcolm at the news, "and what the bloody hell is he doing about it?" No one there dared to ask him what in fact he could effectively do about it.

In fact it was the very good fortune of Malcolm Canmore that he had a good man on the ground there over at Leith as the Hardraada vaulted over the side of his boat and splashed ashore, trailing his son Olaf , his prospective son in law Eyestein Orri and his newly appointed second in command, Stryker, in his wake. Men were coming ashore from the other boats, the two Earls of Orkney, Godfrey Grovan, the leaders of Dublin and Man, the Hebrides and the Faroes.

Lachlan Strachan, second son of old Strachan and recalled from the Monastery when his elder brother was thrown onto his head and killed in a riding accident, was an excellent if accidental choice in dealing with the situation. Down there at Leith, they had known for days, ever since the Norsemen had begun to make their way down the Pentland Firth, that the Hardraada was on his way. Strachan, a man of wit and presence and considerable personal courage, was one of the few to keep his head. He spoke soothingly to the nervous and twitching chief factor standing beside him now. "Well now, here comes the last of the Northmen. You can only die the once, Dougal my boy." He bared his teeth at the oncoming giant in a welcoming grin. To either side of him and the reluctant Dougal he had placed two of his least impression-able servants. They held aloft staffs hastily wrapped around with green ivy and garlanded, a sign of peace in any man's visual language.

Lachlan spread his arms by way of further welcome, thus showing he carried no weapon. Under the circumstances he would have been mad to have done so. Behind him a number of fishermen's gutting tables had been hastily doused with salt water and scrubbed. He had collared a few tardy people from a nearby tavern and bakery and bribed them heavily to stay. They bustled fearfully around now, laying out beef and pork and mutton, fresh bread and strong drink.

"Here we go then, Dougal. Do please try to look pleased and delighted. You have a wife and all those bairns at home to support. Remember, it's not us he's after, its yon beta-iled English in the south. Let us speed the parting guest with honour and praise if we can." Harald loomed up and gazed down at them impassively, hands on hips. Strachan bowed low, elaborately. "My Lord King," he began, "you do me and this place of Leith great honour. I am distraught at the poverty of our welcome." At the sound of the unfamiliar Gaelic, Harald frowned and gestured Paul of Orkney forward.

"You may address your remarks to me," said the young Earl imperiously. "We do not intend to stay here for any appreciable period of time." Strachan murmured noises of dismay and disappointment. "We need to provision, buy things," said Paul. "The King of Norway takes only from his enemies. Here, of course, we shall pay." So far, so good, thought Strachan. "Might I ask your Lordships what you are in need of and when, to my distress, you shall be leaving us?" Paul conferred briefly in Norse with Harald and the others before turning back to him. "The sooner you provide us then the sooner we shall be off. We have things to do."

Malcom Canmore's representative at his Royal Port of Leith bowed low and elaborately. As far as he was concerned, this was excellent news. A group of men had manhandled a large wooden chest off one of the boats and were now struggling up the loose pebbles and shingle of the shore with it. "The King of Norway bids me tell you that there is no need to disturb your King," Paul continued. "Our men will come on shore for a short while only. They shall keep themselves to themselves and there shall be no disturbance. You have the word of the King of Norway on this. We shall take on fresh water. We need salt and fresh meat and bread for the fleet. Fresh green stuff too, anything that you have." The boy Earl looked beyond Strachan to the deserted dockside behind him. "We need also ropes and pitch and tar, this and that. I'm sure you know the kind of thing. Our ship masters will advise."

With a final crunch of the shingle, the chest was deposited at Strachan's feet. He gazed down as the lid was prized off to reveal hack silver and coin gleaming slightly in the watery September sunlight. "That will do nicely," said Strachan, his King's good and unacknowledged servant and a man now about to make a fine personal side profit. "I shall see to everything."

***

On the evening of their sixth day of cruising up and down the north Yorkshire coast, and with no sign of either friend or foe in Northumbria, Copsig, tentatively, ventured a criticism. "We should have stayed and waited in Scotland," he said, looking at his Earl out of the corner of his eye to gauge the response. Tostig's little flotilla of twelve ships lay beached beneath the tall cliffs just below Ravenspur, a godforsaken spot, and with the estuary of the Humber just a short distance to the south. His little army, decimated by death, disease and desertion, sat about their fires and sharing out what food they had. Men had been placed on the cliff top. Warned, they could have these boats away and at sea in minutes, trusting to the power of the oarsmen, whatever the tide. At least there would be no more desertions. There was no one and nowhere safe to desert to. Their only salvation lay in the arrival of the Hardraada. "Peace, Copsig, peace," said Tostig amiably. "It's always the darkest just before the dawn. Any day now and we'll be marching in to York. And after York all of Northumbria will be ours once more. Have I ever been wrong?" Wisely, Copsig forebore to make any further comment.

***

In York the spacious house of the prosperous merchant Thorri Arnulfson lay just across the way from Tostig's own former residence and beneath the shadow of the Minster itself. Men had gathered there in the upstairs room, making their way through the crowded streets and the square with circumspection, for what they were to discuss could be considered treason. They were traders and merchants of the city, Danes and Norwegians to a man.

One of their number, detailed to the task, gazed nervously out of the open and unshuttered window at the activity in the square below. He shivered in the cold and wind of the season, on the watch for any uninvited Northumbrian housecarls out to break up a seditious assembly. He could almost reach down and touch the heads of the people passing by below. In and around York the fyrd of Northumbria and the thegns and their followers had been gathering for days past. Around the open doors of Morcar's hall the activity was especially pronounced.

"So, we are agreed then," Thorri Arnulfson was saying. "We need to be brief. This fight is none of ours, and this city cannot be defended in any way." There was universal assent to this from the gathered men. The once fine city walls were in a truly shocking state, a party of determined children could overrun them, often, in their play, they did. Of all the cities of England, York was fiercest and proudest in its independence of any outside interference. The people of York had come to hate Tostig and their dislike of and contempt for his successor Morcar was now beginning to take a more pronounced turn. None of them relished a visit from the King of Norway either. If the English and the Norse were to come to the shield wall, then let it be as far away from their walls as possible, they could treat with the victors subsequently. Despite the displays of martial power going on all around them, none of them doubted but that it would be the Hardraada who would triumph. In York, certainly in this room, Scandinavian influence and Scandinavian interests were paramount, a smug little mercantile island dedicated to peace and to profit beleaguered in a wild sea of war hysteria. "We can always pay him to go away," said the city's leading leather exporter. "It's always worked in the past." Arnulfson sighed elaborately. "Yes, but first we have to get those two brats well beyond our walls to have their little fight. That is why we have met. I look forward to hearing your suggestions tonight here. Now leave quietly and individually, for the love of God, mind yourselves in your leaving."

The taking of Skaroaborg proved to be immense fun. The little Danish fishing village was not half a hundred years old and where old people could still recall the founder of the place, Skarre, a free booting Danish adventurer from the old days of Cnut and Aethelred. As Haralds's fleet swept inexorably south, it was the high cliffs rather than the settlement beneath them that first attracted the attention of his failing eyesight and his interest. The existence of Skaroaborg itself had to be tactfully pointed out to him. "It's as good a place as any to start visiting," he said. The beach was wide and welcoming, enough to accommodate twenty boats. Messages passed through the fleet. They dropped their sea anchors and paused as the appointed vessels sped towards the shoreline, running up into the gravel.

Naturally, the people of Skaroaborg knew trouble when they saw it, the fleet having been sighted long since.

Recklessly, and in keeping with their fierce independence and bellicosity, the people of the settlement decided to make a fight of it. When, then, the first of Harald's men strode confidently up the shingle and sand they discovered a village not deserted or even in panic struck turmoil, but instead a steep single lane barricaded with overturned carts, barrels and timber and behind which stood a line of determined looking men and boys armed to the teeth, perhaps a hundred of them in all. The women and children were beginning to toil up the steep paths to the headland. A dozen Norwegians, complacent and contemptuous, were strolling towards the barricade when a hail of throwing axes, spears, sticks and stones descended upon them. Half of the men went down in the first moment and the defenders of Skaroaborg swarmed over the barricade and put a prompt end to the dazed survivors.

Harald, just a short distance behind, swore in bemused anger, ducking as a hurled stone missed him by inches. "By the Gods above, they'll regret this," he roared, shedding all pretence of a supposed Christianity. "Kill them. Kill them all." Godfrey Govan had come ashore. Needing no second invitation, he unleashed his Icelanders upon the men and boys of Skaroaborg, making short work of them, sending the survivors in flight. "You," barked Harald to Eyestein Orri and Stryker, as the Icelanders wreaked their swift and bloody revenge, "up those cliffs." Even he had noticed the labouring women and children making their way up the cliff side. Nimble as goats, the Norsemen went swarming up a track of the cliff face after them. Harald was ever a dedicated and devoted pyromaniac. "Burn this place," he said, "and kill them all, women and children as well." And this, obedient to his will, his men did.

***

The news was brought to York before nightfall. At the gate the messenger gathered himself and drew breath. He dismounted, dusted his cloak and with his sleeve wiped the foam and the blood from the mouth and nostrils of his horse. No point in starting a panic, at least not yet a while. He was a sensible and a collected man who had been out in the rebellion the year before against Tostig. Leading his horse, he made his way quietly through the crowded streets without exciting undue attention and straight to the presence of the Aelfgarsons. The two boys received and digested the news, distilling between them a potent brew of fear, excitement and elation, leading to vainglorious threats. Action at last! Had Edwin himself not thrown out Tostig not too long ago? Now Tostig was rumoured to be lurking not too far off again.

Order after countermanding order went issuing out and, at this customary time of curfew and the closing of the gates, the town boiled up and swarmed with men. In the eye of the storm, Staffyd collared a clerk and writing materials and dictated a brief note to Harold in Westminster, copies sent also to Gyrth in Norwich and to the men of the five boroughs. Within the hour messengers went thundering out of the open gates, the traditional curfew being in abeyance on this occasion, on their respective journeys.

Much later that evening Edwin sought Staffyd out. "There you are, then," he called, finding him alone as he was returning to his room after an especially long communion with God at the nearby Church of All Hallows. "Where have you been hiding yourself all day? I've been looking for you everywhere. You're never around when I need you. A message, Staffyd, to the King. Tell him of all that has happened. Ask him what we are to do." Staffyd inclined himself at the waist, stiffly and politely. "Upon the instant, my Lord," he said. "Man alive," said Edwin irritably, "do I have to think of everything myself?"

At first light a mixed force of the local fyrd and with a stiffening of Northumbrian housecarls, perhaps three hundred men in all, left York for the coast below Skaroaborg. It was not a long journey and they moved with speed. What, effectively, realistically, they were supposed to achieve was never really made clear to any of them, but they took a misleading comfort in their numbers. It was assumed, accurately enough, that there would be a Norwegian land force roaming around to the north of them and in this they were proved, disastrously, to be correct. Towards mid-morning the now tired men formed up in a shield wall to protect the main road running south, almost to the very sea edge, disgruntled and nervous men.

Shortly thereafter, the fleet of the Norse swept into view. Even as they gaped in stupefaction at its awesome size, a land force of perhaps three times their number appeared before them, coming on at a screaming run. There was a brief and bloody encounter and then the farm boys of the moors and dales broke and fled, their backs presenting broad and tempting targets for the axes and spears of the northmen. It was a massacre, and over in minutes. Perhaps once man in ten made it back to the dubious shelter of York.

***

"And now there's a sight for your tired old eyes," yelled Tostig to his lieutenant as their boats rocked gently in the lee of the Ravenspur, "and not one you'll see every day of the week." His mouth open and his eyes squinting against the sun, Copsig could only agree. Four hundred sails, if there was a one. By the White Christ, but he never thought he'd live to see such a thing. The fleet surged towards them, awesome and terrible and beautiful to behold. In the van, its large cream coloured sail bearing the sign of the black raven, came a vast twenty bench vessel, forty oarsmen labouring away and inboard a jostling crowd of waving and shouting men. Across the way, they could now make out a war chant, rolling out in time to the rhythm of the oars.

Standing proudly and clutching the prow head was a gigantic and familiar figure. The boats behind him seemed to crowd out the horizon. Tostig barked orders and the starboard rowers of his flotilla set to work while the port side backed water. In moments, his twelve boats stood in line behind, ready to fall in with the Norse fleet. Another order, and the crews began to dig and pull their first long sweep, to build up a speed that would bring them to the same pace as the Norwegians as they passed. Tostig gesticulated and screamed in his delight and was weeping openly as the Hardraada, now level and some five lengths off, favoured him with a single wave. "The estuary of the Humber," Tostig bawled at him, "ahead of us, we'll reach it within the hour." Still weeping, he turned to Copsig and hugged him. Never an emotional man, Copsig endured the embrace and set himself to counting sails once more.

There were English boats in the estuary, twenty of them, an untidy mix of genuine war vessels and converted merchant traders, small and ill handled. They had been pottering up and down river for some days now, aware of the importance of the estuary and the old Roman road at its head that linked the north to the south. Now they had definite news of a sighting of Tostig near to the Ravenspur and were heading for the river mouth to set his head upon a spike. Instead, sweeping round from Spurn Head and the triumph of the rout at Holderness behind them, they encountered the full force and majesty of the Norse fleet. The master of the leading vessel swore vividly, invoking the Almighty at the sight before crossing himself in penitence. He did, however, have full cause. He screamed urgent orders to the boats behind. They backed around, not without difficulty and a fair measure of clumsiness and went racing back up the estuary with as much speed as they could gather in search of a place of safety.

Tostig, Copsig and a recruited local pilot born and bred in the tidal reaches of the Humber and its tributaries stood on the raised deck of Harald's flagship. In this reach of the river, five ships abreast could be accommodated. Shortly, and the order had gone back, the flow and width would permit only two and then thereafter only single file. Ahead of them and prudently out of bowshot a solitary English boat sailed ahead of them, monitoring their progress. On either bank there was a dreary and desolate vista of low-lying marsh and flatlands, utterly devoid of human life. "You'll find the inflow of the Trent just up ahead to port," said Tostig knowledgeably. "Thereafter the channel narrows, lots of mud banks to either side." Emboldened by the presence of his future father in law, Eyestein Orri smirked as he surveyed the empty banks. "Not much sign, as yet," he said to Tostig, "of your loyal followers in their thousands."

Both men glanced across to the Hardraada, deep in thought and clutching the rail. He was, in fact, hundreds of miles away, navigating the Don and the Dnieper in the days of his glamorous youth. The two men had not got on well with each other all those weeks ago in Norway and the events of the day thus far had not reconciled them. "When we move upon York," said Tostig through gritted teeth, "then we shall see. In the meantime, have your helmsman and those in the bows mark their course. Here on in it begins to get difficult." Orri snorted in amusement. He had sailed up and down more rivers and fjords than this Englishman had had hot breakfasts. "As the river narrows," continued Tostig," you'll find more woods on either bank and the river winds more. Good place for an ambush. Look to yourself." Arrogant little Norwegian bastard, he thought to himself, praying for an inglorious death to the man.

Sure enough, the entry of the Tweed now behind them and the English boat up ahead occasionally invisible because of the twists and turns of the river, they were obliged to sail single line ahead. Behind them the men in the other boats were in fine mood. They sang and chanted as the fleet, now backed up for over two miles, progressed along. They had not a care in the world, these men. They were the sea wolves, now with their fangs deep in the English throat. On some of the boats behind men had begun the oar race, stripping naked and challenging each other to run barefoot along the oars from stern to bow as they rose and dipped. There arose shouts of acclaim and hoots of derision as men either triumphed or were thrown into the water. "Last chance for a full turnabout of the boat," muttered the local pilot to nobody in particular. At this Harald snapped out of his introspection. "Last ten boats," he snapped. "Five to face about to the sea and the other five to stand by to carry messages. Give the order." He sank back into contemplation once more as messengers swam to the bank to relay the message back.

They were now fast losing the light and the order was given to halt. Still in excellent spirits, the fleet made fast to the northern bank and men set off to forage, all need for secrecy now long gone. They reported a deserted countryside, just the occasional Englishman scuttling off into the woods and marshes at their approach. They came back mostly empty handed, but no matter. Cleveland and the expanse of coast between Scarborough and the Humber had yielded a fine haul of livestock and other supplies, now being passed amongst the boats. They slept the night in comparative comfort on shipboard and on the bank.

The next morning, in an early mist giving notice of the autumn, they set off once more, making good progress and meeting no opposition. The English boat was still on its station up ahead of them. They grew more attentive as the woodlands began to thicken on either bank and as the river narrowed still further. "Riccall up ahead," said the monosyllabic pilot after a while. "And so?" demanded Harald, turning to him. The pilot, dour and unimpressed, spat over the side, thus winning himself the whimsical favour of the King of Norway. "And so, a settlement," he said. "Most likely it'll be deserted by now. Beyond it you'll find the Ouse going off to the north, all the way to York and beyond. This river way, we call it the Wharfe, takes you to Tadcaster. Either way, you'll be advised to stop here. You'll not get your boats much further in safety." Harald nodded, the previous evening, with difficulty, they had manoeuvred a smaller pilot boat ahead of the flagship. This was now sent off to see which of the two waterways the small English fleet ahead of them would take. The English boat, they reported back, had taken the way to Tadcaster. "Then you have them now," said the pilot, "Bottled up nicely, so they are. They'll not come out again unless you let them." Tostig agreed. "Send ten boats to block them," he urged, "up the Ouse to hold it and you'll have them stuck fast." Orders went back once more. Harald's fleet passed by and the last ten boats took up station to and block the river Wharfe.

The rest of the fleet then carried on to the deserted village of Riccall, a small and mean settlement set on both banks. Jetties revealed the presence of a recently busy ferry crossing. The Norsemen roamed about on either bank in search of food and loot and were, of course, disappointed. At least there was plenty of firewood. Harald stepped ashore on the north bank and looked behind him at his pride and joy, a section of river more than two miles in length crowded with boats.

By a circuitous route, men were sent to scout Tadcaster from the north. Reporting back, they told of a large and occupied settlement in a considerable degree of panic and confusion and of the English boats hopelessly jammed together. They had been observed, but none had moved against them. They had jeered and exposed their buttocks to the spineless English before returning back, killing a solitary and hapless water fowler on the way. A second group, moving in the direction of York, had encountered neither man nor beast.

In a large tithe barn full of winter hay and recently stored apples and pears, Harald contemplated Riccall as winter quarters for his fleet, it now being well into September. "For myself," he told the men gathered about him, "I shall take my ease in York, and then south in the spring." They all roared, banging their fists on whatever came to hand, it was an automatic response to any of the King's more portentous or bellicose remarks. Outside an entire ox was being basted and rotated and roasted over a fire and they had all of them been drinking solidly and steadily for over an hour. The city of York, Harald had been informed, was a mere ten-mile march to the north along the bank of the Ouse. "May I ask, my Lord King, what your next move shall be?" asked Tostig politely, "near as we are to York?"

Harald paused, raising his eyebrows, a mug of strong drink halfway to his mouth. He put the drink down. "Well, now," he said. "Well, now. We have waited long enough for your loyal Northumbrians. In their thousands I believe you told me." His followers all dutifully laughed as one and Tostig flushed angrily. "At least my Lord Tostig," said Orri, "he is a passable pilot and navigator." Perhaps in the battle which must surely soon follow, mused Tostig, this man might meet with a tragic accident. "Ten English miles or so to York," said Harald, "and I wonder what is going through their minds at this moment?"

"I can answer that, I think," said Tostig. "Those two puppies will be spoiling for a fight, and they'll have all the available men of Northumbria and much of Mercia with them. Five thousand men? Six thousand? Perhaps more. They'll not stand behind the walls of York; of that I can assure you. They'll not risk either a siege or a sack, the townspeople will not permit it. No, they'll come out against you and seek to hold you up as long as possible while they get word to the south. The ground will be in their favour and of their choosing. You must move against them as soon as possible, on the morrow for preference." Harald nodded, "that was my thought also," he said. "Thank you Tostig. We shall oblige them."

***

This, the thought came suddenly and chillingly to Staffyd, is the end of all things. He felt cold and clammy with the realisation of it, an undeniable presentiment of an impending and inescapable doom. Not for him, then, a frequently imagined happy and fond old age in his manor outside Tamworth and surrounded by doting grandchildren. There was an inevitability to it all, and he was powerless to resist. Perhaps, he thought, drowning was like this.

The previous day, with the news of the Hardraada sailing merrily up the Humber, the two Aelfgarsons had met with a delegation of the citizens of York. The good burghers, English, Danish and Norwegian merchants, had presented a united front and won their argument with ease in a very short time. York could not stand. In fact, Edwin and Morcar had required very little persuading. They had no wish to be bottled up behind walls which in fact could not be defended. No, with the full weight and power of their combined armies behind them, they would seek out the enemy and crush them like lice. The men of York smiled into their beards at this and then shouted acclaim and encouragement. In a series of secret meetings, they had already all made their pledges to a community chest, a common hoard to pay off the Norse and to save them all from sack and destruction. Staffyd, who had his own secret ways and means of arriving at the truth, was aware of this and he stared balefully at them. Very well then, come what may, let the people of York stew in their own juice. His task now was to win time to allow the King to come up from the south, to persuade these wilful boys not to offer battle, to draw them west to comparative safety west across the Pennines.

Edwin wasn't having any of it. "Enough, Staffyd," he said. "I have heard enough. Run from them? Surrender up the whole of the north without a fight?" His handsome face blazed with indignation, "we shall not stand for it." Beside him, Morcar nodded his agreement. "My Lord Earl," said Staffyd with great patience and restraint, "We do not know their numbers, neither can you place any trust in the men of York. We must win time for the King to come up from the south with all his numbers. Then, somewhere to the west, we can in combination beat them. This, in all our meetings with the King, has always been my understanding." If ever he had any influence over this boy then please God, the Father and Son and Holy Ghost and the Virgin and all the Saints let it be now. Knock some sense into them. He pleaded to the Almighty.

"Our King," said Edwin coldly, "has his own fish to fry, let me remind you. His duty is in the south. The Normans are supposed to be imminent; it would seem that you may have possibly forgotten this minor detail. We reached an agreement, sealed with the surrendering up of our own sister. He is our shield to the south, as we are his, here in the north." His look and his stance clearly indicated that the discussion was at an end. "My Lord," Staffyd was almost begging him, "the King was most specific upon this point. I heard him say the words myself. You were not to engage the Hardraada if he came, save only with either his presence or his authority." Edwin jabbed the man in the chest in his anger. "My brother in law, Staffyd, my brother in law is hundreds of miles away.

The Northmen, let me remind you, are just ten miles from here where we stand. What would you have me do?"

"Take your men, and those of your brother the Earl of Northumbria away from here. Move to the west. Take up a position there and wait." Edwin actually screamed at him. "Wait? Wait? You silly old sod. Those bastards will be in York before you know it. While you would have us run and hide, they'll take the whole of the north. And do you seriously imagine that Harold, even if he could come north, would then simply hand it back to us again? No, we fight. What of Skaroaborg? What of the dead of Holderness?"

And so, that was that and the orders were given. In the morning, at first light, they would leave York and move on Riccall to seek out the Hardraada and burn his boats for him. Unless, of course, he came looking for them.

***

It was done, and God alone knew what would come of it. The men of the southern fyrd were streaming away, back to their badly missed homes and to the remains of the autumn harvest. Only a small force remained, funded and supported by local thegns, guarding the coast from Dover to the lands of Devon. On the morning of his own departure, Harold lit candles and spent more than an hour on his knees before the main Altar in the little and peaceful church of Saint Christopher in Bosham, praying for vital months of winter peace before facing the Normans, as he knew he must, in the spring. He felt that the Saint was not listening and, attempting to rise to his feet, he felt himself stricken in the back, his legs frozen and fused, it seemed, into one single mass of unbendable bone. To his dismay and humiliation, he had to call for help. Presently Willi and the Welsh boy Gavin appeared. They hauled him to his feet and helped him from the church.

Edith would have known what to do, but she was gone. It was the rheum again. All those wet nights on shipboard and crouching in Irish and Welsh mists and fogs. Walking about eased the pain and the cramps somewhat, but the journey on horseback across the downs to Guildford and then Kingston and on to Westminster was a personal calvary to him. At night his devoted men brought him heated stones and massaged his limbs. He put on a brave face for his entry into Westminster, smiling broadly and waving at the yokels in the villages of Chelsea and Kensington and appearing to enjoy the plaudits of the crowd at Westminster itself. "That's enough of that," he muttered. His face had gone ashen and there was a sheen of sweat upon it. "Get me inside now." There was a last cheery wave to the crowd before he was put to bed with a high fever, wracked with a dull and monotonous ache, enlivened occasionally by sudden stabs of fiery pain when he sought to move. This was the pattern of his next few days, public exhibitions and personal torments, until the arrival from the north of a man with news, a man arriving two days ahead of Staffyd's own messenger. The news he carried changed everything.

***

"My darling, my beauty, my only one," crooned Harald the Hardraada dreamily in the privacy of his curtained off section of the tithe barn at Riccall. "Come to me, my sweetheart." The object of his affections was a six-foot pole of finely polished wood. At its head was a firmly secured silver effigy of a raven. Its wings were spread and its beak was open in an angry, silent shout. Its eyes were two shining rubies. Its work, did Harald but know it, was Scythian, ancient and from the far northern steppes. It was an object he had come by many years back during a punitive mission near Thessaloniki whilst in the service of the Emperor. He had kept it with him ever since, had had it carried into all his battles and skirmishes and brawls for twenty years and more. It was known to all as the Land Waster, an object of fear from the Balkans to the Baltic. Old Hardraada played with the linen folds of the banner on which was stitched out the emblem of the black raven. "You are thirsty, my heart, I know," he said lovingly. "But wait until the morrow, little one. You shall drink your fill then."

***

"Gate Fulford," announced young Morcar importantly, glad at last to be the centre of attention in his own hall in his own city in his own Earldom. "It is a mile, perhaps a little more, to the south of here. A small village, nothing to speak of, nothing to speak of at all, but the point is that two roads meet there, both from Riccall. The one follows the Ouse and the other, straighter, runs directly north. If the Hardraada wants York then he must come along one of those two ways. We shall meet him there."

"And the ground?" asked Staffyd resignedly, "what of that?" Morcar shrugged and scratched at his acne, two gestures now so habitual with him that it was too boring to parody. "On the east side of the river? Five, maybe six hundred paces from the river to the boundary dyke. On the one side we have the river and on the other the dyke and marshland beyond." He had been practicing the phrase in his head. "These will hold our flanks." Edwin was more than satisfied with this. "That's fine then," he said, "The Northmen can only get to York by walking over us." Staffyd nodded, that was just what he feared.

***

Over two hundred miles to the south and five days earlier, Harold had briefed Aesegar, his most senior official to hand and a man that he had always had good cause to trust. Aesegar placed the document in his scrip and slapped his hand on it protectively. "God knows, Aesegar," Harold sighed, "I can scarce spare you, but it needs to be someone those bloody Aelfgarsons will at least recognise. Take Haakon with you, it'll be good experience for him. You have my writ, take the men you need and make all speed."

Aesegar nodded in understanding. The message of the letter could not be clearer. Draw away. Under no circumstances engage the King of Norway, whatever sacrifices needed to be made, York even. Aesegar bowed formally. "As you will it, my Lord. Only, I have this in my mind, if I may speak it." Harold, still in considerable pain, nodded irritably. "This is old news now," continued Aesegar. "It is my thought that I shall be too late and that their natures, the Aelfgarsons, the Hardraada, your own brother, will have already brought about an encounter." Within himself, Harold could only agree. He felt this also. "Then you must send me news of it as soon as you can. I myself will be on the road only hours behind you. You know my route and I shall not deviate from it. I shall take the same old Roman way as you to Tadcaster. On the journey I shall gather what men I can, the word is already out." Indeed it was, a summons to the men of Middlesex, Essex and Hertfordshire along the road leading north to gather and wait for him. Messages also to his brother Gyrth and to Waltheof of Huntingdon. Leofwyn would remain in the south to patrol the coast. Please God above, keep the Aelfgarsons from battle, keep the bastard in Normandy. "Away you go now, Aesegar. God keep you safe." Aesegar smiled and gripped his King's hand. He spun on his heel and was gone, calling for Haakon as he went.

***

The boisterous northmen were up before the lark, assembling in their boat contingents. They checked straps and buckles and hefted their weapons in an amiable and lighthearted buzz of chatter. There was an occasional splash as men were hurled playfully into the river. They were like people on their way to a wedding feast, as they lined up on the two pathways leading north to York. Harald conferred with his young and bitterly disappointed son Olaf. "Well, my boy," he said. "This is a serious charge I lay upon you. Keep these boats safe against all comers. Without them we are well and truly buggered. You have enough men here with you. And don't you go pining and fretting either. Today is just the first of the fights we'll be having before England is ours." He pushed to the edge of his mind the memory of old Stump and his prediction of two battles and then embraced his son and threw himself back into the confusion of the departure. The two Earls of Orkney were also staying with the boats. They hovered in the background, busying themselves with unimportant tasks and appeared to share none of the disappointment that Olaf was displaying.

Harald would take the river path with Orri, his brother Nicholas and all the men of Norway. His chief man, Stryker, was delegated to accompany Tostig along the more easterly path through the marshes. There had been a considerable amount of disagreement, now quelled by Harald, when it was learned that in addition to his own Flemings and Northumbrians, Tostig would lead also the men of the Norse diaspora. It took cajolery and finally naked threats, but finally they had agreed and the Orcadians, Icelanders, the Dubliners and all the others lined up behind him. Harald the Hardraada, King of Norway, former Varangian Guard of the Byzantine Empire and scourge of the east, screamed the order. The Land Waster was held aloft and, half a mile separating them, the two divisions of the army, some ten thousand men, began to march purposefully towards York.

The Northumbrians, in the event, made it to Gate Fulford scant minutes ahead of the north men. They had been late in starting out and their departure from York and the cheering and highly relieved citizenry had been a shambles. They made the short journey at a jog trot. As the last of them moved beyond the southern gate, Thorri Arnulfson left off his waving and exhorting and breathed a deep and heart felt sigh of relief. "They'll be back soon enough, with their tails between their legs, some of them at any rate," he predicted to his companions. His own personal fortune, four wagon loads of it and under heavy guard, was presently making its way out of the north gate and in the direction of Ripon where a man who owed him money and more besides would keep it safe. Over to Bootham Bar, one of the main gates to the city, in a large and capacious cellar and buried deep beneath stacks of timber and kindling, lay another small fortune. This was the collective ransom of the city of York, a veritable treasury of gold and silver, plate, bullion, coin and jewellery. Should the brothers Edwin and Morcar not prevail, and to Thorri Arnulfson, who was a betting man, this was a racing certainty, then it should suffice to keep the wolf from the door.

The two brothers bade a brief farewell to each other as they arrived at the meeting of the Riccall roads at Fulford Gate. Time was pressing and their scouts were reporting the imminent arrival of the Northmen, just a short distance away to the south. "I'll see you afterwards, brother," said Edwin. "God keep you safe." He noticed that Morcar's usually ruddy complexion had taken on a slightly green colour and that he appeared to be shivering uncontrollably. In his excitement and through some vague filial attachment, he elected not to pass any comment. Instead he stood on a kneeling servant's back and mounted his horse, a fine and frisky chestnut, and rode the short distance off to the west and to the bank of the Ouse at the head of his Mercians. His own housecarls crowded around him in a cheering and enthusiastic mob, followed after by the less enthusiastic levies of York and an equally depressed looking number of Northumbrians rooted out from their farms and holdings at the last moment and allocated follow under his command.

Morcar watched him go. He felt ill and sick and wished to be away from this place, anywhere else. Behind him, however, and making such an option impossible, there stood, rank on rank and waiting expectantly, were those of the aristocracy of Northumbia as were available, the housecarls and the fyrd. Strong, dour Northerners, they were arrayed in furs and a motley of chain mail and boiled leather and a variety of head coverings. They stared at him speculatively and made comments amongst themselves. He caught the eye of the Lord of Ostdale, who then leaned over the withers of his horse and cleared his throat noisily. He nodded to his Earl, but his gaze was filled with hatred. Morcar made a mental note to himself. The man had a bad look to him. If the Good Lord preserved him this day, then that was most certainly a man to keep an eye on. Behind the quality, the footmen of the Earldom quarreled and jostled in the gateway, backed up into the streets of York leading to the congested gate.

Watching his brother move off with his confident and cheering men about him, Morcar had never felt so alone and so defenseless, despite all those men about him and at his back. Not for the first time he wished he was not Earl of Northumbria. It was so unfair! At least his brother had that man Staffyd for comfort and counsel and guidance. He had no such man to call upon. He had much preferred being the youngest son of the Earl of Mercia. He sighed deeply, fully aware of the hostile stares and glances. Well, there was no going back from here. He brought up bile and spat. "Very well," he said breezily and with a confidence he did not feel and to no one in particular. "Let us be about making a start of it. We haven't got all day."

For nearly three hundred yards, three lines deep and with the wide and fast-moving brown flow of the Ouse anchoring the flank to the right, Morcar's noblemen attempted with difficulty and much profanity to bring the Northumbrians into some vague semblance of order. The men of Northumbria were shoved and cudgelled into line, men and boys, hard bitten professionals and conscripted farm labourers alike. They clutched weapons either loved and well cared for and familiar or else completely strange to the hand and frightening. The unhappy and common men of the fyrd, hastily summoned from the harvest, were for the most part armed with the implements of the farm or the field. They clutched mattocks and scythes and improvised spears, rough affairs of staffs with low quality iron heads attached with baling twine. They settled finally into line and then listened, increasingly fearful, to a sound like an oncoming storm.

In the centre of this uncomfortable mix of professionals and amateurs, the Mercian Staffyd, appointed by Edwin to act as messenger between the two forces, screamed and shouted for order at these Northumbrian strangers. They stared back at him. Their expressions either blank or hostile. His horse swayed and pitched beneath him, feeling his own unease. The lines slowly formed up behind him and with the professionals pushing their way to the front. There was now a stiffening spine of well-seasoned men in the first rank behind a rabble of untried and nervous men. Over there on the left, struggling around the water filled dyke and the bogs beyond it, Edwin and his Mercians struggled to form line. On horseback and on the raised causeway which the advantage of height thus conferred upon him, Staffyd was able to catch a first view of the enemy. He gasped and crossed himself at the sight. "May the good God above preserve us," he breathed. Ahead, in clear view, a boiling mass of men.

The wolves of the North came roaring and screaming up the two track ways and spilling out into the featureless land before the English, a terrifying host of fearsome half naked and painted men, yelling and running to the sound of blaring war horns and throbbing drums. There were far more of them than the English too, perhaps by as much as a third again. The levies of Mercia and Northumbria watched in horrified fascination at their approach as their leaders strode along their lines, cajoling and threatening and encouraging. "Shields up and locked and together, lads. That's the way. Give them the shield wall. They are only human after all, just like us." A Warwick man hefted his shield and grasped the greasy haft of his spear. "They don't look that human to me," he remarked to his neighbour, "Would you allow your daughter to marry one of those?" His companion grinned mirthlessly and thought his own thoughts.

The disparate army of the Hardraada closed on the English shield wall remorselessly. On other occasions there would be pauses and delays and individual acts of bravado. In the ordinary course of events no man would readily hurl himself against a wall of shields and spears. These foreigners, though, fueled by glee and confidence and strong drink and greater numbers, were displaying no such inhibitions. They were big and fearsome men, heavily armoured and wielding awesome weapons which they banged against their lime wood shields, screaming in derision at the sight of the English before them. Within minutes they had filled all the ground opposite and formed up in a noisy mob in front of the English just two hundred paces off.

In the event it was a minor Yorkshire thegn from the Vale of Pickering who poured oil on the flames. His younger brother and a cousin had died at Holderness. He was in mourning and he had a vow to fulfil. "Bollocks to this," he muttered and then crossed himself. He screamed the war cry of his family, swung his axe above his head and then led his retinue off at a run. There was a brief pause and then, caught up in this sudden rush by a small group of men, the entire English left came on after him and roaring their defiance and hatred. Because of the basic geographical facts of the battlefield and the efforts of the keenest and fastest amongst them, the first of the English arrived at an angle and in a wedge-shaped crowd at the uneasy juncture between Tostig's Flemish and Scottish contingents.

The English went crashing into the enemy shield wall, striking down at the helmets and bare heads and up under-neath the opposing shields, seeking to at least hamstring or stab into unprotected groins. They scythed through Tostig's long suffering following like a knife through hot butter, hewing and hacking as they went. Some twenty paces behind Tostig's front line the avenging English then came up against a second shield wall of men, this time a line of Orcadians and Hebrideans with their shields locked tight together and reinforced by a vociferous crowd of Icelanders, Manxmen, Dubliners and Faroese. The fight became now a trial of strength and a contest between men pushing and shoving, each seeking to cut or thrust either below or above the protection of the shield of the man facing him. In the English centre, despite Staffyd's passionate appeals and commands for order, his ill-disciplined men began drifting off towards this promising and enticing fight that they appeared to be winning. Who was this foreign Mercian anyway? He was no man they recognised nor owed duty to. He could go hang, and his desperate entreaties fell on deaf ears.

His own following not yet engaged, Harald smiled to himself in grim satisfaction as he beheld the inactivity ahead of him and the boiling and struggling mass away to his right. With every moment the Englishmen were drifting away to the fight at the boundary dyke. He thanked his secret Gods. Perhaps, even, the irritating Tostig might meet his end here on this Godforsaken spot. Neither was he averse to a further culling of the ranks of some of his other more troublesome allies. The men of Hardraada and Edwin contented themselves with hurling spears and throwing axe and curses at each other, with little noticeable effect. Battle music, the Norwegians called it, the sound of weapons striking shields and armour. Over by the dyke, and like a whirlpool, the growing fight was now sucking in more and more men. Perhaps the tallest man there, Harald nonetheless ordered a man to kneel and then stood on his back. From this vantage point he could see that his own lines were beginning to buckle under the strain. He called his man Orri over to his side.

Not through his orders, the fearsome 'berserkers' had now appeared in his own front ranks, they were unstable and psychotic men made yet more deranged by potions of berries and herbs and secret distillations of their own making. They were a law unto themselves and, as ever, Harald, like any sensible man, chose not to interfere. They howled and leaped before the English. They threw off their armour and exposed their chests, inviting the now hesitant English to single combat. Harald indicated the thinning English centre. "The flying pig," he told Orri. "I think it is time for it." The berserkers were manhandled and otherwise persuaded into the rough shape of an arrow head. Behind them a huge mob of men, Harald and Orri in their midst, formed up. Razor sharp at the tip and with all the weight and impetus coming from behind, 'the flying pig' launched itself directly at the English centre and up went the Land Waster. Screaming and yelling, the formation set off at a run at the English.

The force of the impact sent Edwin's men reeling, forcing them towards the river as the rest of the Norsemen came up in a line. The flying pig went hurtling through the English line, and tore it to bloody shreds. Staffyd, his horse killed by throwing axes and so now dismounted, had the briefest of glimpses of his nemesis, of a veritable giant of a man, his chest and forearms reddened with blood and his teeth bared in a feral leer, coming straight for him. Desperately, he raised his own sword in an attempt to prevent the blow, but the axe came whistling down, nonetheless, shattering his weapon and cleaving him almost in two from collarbone to navel. He sank to the ground, dead in an instant, and bodies tumbled over him.

What there remained of the English centre fled in justifiable panic and the survivors began to stream back up the road to York. By the river, now engaged in overwhelming numbers, the professionals of the Earl of Mercia faced the elite of the King of Norway, finding themselves in turn forced, remorselessly, like the Northumbrians before them, into the fast-moving river and surrounding marshes. Scores of them were now in the water and there, weighed down by wounds and armour, they drowned. At the dyke the seemingly triumphant Northumbrians had found themselves suddenly trapped between two lines of enemy and with the Hardraada tearing at their unprotected backs. Those that could do so attempted to find sanctuary in the bog. They were either struck down with spears and axes or else sucked under by the treacherous ground. The men of Northumbria, the pride of the north, began to die by the score, cut down by the Norsemen or floundering and drowning in the river and the marsh as the shield wall pushed them back. The battle now reached the more hesitant Mercians from the gentler lands of the Welsh borders and the Midlands.

Unlike the Northumbrians, many of them felt that this was not necessarily their fight and they began to fall back. The Ouse was now flowing red with blood and the men of Hardraada were able to leap across it almost dry shod across the mounds of dead and dying. There was of course the occasional ducking and the occasional Englishman who fought back. Always careful to keep a personal tally, Harald himself, as he made his way across the barrier, struck down eight of the English. One of these, a mere boy, to his amazement, actually inflicted a raking cut across his ribs with a desperate swing of his sword. Harald roared with anger, dropped his axe and then strangled him to death with his bare hands, relishing the sight of bulging eyes and purple throat as he forced the last of the breath from him.

Jostled by a crowd of panicked men, grimy and covered from head to foot in mud and blood, the two brothers by chance collided breathlessly at the very same gate they had left not two hours since. Edwin's left arm was broken and dangled uselessly. There was a flap of half severed skin from his scalp loose on his forehead and his face was a mask of blood. Morcar, incongruously, sported a black eye. The noises of battle were still very near and coming closer, the bellowing of horns and the booming of drums. The brothers were swept through the gates by the force of the fleeing crowd and into the thoroughfare that led directly to the Minster, the streets jammed with terrified citizens. "Staffyd," yelled Edwin. "Where is he? Have you seen him? He'll know what to do." But Staffyd, mutilated beyond all recognition and buried deep beneath a mound of English dead, was long past caring.

The victorious army made no serious attempt to attack the city of York, they did not need to. Instead they marched noisily and triumphantly up to the closed southern gates and where they encamped. They jeered and gesticulated and displayed their buttocks and the heads of dead Englishmen whilst the remnants of the defeated English army poured out in panic from the gates leading to the north. Hardraada's men rejoiced, but in fact the army had been severely mauled. The English had put up more of a fight than had been anticipated. They had lost perhaps five hundred men, dead and wounded, and very few of the wounded would survive the next few days. The leader of the Hebrideans had simply vanished without trace and mad young Grovan had lost an eye. He would never walk again properly either, having been hamstrung by a dying English boy. It had, to their surprise, been a tough fight. Who would have thought it? Harald's ribs swathed now in an impressively blood-soaked bandage, were paining him and he found it more comfortable to stand, using Land Waster as a staff. To his great regret he discovered that Tostig still lived. Tostig, sucking at a deep gash on his forearm, was elated. He was back at York and cheered by strong drink. By Christ, but there would be some changes! Would he be permitted to hang the Aelfgarsons from the walls? He would ask the Hardraada when the time was right. There were, of course, certain problems that first needed to be faced. For one thing, his English and Flemings had born the early brunt of the Norse onslaught and now one man in three of his men were now dead, incapacitated or missing. This was greatly to his loss and disadvantage and as he correctly suspected, much to Harald's satisfaction.

"Give the people of York a day and a night to consider," Tostig advised Harald, "and then I can assure you that they will be all over us like a rash. The terms and conditions will be entirely of our own making. God above, I never saw such slaughter, so many dead."

"You should put yourself about a just a touch more, then," said Harald curtly. "We could take this place here and now." He looked up at the walls and the alarmed faces above him. "Yes indeed," said an entirely unscathed Orri. "But we do need the place to be in one piece and with a docile citizenry if we are to make it our winter quarters. Much good it would do us burned to the ground. No, Tostig is right. Let them worry over it and then treat with us. Let them feed and house and pay us." Harald grunted, "very well then, but I want those gates open, quick as you like. If they do not then we shall break them open or burn them down. Then I shall really give the whole city over to my boys. The Gods above know that they deserve it. See to it. I require care and shelter for my wounded, food and drink for my men."

There followed a time of shouting back and forth between the besieged and besiegers before the gates finally swung open, the last of the unwounded English army now safely away and streaming away in any direction apart from south. As Haraald strode masterfully into York there, waiting for him with a commendable serenity, was Ealdred, Archbishop of York. He was fully enrobed and clutching his pastoral crook, surrounded by a huddle of terrified priests and acolytes. Behind were a number of thegns who had chosen to stay and surrender and a knot of York merchants awaiting the opportunity to offer up their ransom. Harald advanced upon the Archbishop. His English was very poor, but he had enough for this particular speech. "York is mine," he announced. "I claim it."

***

Like an avenging angel, Harold, King of the English moved swiftly north. He rode out of London and up the old Ermine Street and with two hundred mounted housecarls at his back. His infantry, rousted out of their billets and gathered along the route, came on after as fast as they could. The road, all two hundred miles of it, would lead him straight to Tadcaster and a reckoning.

Harold was curt and uncommunicative, his face set in anger and a grim resolution. He felt also the constant ache of his rheumatism as he led the way east and then north. In his aching bones he knew that Edwin and Morcar would have forced the issue, and he feared the worst. Fast horsemen had gone on ahead of him to call out the militia and at Brentwood in Essex several hours later there were the first of them already assembling, about one hundred extremely noisy and enthusiastic men lined up behind their thegns. Only the local aristocracy were mounted on sorry looking horses and ponies. Harold gave swift and perfunctory orders for them to follow on and he was on the move once more. Moving at an alternating trot and canter, Harold and his escort finally made Hertford long after nightfall, with men of the home shires coming in at all times in the night and disturbing the rest of all already gathered. A quick and unpalatable breakfast in the morning. and then he was off on the way north once more, his mounted retinue almost doubled in number and with the men of the local fyrds gathering all the time.

***

The all conquering and mighty Harald of Norway and those leaders of his army still on their feet rejoiced and celebrated and then settled down to enjoy a good night's rest in Tostig's own town house which he had gleefully repossessed. It was full of memories of his own time and full of the possessions of the fled Aelfgarsons. Tostig recognised some former servants. He pinched ears affectionately, embraced and rewarded from his purse. Very early the following morning after a Mass in the Minster, attended purely for the sake of form, Hardraada had the principal men of York held at the steps and then brought to him. There was very little that he needed to be told about the rituals and procedures regarding the policing of a fallen town and none summoned there before him would have dared to make suggestions or offer advice. Instead they knelt and prostrated themselves before this formidable figure, lounging and fully at ease, he had appropriated the Bishop's Seat from the Minster and to which he had taken a fancy, conducted in the open before the Minster.

It was some minutes before he allowed them to climb to their feet once more. As was customary on such occasions,

Harald had decked himself out in the usual and formidable style. His cloak was kept to one side in order to display his wound of the previous day. His neck and wrists glittered with gold and he clutched his personal totem in one hand and his terrifying battle axe in the other. Upon his head was a helmet of ornate design. Wholly impractical in battle, it did serve to add further inches to his impressive height and more weight to his menace. He had the York representatives, in bare feet and with halters about their necks, kneel before him and then he made his demands. The Archbishop alone was permitted to sit, albeit on a humble stool taken from a nearby tavern. Standing next to the King of Norway, Tostig amused himself by making eye contact with those who had defied and risen up against him the previous year. It was a glorious moment for him as they paled and flinched at his scrutiny. He had the power of life or death over them, the pit and the gallows, and he enjoyed their fearful realisation of this. He caught the eye contact of a previously particularly troublesome man and slowly shook his head in mock sorrow. To his delight the man visibly turned grey.

Without discussion and in full sight of the victorious army and the cowed people of York, the city was formally given over to the Hardraada, along with all of its wealth and the prudently gathered ransom hidden at Bootham Bar. Harald dismissed the assembly with contempt, viewed the offering without comment and then mounted and rode a gift horse out of the city and back in the direction of the boats at Riccall, leaving trusted men in place to police and garrison the city. The people of York had been at pains to provide him and his chief men with the best of thoroughbreds available, tall and highly-strung creatures, all shining flanks, rolling eyes and nervous movements. This was all well and good for show, but each of them would have preferred a more dependable and solid beast, even if their legs did hang down well below the creature's belly.

The saddles and accoutrements of each horse, however, were well beyond the blood price of an ordinary man in the shield wall, if not two. All in all, it had been a highly enjoyable and entertaining day spent in York for Harald and Tostig. They strutted through a tour of inspection of the main streets and principal buildings of the city and then along the catwalks of the derisory wall. There followed a muted and very uncomfortable feast of welcome in the palace of the Archbishop. Harald remained aloof and stern throughout, whilst Tostig was at great pains to be as unpleasant and threatening to as many people as possible, from the Archbishop downwards.

They rode now through the nightmarish scenes of the previous day. It was a landscape of naked and stiffened bodies, wide eyed and staring, congealed blood turned brown on marble white limbs. In the hours of darkness both the victors and local predators had been hard at work. The bodies had for the most part been stripped naked and many were missing ring fingers and even bracelet arms. Sharp knives had been at work. Behind, beside and before them, came the men of the victorious army, lured away from York by both bribes and threats, and picking their way through the piles of dead. They had left the gravely hurt of the army in York and to the less than expert ministrations of the people there. Even now they were dying by the minute, laid out in rows in the open before the Minster. Those clearly not about to breathe their last came supported either by their companions or else making the best they could of the journey by cart across the bumping ground and causeways. Most of the uninjured were making their way back to the boats, burdened down with portable booty acquired in York itself or else looted from the dead. Out of the south gate came a convoy of twenty heavily laden wagons carrying the gleaned and gathered ransom that would be shared out at the boats that evening. Yet more wagons followed after, carrying bread, meat and drink. The day was glorious, and a holiday atmosphere prevailed.

Harald, Orri and Stryker were inured to the sights and smells of a day-old battlefield. There was no need to tidy up, this task had been part of the many terms and conditions imposed upon the people of York. For all Harald cared, the dead could remain there forever. Tostig was describing, with enthusiasm, a place not far off called Stamford Bridge. He knew it well and he had been instrumental in its selection as a meeting place. As part of their submission, the people of Northumbria had pledged beef and mutton on the hoof, pigs and poultry, ale and mead, charcoal and firewood, grain and flour and twice baked bread. All this would be brought to this Stamford Bridge. More significantly, the people of York and the surrounding districts had agreed to hand over five hundred hostages as a further surety. For the most part these were the sons, the oldest where available, of the leading burghers and local gentry. In this way did York win its respite against the fury of the north men.

Stamford Bridge, Tostig told them, was ideal for the gathering scheduled for three days hence. This was time enough for the locals to come up with the necessary wherewithal, but not time enough for them to gather together and plot resistance. The meeting place lay just seven miles east of York at a crossroads and an old bridge over the river Derwent, another tributary of the Ouse. The people of the Ridings, the rich Vale of Pickering and of York itself could reach the place easily to make their submissions and honour their pledges. There was good meadowland to either side of the Derwent on which to camp out and to secure all the expected hostages and livestock. Riccall lay some twelve or thirteen miles off, a brisk morning's walk. "Not only that," said Tostig in his annoyingly good Norwegian, "just a short way off is a place called Catton. It is a royal manor directly owned by my dear and beloved brother. It is ours now. We may of course make free with it."

Tostig knew Catton well. In less troubled times he had been a frequent honoured guest and visitor and he had fond memories of the place. By now the grain would be in the barns and ready for grinding at the local mills. The prized apples and pears of the district would be nestling in the haylofts, along with the gatherings of onion and garlic, peas, beans and cabbages. He recalled the last occasion that Harold had taken him there and his brother's boyish enthusiasm for and admiration of a herd of highly bred short horns, the much coveted breed of Cheviot sheep. There had also been his particular pride and joy, a collection of Tamworth pigs. Harold had always been especially fond of pigs, to the extent of individually naming them, despite their known and inevitable fate. This planned despoliation of Catton would hurt Harold deeply but Tostig, his soul long since pickled in bile, had no remaining filial sympathy for his brother whatsoever. "And a deer park," he enthused. "My Lord Harald, I look forward to showing you hunting in the English manner."

Harald bared his yellow and fearsome teeth at him. Once, in an idle moment, he had seriously considered having them filed to an edge for military purposes and for greater visual effect but had decided against it. Harald's smile, as was often the case with him. did not quite reach his eyes. "I look forward to it," he said. "I look forward also to the full submission of the north and the arrival of all these loyal Northumbrians of whom you so often speak. Doubtless that will be at this Stamford place." At this point they were obliged to diverge at a particularly large mound of bodies lying under a busy and buzzing halo of flies, the nervous horses baulking and side stepping. As they came together once more Stryker said "Wasn't that Arnie back there? I am sure it was. Do you recall him? The boat builder from Stavanger. He owed us a tax on timber last year that was never paid. If that was him then I guess he won't be honouring the debt now." He and the Hardraada chortled merrily together for a moment. "Oh well," Harald said. "I'll get it off him when I get to Valhalla."

Having had time to gather his thoughts, Harald resumed. "It is late in the year," he pronounced, "even for such a soft country as this. I shall winter in York and near to my boats. From all I can see and from all you tell me, we shall have provisions enough. If we run short, then we shall simply take what we need. If the weather holds then I shall send people west after those Aelfgarsons and bring them back in chains. And yes, Tostig, before you ask again, I shall hand them over to you and you may do with them as you see fit. If we can take Chester then we are in reach of both the Isle of Man and Dublin, and more supplies and reinforcements. But what, my esteemed Earl of Northumbria," Harald's irony was never subtle, "of your brother in the south? What too of this Duke of Normandy of whom I hear so much? Now there is a man I would like to meet, either on a battlefield or across the feasting board."

So, all the way back to the boats, Tostig spoke of his brother and of the Duke of Normandy, predicting, recommending and dismissing in turn possible events and suitable courses of action. For the time being at least his brother would remain in the south. He said this yet again as they took their ease outside the barn at Riccall and watching the glazed skin of a suckling pig bubble and brown. "Not even the Duke of Normandy," said Tostig with an air of finality, "would risk the venture now, not even with a favourable wind. No, he'll make himself comfortable as best he may and wait for the spring. Then he'll come."

"And your brother?" demanded Orri, "what of him?" He had had no opportunity yet to advise the King that the Englishman's use and value was at an end. "Harold?" replied Tostig airily. "He'll leave a force of men, not a big one, all along the south coast for the winter. Poor sods, it'll not be pleasant for them."

"Much I care," sniffed Harald. "What else will he do?" Tostig paused, inhaling the tantalising smell of the roasting meat. "Winter or not," he said. "He'll not leave you alone. Two things in particular he will do. First, he will try to track down Edwin and Morcar before you are able to do so. Either way, it's the end of the road for those two. He will put his own men in charge of that portion of Mercia that you leave to him. How my father would have loved to see that. He'll also move against us in stages. He'll secure what he can of Mercia, the midlands and the east against us and, here and there, move against us. Losing control of the Ouse is a bitter blow. In particular, my Lord, look to your boats here. They are an obvious target. He will also well try to patch up some arrangement or other with King Malcolm. We need to get to Malcolm first. You will find him easy enough to deal with. We also need to secure Carlisle, Berwick and Newcastle as soon as we may."

Finding himself in the position of the expert man on the spot and with good local knowledge, Tostig began to warm to his theme. "Harold himself, I believe, will remain in the midlands, perhaps Leicester. From there he will be free to move in any direction he chooses and according to need. I personally hope that he has to fight the Duke of Normandy first, so much the better for us. I think he'll pass on this job of brawling with us to my brother Gyrth. He'd not trust Leofwyn, he's too hot headed and none too bright. If so then they'll throw up a screen of men from the Wash over the Pennines to Chester, if we don't secure it first. It is my thinking that we are looking at an autumn and winter of armed camps and occasional raids and skirmishes, and then a big confrontation in the spring. As I say, I hope, I do feel. that the first big battle is between the Normans and my brother."

It was at this point, and for differing reasons, that both Harald and Orri began to relax. They were well accustomed to war by stages and both had had fifteen year's experience of this all along the borders and shorelines of Denmark. The North now belonged to them. They had taken it with the edges of their blades. Now, for the next few months, they would have to hold it and make themselves secure. For the moment the cupboard was bare back home in Norway and anyway, there was always that old fox Sweyn to keep an eye on. Come the spring and they could recruit once more, in Alba and Ireland and in the isles.

"For as long as the weather holds," said Orri, "we should secure the estuary at the head of the Humber and all of the river inland. What of those English ships we have bottled up there? What's that place again?" Tostig was anxious to inform. "Tadcaster," he said. "We need to take that as well, it is an important place. The road there runs all the way to London, about two hundred miles south. In parts the road is still good, for as long as the weather holds. At the speed of the slowest man it would take an army well over a week to come up against us."

"Time enough then," said Harald. "We all of us need our rest. We'll sort things out at this Stamford Bridge place first. After that, Orri, I want you to secure the Estuary. To you, Tostig, I shall give men to take and hold Tadcaster. Make it safe for me. Tell me how many you shall need. We shall build an encampment here to secure the ships and I shall settle in York for the winter."

"Please," said Tostig. "Consider my home to be your home." He held his arms expansively, like a welcoming host. "I do already," said Harald witheringly and Orri uttered a brief bark of amusement. "Tell me now. This man of yours, Copsig. Do you trust him?" Offended, Tostig raised his eyebrows. "Implicitly, with my life," he replied.

"Very well then. If you trust him so, then I require him to take a small force of mounted men, all English save for a few of mine, to the west. I require him to seek out those two brats we bested yesterday and find out what they are up to, if anything, and then report back. I don't want him wandering all over the countryside for long. I have him in mind for my provost of York. With your permission of course, my Lord Earl," he added satirically.

"Absolutely," said Tostig gravely. "A wise choice if I may say so, none better. Local knowledge, known and deeply respected, understands how they think around here and everything." This was fine news indeed. His own man on the inside of things, he would be his finger on the heart pulse of the capital of the north. Nonetheless, there remained within him a distinct feeling of unease at the way things were turning out. Orri was growing ever more caustic and aggressive and the King of Norway's own tone and behaviour was far from reassuring. Time now, clearly, to thrash the matter out. "My Lord King," he began formally, "please accept my heartfelt congratulations. You are now master of the north and I can govern it in your name and on your behalf and with Orri here representing your interests, but answerable to me, of course. Should you wish," he ventured, "you could even return to Norway while the weather holds and then return in the spring. In the meantime, I have a few projects in mind which I am sure will meet with your approval."

Harald stared at him in utter stupefaction for a moment while, beside him, Orri seethed in anger. Harald had forgotten what this strange Englishman could be like and why he found him, as he on occasion did, so entertaining. The man's confidence, his arrogance and insolence, was truly staggering. That Orri should answer to him! A nice touch, he liked that a lot. In his own way Harald was quite fond of his prospective son in law, an unsubtle bear of a man whom he had once watched carve out the blood eagle on of the back of a priest for a supposed slight.

It was highly amusing to see someone so enrage Orri in this fashion. He laid a restraining arm across the man's chest, for he knew that Orri was quite capable of rearing up and tearing Tostig limb from limb. There was, Harald knew, a strain of berserker madness lurking in Orri's family, doubtless a result of all that inbreeding that took place in the lonely winter months in the uplands he came from. As for the suggestion that he simply sail back to Norway again! He loved that, it was priceless. He hooted with laughter and slapped his thigh. Tostig, who loved people to laugh with him but never at him, was deeply offended, Dear God, he thought to himself. What now? Did I say something funny?

Patiently, and with some unease, he and Orri and the others waited for the Hardraada's mercurial good humour to subside. Orri and Stryker, if not Tostig, were well aware of the man's dramatic mood swings and braced themselves for a shift to ungovernable rage. On this occasion, however, this failed to erupt and instead Harald patted Tostig on the knee in a companionable manner. "Thank you for your concern," he said. "But I shall be stopping here for the present. I have a feeling, my Lord Earl, that there will be plenty enough to do for the both of us."

***

Over the past few years, the oldest surviving sons of Godwin had begun to underestimate each other with an increasing frequency. Once, when they had been in perfect harmony, it had been as if each were able to read the mind of his brother. Here, and now, Tostig was wrong, utterly and disastrously. As he sat in anticipation of the roast pork and the taking up of his old lifestyle once more, his brother was in fact leading a mounted force of a thousand housecarls and thegns into

Huntingdon after yet another painful and wearying day on the road.

All the way along Ermine Street and through the Lea valley the men of Middlesex and Essex waited to fall in line behind him, summoned from their preparations for the winter by their king and the obligations they had to him, each settlement and district, each hide of land equipping and providing for the stated amount of men required. Others, unprompted, came anyway and they stood and waited, it seemed, at every turn of the road and at every settlement. Harold, at the head of all this, looked gaunt and menacing, still suffering a constant aching pain exacerbated by sudden movements or gestures. He was irritable and tetchy with even the most devoted and beloved of his companions as he gazed ahead constantly, searching for messengers from the north.

At unwalled Huntingdon as they clattered in over the rough cobbles that replaced the habitual mud of the track, there was Waltheof waiting for him with a force of five hundred Cambridgeshire men and with food and drink laid out on tables at the small market cross. The young Earl had achieved a minor miracle in the two days since he had received the message and Harold was fulsome in his praise at his efforts. Waltheof flushed with pride, "and more coming in all the time," he said. "By now your brother Gyrth will have had the word. I suggested that he meet with us at Lincoln, though I am sure that you would have thought of that already. I can organise provisioning until then." Harold gripped the boy's shoulder. "You have done well, and now for some sleep. We still have a long journey ahead of us."

***

To the north, those of the King of Norway's army with time on their hands skylarked around the boats or else went off on private and unauthorised hunting and looting expeditions in the surrounding countryside. Others began the construction of a proper winter encampment and the building of a stockade on the north bank of the river. Minor repairs were carried out on the boats and equipment and food and supplies continued to arrive from York.

Tostig found time to instruct and confer briefly with his deputy before Copsig left for the west in search of the elusive Aelfgarsons. "Just do not be too long about it," he instructed him. "I need you here with me. If anything unfortunate or fatal should happen to either Edwin or Morcar, then so be it. Such a thing would be sad, but we all have to live with sad things, if you get my meaning. How do you feel about being my man in Mercia?" Copsig's unlovely features crumpled up in concentration and he shrugged. "Don't really know the place," he said, stolid and practical as ever. "If old Staffyd survived that fight then he'd be your best bet." Tostig laughed and sent him on his way with a slap on the back. The King of Norway, meanwhile, continued to relax in the late sunshine, admiring his new scar. It was healing up nicely, a welcome addition to an already impressive collection and something new to show to the adoring women back home.

CHAPTER FIVE :

The Road to Stamford Bridge

Yorkshire: September, 1066

Early on the morning of the same day that Tostig conferred with his deputy and whilst the Hardraada dozed peacefully, Harold was on the road once more, now beyond Lincoln and circling west to avoid the Humber and heading for the first rise of the Pennines. Gyrth and Waltheof rode to either side of him. It was now their sixth day on the road north and their numbers had risen to over five thousand men, the hooves of their horses and ponies churning up the decaying surface of the Roman road and making the passage difficult and unpleasant for the footmen who followed after. Here and there along the way people waited with gifts of twice baked bread, ale and fresh water. Gyrth, too, had done him proud, with both men and supplies. There was no time to wait for the baggage or for lunchtime halts. They ate and drank as they rode, the insides of their thighs chafed by the saddles and the sweat of their horses. They turned aside to attend to the needs of nature in the surrounding fields and hedgerows when so required.

As the army rode into the bleak upland expanse of heather and gorse of the Hatfield Chase and with a threat of rain in the air, Harold finally received his news from the north. Beneath all the accumulated sweat and grime, he could just recognise the man as one of Aesegar's messengers. He had seen him around, here and there, on previous occasions. The horse the man rode was lathered and bleeding from the mouth and nostrils as he reined in. "You of course have news, and hence your haste," Harold observed unnecessarily. He led his brother and Waltheof ahead and out of earshot of the crowd behind them. The messenger began to dismount, doubtless a preliminary to kneeling before his King.

"No, no." Harold said. "Stay where you are. Just the message, if you please." The man took a deep breath. "It was a battle, my Lord. A great battle at a place called Fulford Gate just outside York." Harold nodded, he knew the place and there was a certain logic to the location. "And? It went against us. Would I be right?" The messenger swallowed. He was swaying in the saddle and looked to be in desperate need of a drink. "Waltheof, a drink for the man, for the love of God," said Harold. Gratefully the man poured the thin acid wine down his throat, spat and wiped his mouth. "Indeed so, my lord. It went against us, I grieve to tell you. My Lords Edwin and Morcar led their men out of York against the Hardraada. He had come up the Ouse to Riccall, hundreds of boats, thousands of men. Ten thousand at least, they say. Earl Edwin had all of his housecarls of Mercia and those of the fyrd he could gather in the time. Likewise, the Earl Morcar, with his men of Northumbria and the men of York." He fell silent, as if his report were at an end. "Yes, yes," said Harold impatiently. "Go on."

The messenger continued to stare at the ground beneath his feet. "My Lord King, it was a complete slaughter. They were cut to pieces in their hundreds. They say that the river was choked with dead and that the Norwegians crossed a dyke there dry shod because of the English bodies beneath them." Gyrth began to swear monotonously under his breath and Waltheof had turned ashen. "Come now, come now," Harold chided him. "Surely you exaggerate. You were not there yourself, after all." The messenger was almost defiant in his reply. "I have all of this from men who were there. The army of the Earls was completely destroyed, and the survivors are scattered, fugitives, all over the countryside. Edwin and Morcar are believed to be somewhere to the west of York, trying to rally their men. York is in the hands of the King of Norway and of your brother."

Harold shivered. There was another implacable enemy waiting for him in the south, a man who was still capable of arriving on his shores this year and who had proclaimed his intention and dedication to the complete destruction of Harold and the English. He himself was under the threat of excommunication, in risk of his soul and of Salvation and of the hope of the everlasting life to come. His own people of England would go to their graves without unction or consolation or sanctified burial. Baptisms would be null and void and thus be shunned by the Creator. All children from illegal marriages would remain bastards for all their lives. His two leading Prelates of the Church in England were alternately already excommunicated and in hiding, or else presumably a prisoner and puppet of the Hardraada. Mercia and Northumbria were a spent and destroyed force and a vicious enemy, aided and abetted by his own brother, were in possession of the second biggest city in England. All behind him was an untested force, footsore, weary, hungry and frightened. If he failed in this then he was without doubt damned in this life and in the life to come. How he yearned at that moment for the comforting and reassuring presence of Wulfstan of Worcester. "When was this?" he asked.

"Two days back. I had word from Tadcaster only yesterday. There are some boats of ours there, trapped by the

Norwegians. Men have rallied there, perhaps five hundred of them. Aesegar is with them. They pray for your coming and await news." Harold sighed.

"Well, they will just have to carry on waiting. I want no news of us reaching the ear of the Hardraada just yet." He fumbled in his tunic and threw a small purse of coin to the man. "You have done well, I thank you. Rest up now and join us later. In the meantime, I command you, as you love me, to keep this news to yourself. I myself shall inform the army." He turned and beckoned forward a small group of thegns that had been desperately trying to eavesdrop and told them the news briefly.

It was pointless trying to paint anything other than a truly grim picture and he ordered the information to be spread to the army behind them. Slowly, after this halt, the army picked up the pace once more and moved on. "This is bad," said Gyrth with massive understatement. "Brother, it is the worse news there is," Harold agreed. All those men. All those men now dead or scattered. Those men of the Midlands and the North that he had been relying upon to guard his back door for him, and to come south when he needed them. York, the second biggest city in the country, in enemy hands, along with one of the finest water routes in the country. Tostig back in the city from which he had been banished. Ten thousand men! Surely. they must have had a bit of a mauling in the process. What if William were to come now? "The little bastards. Couldn't even do the honourable thing and get their silly selves killed," said Gyrth bitterly. "Alive or dead," Harold announced, "they are of no further use to me. They will never be a force in the land again. I shall see to that." Waltheof was puzzled. "But why? Why did they fight without you? Your orders could not have been clearer."

"The only person Edwin has never underestimated is himself," said Harold. "It is also in my mind that they perhaps did not have too much choice in the matter. The defences of York are a disgrace and the people there would have done everything in their power to prevent a battle in their streets and then the destruction of the whole place. Can you imagine that happening? In York? I can. Things had obviously moved on too quickly for the pair of them. They could not risk being trapped in York and the Hardraada, so they say, has carried more towns by force than can be named. No, I imagine that they believed they had to fight, both out of vanity and fear."

Jesus Christ and all the Saints above! Two silly, vain-glorious little boys and a hastily assembled force that was most parts farm labourers up against the most fearsome living fighter in Christendom. He looked back behind him, seeking out a man with local knowledge and, finding him, he beckoned him. The Humberside thegn nudged his horse forward. "Lord?" he enquired. "We have four, perhaps five hours of daylight left to us," said Harold. "Where will that take us?" The man considered for a moment. "Burford," he said. "Burford, where the hills begin that separate us from Cumbria. The town there has good grazing and plenty of water. I cannot answer for how well provisioned it is. It is a tidy way, though. We'll not be there before nightfall."

"We shall not stop until we reach it, and we shall leave it again before first light. Send men ahead to warn them and pass the word back that we shall stop there." The thegn nodded and turned about. "The men are very tired," said Gyrth. "God damn their tiredness," said Harold in a fury. "They can be tired all they wish after they've met the Hardraada. And pleased enough they'll be then if they find themselves still alive to be tired. In the meantime, be so good as to place a cordon of mounted men about the column. I want no strag-gling, deserting or looting on this little journey."

***

The morning of the twenty-fourth promised no let up in the unseasonably hot weather. All had been decided that previous evening. The young Haraldson and the Orkney Earls would stay with the boats once more, and, with them, one third of the men. It was painfully apparent that Harald had nothing but contempt for the two Orcadians. He tolerated them for the men and the ships they provided and absolutely nothing else besides. Orri would watch over them all. Orri took the decision very badly and was now spectacularly sulking. Harald and Tostig would take the majority of the army to Stamford Bridge, some six thousand men, and there intimidate and receive the submission of the beaten English. They would return in two or three days time with their hostages, booty and provisions. The men were clamouring for women. They would have to see about that, and soon. Harald had seen many a successful war party break up and fight amongst itself over just such a thing. After Stamford Bridge, Tostig said, he would personally arrange things in York.

Watching the men forming up, boat crew by boat crew, Orri expressed concern. All were armed and carrying their favourite weapons, but few had elected to wear mail or carry a shield or helmet. These they had decided to leave with their comrades at the boats. "I would say that was rash," Orri said "wandering about half arsed like that." Tostig agreed. After Gate Fulford he had just over two hundred men left under his direct command, Northumbrians, some who had rallied to him since and the scarred and embittered remnants of his Flemish and Scottish mercenaries. "Mine will go fully armed," he said. "I have ordered it so." Harald shrugged, "and I and my bodyguard. As for the rest? Well, I see little harm and one valuable lesson I have learned from life is never give an order that might not be obeyed. When next you come to give one that is truly important then the results can be very unhappy."

He was tempted to relate such an instance in Cappadocia that he had witnessed, decided against it and instead flung out an arm to indicate the river and the noisy and exuberant horde of men now assembling. "Look at them. Go on, take a good look. Six thousand men, the best fighters in the world. Those sheep faced buggers we'll be meeting will soil themselves at the sight of them." He crossed his arms with an air of finality, and that was the end of the matter.

***

At that very moment, Harold and his vanguard were by now some six hours from Tadcaster, his exhausted army strung out for miles on the road behind him. Grey with dust and fatigue, the Englishmen swayed and rocked in the saddle, sleeping as they went and occasionally falling from their saddles and tumbling to the ground. In the small hours Maerlswyn of Lincoln had ridden into Burford at the head of five hundred men. He had been off levying and recruiting and kidnapping in the Five Boroughs before setting off up Ermine Street at an astonishing speed. Harold half hugged and half supported the man as he dropped from his horse to make his report. Harold felt humbled by the efforts and the loyalty of this man and all the others along the way. Off went the messages at last to beleaguered Tadcaster by separate routes, with strict instructions to their carriers to avoid all contact with the enemy. Absolute secrecy had to be maintained at all costs. Your King is near, the message ran, be ready for our arrival and wish God speed to us. Food and drink for the men. "Lie if necessary," Harold instructed them blithely." Tell them we are ten thousand. That'll encourage them. They'll also have the absolute conniptions trying to find enough to feed us. They'll never do it, of course. What they will do, and impress this upon them, is to make sure that they look after our mounts. Elsewise I shall hang them upside down by their balls. Tell them this, we shall be there by nightfall."

Heartened by the news of the prospect of Tadcaster and the proximity of the enemy, the men began to sing and chant in a multiplicity of dialects. Head cocked to one side, Willi listened appreciatively. "It shouldn't really sound as good as that," he remarked to the tone deaf and completely indifferent people riding at his side, "but it does." He joined in the next available chorus, and if the words and the dialects of the Epic of Maldon varied according to the Shires and districts of the men singing, then the rhythm and the cadence remained the same. The choruses and refrains went booming and rolling like thunder up and down the long and ragged line. Ceofwyn, a Cornishman and thus not even English, shrugged. Instead he preferred to invoke the patronage of one of that strange country's many and obscure saints.

When, finally, they arrived in the pitch dark at Tadcaster the situation proved to be as much as Harold had foreseen. There was total confusion and flaring torches and hissed orders. Possibly Norwegian scouts were out and they did not wish to advertise their presence. Perhaps, even, there were spies in the camp. It was, in any event, hard to see how they could disguise this night-time arrival. The provisions available proved to be wholly inadequate, though under the circumstances it was difficult to see what more could possibly have been done. Many of Harold's men simply dismounted, handed over their reins to waiting helpers and sank into a deep sleep on the spot. Others made their way to where what food there was available had been set out and Harold, Gyrth, Waltheof and Maerlswyn entered a customs shed where, in happier times, merchants and drovers had argued the toss with local officials.

A small committee was awaiting them there, headed by Aesegar, looking as gaunt and as awful as Harold himself felt. "My Lord," he said, arms wide open in welcome. "It gladdens me more than I can say to see you here. Welcome," Haakon was there also and looking equally terrible. He too had had an extremely trying time of late. With them there was a thegn from over to Theakston who had been at Gate Fulford. He was grim and foul smelling and had a blood encrusted bandage swathed about his head. Cerdic, the notional head of the trapped boat crews, hovered behind them, a heavily bearded bear of a man, and two of York's most influential English burgesses who had slipped away from the city. Harold listened to each in turn and, from their separate accounts, was at last able to build up a reasonably coherent picture of the chaotic events of the past week.

As he had predicted in London, Aesegar had arrived too late to head off the Aelfgarsons, let alone talk them out of a pitched battle. He had arrived in Tadcaster a full day after the fight. Between then and Harold's arrival now, he had been the prime mover in the gathering of intelligence and the preparations for resistance. The ship man, Cerdic, had left a screen of men all around Riccall and from him Harold learned that the northmen had been busy putting up fortifications there and he also received a fairly accurate assessment of their numbers. From the Theakston thegn, who had lost two sons and a brother at Gate Fulford, he heard a first hand account of the full horror and muddle of the battle. From the two York men, finally, he learned the most important news of all. A peace had been brokered and the army of the Norse would receive full submission upon the meadows at Stamford Brook the very next day. The ship man confirmed this, reporting great activity around the boats and of many men preparing to move. Harold pounded the rough table at which he sat. "Now we have them," he said exultantly. He seemed to have tapped into some inner reservoir of stamina and determination. "Are any of them still at York?" One of the York men answered, "No, my Lord," save only their wounded and those who tend to them. This was part of the terms agreed with the Hardraada. York is barred to all others for the time being."

Harold paused to consider and calculate. "And here to Stamford Bridge is fifteen miles, I would say, give or take. If we push them then I guess it would be a four-hour journey for the foot, perhaps slightly more. We'll give Riccall a wide berth and move around York to the east and then pick up the coast road to Skaroaborg. So then, we shall skirt York, though doubtless their leaders there will come out to meet us. I'll talk to them then. Before the main force I want pickets at all the gates by dawn tomorrow. Absolutely no one is to leave or enter. Aesegar, I leave this to you and Haakon. I want that place completely shut off. Fifty men to a gate. Join us once we are past York."

He looked about him at the exhausted and haggard men gathered there. "We are all of us tired and we can sleep soon. I shall take but just a few moments more of your time. We have ahead of us yet another departure at first light." He held up his hand at their dismay. "Just one more time, my friends, I beg this of you. Local guides will take us clear of Riccall. After York we shall then move in four formations. Two mounted, then the foot and then Aesegar as rearguard. I shall lead with my own housecarls and the Middlesex, Essex and Hertfordshire men. Gyrth and Waltheof, you are to follow after with all of your people and those others with mounts. Maerlswyn, see to the rounding up of these people. If you find that you cannot be gentle with them then so be it." Harold turned to the wounded and bereaved thegn. "As for you, I charge you to keep good pace with all of those of the foot that remain and all of those of mine still coming in. Without a doubt you will have a hard time of it. Try two hundred paces at the walk and a hundred at the run." The man nodded, "My Lord King. We shall keep up with you. Have no doubt, we shall be right behind you."

Harold afforded him a smile. "Good, very good. Then we go straight there. We don't stop and we pitch right into them at the run. Do what you have to do now for your people and then get what sleep you can."

***

Stamford Bridge was a pleasant and a pretty place. The area was a lush bowl of land with the river Derwent meandering lazily through its wide, green meadows. To the east the land began to rise gently to the Wolds and over to the west to a steeper ridge and the village of Gate Helmsley. Two roads converged upon the wooden bridge, a bridge wide enough to permit three men abreast and crossing the wide stream fringed by steep banks and a forest of reeds. One road, passing through Gate Helmsley, ran from York to devastated Skaroaborg. The other, arriving transversely at the bridge, ran north east to south west. The location was a natural arena and meeting place for people travelling from any direction. Because of its nature and its location Stamford Bridge had often played host to large gatherings of people. There were fairs and folkmoots and on certain occasions in the past the fyrd had rallied there against marauding Norse or Danes. Until now, though, it had never played host to so many men. They sprawled and relaxed and skylarked on both banks of the river. Others roamed the fringes of the area aimlessly or cast lines into the river after fish.

They had arrived the previous evening, laying waste to both Gate Helmsley and Harold's estate of Catton on the way. Catton had indeed yielded up a great deal of mouth-watering livestock, prize Tamworth pigs included. The men gorged on beef and pork and mutton and awoke to gorge once more. At least they had had the sense to use the banks and river downstream as a latrine. Harald had insisted upon this, having had plenty of experience in the past, if no explanation for it, of the sickness that could strike out suddenly and savagely at large numbers of men gathered together in one place.

He had had a tent pitched on a slight rise of land a few hundred yards east of the bridge, his beloved Land Waster standard firmly planted into the turf outside. On his invitation Tostig had also spent the night there and now, in the fine mid morning and with the shouts and yells of men at leisure around them, they took their ease and awaited with anticipation the arrival of the last of their English supplicants and hostages. Nearby, Orri's brother Nicholas was practicing with a throwing knife and a log, a monotonous thudding. Englishmen had in fact been arriving in small groups at the meeting place since early morning and were now corralled together under armed guard, small huddles and knots of furtive and muttering men sitting upon the ground. Children, noisy as crows, were running about and playing, hostages to the capricious King of Norway.

Mysteriously, there had been no activity on the road that led to York, but from the east and the coastlands a steady stream of men arrived to surrender up their hostages and to convey and escort the wagons laden with food and livestock on the hoof. For the young hostages this was very much something out of the ordinary, an adventure. They roamed about exuberantly and, save for the occasional cuff and curse, were treated indulgently enough by their Norwegian captors. It was largely a peaceful scene and only on the other side of the bridge and slightly up the incline leading to Gate Helmsley was there any real semblance of military preparedness, a force of some three hundred armed men. Strange, though, thought Tostig to himself again, that there had been no sign of movement on the York road. He had mentioned this already to Harald. "They'll be here, by and by," said Harald peaceably. "It takes time to move men laden down with carts and beasts and brats. But if it concerns you so much then by all means send men out to scout."

Such a group of men was indeed already forming up to cross the bridge when there came shouts from across the river from gesturing men. Both Harald and Tostig looked over. There, on the ridge, was a definite movement, of rising dust and the glint of metal. Seconds later this movement had resolved itself into a mass of men, mounted and moving downhill fast. "There you go," said Harald, with his poor and failing eyesight. "Told you so, the good people of York." Tostig looked just one moment longer. "The good people of York, my arse," he said. "That's an army up there."

Across the river there came cries of alarm and warning and the Norwegians there began gathering themselves up and running for the bridge, the slowest of them even now being overrun and cut down by the mounted English. "By the White Christ, do you say so now?" exclaimed Harald. Around them the scattered army, the bathers and the fishers and the idlers, began to react, an initial panic and then a rush to their weapons.

"Nicholas," shouted Harald. "The horn, man. Blow the horn to assemble." The great ox horn began to boom out over the meadows and fields, summoning men to it as yet more English continued to pour over the ridge and down the short track to the bridging place. The first of the enemy were now dismounting and forming a shield wall prior to advancing on the bridge itself. "But who are they?" demanded Harald incredulously as attendants rushed forward with his chain mail. "What are they doing here?" Tostig replied, his voice grim. "I think I can answer that" Two large banners had now appeared on the ridge and were being waved aloft at them, the Dragon of Wessex and the Fighting Man. "It is my brother Harold, come calling on us. Short notice, but let us prepare a feast for him."

***

The English had made excellent time from Tadcaster, moving at the trot and canter and with the infantry behind them struggling manfully to keep up. At York, just after daylight and alarmed by the arrival of Aesegar's pickets at all of the gates, the citizens crowded the crumbling battlements and catwalks, peering out at the oncoming army. At Walmgate Bar Harold permitted a small delegation to come out to him. They approached, obsequious and fearful, scuttling in a sideways manner like crabs, as the army continued on its way along the Scarborough road. Harold remained mounted and looked down upon them coldly as they bowed and knelt. "Time is pressing," he told them, "and I do not have the luxury of talking to you overlong. I understand that you have already played host lately to the Hardraada and to my brother." Alone among them, Thorri Arnulfson looked him in the eye. "You have the right of it there, my Lord King. That we did. And what would you have had us do? They came upon us in their thousands and tore the men of Northumbria and Mercia to pieces in our sight. It was either that or have them burn this city, the second in your kingdom, to the ground." Harold nodded, acknowledging the fact and also the bravery and logic of the man standing before him.

"Quite so," he conceded. "You are, I presume, the spokesman for the city?" Arnulfson nodded, his eyes not leaving the King's. "Then know this," said Harold. "No person is to leave York this day, not your hostages for the Hardraada you have been busy gathering, nor any of the enemy. Any of these within your walls are to be held and all other ablebodied men capable of carrying arms are to assemble fully equipped and provisioned before the Minster. They are to be prepared to follow on with all speed when I instruct." Harold prepared to depart, swinging his horse around to gallop to the head of his column once more. "We go now to seek out the Hardraada and my brother and settle things." Arnulfson bowed gravely. "As my Lord King instructs," he said. "It will be done, and may God go with you today and always."

"Thank you, whatever your name is. And one more thing. I understand that you handed over a considerable fortune to pay off the Northmen. Such days are over. I shall now take this for myself, for my war chest. Look upon it as payment for services rendered."

***

There was desperate and savage fighting at the bridge now. The Norwegians were still streaming across it as a group of some fifty diehards swung their axes and swords against the oncoming mob of English. The first two divisions of mounted men had handed over their horses and had formed a curving shield wall five men deep as others crowded up behind them. The first of the infantry were now appearing on the ridge, with archers hurrying ahead to take up position on the flanks to shoot down the defenders of the bridge. The English beat their weapons upon their shields of wood and leather, shouting in unison the English battle cry, "Out, out, out!"

On the meadow and the slight rise of land, Harald and Tostig were busy rallying their panicked and confused army, both men now in full chain mail, helmeted and armed. "Take men and horses," Harald instructed Orri's brother Nicholas. "Ride to Orri at the boats at all speed. Bring him back here with all the strength he can spare and as fast as he can. We shall try to hold them at the bridge." The assembling Norwegians were now forming their own defence, a wide and curving wall, and shrieking back their own defiance. It was not, in truth, the shield wall of the epics at all. Very few of them possessed either shields or armour or helmets, these were for the most part back at the boats. "Pray to God they do not have many archers among them," said Tostig. Harald, the old blood lust once more upon him, threw back his head and laughed. "At such moments," he boasted, "I pray to the old Gods. The Gods of battle with whom we may presently feast." As had Staffyd back at Gate Fulford, he in fact felt a presentiment. He remembered old Stump back in Norway and his prophecy. He felt no fear, only an elation. One last glorious battle and perhaps an end to things, with all wounds to the front. This was how things ought to be. In either event, victory or defeat, his immortality was assured. The poets would sing of this in the great halls forever, the song of the last of the Vikings. He pulled Land Waster from the turf and waved it aloft. "Do you see them, you old bitch?" he addressed it, to Harald his personal totem had always been female, "let them come on and you shall feed on their flesh."

Tostig, watching the English now gathering in numbers, watching them as they poured down the trackway and sending out contingents to either flank of the bridge, was less sanguine. "We cannot meet them here," he urged Harald. "This is no place to seek a battle and we are ill equipped for it. We should cut and run while we may, make for the boats. I know a way around south east of here." Harald looked at him scornfully. "Cold feet, Englishman? No, absolutely not. This was fated to happen and I stay, come what may. They have us at a disadvantage, to be sure, but let us make an end to this, one way or another." He turned to roar encouragement and good-natured abuse at his men as Nicholas and a small group made off at the gallop, seeking to ride around the English and find a safe crossing over the river. "Ride like the devil," Harald screamed after him, "as if Loki himself and all his creatures were after you."

The Norsemen of the wall began to sing and chant in unison as more men came running from every direction to join them, throwing out from their ranks the ubiquitous leaping and capering berserkers. Ahead of the Scottish contingent, men had laid out broadswords upon the turf and were dancing across them as the pipes moaned and skirled. Tostig's veteran Flemings, a hard and embittered group more accustomed to a different and better ordered type of fight, were fully armoured. They leaned upon their swords and spears and awaited the outcome at the bridge and the final onslaught. They had followed this mad Englishman up and down the coast for months now and each man among them was bracing himself for the worst. A chaplain of suspect credentials walked along their line, blessing them and their weapons. Tostig continued to plead with the Hardraada. "We cannot stand here. Let us at least attempt to parley." Harald gestured towards the bitter fight at the bridge. "Try telling them that," he said.

On the other bank, and with the advantage of height that their horses gave them, Harold, Gyrth and Waltheof gazed down at the struggle around the crossing of the Derwent as Aesegar and Maerlswyn hurried to join them. The lines had drawn back from each other and now the English bowmen, with a clear field at last, were beginning to whittle away at the defenders of the bridge. They were reduced now to a score of men and the bank of the river was already thick with dead and injured men. "Enough of this," said Harold. "I want that bridge now. Take it."

Bjarni Eriksson was a veritable giant of a man, nearly as tall as the Hardraada and far broader, massive legs and arms like the trunks of young trees. He stood now upon the bridge, blocking the way as all around him men continued to fall to the English arrows. He was the acknowledged and wholly undisputed leader of an unruly and independently minded settlement to the north of Trondheim and in this capacity had taken over to England two boatloads of warriors. Once, remarkably, he had actually bested the Hardraada himself at the arm wrestling, thus winning a tax exemption for his community for a whole year. Now he stood alone, helmeted and in mail shirt. He swung his axe above his head, jeering at the English and daring them to come against him. Four men had already fallen to his axe. "You want some?" he yelled. "Here I am, you worms. Come and get it." Three men, one with a spear, closed upon him in a rush. The jabbing spear cut a raking wound in his side. Almost absently, he barged its owner into the river, chopping his free hand down onto the man's neck as he fell. The two remaining Englishmen drew back slightly and he went on to the offensive, charging into them and knocking both off balance. With an experience that was second nature, he stamped on the throat of one of the sprawling men, crushing his windpipe and snapping his neck. His axe rose and fell on the other, a killing blow that cut through the top of the man's helmet as if it had been butter. Cross eyed, the man fell back in a spray of red foam and brains. Eriksson roared in delight. "Who's next?" he demanded. A few arrows flickered at him. They passed by harmlessly, but one took him in the arm. Contemptuously he snapped it off at the haft and tossed it into the river. "Tell the Hardraada," he shouted at those Norwegians who had now reached the comparative safety of the far bank, "that I die hard."

Harold gasped and gripped his reins as he saw that the next man onto the bridge was none other than his own Ceofwyn, the gigantic Cornishman "Mind yourself, Ceofwyn," he muttered to himself. Ceofwyn, who had once beheaded an ox for a bet back in Rouen and who straightened horseshoes with his bare hands, approached the solitary Norseman in a Cornishman's wrestling crouch. Eriksson, sensing a worthy opponent at last, hooted with glee and dropped his axe. Instead of going hand to hand, however, he moved with a speed that belied his size and bulk and produced a throwing knife from his belt. It was an unexpected movement and he threw with precision. The knife buried itself to the hilt in the Cornishman's forehead. Ceofwyn grunted with surprise and fell to the planking, the Norseman's triumphant yell the last sound he ever heard. "Dear God Almighty," murmured Harold, part of his past wrenched from him. The giant man danced a little jig and pulled off his chain mail tunic. He threw it to the planks and derisively displayed his bare chest. "Any more for any more?" he called out mockingly.

Slightly upstream, Leofgar and Alfi had located a forgotten and abandoned fisherman's coracle. They clambered into it and, with spears for paddles, made their precarious way in the flimsy craft to midstream and then to under the bridge. Alfi thrust his spear into the bed of the Derwent to anchor the boat. There were wide gaps in the planking of the old bridge and they had positioned themselves directly beneath the giant Viking who was roaring out for fresh opponents. Leofgar the Mercian, possible kin to the Aelfgarsons themselves, had ever prided himself on a sharp and bright edge to his weapons. Now, having judged carefully his moment and place, he jabbed savagely upwards through a gap in the planks. The vicious and carefully honed blade of his spear entered the Norwegian at the base of his spine. With another savage thrust the spear severed his spine and entered his vitals, the blade and part of the haft emerging finally beside his navel. Transfixed and held upright by the spear, Bjarni Eriksson took a long time to die, wordless and in agony, as a rush of triumphant Englishmen poured by him and on to the other bank, spitting at him and tugging at his beard as they went. In the boat below Leofgar glanced at Alfi. "He shouldn't have done that to our Ceofwyn," he said laconically.

Harald the Hardraada, having on occasion been obliged to do so, never liked to fight upon the defensive, which partly explained why he was heedless to Tostig's urgings that they should close up on the bridge if they were after all to stand and fight. Outnumbered and with his men poorly equipped, he now had no option other than a defensive action. He stood at the head of his men as the English crossed over the bridge in force to line up on the meadowlands of the once peaceful Stamford Bridge. The Yorkshiremen and their children hostages had scattered in all directions, occasionally cut down but for the most part largely unheeded, and the cattle and sheep milled about, adding to the confusion. As the last of the northmen at the bridge reached their own lines, the English formed up in a shield wall once more, stretching significantly beyond either flank of the Norwegians, and with more men coming up behind. Harold, his brother and Waltheof had now dismounted. They stared at the chanting, jeering men opposite. "Come," said Harold. "Let's go talk to them." Gyrth was incredulous. "About what exactly? I wouldn't have thought there was that much to discuss." Harold was firm "That's our brother over there," he said. "Let us give him one final chance to see reason. I promised our mother, Gyrth. I do not seek his death. I want him alive, in dishonour and exile, but alive nonetheless. Perhaps one day his son will have Northumbria or Mercia. As for the rest of them, they'll rot here, by God." Gyrth shrugged and sighed. "This I must see," he said. "And I've always wanted to meet the King of Norway."

Tostig's eyes narrowed as he recognised the three men slowly approaching, arms spread wide to show they carried no weapons. His older brother, he noted, was walking with a decided limp. As he came closer, he seemed also to have aged considerably since last he saw him at that furious encounter at Oxford the previous year. Suddenly he felt old himself, felt like giving up this constant struggle and settling instead for his brother's justice, knowing that Harold did not want him dead. An exile somewhere. There, in that far flung corner of northern England and with a baying mob both before and behind him, Tostig experienced a sharp pang of regret, a brief flash of memory and nostalgia for the pine laden and sunlit hills of Rome, fine food and wine, elegant and polished discourse with learned and erudite men, and the dark and shining eyes of beautiful women."Who are they?"

demanded Harald, breaking into his personal reverie. Tostig thought quickly as his two brothers and Waltheof, of whom he was fond, drew close. It would most decidedly be tactless to identify them at this stage to this unpredictable man. He shrugged, "emissaries," he said, "come to seek peace terms." Harald smiled bleakly. "Then I shall listen to the terms they seek in return for their surrender," he said. As was natural and customary with him, he stared down contemptuously at the three Englishmen now standing there, staring at him and Tostig with undisguised curiosity. "Ask them what they want," he ordered Tostig. The erstwhile Earl of Northumbria chose to ignore Waltheof. "Gyrth, Harold," he said. "You are well, my brothers? I confess it does not gladden me to see you here in this place and at this time." His tone was genuinely sad.

"We are well enough," replied Gyrth grimly, and Harold raised a restraining and admonishing hand. "I find you in poor company Tostig," said Harold, "and I would separate you from it." Tostig laughed bitterly. "On the contrary, brother. I find myself in excellent company. Tell me what you want." Beside him he was conscious of the King of Norway fidgeting irritably and behind him a tangible increase in the shouts and chants of abuse and aggression amongst the men behind.

"Come away, Tostig," said Harold gently, and there was compassion in his voice. "Come away from these people now. Tell them you come with us to discuss matters." There was a bark of sour laughter. "You expect them to allow me to simply walk away from this? What would you do with me? What do you offer?" Harold gazed at him levelly. "I offer you your life, if not your honour. Your life to live in exile some place, never to return to England. You may keep your own boats and I shall give you money. Denmark is barred to you. Doubtless so too is Flanders now. I doubt that your big friend here would have you back, not that he has long to live now anyway. Upon your oath to me, you will go neither to Scotland nor Normandy. You might try Sweden, or the Empire, Rome even. As I recall, it suited you there."

Tostig was stung to one of his occasional furies. "You talk to me of oaths? You, of all people? And why would you do this? After all that has passed." Harold sighed deeply. "Because you are my brother and because too of a vow I made to the woman who brought us both into this wicked world." Tostig was silent for a while, at this invocation of his mother. With a slight nod he indicated the great Viking standing beside him. "And what, brother, do you offer him?" Harold's eyes flickered up and down the restless form of the man standing there, irritable and impatient to be at things. "In truth," he said to Tostig. "He is a very big man indeed. Seven feet of good English earth is what I offer him, to lay his thieving carcass in. Nothing more and nothing less. Now, I urge you. Come with me." Once more Tostig's ungovernable pride rose up. "I shall not walk away from him," he said. "I shall remain here with a man who holds me in greater esteem than my own brothers do. Farewell to you both. It may be that we shall not meet in this life again. Leave me." Their eyes locked for a brief moment, regret in both faces, before Harold turned on his heel and returned to the English lines, Gyrth and Waltheof in his wake. "Well," asked Harald, "what was all that about then?"

"They offered terms," said Tostig. "For me, my life. For you, your death. I stay here with you." Harald seemed unimpressed by the sacrifice. "And who are they, to speak with such authority?" Tostig was gazing at their backs with a fierce longing. "The young one," he said, "is Waltheof, Earl of Huntingdon, son of Siward of Northumbria. The other silent one was my own brother Gyrth, Earl of East Anglia, and the third was my brother, Harold King of England."

He should have seen to it that they had brought more bowmen reflected Harold gloomily. They had by no means enough of them. For nearly two hours the two armies had been hacking and hewing at each other like enraged beasts, with occasional and much needed pauses when they drew back and crouched, fighting for breath before hurling themselves at the enemy once more. Now the ground between the lines was a muddy mire thick with dead and dying men. Three times they had attempted to force the wall with mounted men. Each had proved to be a costly mistake. The Northmen went for the horses, targeting the unprotected heads and necks. Some of the Norwegians had managed to snatch up shields and helmets and they were placed in their greatly depleted front line into which the English bowmen shot their shafts when the opportunity, such as now, arose. Casualties were about even, and heavy. But the English were more numerous, and with the levies from York by now presumably on the road. First Fulford Gate, and now this, the thought was constantly with Harold. The much needed housecarls of the Earls, the trained bands of the thegns and the fyrds of the home counties, the midlands and the eastern marshes now joined the dead of Northumbria and Mercia. The northmen broke into a bellowing war chant once more and their horns boomed. The skirl and wail of the Scottish pipes wove through the sound. "At them again, then," ordered Harold, and once more the English came on at the run.

There was another clash of weapons and the sounds of struggling and injured men. Gyrth, sporting a spectacular gash to his head, less life threatening than it appeared, made his way to his brother's side. His sword was bloody and his sword arm reddened up to the elbow. "Waltheof is down," he announced. "He'll live, but it's a nasty wound he's taken. His men are taking him away." He glanced over at the struggle some fifty yards off. "They are much less than before, and weakening," he observed. Harold attempted a smile. It emerged like a drunken leer on his exhausted face. "As are we, Gyrth, as are we. I have never seen the like of it and hope I never shall again." Between them both fell the thought of the inevitable fight still to take place, and all those irreplace-able men of Fulford and Stamford Bridge. "Aye, well," said Gyrth, "If we pull this one off then they'll not come calling again in a hurry."

At about two hours after noon the men of York finally arrived, much needed fresh reinforcements and additional bowmen keen to avenge the humiliation of their city. Gratefully, the English army drew off to allow men with bows, much maligned men who were mocked for doing their killing at a distance, to whittle away at the outflanked and exposed edges of the enemy. Every so often, in their frustration and rage, individuals or small groups of men rushed from their ranks to hurl themselves at the English. If they got past the arrows, then they took numbers of the English with them before finally being cut down. In the midst of the enemy army the Land Waster still waved. "A fine ornament for a Royal Hall and a victory feast," said Gyrth as the grim and foreboding object continued to move defiantly. The standard of which they had heard so much was attracting men, drawing them from the flanks to the centre as the Norwegians closed up. Harold wiped the blood of some unknown enemy from his forehead. "They're up to something," he said.

Indeed, they were. Harald, frustrated and goaded beyond all reason, was contemplating the flying pig once more, one last savage and barging leap at his tormentors and a break for the river. It had always done the trick in the past and, doubt-less, would work again. It was good fun and also scared the wits out of the opposition. Tostig, grimy and now carrying several wounds, was at the King's side, pleading for a fighting retreat to the higher ground of the north and a narrower and more defensive position until Orri came up from the boats at Riccall with reinforcements. Privately, Tostig had his doubts about Orri. His brother Nicholas had been gone a good three hours now. Harald, in between raining blows on the helmets and shields of the English, would not be argued with. "If you don't like the way I'm doing things then why don't you just bugger off and join your little English friends? I'm having him, that brother of yours. He's dead meat. I'll leave him for the crows to pick clean."

In the event, Harald was not to be permitted to have much further to say on the subject and Tostig won his argument for a greater influence and say in the way things were going. The sharp end of Harald's battle formation was already beginning to shape itself. He paced up and down before them, cursing, cajoling and punching the ribs and the shoulders of the men in his playful fashion, his back to the enemy. He had removed his helmet and neck cover to allow the sweat to cool upon his head and his yellow and white hair as he good humouredly disputed the parentage of one of the Oslo Jarls. The arrow, perhaps deliberately aimed but in all probability not, came whistling down from a high trajectory.

At the very last, Harald was denied the glory and honour of taking his death wound to the front. With great speed and force the wicked leaf shaped blade of the arrow pierced the back of his neck and emerged once more, followed by four inches of haft, through the Hardraada'a mouth like the tongue of a serpent. A gush of blood poured out and drenched Tostig, standing just inches away from him. Without comment, without any final rousing words to ring down the centuries, Harald the Hardraada, last of the Vikings, was stone dead before he crashed to the ground. "Well, isn't that marvellous? Isn't that just marvellous," was Tostig's first shocked thought in that dreadful instant. "What, by all that's holy, do I do now?" Instinctively his own body answered the question for him as he snatched up Land Waster as it fell. As the shock waves of the finality of that moment began to ripple through the stunned warriors gathered around their fallen and stricken King, the English came on at them once more.

Few options were available to a leaderless and demoralised army trapped on a lost battlefield far from home and
ringed about by enemies. There was flight, if possible, and
surrender, if accepted. Here neither appeared to be a realistic
or viable choice. They were the Viking, and their duty was
to their dead Lord. Thus they fought on, the Land Waster
still flying above them, long after the arrival of the fresh
York levies. None there had ever experienced a fight of such
length or ferocity. None there had seen so many dead. With
less than an hour of full daylight remaining, a stir went
through the rear ranks of the English. There were more men
on the ridge road leading to York. This time, belatedly, it was
the brothers Orri and Nicholas, bringing with them such
men as they had been able to gather at the boats and who
had not dropped by the wayside in their punishing run in
full armour from Riccall, perhaps a thousand of them. It had
been a marvel of effort and endurance. The hearts and lungs
of the running men were at bursting point and the blood
sang in their ears. Many of them had not made it as far as the
gutted village at the top of the ridge. Some had actually died
of the effort and others had fallen in utter exhaustion, to fall
easy prey to vengeful gangs of local English.

By now the ferocity and the unpredictability of the
northmen held few surprises for Harold. He noted the
ragged arrival of the newcomers, no concerted and massed
charge here, and gave a series of swift and crisp orders. He
detached a third of his remaining force and had Maerlswyn
and Aesegar lead them back over the bridge to meet them.
They formed line and actually charged uphill in their rage.
There was another savage clash of shields and weapons and a
boiling mass of desperate men. From the fight came renewed
English cries of 'out, out, out' and in a quick glance Harold
could see that they were holding them. "Up there, Haakon,
my boy. See what's happening, and report straight back," he

yelled to his nephew. "I have things to see to here." Haakon grinned, waved and was gone.

The arrival of Orri and his failure to break through the English had been duly noted in the Norwegian ranks. There came another flurry of arrows and throwing axes and spears and the lines of the northmen seemed to shiver under the blows. At the edges men could now be seen to be running. The horns and pipes had long since fallen silent. The English, without orders, were gathering themselves for yet another surge forward. "Pull them back," screamed Harold urgently at his own surviving thegns, "keep in line." It seemed to him that the impossible, the unthinkable, was about to occur, a surrender of the Vikings. The noise of the battle on the ridge floated over to them but here, on this part of the battlefield, a sullen silence had fallen, punctuated by the screams and groans of the dying and injured. "No more, enough. They are giving up," he yelled.

Sure enough, a solitary figure stalked to the front of the defeated northmen, ostentatiously throwing helmet and axe to the ground. He held out both hands to the English and then to Harold as he thrust his way through the ranks. Harold stepped over the dead and dying to come within hailing distance of the man. He spoke in Danish, confident in the belief he would be understood. "Be at peace a moment," he said. "Do you understand my words?" Stryker, Harald's deputy, frowned and attempted to form words in the language. Stryker was another devoted follower who had grown old and grey in Hardraada's campaigns, a sensible and canny man who saw the ruin of it all and the folly of carrying on. Perhaps something, some honour, could be salvaged from this. His duty now was to the sons of the Hardraada and to carry away those who remained to the defence of their homeland. Already he was envisaging renewed attacks by their old enemies the Danes, emboldened by this defeat, of the return of rebels from the court of the King of Sweden and from the barbaric sanctuary of the Lapps.

The two men faced each other. Old Stryker's Danish had, finally and haltingly, returned to him. "You are the King Harold of the English?" Harold bowed formally in response to the old warrior. "Then there is my axe, there at your feet. It was a hard fight, no? We have hurt each other much." Gravely, and with a compassion that surprised him, Harold nodded. "But you have the better of us and now we place ourselves in your hands," said Stryker equally gravely. He turned and barked a series of commands at the men behind him. There was muttering and upraised voices, but the surviving men began to hurl their weapons and their shields to the ground. "You speak on behalf of your King?" asked Harold. "Our King," said Stryker, and there were tears in his eyes, "is dead."

Over across the river, both Orri and Nicholas lay dead, lying among their own men. Only a few hundred remained by the time Stryker was able to get a message to them to lay down their weapons. On the now muddied and scarred meadows the Faroese, the Orcadians, the Icelanders, the Dublin men and the confederation of the western isles were most of them dead, lying in mounds along with the Scots and Flemings and Norwegians. Perhaps one man in five who had made that carefree stroll from Riccall to Stamford Bridge was left standing.

With a ring of jubilant English now surrounding them the defeated survivors moved away from that place of death to an uncluttered area not far off and there slumped to the ground dejectedly to wait upon events. The following morning Harold's own provosts would make their own report, upwards of two thousand English dead. All those fine men who had made that truly heroic march from the south, an irreplaceable loss.

Depressed, dismayed and exhausted beyond measure, Harold and Gyrth roamed the battlefield, searching among the dead and dying and at last finding their brother where the bodies lay thickest and where the fight had finally ended. A ring of dead housecarls surrounded the bodies of the Hardraada and Tostig. Unlike the one time King of Norway, Tostig had clearly not had an easy end of it all. He had died hard, his right arm, severed just below the shoulder, was missing and one of his legs twisted at an impossible angle. Some blunt object wielded with force had turned his chest into a concave mess and there was a vast gaping wound in his side, obviously the work of an axe, from which had slipped a hideous coil of pink and blue and grey intestines. Any one of these wounds on its own would have been sufficient to have snuffed out the life of the mercurial, talented and tormented former Earl of Northumbria. His face, his open jaw and staring eyes, was fixed in a feral scream of rage and despair.

The brothers, helplessly, knelt at his side, their eyes meeting across his mangled body. Another Godwinson gone. Harold, the pain of the once forgotten rheumatism now returning to him, tried in vain to close his brother's eyes and then gave up the attempt. There was a discarded shirt nearby, thrown off perhaps by a berserker. Gyrth fetched it and placed it gently over Tostig's face. "What," he asked, "do we tell our mother?"

Harold wasn't listening, his thoughts were elsewhere, far away. They were thoughts of a shared childhood, Bosham and Winchester and all those many places that they had fetched up in as they followed in the wake of their itinerant father. He was thinking of exile in Flanders and Ireland and of their partnership in Wales, and of other things besides. Aesegar had suddenly materialised at his shoulder, staring down at the corpse in fascination. "Have him taken up," said Harold, now aware of his presence. "Mind how you do it, there's enough of him missing already. We shall bury him in the Minster at York." Tentatively Aesegar began to recite a long list of the known dead, Thegns and ealdormen, an

Abbot. A dying Cambridgeshire thegn was requesting to see him and Waltheof was looking none too clever at the moment.

"Yes, yes, yes," said Harold abstractedly. "We shall see to all things presently, but this thing first I ask of you." With his eyes and a brief gesture of the head, Gyrth motioned the Shire Reeve of London away. "Up with you now, brother," said Gyrth gently. "There's the living now that need you, and your guidance and strength." With difficulty he hauled his brother to his feet. Before they could reach the soothing babble and chatter of the river to bathe there was just one more ordeal to face, the screams and the yells of acclaim and triumph of the English he had led to this place. He stumbled amongst them, slapping backs and pinching ears and grinning broadly. To do anything else would have been a weakness and a betrayal.

CHAPTER SIX :

The Point of No Return

The River Somme: September, 1066

There came a brief period of bad weather and unseasonable rain, transferring the camp into a dismal and malodorous morass. On occasion the wind veered, briefly and tantalisingly, to the west and south west, but never for long enough. A small and battered fishing smack blew in from Romney by way of Flanders. It carried with it momentous news. Harold, forced by circumstance and political pressure, had at last disbanded his southern fyrd. The men of the fyrd were returning home in droves to their homes and farms to bring in the harvest. Only a rump force of local thegns and their retainers, stiffened here and there by small detachments of housecarls, remained. There were also rumours, as of yet unsubstantiated, that a number of English warships on their way to their base at Sandwich had been wrecked in a gale.

In turn William rejoiced and raged. The coast of England lay largely undefended. Most certainly it could not defend itself against a large force of determined men arriving all in the one place. Yet here he was, pinned to the coast and waiting for a wind that would not come. Most of his armoured force was now in camp at St Valery, from where he received daily news. There FitzOsbern, his brother Robert and Beaumont kept them in strict order. Here at Dives, some one hundred and sixty sea miles west along the coast, the rest of his force were allowed little time for leisure and idle pursuits. Despite the discipline and the awe in which he was held, there were a number of desertions among the bored and leaderless free-lance knights and among the conscripted peasantry, themselves also feeling the lure of the harvest. William could do little about the mercenaries and free lancers, they were their own men and bound by no fealty. Common men were tracked down where possible and mutilated upon a second offence, usually the loss of a hand or a branding.

In the very small hours of one late summer night William, in the upstairs solar of the Manor House at Dives, was awakened by a commotion in the hall below. He had the warrior's gift of sleeping through the noisiest of events if they were explainable to his unconscious mind, and unthreatening, but he would awake, fully alert and on the instant at the quietest sound of anything unusual. Even so, not even the soundest sleeper could have slept through the gathering noise below. It was the noise of many men speaking in what they fondly believed to be whispers. The main door opened and shut noisily on a number of occasions and the sound of men hoarsely whispering to keep their voices down.

William's two squires, the fourteen-year-old twins, Hugh and Drogo FitzPons, were shifting and fidgeting on their straw mattresses at the foot of the bed, murmuring sleepily to each other. William sat bolt upright and then levered himself to place both feet on the planking. He swore colourfully as a loose splinter entered the sole of his bare foot. "Well, one of you then, for the love of God. Christ's wounds! What do you think I keep you both on for?" Both boys were fully dressed but for their boots. Drogo, always the quicker of the two, went down the ladder like a squirrel. Hugh, still bemused by sleep, hovered uselessly. William snarled at him and reached for his cloak. Presently, Drogo's tousled head appeared at floor level at the top of the ladder, looking like a disembodied apparition. "It's those Flemish shipmen," he announced excitedly. "They say the wind is in the west, and likely to stay for a while. Is that good?" Despite his ill humour at the rude awakening, William smiled at him. "By all accounts, my boy," he said. "By all accounts. Away with yourselves now and find something useful to do for a change." The twins vanished, like wraiths at the dawn.

The men, experts in the vagaries of the wind, had in fact waited some time before electing to go in a body to awaken the Duke. Years of experience and disappointment and surprise had made them cynical and suspicious of seemingly favourable sailing conditions. The Duke had been abed for some four hours before they finally decided to awaken him. There in the hall they conferred with William as the FitzPons boys and other servants bustled about and brought lights and food and drink. "The wind is in the right quarter, sure enough," said the Flemish master mariner, Martin. "And at this moment it shows no sign of shifting. I'd give it a day or two, maybe a short while longer. It is time to move, your Grace. I cannot say when next you might get this wind again. Best it was now, for fear of losing it."

***

The camp was by now well accustomed to night alarms and sudden practice drills of various types. It was a habit of William's and in which he was indulged by his principal deputies. All, particularly the more senior people and the very prickly mercenaries, took serious exception to this habit, but none dared complain directly and all were far more proficient through practice in such skills as the striking of tents and the saddling of horses. Thus it was that some three hours later, and with the first pink of the dawn appearing, the activity about the moored and tethered boats was frenetic. William's appointed beach marshals moved amongst the cursing and labouring men with clubs and switches and belaboured the shoulders of the slow and the clumsy and the sullen. The first of the boats within the estuary at last unfurled their sails and began to make out into open water, made slower by the lack of oarsmen. The brisk west wind caught behind them and set them on their journey east, with the specialists in the stern leaning on the tillers. Latecomers splashed into the shallows and were hauled aboard. Close on to seven hundred heavily laden boats of varying size and seaworthiness jostled for space and collided in midstream.

Observing the chaos, William winced and swore colourfully. His language was, however, by no means equal to that of Montgomery, as he roamed up and down and kicked and punched and cajoled. He was experiencing the effects of a crippling hangover and had never been a good man for work in the early morning.

Up to their waists in the rising dawn tide, men laboured with staves to assist the boats off the mud banks. One boat crashed broadside on to a ramshackle jetty, bringing the luckless men standing on it waiting for embarkation hurtling into the water. Another boat, inexplicably, turned on its side and sank in moments. Men and horses laboured towards the safety of dry land. "Dear God," murmured an exhausted and demented looking Montgomery, now back and standing at William's side. Even so, the bulk of the fleet, seven hundred boats or so, was now underway. It made for an impressive sight, and the like of which none had ever witnessed before or would ever again.

From first light to the ringing of the Angelus bell and beyond the fleet was still setting out, to hug and claw at the coastline on their way east. Those boats that were best equipped and manned, with the most expert mariners and tillermen aboard, were first off. The instructions to those following after were to keep in sight if they could and to find a safe harbour before St Valery if this proved necessary. May the good God above help them if the wind veered to the contrary or if the English chose this time to sail in close.

The sight of all those boats may well have been an impressive one, but no one viewing from the estuary head had any doubt of the fleet's vulnerability and inexperience as they watched it go. Boats were still putting out as the light began to fail and, aboard them, lanterns were raised to the mastheads. Dives was now beginning to resemble the site of a large country fair after everyone had gone home, a vast expanse of churned up mud and litter and the excrement of men and beasts.

"We can now but pray to Almighty God," observed the Abbot of Fecamp portentously. "It is now all within His most loving and generous hands. More than this we cannot do." The good and saintly abbot and his followers, and other men of God besides, had been busy all day with individual confessions and absolutions and group blessings and benedictions. There were deep, purple rings under his eyes and his hands shook. They were all standing on the east bank of the Dives estuary and with the smell of mud and salt and decaying marine life rich in their nostrils, as disturbed and outraged gulls wheeled noisily above them. From time to time, with slight changes in the wind, snatches of singing, both sacred and profane, drifted on the breeze over to them, a 'Nunc Dimittis' or a tribute to the qualities of a wharf side whore. "God keep them all indeed," said William. Montgomery touched him gently on the shoulder. "Time to eat," he said. "It's been a long day, and we have a hard ride tomorrow."

Before dawn the following morning William was on the road again. His favourite destrier, a huge muscled giant of close on seventeen hands and upon which he would go into battle, had gone on ahead to St Valery, led by two highly nervous squires. Instead, he rode a spirited bay that threw clods of earth up into the faces of those behind and attempted to nip any other horse coming too close. He was heading for Lillebonne, hoping to reach it by nightfall. If his horse foundered along the way, then there would be others available. He hoped to be on the border at Eu by noon of the following day and at St Valery itself by that nightfall. In his wake there came those remaining notables who had not already left for Ponthieu. What had happened to his fleet, the bulk of his army and his power? Without it, without them, he was lost. He had placed everything on this gamble. If he failed in this then he was truly finished, an easy target for all his currently dormant enemies, and with the Duchy reduced once more to the anarchy that he had been born into.

At noon he surrendered up his exhausted bay and transferred to a less spirited and more biddable beast. He rode tirelessly, eating up the miles at a canter as other men and horses fell behind. They crossed the Seine at Lillebonne. As they rode through the crowded township nestling up against the walls and towards the citadel, scene of William's great diplomatic triumph a few months back, they were mobbed and cheered. The final flowers and blooms of the summer were flung at them and people pressed up against their stirrups, offering up leather flasks of wine and cider. Montgomery cursed as a stale loaf, enthusiastically but inexpertly flung, struck him on his bared head. It was approaching dusk. There was still no news of the fleet.

William waved aside all attempts at ceremonial and offers of feasting and went to bed while the last of his following continued to straggle in. Before daylight he was off once more and heading for the small town of Arques.

He was there before noon and receiving reports at last from the nearby coast. A vast armada of ships had rounded Cap D'Antifer, sailing in line and appearing to be making good progress. Between there and the coast north of Arques, so seemingly reliable reports told him, the wind had changed. Many of the ships, bearing their crews and seasick passengers had been driven ashore. There were reports of ships lost and drowned men bobbing in the shallows along the shoreline. The news was unremittingly bad.

At Eu, at the crossing of the river Bresle and at last into the lands of Ponthieu, the grim faced Duke brushed aside a hastily assembled welcoming party. St Valery itself was now just a short journey away. William took the coast road, hoping for further news. He overtook a small group of bedraggled men trudging painfully towards St Valery and interviewed them from the saddle. They were, they told him, the survivors of two small boats that had collided as both were attempting to claw back out to sea and away from the rocks. One of the boats, with a minimum complement of men and heavily laden with arrows, had sunk like a stone. The other was an equally crammed troop ship. Between them, both boats had carried fifty men. At least six of those men were now unaccounted for. They had been arguing and bickering as William had ridden up.

William was strangely comforted by this individual story of loss and tragedy, the crisis was now assuming a more human rather than a cosmic dimension. He reached into his tunic and threw a small purse of coin at the men. Neel of Herve, fast rising in the Duke's estimation as a valuable and inconspicuous mover and shaker, was there with him and was summoned forward.

"Herve," William told him. "Take what men you need and trust and what money you require from my clerks back along the road. I want this coastline scoured all the way between St Valery and Dives, and with a minimum of fuss and attention. I want the dead buried and the living persuaded to hold their tongues. I want all evidence burned or otherwise removed. That which is salvageable you will have sent to St Valery. I shall want a full reckoning of men and ships and equipment lost. Above all, I want discretion. Have you got all that?" Herve, saturnine and sardonic as ever, touched his forehead with his index finger and wheeled his mount. William, at ease in his selection of the right man for the job, watched him go and then set about completing the last leg of his journey. Time, once more, for a change of mount.

Throughout his headlong chase along the coast in pursuit of a fleet which might or might not have come to grief, William had been making frantic contingency plans against the time he might find himself isolated and alone once more against a mob of enemies, both domestic and external. He could, perhaps, fortify Mont St Michel against siege and build himself up from there. In extremis, he could perhaps punch his way south and make his way to his obscure cousins in Italy and Sicily. From the saddle he dictated and then dispatched a sealed letter to his wife. There were caches of hard cash and disposable gold and jewellery that he had left in secret places against such a contingency as this. Take the children and shift for yourself until such time as I can join you if things turn out ill, tell me where you have gone, the message concluded. The sight that greeted him on the broad banks and meadows to either side of the wide river Somme was, therefore, a deeply comforting one, a sight that lifted his spirits and caused him to most uncharacteristically cry out in delight. In many ways the place resembled Dives, with an encouraging bustle and mob of men and an array of moored and tethered boats. Even as he reined in for his first proper view he could see further boats, distinctly battered and travel worn in appearance, putting in at the estuary head. There was a positive swarm of gratifyingly busy looking men hard at work in unloading and setting up camp. The noise and hum of their activity and the mournful lowing of cattle drifted across to him. It was music to his ears.

In the broad meadows of the opposite bank the tents and pavilions of the lords and their contingents were in the process of being erected. He could sense the feeling of order arising out of the confusion and an immense sense of relief and then satisfaction overwhelmed him. Pennants and battle standards had been raised before the temporary canvas homes of the principal men of Normandy. In the stiff breeze these brave insignias of wolf and bear, lion and dragon, white bull and black horse, were all, uniformly, flying in the wrong direction, away from the grey and drizzling coast and the Kingdom of England beyond. No matter, in his pleasure at the sight of the greater portion of his army and fleet gathered together in one place again, William paid little thought to this. Instead he dismounted and knelt, bending his head and offering up a prayer to God and His Son, the Holy Mary and all the saints above. His lips moved in silent thankfulness. Adverse winds could wait for a while. For the time being he was safe, he was vindicated. Blood of Christ. Pity the man who would move against him now. He would squeeze him in his fist like soft mud, he would chew him up and spit him out. Those of his followers who had managed to keep up with him on this last frantic chase across the headlands glanced at each other uncertainly and then slid from their saddles to kneel likewise upon the ground, remaining there for what they hoped was a suitable length of time.

***

His brief communion with God concluded, William rose, triumphant, his eyes scanning the pavilions once more, itemising them one by one. His arrival had been noted on the far bank. Already there was activity around and about a number of the flat-bottomed barges. He could make out men running aboard and preparing to put out to the bank upon which he waited. He turned to discover his entourage still bent and kneeling in gestures of piety, both genuine and feigned. "Enough of that," he roared exuberantly and clapping his hands. "Work to be doing. Work to be doing."

He strode through the encampment, cheered to the echo, and towards the space possessed by Guy of Ponthieu, that most reluctant of all his vassals, The Count had pitched his tents on the highest ground available, in an attempt to make at least some form of statement and protest. This was his territory, after all. William was able to afford his prickly and sensitive subject a certain amount of sympathy, but not too much, as he loathed the man.. Doubtless Guy had taken a fair old battering over the past few days at this uninvited invasion and the less than sensitive treatment he had in all likelihood received from those experts in coercion and demoralisation, FitzOsbern and Robert of Mortain. Even now, as he stalked up the greasy incline to where Guy's banner flew, FitzOsbern was recounting with relish the Count's reaction, delivering also a swift situation report. Seven hundred and thirty-eight craft of various size, manpower and content had set out from Dives. "We have now six hundred and eighty safely moored or else in sight," FitzOsbern informed him, "and watchers all along the coast." He paused, "it could have been a disaster, William, one we could not have hoped to have recovered from." William nodded sombrely. "I know, Fitz," he said. "Don't I just know."

And here was Guy himself, standing before his tent in supposed welcome and bristling with injured pride and importance, his slight and twisted figure like a spavined game bird bested in a fight. Crowding around the deeply unhappy man was a group of William's own men. His half brother Robert was there, along with a happily beaming Beaumont. There were other allies, both willing and unwilling. Aimerie of Thouars and the Breton Alan Fergant stood next to gloomy old Eustace of Boulogne. Ponthieu vassals, unhappy and resentful, hovered at the fringes, a sullen knot of mailed men.

"Guy," William called out cheerfully. "God's Love! You are looking well, aren't you just. Must be the sea air." Robert of Mortain, uncomplicated and totally lacking in either guile or diplomacy, chortled merrily and slapped the little man on the back, causing him to stumble. "That," he said, "and the delight of having us all here as his guests." Guy smiled a sour little smile that failed entirely to reach his eyes and then bowed with elaborate formality. "Your Grace. I am of course delighted to welcome you, and to see you once more. I offer you as much hospitality as I am capable of within my small means, until, that is..." He lapsed into silence and so William mischievously chose to help him out with the incomplete sentence. "Until such time as the wind shifts to the direction we require it to shift to. Now then, my good Lord Guy. This hospitality of which you speak. Shall we go in?"

The time they spent there at the mouth of the Somme proved to be longer than anyone would have expected or desired. In Normandy and along the coast of France and across the water in England the crops and fruits and vegetables were gathered up in a long and glorious summer. It had been an exceptional harvest, the best many could remember for years. The grapes, apples and pears had yielded an excellent return there in Ponthieu and went to the presses to produce wine and cider and raw spirits. Guy's own forest lands were forbidden to his guests. Unhindered, the pigs of the area, both wild and domesticated, gorged upon beechmast and acorns and the horse chestnuts blown down by the gales.

A few days after William's own arrival in Ponthieu, an extremely weary Neel of Herve, battered and care worn in appearance, reported back. In the event, or so it would seem from his report, that although the damage caused by the fraught and dangerous journey from Dives to the Somme was serious and costly enough, the damage caused was not as great as it might well have been. Both men, for their own separate reasons, drew satisfaction from this and chose not to reflect too unduly upon the dead.

Out of William's fleet of invasion perhaps thirty of the smaller and more unseaworthy craft had been lost. For the most part these had been flat bottomed craft and wholly incapable of withstanding the storm. It seemed that upwards of perhaps three hundred men had disappeared. They had either drowned or else, angry and depressed and reaching the shore safely, had drifted off to disappear into the interior of northern France. These fugitives would prove to provoke serious policing problems for weeks and months to come, with robberies and rapes and murders and a large crop of men hanging from the market crosses of the towns and villages of the surrounding districts. With the minimum of fuss that the Duke had commanded, Herve had the dead tumbled hastily into communal pits and those survivors that could be found and rounded up were sent to obscure garrisons in the lonely fortresses along the borders of Anjou and Brittany or on pointless patrols deep into the countryside.

Over the next two weeks Guy raved and fumed and fretted to himself and to the closer of his associates as this most unwelcome of armies continued to make ever more serious and punishing demands upon his provender and supplies. His guests, knowing of William's personal disdain for the man, challenged each other to see who could consume and waste the most. Most wagers were won easily by Robert of Mortain until finally he could find no more takers. William, by way of recompense, pledged over the crucial stronghold of Dover and a large swathe of the coast of Kent and its hinterlands to Guy, along with the tolls and customs of the Thames estuary and certain privileges in the city of London itself. In the meantime, the wind kept them all firmly pinned to the coast and anger and frustration and increasingly more serious breaches of camp discipline grew in number and severity.

The army was bored and listless and the camp provosts were once again put to work with their cudgels and their threats. Once, spectacularly, an incomprehensible and clearly deranged Lithuanian adventurer attempted to pull Beaumont, of all people, from his horse over some imagined slight and was promptly beaten to death on the spot by Beaumont and his men. Had the man had sufficient French to understand then he would have known not to tangle with the highly unstable Beaumont, who received a mild reproof from the Duke that same evening. A few melees and other warlike sports were arranged for prize money in the meadows. There were the usual broken limbs and maimed horses and two more deaths.

Matilda arrived from Rouen with the children. Bustling and businesslike, she had all the unnecessary clutter heaved unceremoniously out of William's pavilion by his own cowed servants and set about making herself comfortable. He himself was away inland at the time, bullying the locals and so in no position to interfere. Half repaired harness, scouring sand, other items of equipment, two bull mastiffs and the FitzPons boys were all thrown out or evicted and, instead, in came Matilda and the children, Agatha and the baby William, and all that pertained to them. The boy Robert was back in Rouen, ostensibly under the tutelage of the kind and well-meaning but immensely tedious and dull Bishop. Arriving back late in the afternoon, William dutifully greeted his wife and decided privately that henceforth he would spend more time in the tents of his followers. His tiny and doll like wife was the only person on God's earth capable of subduing him. On occasion, when and where necessary, she took pleasure in reminding him of the time she had stabbed him with a knitting needle during his tempestuous wooing.

Matilda sat now sedately as William, readmitted to his tent, ranged around and cursed the weather and occasionally kicked things. Amongst her many other talents and accomplishments, Matilda was also a botanist and a distiller of strange concoctions and liquids and an amateur artist of some considerable skill. In her busy life she had amassed an impressively comprehensive knowledge of flora and fauna and of how best to use readily available herbs and weeds and flowers for a variety of ailments and preventatives. Thus, for example, she could treat either constipation or else loosen bowels. She knew how to either hasten childbirth or prevent it altogether. Favoured people approached her furtively to ask for advice and assistance on a multiplicity of ailments, on acne and other skin complaints, on warts and haemorrhoids.

Matilda prescribed and applied tincture of cloves for toothache and henna and lampblack to the wives of noblemen. On each occasion she probed also with considerable skill for family details and stored away all useful information, along with a mental note of who was thus indebted to her. She possessed also a slightly alarming knowledge of fast and slow acting poisons. At this particular moment and while William, now seated morosely on his campaign stool and staring into space, she was seated at a small portable table and working painstakingly on a little book of vellum, the size of a book of hours. On one page, spread and dried, was a single stem of juniper, the dried and flattened berries still attached. On the other side, with pen and ink, she was sketching and making occasional notes in good Latin in a tiny and spidery script. William had always resented and feared her literacy. She paused and sighed. The poor light made her eyes and head ache. Outside were the usual noises of men in camp settling down for the night. The baby William slept fitfully and whimpered in his cot and their darling daughter kept to the shadows and played some secret game of her own with beads and her beloved rag doll. Only she and her mother knew it was named after the girl's poor pronunciation of the present King of England. It was their little secret.

William looked across at her. "Do you know," he said, breaking the silence in the tent, "that anywhere else and married to anyone else, you would have been long burned by now for the witch you undoubtedly are in some town square. Anyone else and I too would have watched and cheered." Unruffled, Matilda glanced up and smiled at him sweetly. "But I would not let them," she said. "Were I a witch then for sure I would turn them into pigs or donkeys or some such. Tell me, was it wise to let our Robert out after wild boar that time? I did mean to ask you before." William shrugged. "The boy has to learn. He's old enough, and Fitz and his uncle Robert will keep him safe enough while I am away."

"William," said Matilda evenly, "if he comes home with so much as a scratch then I shall, seeing as I am a witch, put something in your drink that will make your eyes melt and steam to come out of your ears. You have my word on it." William uttered a brief bark of laughter and rose to walk over to her, tripping over a small lapdog on the way. It rose and snapped and yelped at him irritably. "Why is that thing, that abomination, bright blue?" he asked as Matilda put down her pen soothe and appease her outraged pet. "It is the fashion," she replied. "Besides, I thought it would wash off. It hasn't though." William snorted. "Small wonder it has a temper." Matilda raised her eyebrows. "And you have not, I suppose. All this blaspheming and kicking the servants. It's enough to try the patience of a saint. Speaking of which, why not try Saint Valery for a wind? At least he lives locally"

William knew that Matilda never made idle suggestions and so, two days later, and after considerable negotiations with the custodians of the blessed Saint Valery, the desiccated and mummified corpse of the saint was disinterred.

Preceded by chanting clerics and acolytes swinging censors of expensive incense, the Saint was paraded on a bier throughout the camp. Everyone turned out for the event and knelt and prayed and doffed their caps. The crimson carpet upon which the bier finally rested became near to invisible under a shower of coin and jewellery and flowers. "It might work, I suppose," observed Montgomery sardonically. "At least it is a diversion of sorts."

As if in response to the supplications and appeals made to the Saint, the indefatigable Gilbert of Lisieux, that peerless traveller and diplomat, appeared in the camp the very next day. Trailing in his wake was a Papal delegation from the Holy Father himself, creased and rumpled and exhausted on their mules, but decked in their soiled and muddy finery for the occasion. Before William's pavilion, and with great and solemn ceremony, an object was removed from a large oaken chest with veneration and then held aloft. The tall and angular Bishop brimmed with pride at this major coup as one of the Cardinal Legates unrolled a scroll and began to intone in a ponderous Latin that few of those close enough to hear could understand. Attached to its cruciform frame, the Papal banner, the "Vexellum", was displayed for all to see. On a background of white linen, a crimson cross was displayed. Holy medals swung below it; kissed and endorsed and blessed by the Pope himself.

Thus was the venture transformed. No longer was this simply a military adventure, though larger than most. Now, and with this banner displayed before the whole army, the enterprise assumed the proportions of a collective act of faith. Now were they all transformed from marauding and feckless soldiers of fortune into a host gathered together in the service of God. This, now, was a 'Sacra Bellum,' a holy war and with all the honour and the remission of sins to those participating in this truly blessed campaign against the godless English. Hardened men, well-seasoned in the dark arts of war, knelt and wept like children. Caught up in the solemnity of the occasion, they beat their heads against the earth and called upon the blessing of God above.

Naturally, William was the first in the queue to kneel and kiss the banner that two priests held aloft. Behind him there formed a solemn procession of the greatest of Normandy and its allies. Looking on, as the Latin chants and the cries of the mob rose into the air, Gilbert felt a glow of sinful but blissful and understandable pride. Beside him, Odo simmered and boiled with resentment and jealousy. He would have killed in order to be able to preside over an occasion such as this. One of the Cardinals, vaguely and wearily, blessed the crowd. More incense and indiscriminate flinging of holy water. "In the name of the Father, the Son, and the Holy Ghost."

At the very fringes of the crowd, a small knot of mercenaries, thrown into the company of each other by their very alien backgrounds, and collective lack of French, attempted to make sense of this latest bizarre manifestation of pomp and ceremony. Over the past few weeks they had kept themselves very much to themselves and were now able, painfully, to communicate with each other in a fractured form of bastard French. There was a man from Novgorod, a man from pagan Riga, a brace of Lotharingians, a Hungarian, a Bulgar and a dark and voluble man who maintained he was no Moor, but a God-fearing Spaniard. "So what is? What is now?" demanded the Hungarian. The Riga man spat and shrugged. None had a satisfactory explanation and so they returned once more to one of their interminable games of knucklebones, a game that required only the very minimum of speech.

***

William resumed his geography lessons, calling once more upon his Flemish experts, Malet and the monks of Fecamp.

To the east of Beachy Head, he learned, he had some forty miles of coastline to choose from for a landing, as far as the high cliffs of Dover. To the west a very promising harbour at a place called Shoreham. West of that he would be chancing his arm, with a concentration of English ships likely to be prowling around the island called Wight. Together, he and his advisors pored over rough maps scrawled upon scraps of parchment. Pevensey Bay would seem to be a reasonable choice. The preferred choice was a place called Bulverhythe. Smaller than Pevensey, it appeared to afford easy access to the nearby towns of Hastings, Rye and Romney. The Flemings knew the settlements there well enough. It was not a place where they would seek to spend their leisure time. Huddles of raw, mean cabins of turf and mud and thatch inhabited by equally raw and mean people spreading seaweed over their sour little fields and attempting to squeeze a living from fish. A road of sorts ran north out of Hastings, William learned, diverging some seven or eight miles inland at a small settlement on a ridge called Senlac, bordered to the east and north east by the forfeit lands of both Malet and the monks of Fecamp.

"Senlac," William mused. "Strange name. French almost. 'Lake of Blood.' Do we have an omen here, I wonder?" Malet, who did not care for such observations, crossed himself hurriedly. From the ridge, it seemed, two small trackways made their way through the dense Sussex weald towards London.

In his time with the army, Martin's command of French had made little progress but was now heavily peppered with local colloquialisms, mostly inappropriate for present company. "Bulverhythe," he said, jabbing at the map, "would be good. But the wind you are most likely to get is a south westerly and, as I keep saying, you have no fucking oars." William, the monks and Malet, winced. "This means you'll fetch up somewhere along here." He waved his hand over the crude map and above the places indicated with a red spot. "Rye, Dover, Folkestone. I could get a single boat to any of these places, no worries. I can't say the same for an entire bloody fleet. Fearsome cliffs they have thereabouts, and marshes and tidal reaches and what not. Real bastards to navigate. We could even fetch up in Sandwich, like as not."

"Sandwich would be fine," said Arnaud, "but for the fact that there is an English fleet there, and a strong local militia." William nodded. "What I want," he said, "is a stretch of coastline, any coastline, where I can get all of my people ashore in one piece and where the English are not mustered in force. Then we can shift for ourselves." One of the monks spoke. "And with the blessing of Almighty God, who rules and directs us all," he observed, feeling that God had been kept out of the discussion for long enough. "I thank you for the reminder," said William piously.

***

"Surprise!" shouted Matilda. She clapped her hands together delightedly and then attempted to reach up to remove the blindfold. William sighed resignedly and removed it himself. Only for his wife would he have submitted to this. Only for Matilda would he have agreed to be hooded in his tent and then led, stumbling, down a meadow packed with his entranced soldiery and with his immediate deputies sniggering and muttering witty asides behind him. But that was Matilda, a determined woman who would brook no opposition when the mood was upon her. William flung aside the blindfold and peered ahead of him. The mob erupted and boiled in delight, the Duchess of Normandy had ever been a great favourite with them. Matilda smiled contentedly. "So what do you think then?"

They were standing now on the treacherous south bank of the river Somme. Before them, smelling of fresh pine and undried pitch and paint, there was moored a sleek single masted vessel. It was some sixty feet long and narrow in the beam, a true Viking greyhound and built for speed. On either side of the boat was a bank of six oars and a raised poop in the stern where a tillerman and a number of others stood stiffly to attention. It made for an elegant sight, bobbing up against the crowd of ungainly mongrel vessels, like some high-quality courtesan fallen in amongst low harlots. There was a brief barked order and, with a satisfying crack and rustle, the sail was unfurled. On the pristine surface of the cream coloured sailcloth the large red outline of a leopard rampant had been skillfully stitched. "My gift to you," said Matilda. "Many happy returns." William took her hand in his. "I have not the words. It is most unexpected." Matilda stamped her foot in mock exasperation. "Well, it is your birthday."

"It is? I had forgotten. What on earth is that thing?" William pointed at a gold painted figure at the prow. From where he was standing it looked like a pig blowing into some sort of shell. "That," said Matilda, "is a cherub. A child blessed by God and taken unto him." William nodded. "Then what's it doing there then?" he asked ungraciously. "The boat," said Matilda. "It's called 'the Mora.' A fine name."

At the back of the crowd Martin massaged his jaw appreciatively. "A pretty enough thing," he muttered to Arnaud at his side. "You may be sure that yon craft will shift some. She'll get him killed yet, that little dwarf duchess of his. In a thing like that he'll be out of sight of any of his fleet and a sitting duck for any loose Englishman." Matilda picked her way daintily down the bank to the stern of the 'Mora,' William trailing awkwardly after her. A large grey flagon was attached to a rope. She picked it up, felt the weight, and then hurled it against the timberwork. It smashed gratifyingly and wine splashed down the side. "There you go," she said.

***

Two days later, at about the time of noon, a strange boat appeared off the estuary. It was a safe distance out, about a sea mile from the entrance. It rocked lazily there, with its oarsmen occasionally back paddling against the sea flow. The keener sighted of those on the shore could discern the trim lines of a warship, a twin bank of six oars. The sail carried no device and no banner flew from either the poop or the mast-head. Martin spat over the harbour wall. "English, can only be English," he said. "Come over here on the north wind for a good old look at us. And with those lines and those oars they can go where they want when they want. We'll not catch them." As if to prove the point, the ship began to cruise arrogantly across the estuary mouth at its leisure, oars rising and dipping lazily. It made a number of passes before turning once more to the north and, by degrees, disappearing. "Well then," said FitzOsbern, summoned by the excitement the foreign ship had caused. "They know where we are and what we have, more or less. They'll not be slow in reporting back." William shrugged dismissively. "Good. I'm glad. I hope also that that spy priest of theirs got home safely. I want them worried, Fitz. I want them scurrying about over there and fouling their breeches. False messages, false alarms, sleep-less nights, arguments at their councils, that sort of thing. Their army and their fleet is disbanded. They know where we are, but they do not know where we'll arrive, or when." FitzOsbern smiled pacifically. "You know best, William, as ever. But we all of us want this settled as soon as possible. We want to be off. We want the right wind, God grant it."

For FitzOsbern's wish to be realised they had to wait a further week, and with the army growing more frac-tious and frustrated than ever, despite their new identity as God's anointed. On the morning of the twenty-seventh the wind changed at last. It began with the faintest of sugges-tions, a light breeze beating up from the south. Men had been flinging sand and dust up into the air for weeks past, checking the direction of the many flags and pennants and the weathervane set atop the uncompromising square tower of the shrine of Saint Valery. There was a cautious air of excitement about the camp, heightened when William convened an emergency meeting in his pavilion at the hour of Prime. They were crammed in, shoulder-to-shoulder and malodorous in the unseasonable heat. There was a growing crowd of lesser men gathering outside. William stared about him impatiently. "Just get back there," he shouted. "Give me some space and some silence, for the love of God. I can barely hear myself think. Let my man here say what he has to say." Martin, unhappy at being the focus of so much attention, stared at his boots and made to spit, and then thought better of it. "I've seen this before," he began. "It's not so unusual, even at this time of year. I'd give this wind two to three days, I reckon. Enough to serve your purpose, all being well." The men there howled and whooped and thumped the shoulders of their neighbours.

"Silence," William roared above the clamour. Once more he was in a decisive mood, that same determined man who in earlier days had beaten off his own rebels, the French, the Angevins, the Bretons, the Pope himself. "Well, my Lords," he said in more measured tones, "it would seem that we can be off at last. Our day, it would appear, has finally arrived. We have the wind we need and a good tide at dusk, so I am told. We must all of us pray that the present conditions prevail. Not now, please," he said hastily to the good Abbot of Fecamp, who had begun to sink to his knees. He wagged a warning finger at those present. "St Valery is not to be another Dives. Dives was a shambles, a disgrace, a pig's arse. It is not to happen again. I require calm and order. You all of you know what to do. God knows but we've practiced it enough. From now on take your direct orders from my marshals and beach masters. I shall lead out in my own ship. Follow me on out and keep in line. Do not crowd or bunch.

I shall require mast head lights when the light fails." He gazed at the eager men crowded before him, men whom, for the most part, he had coaxed from apathy and downright disobedience in a few short months. It was one of the most crowning and proudest moments of his life. "You shall join me on the open sea and on the shore of the country we shall take by right and conquest. I thank you for all you have done, and for all that you have yet to do." Unprompted, there came the old deep chested guttural shout, the war cry of Normandy. 'Deux Ai! Deux Veult!' 'God aids us. God wills it!'

The complicated work of embarkation took place throughout the long day with an admirable calm and efficiency, a far cry from their previous attempt. William made his private farewells to Matilda and the children. Matilda was used and inured to such events. Agatha cried and was cuffed, fondly, by her mother. "Time to go," said Matilda briskly. She held out the infant Rufus for William to kiss. "Keep warm," she said. "You know how the cold and damp gets to your chest. Come back safe to me when you can. I shall pray for you, every day." Without another glance she turned and left, removing herself from the camp immediately and without ceremony in order to spare William a second farewell in what would without a doubt prove to be a very taxing day.

Later William sat with just Montgomery and Beaumont for company, with a jug of cider, a large wheel of soft cheese and fresh bread. William, not a drinking man, nonetheless lifted his cup to the pair of them in salute and drained it. In a short while he would step aboard his gleaming new flagship and lead his army of invasion out onto the open sea. It was late afternoon. By now most of the men, the horses and the impedimenta had been crammed aboard the vessels in the crowded and teeming estuary. It was just a short walk across the churned-up water meadow to his waiting boat. "I am in your debt, deeply, to both of you," said William, "for all you have brought about and for the knowledge that you will keep Normandy safe while I am gone." Beaumont scowled in embarrassment. "It's all been most informative and instructive," said Montgomery. There was a bark of laughter from William. It had more or less the reaction he had expected from both men. "We both of us want to know," said Beaumont in his slow and ponderous manner, "when we might expect to join you." William smiled at them, almost fondly. "When things are settled over there," he replied. "There will be hard times to come, devil a doubt. But, when I can, I shall send back FitzOsbern or some other, or one of my brothers. There will be land and honour and riches for you both in England. As for you Beaumont, your son will be with me and at my side at all times. He will be an ornament and a source of pride to you and your house."

William slapped his hands on his thighs, as if to dismiss this cloying sentiment. Time, now, for practicalities. Keep a close eye on Belleme in the south there, he told them. Belleme was a most unpredictable man and one given to strange quirks and ill judged fancies. Under no circumstances was he to be allowed to stir up trouble in Anjou. Come down on him hard if he does.

Brittany was quiet, but it would be best to maintain full garrisons there. No trouble was anticipated either there or here in Poitou, or in Boulogne. Eustace, of course, would be travelling with them, his heir a hostage to good behaviour. Baldwin of Flanders would use all of his considerable influence to keep things sweet in the Ille de France. Briskly, they dealt with a number of other, lesser, issues in short order, a final review of a checklist. William arrived at his conclusion, conscious of the need to catch the tide and anxious to be off. "Above all else," he told them. "Look to my own Robert." Again, that nagging memory of his own feckless father, dead of a fever years past and bundled into a mean little grave in an obscure Spanish church yard. All those years of ducking and weaving. Narrow escapes and frantic nighttime gallops just ahead of murderous assassins in a countryside made anarchic by warring factions. Both Montgomery and Beaumont had their own vivid memories of those times, and from different ends of the divide. "We shall be a second skin to the boy," Montgomery assured him. "Then," said William, "I am content."

With the two men following, he strode out of the tent and across the field to the riverbank, thrusting his way through a jostling and cheering crowd of stragglers and burdened down servants. The FitzPons boys, proud and portentous, came scurrying after, their arms laden with their master's more immediate needs and possessions. William paused at the gangplank leading down into the packed belly of his boat. He looked downstream at the crowd of rocking boats awaiting the order to sail and feasted his eyes upon the spectacle. Never in all of his life had he seen a finer sight than this, the cream of his fighting men, the wealth of his Duchy. William could never be described as an emotional man but, as his eyes registered the scene, they misted with tears for a short space of time. God was good. In fact a priest was saying precisely that as he splashed holy water over 'the Mora' and as acolytes swung yet more incense. William paused, offered up a brief prayer and crossed himself. Self consciously, he knelt and kissed the turf and all those within sight of him set up another roar of acclaim. William was handed down into the boat. He had brought all of this in to being; he, the bastard son of a tanner's daughter. An impious thought, perhaps. He crossed himself once more for luck and held up his hand in farewell to Montgomery and Beaumont on the bank there and all the others who would be remaining behind.

The order was given. Matilda's birthday present cast off and swung into the gathering tide, the oarsmen taking up the rhythm. Slowly, jostling against one another and to the accompaniment of shouts and curses and songs, the large fleet began to make its way out of the estuary and into the open sea and the gathering dusk. Lights began to be raised to the mastheads and it was completely dark before the last of the boats cleared the headland. Beaumont and Montgomery stood and watched until only twinkling lights were visible. Wordlessly, they then turned and made their way back to their own respective tents.

CHAPTER SEVEN :

The Goad and the Lure

London and Hastings: September 28th to October 13th, 1066

"Beachy Head," announced Martin, the laconic Flemish Master of the 'Mora' with a deep and personal satisfaction. "Over there to the port side." He smiled complacently to himself. He had of course been marked down to sail with the Duke in person and had come in for a considerable amount of criticism and abuse from his passengers ever since they had set out from St Valery the previous evening. He had noted earlier the likely swiftness of this vessel and, sure enough, they had soon outdistanced their own fleet and the 'Mora' had spent quite some considerable and nervous time alone on the open and rocking sea before the rest of the fleet had caught up. Apart from Martin, only the Duke had displayed a lack of concern, acting with commendable sangue froid and composure and demanding food and drink.

Sure enough, there in the faint light of the dawn, the huge, white towering cliffs could be discerned through the gloom. Beachy Head, one of the finest landmarks known to the mariners of these waters. To head for this very visible point, when planning a course to either east or west, they would thus be allowed to drift in, according to wind and tide, to a suitable place of safety. And who should know the ways and means of this better than he? He had made this trip many times in the past, though not in this fashion and for motives best left unexplored. Instead he found himself, not for a swift and furtive drop off or collection, but with this improbable collection of unfeasible and unseaworthy boats in his wake. Martin turned and stared behind him once more, observing with a mixture of gratification and alarm a forest of masts and a profusion of sails following after. It was one thing to land a cargo of wine or take one on of fleeces or a consignment of tin, it was altogether another thing entirely to pilot in an invasion fleet such as this. William had been an imposing and intimidating presence throughout the journey from St. Valery and he stood now beside him at the rudder. "And now what?" he demanded of him impatiently. The Duke rubbed his hand against the harsh, blue stubble of his unshaven chin. Martin was being paid handsomely for his work and, for the time being at least, it was he who was in command and he who made the decisions. "The wind is blowing due south at our stern," said Martin. "We can make a few points to starboard with some clever handling, but what is directly in front of us is where we must land, more or less."

"And what is in front of us, may I ask?" Hugh Margot, the dubious monk of Falaise and William Malet were at William's side, supposed experts, the pair of them, as the boat was carried slowly towards this stretch of the English coast. The sweep and the swell of the sea at this moment was gentle enough and Martin had marvelled inwardly at this throughout the later part of the voyage, but both the landsmen were green and clutching at the rigging. William Malet, that most unhappy of men, carefully considered his answer. He was no longer sure any more if he were Norman or English, with all his old associations with the south coast and with his tortuous family links to the house of Mercia itself. He was, after all, an uncle of sorts to Edwin and Morcar, and there was also his former deep friendship with the King of England. He still possessed land, in theory at least, in the very direction in which the ship was heading. He thought over all of this before replying. "It is much as we had supposed, your Grace," he said finally. "If your man, the master here, is right, and I suppose that he should know, then we shall not make the harbour at Hastings as intended. We shall fetch up instead east of there. The bay at Pevensey, by my reckoning."

Martin nodded in agreement and approval. This man Malet was clearly well informed. "That is my reckoning too. I know the bay at Pevensey well enough. It will suffice for our needs." William folded his arms across his broad chest. "By now," he said, "I too know something of the place. But tell me again." The scrawny little monk opened his mouth to speak. "Not you," said William hastily. By now he had had more than enough of the man and his pious mutterings and exhortations to the Almighty all the way across the Channel. "You, Malet. You tell me." In the growing light they peered ahead at the unpromising looking lowlands and mudflats directly ahead of them. "It is a peninsular, your Grace," said Malet. "Nothing to speak of, poor and sour land. It is all mud flats and lagoons and river tributaries. Good for eels, but it is a hard place, not one where I would choose to live."

"I am not interested," said William acidly, "in where or where not you would choose to live. Just tell me what I need to know." Malet apologised hastily. "Quite so, your Grace. Hastings itself lies to the east of here. Between there and here are two more headlands. We cannot see the nearest just yet, but over there is the place that the English call Bexhill and beyond that is Hastings, which is where we should be." Martin felt moved to protest. "I thought I told you," he said. "We have no oars, just the tiller. We go where the wind takes us, and that place is Pevensey Bay. With oars now, then that would be different." William gazed at him enquiringly, one of his extensive repertoire of intimidating expressions and gestures. The master fell silent and gazed ahead once more. "Do go on, Malet, I pray of you," William said. "The bay is wide," Malet continued, "with good shelter for the fleet. Last time I was there they had wharves and jetties for the locals and for the King's ships. Lots of merchantmen call. There is a fair old trade between Pevensey and the other side of the Channel."

"Sleeve," said William firmly. "We call it 'sleeve.' So, will they in time." He jabbed a thumb at the English coast. Malet corrected himself. "Sleeve. Pevensey as a place isn't up to much, but there is an old Roman castle there. Perhaps we could use that as a place to rally." The monk was keen to participate in the conversation. "Anderida," he said helpfully. "It's called Anderida." William, as ever, ignored him. "But," said William, "it is not where we should be." Martin detected a possible slight to his skills. "Like I said," he began. "I only pilot this vessel. I am not responsible for......." Again, he broke off as he faced another icy Ducal stare. "Surely," said William, "at this urgent point there must be many things for you to be attending to? I feel we have detained you enough." In that confined space it was in truth very difficult for the master to make himself scarce, but he did his best. He yelled directions at the man at the tiller and retreated to the stern to yell instructions and to indicate the way to the boats that were immediately behind were to go. There in the 'Mora' the south wind carried to them the shouts of jubilation and thanksgiving from the men in the fleet astern. For all of them, despite the clemency of the sea, the evening and night since they had left St Valery had been a terrifying and nightmarish journey, one of vomiting men and panicked horses, shifting cargoes that had broken limbs, masthead lights that appeared and disappeared and appeared again without warning. "You were saying, Malet?" enquired William politely.

"You are perfectly correct, your Grace. Hastings is where we need to be, but Pevensey is where we are driven." He pointed at the coastline now slowly looming up before them. The increasing light revealed a grey and brown and slightly diseased looking expanse of lowlands. "I've ridden often enough between Pevensey and Hastings," said Malet. "It's not an easy journey by any means. It gets easier inland, once you reach an old Roman road running across to the village of Lewes. Before that it is marsh all the way and bad country for horses. When you reach the road then you turn east to Hastings, past two settlements, as I recall." He struggled for the names and once again the monk was there to help. "Herstmonceaux and Ashburnham," he said. "Beyond that the road continues and then runs south and east directly to Hastings. The road goes through our own lands, those of Mother Church, of the Abbey of Fecamp." The Abbot back at Fecamp had been at great pains to impress upon Margot the importance of reminding the Duke of this fact at all available and appropriate moments.

"It is a good thirty English miles," continued Malet, "much of it hard going. You ask for my advice? Then fortify Pevensey, you can use the Roman fort there. The harbour there is good enough, but not as good as Hastings. Take your footmen across the way by ferry to the place they call Hooe, and from there to another place called Crowhurst." He paused to reflect. Crowhurst was Harold's personal property. He had been there on several occasions as his guest, walking his fields and admiring his livestock. "The

foot and the horse can meet at Crowhurst and go on to
Hastings together. The fleet should sail direct when the
tide is good. Too much to do today, it will have to be
tomorrow." They all flinched as a rogue wave slapped over
the gunwhale and over them, tasting salt in their mouths.
Neither William nor Malet were wearing mail. Salt and
water, a valet's nightmare. Martin reappeared at their side.
"We'll be inshore in just over an hour," he said. "We need to
close the boats up." William continued to stare ahead. "Your
job," he said to the master. "See to it. I understand none of
these matters."

There was England ahead of him, a country his by right
and his promised legacy, his destiny. There had been all
those years of frustration and expectation, of planning and
scheming. Then had come Harold himself, served up on a
plate to him by Almighty Providence. There had been that
strange and eventful time with him as his guest. He had
liked the man, admired him. He remembered often how
the Englishman had saved those foolish boys out after gulls'
eggs on the treacherous sands at Mont St Michel. He himself
would not have bothered to save them. The man had sworn
an oath, he had sworn an oath on holy relics, on an altar, in
his hall. And then had come the whole wearying business
of whipping his own fractious aristocracy into line. Eight
months of precious little sleep, spending money like water,
banging tables and banging heads. There was no going back
now. His entire reputation, his very existence, depended
upon this venture beset by imponderables. If he failed now
then he was finished forever. By Almighty God, he would
take that forbidding looking land coming ever nearer or else
die in the attempt. Were he ever to limp back, mauled and
empty handed, then he knew he faced the very real prospect of revolt and rebellion and, ultimately, the knife or the
arrow or the poison of an assassin. That had been the pattern
of his dangerous and desperately unhappy childhood. At the

very least, failure would make him the laughing stock of Christendom.

By God! He would not allow this to happen.

The boy Drogo FitzPons appeared at his elbow, one of his many tasks being to assist to arm the Duke when necessary. "Presently, Drogo, presently" said William. He pinched the boy's cheek. "Let us first see if there are any English here to greet us." This was a question that was exercising the thoughts of all the men in the fleet. A forced landing against a determined wall of English waiting to hurl them back into the sea was not an attractive prospect. The general fyrd, they now knew, had been demobilised, but garrisons of professionals would undoubtedly remain at certain points, Sandwich, Dover and Rye for a certainty. What about little Pevensey? William changed his mind and recalled the boy. Full mail it would be. After all, it would not be his job to remove the rust afterwards. That was what servants were for.

Ahead of all the rest, the 'Mora' rounded the point and headed into a wide bay. They could just discern a small and low-lying settlement still hundreds of yards off. Other boats were now beginning to close up on them. "Will you mark that now?" said Martin suddenly and pointed back to Beachy Head. They all looked across at the distant landmark. There on the heights of the headland, a thick cloud of black smoke, now turning grey, was boiling up into the air. "Warning beacon," said Martin unnecessarily. "They've seen us, and that news will back in London in a very short time from now." William shrugged indifferently. "It was only to be expected," he said.

In the event, there was no garrison at all at Pevensey and at the wharves and jetties there were just a few hastily abandoned fishing smacks lying idle and rocking in the tide. As the fleet came nearer, heading straight for the shallows and the shingle, it became evident that the place was in a complete panic. They could now see and hear people as they fled inland, carrying what they could with them. After all the months of argument and preparation, the men of Normandy had finally come to England. Eight of the boats beached on the shore almost simultaneously whilst others headed for the piers and jetties. First over the side, either waist deep in water or else relatively dry shod, went a small protective screen of bowmen and arbelists, followed in increasing numbers by a crowd of thankful and cheering footmen. From the jumble of boats behind and carried on the wind came the Norman war shout from hundreds of voices; 'Dex Vult, Dex Aix.' Boats were now berthing in a more orthodox manner, oars raised and tying up to the jetties. Men came clambering uncertainly but thankfully, out and thumping along the wooden planking to secure the by now almost deserted village.

The 'Mora' itself had also fetched up, grounding on the shingle of the beach. Now fully armed and mailed, William hauled himself over the side and into the shallow water. He righted himself, his head full of marvellous and historic things to say to mark the occasion. He took two or three steps and then fell flat on his face. He tasted salt and blood from his own cut lip as he lay there floundering and cursing and a collective gasp came up from the men around him, witnessing this worst of omens. "You stupid prat," William thought to himself. From another boat the ever reliable FitzOsbern appeared beside him and, with difficulty, hauled him to his feet. "Well, William," he remarked, indicating William's hands, "I see that you have finally seized England." William saw that his hands were gripping shingle and sand after his fall and both men laughed delightedly. "Note it down for the poets and the scribes then, Fitz," William said. FitzOsbern clapped his old childhood friend on the shoulder. "So then," he said. "We are here at last. I can't say as I enjoyed the journey that much, though." Together, companionably, they strode up the beach.

Despite its modest size, Pevensey yielded up a fair haul to them. As the army of invasion roamed through the small settlement they discovered sheds and barns packed to the rafters with salted and smoked fish and meat, grain and winter vegetables, some livestock. Cured hams hung on ropes and freshly made cheese nestled in baskets of straw. There were carefully stored kegs of ale and a small quantity of honey mead, which its discoverers sniffed suspiciously before meriting it fit to drink. The small settlement had long since been designated as a point of provision for Harold's men, but to the victor went the spoils. There was by no means sufficient, however, to feed a hungry army of ten thousand men, not even once. This would not do, clearly, and so William, in one of the first decisions made in what he prayed would be his new Kingdom, sent out scouts on horses and ponies, still shaken and out of sorts from the sea journey, to the north to seek both the enemy and further supplies.

In his role as appointed Beach Master, FitzOsbern, roamed around, cursing and encouraging, as he supervised the disembarkation of men and supplies and arranged a provost guard and picket line. As they had all expected, cajoling the giant cavalry horses proved to be a nightmare of swearing men and screaming and kicking beasts. Men were stamped upon, butted, bitten and kicked, with a few of the horses, ostlers and grooms receiving serious injuries and broken bones. William turned his back on it all and walked up the steep incline above the settlement with his half brothers to the old fortress of Anderida. He found that the ground still pitched and swayed slightly beneath him after his time at sea. When, breathing rather heavily from their exertions, they finally arrived at the place they found an expanse of tumbled down and eroded walls of shale and flint enclosing a weed and rubble strewn enclosure. The passing of many centuries had made the place far from secure against any serious and determined attack. They paced the satisfyingly flat and even enclosure within the ruined walls. "It will perhaps do at a pinch," said William. "Get Thibault up here. Time for him to earn his keep, let us see what he can make from this."

Thibault was an obstreperous and astoundingly bad tempered and foul-mouthed eccentric from Caen, a dwarf of a man with occasional displays of pure creative genius. As was often the case with relations between the great and the humble, William tolerated the man and was amused and diverted by his waspish and irreverent behaviour. Indeed on occasions he positively encouraged it. Matilda had ever had a flair for unearthing the unusual and the talented and Thibault had been one of her finds. The man was a mason by trade, but he was also a carpenter and an engineer of rare and exceptional talent. It had all begun with a doll's house commissioned for Agatha's birthday and a brightly coloured spinning top for the baby Rufus. A short while after the man produced a strange concoction of wheels and cogs and levers that caused a wooden dog to emerge from a kennel and nod its head. It was a pleasantry, a diverting plaything to be viewed after supper and William had indulgently admired it. He sat up and began to take notice, however, when Thibault next produced a portable and retractable ladder, a complex affair of ropes and pulleys and mysteriously shifting parts which when folded out to its full length extended to the height of five men. It was, Thibault told them in his brusque and offhand manner, a device to aid roof tilers and builders. William saw other uses for it and immediately had it set against a wall and ordered five men in full mail to climb it. It held their weight admirably and the little angry man was immediately put on the Ducal payroll.

Here now was Thibault's ultimate moment, his crowning glory. He looked an unlikely candidate for lasting fame as he shuffled up to the Duke, fuming and scratching at himself.

"Here, Thibault," said William, indicating the enclosure. "Put it up here." Thibault looked about him. "No," he said. "Not here, best outside. Flat on the level ground by the south wall. No point in putting a defence within a defence. At least, not yet awhiles." William raised his hands in acquiescence. "Well, you know best. At least it can be seen out there." Within the hour a long file of cursing and sweating men were labouring up the slope. They were carrying pickaxes, mattocks and spades and large sections of timber of all shapes and sizes as Thibault, armed with a thick sheaf of parchment scraps, cursed and railed at them for their clumsiness. All of the wooden sections carried strange symbols and latin numerals, crudely daubed in paint. Thibault danced about in rage. He roared instructions and had men join piece to piece whilst others set about to dig a three-sided ditch outside the wall and to hammer in supporting stakes. A prefabricated wooden keep, stout and complete with gate and two towers, began to rise up, secured by wooden pegs hammered into prepared holes and with exquisite tongue and groove work and dove-tailing. It was a masterpiece. The height of four men, it awed its constructors as it slowly began to take shape. Other men, drafted in, began to knock down those sections of the old Roman walls which threatened to hamper its progress and security.

William did not stay to watch, he had once seen it secretly assembled before. He was away now on the rough track leading north and through the foul-smelling marshes with a strong force of cavalry and accompanied by Odo and his favourite terrorist and intimidator, Robert Count of Mortain. The land was low and largely featureless, with drainage ditches and wide expanses of fields stripped now of their autumn yields. Dotted about the fields and mudbanks and stream courses in a seemingly random fashion, at least to his well-ordered Norman eye, were small huts of mud and wattle and thatch. A group of ten men had been sent ahead to investigate a small hamlet and now reported back. Nothing, they said. Nothing, there were signs of a swift evacuation, a rotting pile of green beans, some stacked hay and a scrawny cow in a byre. They had found also an equally scrawny woman, blind and deranged by her advanced years. "She could perhaps tell us something," William said. "Not that one," said the leader of the scouts. By his accent he was a Breton and therefore a mercenary. "She's dead now. The cow still lives, but it'll make for poor eating."

William shrugged dismissively. This had not been the first English casualty since they had landed a short while back. There had been a number of English dead, mostly old men, women and children, lying back there in and around Pevensey. "This won't do," he said. "Get Malet up here, not that monk, mind. He annoys me." After a fairly long wait Malet finally appeared, hot and sweating. This was no place for horses, and so, like their own mounts, his horse was caked with mud. "I daresay that you will be wanting to know what's up ahead," he said. Robert roared with laughter, leaning across his saddle to swipe Malet across the back. It was a gesture of sufficient force to make Malet's horse start and nearly throw him. Malet had always been an ugly rider, too much time spent in England, far too much.

"You're the one for the local knowledge," said Robert. "Please do enlighten us. Which direction is London then? Any direction is good enough for me as long as it is away from this shit hole." Malet pushed his helmet up his forehead. "As I have told you," he said. "There is no real path to speak of until you reach the road that runs to the place they call Lewes. That road is north of here, running east to west. Between here and there it is all much the same. Marshes, some woodland. It is bad country for horses, my Lords. About an hour from here is a fair-sized village called Hailsham and beyond that the Lewes road itself. That will take us through two more settlements, Herstmonceaux and

Ashburnham, both in the gift of Harold. Most places around here are. Then you come to a meeting of roads, one north to London in two directions and the other south to Hastings, with a few more settlements on the way. Just north of here is thick forest. The English call it the 'Andredsweald' and it goes on for miles. God alone knows who might be lurking in there. You simply would not know until you walked over them."

Fully armed and mailed, a kite shield slung across his back and carrying a heavy iron mace, Odo of Bayeux bore no resemblance to the Prince of the Church he was meant to be. His Bishop's vestments, all the paraphernalia of his office, the vessels and candles, the portable folding altar and the banner blessed by the Holy Father himself, were back with the baggage. Here in his present incarnation, he was pure fighting Norman, and possessing all of the guile and violence of his none too distant pagan ancestors. He sniffed fastidiously. "Thus far it's not up to much, is it? This England. This is all Harold's land, you say? Then we must destroy it, as he would do ours." Robert was more than eager to comply. "Agreed," he said. "How far is this London road then?" William was silent, fiddling abstractedly with his gauntlets. "Too far for today, that's for sure." said Malet, "It would be a good two hours from here in these conditions, probably more, especially if we meet with resistance."

"Enough, then," said William with finality. "I see no enemy to fight yet awhile. Back to the boats with us. Tomorrow we shall take the cavalry to secure Hastings. FitzOsbern will arrange for the foot to be ferried across the bay. Once they land they are to destroy everyone and everything in their path that is of no immediate use to us. We shall act likewise. The rest of the ships are to sail direct to Hastings, I wish neither to hear how this is managed or any moaning from those ship men. I simply require it to be done. We shall all meet up there."

"Crowhurst," said Malet. "There is a village called Crowhurst just north of Hastings. With your permission I should go with the foot and you take the monk." William nodded.

"Agreed," he said. "Until nightfall I want cavalry out here. Take anything of value and burn the rest. Robert, you have a flair for this sort of thing. See to it. Tomorrow we all go to Hastings." He wheeled his horse. "My good Lord Bishop," he said sardonically, "a service of praise and thanksgiving might not go amiss, an appropriate time of thanksgiving, do you not think?"

Fire and destruction and death had come to England and what little desperate and isolated resistance that was offered was crushed brutally underfoot. Way over to the west, an isolated Norman boat, separated at night from the rest, had fetched up in the Romney marshes and there its crew and passengers were summarily butchered by the irate locals. It had contained also a professional soothsayer and teller of fortunes recruited by William. When the news of this percolated through the rank and file it was the cause of much sardonic amusement.

Around Pevensey no English came together in a band to challenge or contest the invaders and the small garrison of housecarls and select fyrd at Rye and elsewhere withdrew into the dense fastness of the Andredsweald forest. Between Pevensey and Hastings the horse and foot of William's army created a wilderness and no person caught up in their path was permitted to live. William and his brothers led a large party of horsemen in person into the settlements that lay before them. Hailsham, Herstmonceaux and Ashburnham were all in turn utterly destroyed. Other flying detachments roamed further afield to the north and did likewise. This was a style of campaigning they all remembered with fondness and in which they were expert practitioners from the troubled times of the civil wars in Normandy and the wars in Maine, the Vexin and Brittany. No restraint was placed upon them and on that second day a horror of biblical proportions was visited upon the countryside. At the village of Netherfield on the road leading to London the raiders resolved to move no further north. On the edge of the forest they hanged all those of the English they had been able to catch, men and boys, and left them dangling from the trees for Harold to find.

With the Falaise monk acting as interpreter, William interviewed the head man of Netherfield. The man, his family dead and his livelihood destroyed, had gone beyond fear. He had no further need for either courage or indeed for life itself. There was also a certain grim elation about him, having brained one of his attackers with a mallet and skewered another to a wooden fence with a pitch-fork. He was bleeding from a variety of wounds and he counted his life in mere minutes. "Your King, Harold," William demanded through the monk. "Where is he?" The Englishman shrugged. "And how is it for the likes of me to know? I am not privy to the dealings and doings of the great," he replied. Knowing that death awaited him just a short time away and fully resigned to it, he stared William full in the face without fear. "What I do know is that he will come. He will come in his thousands and he will make bleached bones of you all. You shall be manure for our fields." He cleared his throat and spat at the Duke's feet. "Kill me now. The good Lord above will gather me to him." William gestured to the guards at the man's side. "Kill him," he said. "I like his spirit, though. Make it quick and clean. A knife behind the ear will do the job."

Earlier that day William's infantry had crowded into the oared boats seized at Pevensey on the tide just after dawn and were relayed across the bay. It was a long and complicated business and the Norman barges they also used had a particularly difficult time of it. Their orders were explicit. Take what you wish and destroy all else. Humphrey of Tilleul had drawn the short straw the previous night and had been ordered to remain behind with two hundred men to garrison William's plaything castle and secure Pevensey. Led by FitzOsbern, they disembarked at Bexhill, duly laid it waste and killed all they found remaining there and then set off north on a difficult route along the coast. The settlements of Hooe, Ninfield and Catsfield suffered similar fates and now behind the column there came a chaotic and tangled convoy of men herding and prodding cattle. There was no point at all in trying to reason with the sheep or pigs. These were slaughtered on the spot and their carcasses hurled onto commandeered carts. The chickens, the geese and the ducks were strangled and then hung around the necks of the men or dangled from their belts. The army would eat well tonight at least.

At Ninfield, incensed and outraged by all that he saw, Malet faced off a mob of angry men, a mixture of Normans and Flemings. He clutched a little girl of perhaps six years of age close to him. The rest of her family, their blood seeping into the earth, lay around them. He attempted to speak soothingly to the child in his own excellent English, laced with the local accent. Three of his servants, one just a boy, attempted to form a cordon around him as the soldiers, now beyond all sense and reason, pressed up against them. The child raked at his face, drawing blood. "Do you know who I am?" demanded Malet. "You sons of bitches. Do you know who I am?"

"No, and I don't give a shit neither," said a particularly menacing looking individual in the accent of the Rouen gutters. "Just hand that brat over, now." Things, Malet realised with a sick despair, were turning ugly. There was a stir and a whirring sound at the fringe of the crowd and a crossbow bolt suddenly buried itself with a sickening thud in the back of the Rouen man's head. His face disappeared as the bolt tore through it and went careering off into the side of a burning hut. The man crashed to the ground and his companions scattered in search of easier pickings. Malet, tired, exhausted and depressed beyond all endurance, looked up to see a languid figure on horseback at the head of a group of men. He recognised him immediately as the horseman tossed a crossbow to one of his followers and elegantly hooked one leg out of his saddle. It was that dangerous looking adventurer, the man named Neel of Herve, the one that the Duke had taken such an unaccountable shine to.

"My Lord," said Herve in a tone of mild reproof. "It does not do to separate yourself from the leaders at times such as this. There can be most unfortunate consequences. My Lord FitzOsbern is calling for you. Would you please agree to join him?" Malet, sickened and his heart palpitating at this brush with death, voiced his thanks. "And that little pretty one there," enquired Herve with a genuine interest. "What will you do with her?" And to this question the heartbroken Malet had no answer.

At Ashburnham the warrior minstrel Taillefer met and raped a witch, for such was his judgement of the woman. He had seen her scurrying up an alley between the burning thatch, skirts held high and her hair as flaming red and gold as the dying village she was fleeing from. He cornered her at last in an outlying byre that reeked of livestock and dung. He threw her to the ground and took her roughly and urgently on the fouled straw. The woman made no resistance as he panted and heaved above her. Her skin was incredibly smooth for a peasant, cream coloured and freckled, though she herself smelt appallingly. She lay there passively until he clambered to his feet once more and hauled up his breeches, fiddling with the drawstrings. Now what do I do with her? he pondered as he made to leave. She spoke then, dreamily and drowsily, in English; a language he did not understand. "You are going to die," she said. "I see so many dead, but you are the first of them." Some strange mechanism working within his brain, Taillefer understood. It was as if she had spoken in the purest French. He crossed himself and then spat for additional luck before, hurriedly, he left her for others to find and be cursed by.

Past Catsfield, they headed east and soon the van of the footmen met up with the first contingents of William's cavalry. By now it was midafternoon and time was pressing. The people of Hastings, nestling beneath the tall cliffs there, had known since the previous day of the arrival of the Normans. In the late morning a huge fleet of boats had arrived offshore and dropped anchor and now desperate and deranged refuges were arriving from the interior and along the coast with horrifying stories of the armoured and bestial giants descending upon them in fury like legends from their own past. The fighting men of Hastings were away with the fleet, in Sandwich, Deal and London and the town itself was exempt of any duties to the land fyrd. In all of Hastings there were perhaps fifty men capable of bearing arms. Men from the boats began to wade ashore and into the town. A veritable host was reported also to be descending upon them from the direction of Crowhurst.

With a truly admirable courage, the leading men of the community, a priest, a baker, a blacksmith and a wool merchant, went out to meet them and to offer the submission of the town. It was their misfortune that the first of the enemy they encountered was a group of hardened mercenaries led by a renegade Frenchman, himself proscribed within the Ille de France for known and proven murder, rape and theft. They had no French, these four men of Hastings. Even if they had, the mercenaries would not have been inclined to stop to listen. As a consequence, their mangled bodies lay in the roadway as William and his brothers and their attendant aristocracy approached Hastings from the landside. They rode past them with indifference as they entered the town.

Possession of this town was important and the army was under the strictest of instructions and pain of death to cause it no unnecessary damage. An invading army of nearly ten thousand men along with the men of the fleet and all the many other servants and camp followers swamped and overwhelmed the small fishing town. Those very few houses of the better heeled were now crammed with a jostling and bickering aristocracy, the noblemen and knights of Normandy and Flanders, Boulogne and Eux, of France and Brittany and France and the Norman diaspora beyond the French speaking lands. Yet more men brawled and roistered in the narrow streets and along the harbour side. The common soldiery shifted for themselves as best they could. The horse lines outside the town were vast, some four thousand fighting destriers, the palfreys and mares that the knights rode when not in battle, ponies and pack horses and mules. To be caught attempting to steal or kill any of these animals brought an automatic death sentence and so no such offence was attempted.

As night fell, men still moved about the horse lines, fretting and fussing amongst the giant and overbred war horses. As stable boys rubbed them down and fed and watered them, the knights poked about, slapping rumps and offering wrinkled apples and pears taken from haylofts. They ran their hands down the shivering legs of the horses and inspected mouths and hooves like anxious parents. These horses were the basic reason for the very existence of these proud and touchy men. With their lands and their lineage, very often of a suspect nature, these horses were a badge and a reason for their being. Without them, they would sink back into the morass of the peasantry from which many of them had emerged. With these beasts beneath them, they would crush all that stood in their path and win further riches and rewards. These horses, neurotic and sensitive, were in a sorry state after a night at sea and a very trying slog through the marshes. Small wonder that many men, solicitous and clucking, stayed with them all night.

Beyond the horse lines, where the unbidden did not venture on their own, the mass of the army was encamped. Wood for burning was scarce and at a premium and had already led to a number of fights and one serious stabbing, broken up by FitzOsbern's pickets. The men now pooled their resources and grilled lumps of mutton and pork and whole chickens on water soaked wooden skewers or on the points of their knives or arrows stolen from the archers. Quartermasters had moved amongst them earlier that evening with bread and sausage and thin sour wine in sufficient quantity to cheer and console but not enough to provoke. Though exhausted, they were still edgy and excited by the events of the day and from their lines shouts and oaths and laughter rang out late into the night. Beyond their lines FitzOsbern had placed a further screen of trusted men, his own and some borrowed from William and Robert. On this, their second night in England, the army eventually settled down to sleep.

At the hour of Sext, Odo officiated over an open-air Mass, his exhortations and observances lost to the vast majority of the assembled crowd. He offered the Sacrament to his brother and to the other leaders whilst chaplains moved amongst the army with the blessed wafers and wine. Shortly after, William convened a meeting of his lieutenants in the port reeve's house, the largest in the place. It was a tight fit, for they were all there. The disappointed Humphrey de Tilleul was over at Pevensey, garrisoning the fort and port. Young Beaumont, along with Roger FitzTurold, Robert de Vitot and Geoffrey FitzRotrou were out at the head of scouting columns. All of the others, all those against whom William had won his arguments earlier in the year, were crammed into the downstairs room or else crowded at the doorway, necks craning. There were seats only for William and the two Bishops, Odo and Geoffrey of Coutances. William Warenne, a man well advanced in years, had brought his own folding stool upon which he sat himself defiantly and looking around belligerently for any sign of criticism. As a preliminary to speaking, William scanned their faces, noting the blend of grey fatigue, excitement and apprehension. Not counting the Falaise monk and the FitzPons boys crouching at the Duke's feet, there were close on forty men present. They represented the flower of the Norman aristocracy, heads of families or eldest sons.

There was also a sizeable contingent of foreigners present. Aimery, Vicomte of Thouars, was an exuberant, dark and high-spirited man from the lands of the southern French, lured to this place by the prospect of adventure and further wealth. He was conferring with his two sons in the impenetrable buzz and whirr dialect of the southern French. William's gloomy and half hostage kinsman, Eustace, Count of Boulogne, fidgeted irritably with a leather strap and next to him stood another equally unhappy man in much the same predicament, Enguerrand, son of the despised Count of Ponthieu. The Flemish and Breton contingents were represented by Hugh of Ghent and a savage and charmless lout named Igraine of Dol. His master, Count Alan, the true leader of the Bretons, was currently indisposed by a bout of dysentery. There arose from that pack of men a tangible emanation of sweat and horse and leather, wine fumes, bad breath and body odour. Less tangibly, the scent of expectation.

"My Lords, good morning," William began cheerfully. "I trust you are all well rested, for we have a busy day ahead of us. We must now address a number of critical questions. After I have spoken you may all offer your comments one at a time, but not until I give you leave to do so. First then, where are we and how long do we stay? Malet and our good brother in Christ here," he gestured contemptuously towards the monk, "may best answer that question. Second, where on earth are the English? All other questions subsume themselves to these two. Malet, you may begin."

Primed in advance to speak slowly and clearly for the benefit of the less agile minded of the assembled men, Malet embarked upon an explanation of the local geography. They were now at the tip of a narrow and waterlogged peninsular. Their efforts of the previous day had been strenuous and had in all probability prevented them from taking in the finer points of the local scenery. We find ourselves, he told them clearly and slowly, at the very northern point of a peninsular some ten English miles long and six miles wide. By now their army outnumbered the local population many times over. A short distance to the north, two rivers, the Brede and the Bulverhythe, further narrowed this natural bottleneck, an infelicitous word which caused William to frown. That same rough track they had ridden down the previous day led north through hard and hilly country between the two rivers to a high point at Caldbeck Hill. Here two better routes were to be found, running east and west to curl around the forbidding Andredsweald forest. To the west ran the London to Lewes road and to the east the London to Maidstone road. By either route, he assured them, London itself lay some sixty English miles away on reasonable tracks. London was a three-day ride in good conditions, barring opposition. There was only one route in and out of this peninsular. Whomsoever secured the meeting of roads at Caldbeck Hill held the advantage.

"My Lords," said Malet. "If we can but make that place our own then we may move either east or west in perfect liberty and secure the hinterland. If, for their part, the English take it for themselves then we find ourselves caught here with only our boats as our salvation."

"Fascinating," said William. "An excellent summary, Malet. Thank you, I shall shortly inform you all of what I intend to do next. In the meantime, your questions please." At the back Geoffrey Fitzrou raised his hand. "Where are these sheep shagging English, and when do we fight them?" William smiled at him with an amiable smile which belied his personal distaste for the man. In fact, he had no answer to the question. Where, indeed, were they?

***

A partial answer to this question came the following day. Immediately William closed the meeting he sent Grandesmil, Montfort, FitzErneis and de Tosny, all of them particularly aggressive men, with their followings up the track to Caldbeck Hill. There they separated, moving west and east and harrying and destroying as they went. They had received strict instructions to return by nightfall, preferably with food, prisoners and information. William, meanwhile, sent for Thibault and set him to work once more, this time to construct a fort from new on the high cliffs above Hastings. All morning workmen roamed about, removing nails and timbers from the houses far below and while others hacked out a circular ditch, piling the chalk and flint and spoil behind them to form a mound. Hastings, never a big place, was all but empty of its former inhabitants and the able bodied of those that had survived and been rounded up were now toiling away under Thibault's supervision. Many had died at the hands of the invaders in the first few minutes of the attack and those who still had it within their means had fled north. Even now they were being chased and cut down without mercy by the cavalry patrols, despatched as casually as vermin. The food gathered at Hastings and at Pevensey had now all but gone and so large and well-armed bodies of the infantry were sent to forage in the peninsular. Barons and knights led them in order to prevent individual acts of theft. There was a very real danger they could be starved out if they remained where they were, the threat of actual starvation spurred them.

William, his two half-brothers and FitzOsbern were out on the track north of the town. At intervals they paused and reined aside to allow livestock to be herded past them and, once, three wagonloads of grain. It was a gratifying sight, but much more was needed. "Were it me," Robert said, "I'd have been down here long since, chewing nails and looking for blood." He was referring, of course, to the absent King of the English whose own lands and people they were so systematically plundering and destroying. Robert was, however, content enough. It had been quite some time since last he had been given a free hand to release his energies upon an enemy. Robert was never given specific orders, but instead simply unleashed. "Is he scared, or what?" he complained. FitzOsbern too had his own personal memories of the Englishman, from that time in Normandy two years back. "No, not scared," he replied, "not him. Cautious, perhaps. It may be that he is simply waiting for us to go very hungry. Perhaps even now, as Malet suggested, he is plugging the gap, seeking to bottle us up in this god forsaken place."

Odo was squinting ahead. "Cavalry patrol coming in," he announced, and pointed. The English rode horses too, it should not be forgotten, and they also wore mail. William shouted a command to their following of twelve men. They swung their kite shields to the front and gripped their lances. A cavalry skirmish here on this narrow track way and with uncertain marshland to either side was neither a pleasant nor a desirable prospect. The only course of action would be to meet the newcomers at the gallop. A man on a horse standing still had little chance. William prepared to give the order. "Hold up," said Robert, "that's Beaumont's boy there. Bugger me if he hasn't gone and got himself reinforcements."

Sure enough, it was young Beaumont, the youth to whose deeply disappointed father William had made such great and solemn promises. He had set out with a command of twenty men the previous day and was now returning with what appeared to be more than twice that number. They waited as the boy and his companions approached. A thick set and burly man, blue chinned and with the distinctive shaven head of the Normans, rode beside Beaumont. The newcomer was grey and brown with exhaustion and from the dust and thrown up mud of his journey and there were flecks of rust on his mail. Despite all the dust and grime, William, with his excellent recall of faces to names, recognised him.

The two parties pulled up and the man dismounted wearily and knelt before him. The Bishop of Bayeux shared his half-brother's gift. He, with his truly encyclopaedic memory for people and how they all fitted into the greater scheme of things. "Well, well, well," said Odo. "Robert FitzWimarc, as I live and breathe." FitzWimarc, having with all due protocol acknowledged the Duke, now kissed the ring on the Bishop's podgy finger. "Indeed so, your Grace, and glad it is that I have found you at last, though I fear your arrival is both inopportune and ill advised, if you will forgive me for so saying." He climbed to his feet with difficulty. Clearly, he and his retinue of knights had had a hard journey of it from wherever they had travelled from. William frowned, both at the man's presumption at challenging his actions and at his memories of him. Despite being a frequent correspondent, they had met only a handful of times in the past. On one of these occasions, deep in his cups, this Norman Breton adventurer and speculator had asked him, his own Duke, where the best and easiest women in Rouen were to be found and had leered distastefully. William, ever an upright and God fearing man, now recalled the occasion with disdain. FitzWimarc, like Malet, had lived in England for many years now, sending back reports to Odo of the doings of the great within the court of old Edward. Indeed, his had been the message announcing Edward's death. He had been there and had witnessed it. The man had extensive lands and financial interests in Kent and the Sussex Weald, but since January had kept his head down and living quietly until this invasion had upset everything and flushed him from out of his bolt hole like a startled deer from a covet. With all the urbanity that he undeniably possessed and of which he was so proud, Odo waved him into silence, lest he say anything further that was unfortunate. "Enough, enough, FitzWimarc. Well met. We are delighted to see you. But you look all done in. You and your people, by the look of them. We need to get some decent food and drink inside you. Then you can tell us all about it. Ride down to Hastings and we shall join you later."

With a large portion of pork belly and beans inside him and about to finish his third large mug of wine, the normally ebullient and good natured FitzWimarc had at last regained an element of colour and composure. He remained, however, a scared and startled man and he was also the bearer of the first real news that William and the others craved. Last he had heard, he told them, Harold was in the north, and at York. "The Hardraada came, my Lords," he explained, "as it was broadly feared he might." William sat bolt upright. This was news indeed. "He came, I was told, with a mighty army and fleet, hundreds of boats. He tore the Earls of Mercia and Northumbria to pieces at a battle and then he took York." He paused to drink, relishing the dramatic impact of the moment. FitzOsbern rolled his eyes at the theatricality of it all. "Be that as it may," said William, there was menace in his voice. He wanted immediate news and not a rambling discourse. "What then?"

"They had the news in London. I have people there who keep me informed. I knew Harold for a fast and crafty man, but not that fast, not that crafty. He was up that road north before you could say knife. Like a rat down a privy," he added obscurely. FitzWimarc had clearly gone native in all his time in England and the colloquialism rendered into French left his listeners baffled. "Next up we hear there's been this bloody big battle near York. Your Graces, my Lords, I can tell you now that King Harald Hardraada and Tostig are both of them dead, and thousands of men with them. The Norwegians were destroyed. The English took a right hammering too, which I suppose is all to the good as far as we are concerned."

"And when was this, this battle?" demanded William. He found the man, with his portentous remarks and silences, extremely irritating. Much more of this and he'd simply hand him over to Robert for all the answers he required. He would never now, he reflected, meet the mighty Hardraada, either in peace or in war. It had been one of his ambitions. "Just five days since," said FitzWimarc. There was an audible intake of breath from the other men. FitzWimarc's boorishness could perhaps be forgiven. By Christ but the man had moved fast, in response both to the news from the north and to arrive here now on the south coast. Smug with satisfaction, FitzWimarc enjoyed the moment. Apart from a privately bankrolled team of expert messengers, he had an even more proficient and clandestine team of highly trained carrier pigeons whom he loved and cherished as if they were his own children. It had been a relatively easy matter to insinuate a few of these and the men who hid them about themselves into Harold's army of the north. One such pigeon had flown contentedly back into its loft, cooing happily to be back at his manor in Essex only the previous morning. Only the day before that had he been informed of the Duke's arrival and had immediately set off at all speed for the south coast. FitzWimarc, however, kept his council on all of this, happy to spread a heady whiff of desperate courage and the occult about him like a fog.

"My compliments and congratulations," said William, speaking for all of them. "And, what now?" FitzWimarc belched and begged his Lords' pardons. "Three days you have been here now, and with the warning beacons lit and blazing between here and the north. Devil a doubt but that Harold has the news of you by now, or else he will receive it shortly." He put down his mug. "I have had a right sod of it," he complained bitterly, "creeping around the forest between here and the Thames like a brigand. I've killed my fair share of Englishmen on my way here and now I am what they call a wolf's head. Any Englishman is permitted by law to take my life and indeed is encouraged to do so in return for a reward. My lands and my money, all gone. All of it." William attempted and failed to look sympathetic. "You have kicked up a right hornets' nest, your Grace," said FitzWimarc. "Between here and London, in all of the Andredsweald, the place is swarming with Englishmen, in great numbers and not best pleased either. Harold will now come south with all of his force and gathering more men to him as he comes. They will be here shortly, and in numbers too great for you to resist." He glanced around at his listeners. "My Lords take to your boats, I urge you. Get off this island. You cannot resist them."

"You great big fairy!" Robert exclaimed. He had never been a man to stand on ceremony and thus felt fully entitled to address this craven menial in any way he saw fit. "Bollocks we will. We are all of us in this far too deep." FitzWimarc sighed and scratched his ear. "Very well then, my Lord. If that is the answer of all of you here, then for the love of God look to yourselves. Guard your boats well. I have heard that English ships are even now setting off to blockade you here. To hold this peninsular you must have food and provisions. If not then you must break out into open country before the English trap you here on all sides and starve you out. Is Malet with you? If he is then he will agree with all that I say. If the English are victorious then my life here is forfeit, not worth a fart. For what it may be worth, I pledge myself and those of my men that remain to me to you once more." He made to kneel before the Duke. FitzWimarc was clearly exhausted and fighting sleep. William prevented him from the gesture, "My thanks," he said, not unkindly, "go now and find a place to get your head down. We shall need you and your knowledge and will reward you handsomely for it. Your lands are merely under a temporary change of ownership."

In the days that followed, meeting no resistance and driven by the desperate need for food and to provoke the English into some form of reaction, William's cavalry columns roamed on an ever-widening arc. Growing more daring, they reached the road that cut west and east and raided along it in both directions. Malet and FitzWimarc and the Falaise monk were much in demand on these expeditions, directing and informing and translating the words of those few English brought back alive. Inevitably the invaders were beginning to be stretched ever more thinly and, equally inevitably, they began at last to take casualties.

A few miles up the road towards the settlement of Tunbridge, a mob of English came leaping and screaming out of the tree line and fell joyously on a group of twenty mounted knights and their following of footmen, men of Ralf de Tosny's contingent. In the confined space and in the suddenness of the moment the knights and footmen could neither deploy nor manoeuvre and the whooping English waded into them with axes and spears and farm implements. The outnumbered Normans fought back but were soon overwhelmed by weight of numbers. The jubilant English took back into the forest those horses that had survived the encounter, along with weapons and mail and personal possessions. They left the dead where they had fallen, and with their severed heads placed neatly in a little pile for the next enemy patrol happening along the path to find.

Such acts of revenge served only to raise the level of death and destruction that the Normans brought to the countryside. By the end of that first week the open country between Lewes and almost as far as Rye and Romney had been transformed into a smoking and blackened desert, the inhabitants either lying dead in their fields and farms or else scattered, roaming the dark and ominous oak of the forest of the Andredsweald as, slowly, they starved to death.

Senlac Hill. William remembered the name from his briefings back in Saint Valerie. He stood now gazing across at it from the heights of the hill that Malet told him was called Telham by the local people. Senlac, sounding so similar to his French ear to 'lake of blood.' Behind the ridge, so he had been told. there was a short track leading to the main London roads. Clearly, the ridge and Telham Hill, commanding the route back to Hastings, was a critical focal point. Harold's possession of this Senlac ridge meant that he could contain anyone moving up from the south, whereas for William it was his doorway to good open country, skirting the forest and a choice of two directions for London.

Looking now at the land that separated the hill from the ridge perhaps one English mile away he didn't like what he saw.

The ground dipped gently away from him into a shallow bowl. It was wide enough for deployment, but broken up by dips and folds and copses and looked to be marshy and waterlogged underfoot. To the east and west he could see a number of shallow streams running off the ridge to feed the brooks of the Brede and the Bulverhythe. Almost immediately below him were a number of pools and ponds of unknown depth. Beyond all this, to the north, the land rose up once more to the Senlac ridge. It was a deceptively gentle looking incline, but he knew his heavily laden horses would find it hard going.

"I know what you are thinking," said FitzOsbern. "It's a bugger, isn't it?" William nodded in agreement. He had been spying out battlefields since he was a small boy and had a natural gift for it, a flair. "This is where it will be, Fitz," he said. "Of that I am absolutely certain." He scratched at an annoying itch. "Or rather, it will be if we decide to stay. Harold would be God's own fool not to hold that ridge, and so would I if I didn't try to stop him." FitzOsbern looked at him quizzically. "How do you mean? If we don't try to stop him?"

William smiled. "It is decided," He spoke as if the decision had been arrived at by someone other than him. "We could advance on London right now, if we were so minded. As far as I can see there is nothing to stop us. But God alone knows what is waiting for us there in that forest and along that road. We would be an army strung out on the march for miles, an easy target. No, I prefer to see what we are up against in broad daylight. I want the man to come to us, Fitz. We are, by being here and by doing what we are doing, the goad and the lure. I want him to come to us and give us a headcount. Let him have his little ridge over there. He must have been hurt badly by those two battles in the north and he will not be coming up against us with anything like the power he had two weeks ago, going on from all that FitzWimarc tells us. But I will wager anything I possess against anything you care to put up that he will come against us as soon as he can. We both know the man. Fitz, We know his spirit and his moods. This is his England and this," William waved his arm about him vaguely, "happens to be his own land, owned by him personally. We are making a desert of his own lands and property, for God's sake. Would you or I stand for that? Of what use is a Lord if he fails to protect his own people?"

Naturally, FitzOsbern saw the logic of it. He too could cite any number of examples drawn from personal experience of men in Maine, the Vexin and Brittany, Normandy too, who had set off with half a dozen doomed followers against entire armies in defence of exactly that principal. "Then too," said William dreamily, "then too, we have the

Holy Father in Rome himself marching with us. We have his blessing, his mandate, the banner which he himself blessed and consecrated. I wear his holy medals about my neck, and the relics of the saints which Harold swore upon. You just wait until Harold discovers he is judged and damned by God's Vicar." He chuckled to himself. "I would love to be a fly on the wall when that monk tells him so."

"You are sending Hugh Margot to London?" FitzOsbern was incredulous. William smiled. "How could I not? How could I resist it? And his friend from the old days, Malet, along with him. Just as soon as I know that Harold is there. It should cause quite a stir and with any luck they'll hang that accursed monk. For two pins, I'd send that clown Eustace of Boulogne along with them." FitzOsbern uttered a short bark of laughter. "So, we stay here, and the raids go on."

William nodded as he continued to gaze across the unpromising expanse of land that separated them from the ridge in the distance. He was calculating how to place his men, which areas to avoid and which to exploit. "Just so. The raids go on. I want one battle, Fitz. One confrontation, one battle; and it will be here." FitzOsbern followed the Duke's gaze across at the ridge and the uncongenial ground beneath it. "Well then, in that case I would want to be on that ridge, and not attacking it." William continued to survey the ground carefully with an expert eye, memorising contours and features. "I want a permanent camp here on this hill," he said. "Someone good, someone we can trust neither to panic nor take foolish steps. I also want a post on that ridge and on the hill that lies beyond it there." Just behind them Malet, chilled at the news of this latest task required of him, spoke. "Caldbeck," he said. "Caldbeck, "That's what it is called." William replied with absolute certainty and a finality. "Whatever it is called," he said, "that is where he will gather, and that is where we shall meet him."

CHAPTER EIGHT :

The Vision of the Holy Cross

York and London: October

1ˢᵗ to October 6ᵗʰ, 1066

A nd so it was over. The aspirations and the ambitions of both Tostig and Harald the Hardraada had been brought to a ruinous end there on the gentle meadowlands and all along the blood red running river of the Stamford Brook. In many respects they had been very similar men and the ambitions of each had led the other to his death. The men of the levies of York roamed the banks of the river and the meadowlands to either side with neither compassion nor mercy and knifed those of the enemy wounded unable to climb to their feet. It was a task that the men of Harold's army, who jeered and spat at the disgraced men of York, would have refused to undertake had they been so ordered. The dead Hardraada had been right, never give an order that might not be obeyed. The able bodied and defeated men of the coalition of the north men were rounded up and led in a shambling and humiliating column back to Riccall. They passed the burnt-out farms and villages and then the city walls of York and across the fields and marshes of Fulford Gate and the mounds of rotting dead. A desperate pack of Irish and men of the western isles had made a doomed break for the west, with the jubilant English in hot pursuit. Small groups of Norwegians wandered aimlessly in the woods until they were hunted down and killed, the small garrisons at Skaroaborg and Holderness turned themselves in. Copsig and his men came finally to hear of the disaster as they laboured over the Pennines in their wild goose chase after the Aelfgarsons and promptly headed north for the highly dubious sanctuary of King Malcolm Canmore in Scotland.

It all ended there, the power and the might and the paralysing fear in which people of softer lands held for the north men. For two centuries and more the Norse had fought their Danish and Swedish neighbours tooth and nail. They had terrorised and colonised as far away as Iceland and Greenland and for generations wilful children had been threatened with the hairy men of the north and monks had prayed for deliverance. Norway would now recede back into a historical backwater. As promised, Hardraada, the last of the Vikings, was duly awarded his seven feet of English earth. With reverence, Harold and Gyrth had the mangled remains of Tostig taken back to York in a handcart. They wrapped him in a dirty and soiled blanket and had some flagstones levered up in the nave of the Minster so a pit could be dug into the Roman foundations. Then, after a brief and stilted ceremony conducted by the Archbishop and with no accompanying plain chant or incense or eulogies, they laid their talented and mercurial brother to eternal rest, the flagstones falling back with a resounding crash.

When finally he received the news of Stamford Bridge, old Sweyn of Denmark embarked upon a monumental and celebratory binge of epic proportions and managed to stay roaring drunk for close on to a full week. When, finally and blearily, he emerged like a bear out of hibernation, his still agile mind was reeling with options and implications. None of these boded any good at all for Norway, with its children Kings and a land robbed of its fighting men.

At Riccall, among the crowded boats and the sheds full of plunder, Harold took all the necessary submissions. Strykker, the Hardraader's last surviving senior man, was stiff and unbending and punctilious. This was the worst moment of his life for the valiant old man. In his own grief and rage, however, Harold was in no way inclined to be magnanimous. All of the treasure, the gold and the silver, the jewellery, the church plate, the icons brought from Norway or else seized in England, along with York's own ransom, was piled up and carted off for safekeeping in York. Paul and Erlend, the young Earls of Orkney, made it very apparent that they could not wait to be off and away, even though they both knew they would have a very hard time of it indeed back home. They were already rehearsing their speeches of appeasement to the chief men and the tribal leaders of Caithness and the islands. This whole venture had not been of their making and from the very offset they had wanted no part in it. There was a mercifully brief but humiliating interview with Harold. They had no English and Harold no Gaelic and so a badly wounded Hebridean lying on a hurdle and who had both languages provided the words which curtly dismissed the boys and provided them with just enough ships to carry them and the remaining men of Caithness and the Orkneys north and to a very cold welcome.

Young Olaf Haraldsson would come to be known in his later and declining years as 'the Peaceful.' It was a title that would have turned his father crimson with rage and reaching for his axe. The boy knelt at Harold's feet and swore a permanent and everlasting peace between England and Norway. Harold raised him up and administered a begrudging kiss of peace upon him. Harold's ship masters, meanwhile, were hard at work in selecting a number of boats from the Viking fleet in the same way that skilled farmers culled frail and diseased cattle from the herd. The task of getting these boats, the runts of the Norwegian litter, headed about and out of the jam of vessels on the crowded river at Riccall took up the entire day and well into the evening.

Three hundred longboats had sailed into the Humber. Just twenty-four sailed out of it again and into a humiliating oblivion. Harold and his army stood on the banks of the river, surrounded by piles of treasure and discarded weaponry, and watched them go, this sullen postscript to the greatest of all English triumphs. Not even the mighty Alfred of glorious memory had done as well after crushing the Danes at Ashington. "What on earth," said Aesegar, thinking aloud, "are we going to do with all of these boats?" Harold laughed and clapped him on the shoulder. "I am sure that we will think of something," he said.

With the sick and the wounded of the English army lying in the commandeered houses of York, Harold had the Archbishop's normally austere and sedate hall turned into a place where he might feast his still stunned and disbelieving heroes. Edwin and Morcar, he had been informed, were skulking and licking their wounds and nursing their injured pride at Chester. They had put a lot of distance between themselves and York and Harold was in no mood to meet with them just yet, though he knew he must. Those boys, by their actions, had cost him dear. His men continued to marvel. Had they really achieved all of this? They had made an epic march to the north at a speed which defied all logic and had then fought the biggest and hardest battle since first the Angles and the Saxons and the Jutes had come to these shores. It was small wonder then that the men roaring and wassailing before their King on his high dais were in such fine form and voice. There was good food and drink under their belts and even more now being set before them. The horrors of the Stamford Bridge were now seven days in the past. Since then Harold had slept perhaps three or four hours each night. In the daylight hours he was never in the same place for more than an hour or so at a time, striving to bring proper governance once more to the turbulent and traumatised north of his kingdom. He spent much of the time in the saddle and his rheumatic and swollen limbs and joints were a constant and nagging and occasionally excruciatingly painful accompaniment to all of his movements. He spent his waking hours in seeking to pacify and mollify the sullen and humiliated people of York and the surrounding area. He toured and inspected and admired babies and livestock. He devoted time also to the revision of the City Charter and the additional clauses and those either amended or removed were greatly to the benefit of the citizens. The people of York came out to celebrate in the streets and once more acclaimed their noble and virtuous King.

In Edinburgh, the neurotic Malcolm Canmore, on this occasion justifiably nervous and fretful, was chewing his fingernails to the quick and fearing an English invasion of his lowlands. He required sensitive treatment and a conciliatory document was framed and despatched to him by Harold and Gyrth. It did, nonetheless, touch upon his recent indiscretions and required of him a formal renunciation of any Scottish claims upon English territory and a requirement of compensation for recent depredations. Gone forever were the promises of Tostig.

All the while in those days after Stamford Bridge there were crowds of litigants and supplicants seeking redress from the depredations of the north men and forming ill-tempered and argumentative lines outside the Bishop's residence long before each dawn. In the first two hours of his working day Harold sat and listened with ill-concealed impatience and then pronounced judgement. Men occasionally protested at his decisions and for their pains were then bundled out and, as often as not, subjected to a thorough beating by Harold's exasperated court ushers.

And in the evenings, of course, there was always the mead hall to preside over. Each night, aching all over and with a throbbing head, he needed to be present in order to honour and praise and feast his men. They were chosen by lottery each morning from amongst the thegns and merchants and local landowners because of the limited seating available. Harold was not well and feeling decidedly liverish and so he ate sparingly and took his wine heavily watered.

On this particular evening, with Gyrth and Haakon sitting either side of him and neither of them showing any restraint at all with regard to food and strong drink, Harold surveyed the high-spirited crowd before him and smiled and waved and nodded his acknowledgements. Waltheof was still absent, laid up with a dangerously high fever. The wound to the thigh he had taken at Stamford Bridge had been a bad one and it was slow in healing. The men in the hall needed both time and praise in large amounts, but Harold was restless and anxious to return to the south. He would, he had decided, leave Maerlswyn in the north to look after things. The locals seemed to like and trust him and he had been instructed to patrol the border with the Scots in an aggressive manner. What to do with the Aelfgarsons? Sooner or later Morcar would return in the hope of resuming his Earldom and one of Harold's first acts after Stamford Bridge had been to send a message to Chester where the brothers were now said to be and urging them to attend upon him here at York with all speed. He had no answer to the troublesome problem of the Aelfgarsons as of yet and it worried him. He had no doubt that the Northumbrians would display little enthusiasm in welcoming the irritating little brat back and would instead approve his own personal choice of Waltheof. The young Earl, however, might not in fact survive his wound.

The Hardraada was gone forever and it was very unlikely that Malcolm Canmore would move against him, Northumbria now lay within his gift, but Harold could not afford to upset the Mercian apple cart just yet. There was still the Norman bastard to deal with and so he still needed Edwin and Mercia, even if Northumbria was to all intents and purposes his. A stumble or a fall, a better aimed spear or sword thrust at Fulford Gate. Any of these would have solved many things regarding his problematical brothers in law. Aeldyth with a child growing in her belly, that had been the bargain. No, let sleeping dogs lie. Regrettably he still needed the Aelfgarsons, for the moment at least, even though, between them, they had lost the best of the men of the north at Gate Fulford. Settle the Norman issue first and then he could move against the sons of Aelfgar. He would then take an immense pleasure in encompassing their end.

Why couldn't Edwin and Morcar have gone and got their silly selves killed at Gate Fulford and done everyone a favour? He shook his head vigorously and dismissed the subversive thought. Misinterpreting the gesture, a servant hurried forward and filled his cup once more. Harold smiled politely and thanked him. Last night he had had that dream again. Despite the absolution of Wulfstan, the dream had been more potent and terrifying than ever and he had awoken from it abruptly, drenched in sweat.

The men in the hall were singing once more, demanding his attention and his praise like young children. He smiled upon them and raised his heavily diluted cup in salute and acknowledgement. A different servant appeared now at his shoulder, a man he didn't recognise. The servant leaned forward and muttered into Harold's ear. A messenger from the south had arrived, his sincere and respectful apologies for the interruption, but the man needed to deliver a message regarding an urgent and sensitive matter. Harold frowned and put his cup down heavily upon the table. Full of foreboding, he rose to his feet and descended the steps from the raised dais. As he made his way through the main body of the hall and amongst the crowded trestle tables and stools, the shouts and cries of his happy and victorious men rang and reverberated in his ears. As he made his way between cheering men, he felt a sense of doom. He had known even as he made his way from the feasting hall and to the stables that a new horror and challenge lay ahead of him. This was now confirmed to him by the grimy and foul smelling young messenger, from Essex by his accent, who knelt before him in the straw and horse dung with his head bowed and who gave him the news he had always expected and feared since he had become the anointed and crowned King of England.

The Normans had come. They were landed upon the south coast and were bringing death and destruction to all within their reach. Harold dismissed the boy with thanks and the promise of a meal, a good night's sleep and a purse. He had thought the Hardraada to be his worst nightmare and in the past days he had understandably paid little heed to the danger of the Duke of Normandy. Now, out of season and against all sense and logic, the Normans had come at last, as William had vowed they truly would. Knowing the man and his towering ambitions as he did how could he ever have doubted him? Alone in the stables, Harold felt numb, with a cold sweat breaking out on his forehead. The losses at Stamford Bridge had been appalling. So many of his best men, his personal housecarls and the thegns of the midlands and the south, had fallen before the desperate, swinging axes of the north men. The slaughter had also been great amongst the prized horses and remounts, so painstakingly trained to ride against armed men. Perhaps he should have treated with the man, but he knew in his heart that the Hardraada would have had none of that. At one stage in that crippling encounter the Nowegians, goaded beyond measure, had hurled themselves upon his corps of bowmen.

They had come in close and the slaughter of his archers had been appalling. Rushing north against his brother and the Norwegians, he had drained the Midlands and East Anglia of the fighting men of the fyrd. How desperately he needed those men now.

***

By mid-morning of the following day he was on the road again with fifteen hundred grim faced professionals riding behind him. The rest, the foot, those now deprived of horses, the walking wounded, would have to follow after with all the speed they could manage and sustain. He remembered that campaign in Brittany and the absolute awe and terror inspired by those mailed and mounted men, a ton and a half of fighting excellence. Now those same men were here in his England. They had been there for four days now. He could well imagine the results.

Ahead of him went fast moving and wide-ranging messengers, riding hard in order to mobilise what was, in effect, the fourth English army of this extraordinary year. The routes they passed along were virtually denuded of men, though here and there they encountered small groups of yokel volunteers and conscripts led by minor thegns on their way north to do battle with the Hardraada. These he turned around in their tracks, ordering them to march instead to London. He shouted encouragement and thanks at them from the saddle as he passed by, rewarded by their answering shouts as he made his way south.

The next levy would fall squarely upon the men of London and the home shires. It would fall also upon the men of the Welsh marches and the far west, the men of Gloucestershire, Hampshire, Dorset, Somerset and Devon. They would have a hard and long and difficult journey. He found himself arguing more and more with Gyrth. On each day of their journey, covering some forty miles by nightfall, the disagreements became more bitter and rancorous. The root of the argument lay in Harold's insistence on speed, his insistence on bringing the invaders of their land to battle as soon as possible. At Huntingdon, fractious and bone weary and out of sorts, they all but came to blows. Aesegar, Haakon and Aelfric joined them there, distressed on lookers. Once again Harold repeated his intention to pass directly through London, picking up men there, and continuing straight for the south coast. "Man alive," Gyrth stormed at him, "have you taken leave of your senses? For the love of Christ, brother. Just look at the state of you." He actually jabbed Harold in the chest, causing him to rock slightly. The naturally red and ruddy Gyrth was incandescent with rage and frustration, he positively seemed to glow in his passion. "At this moment an ancient nun could take you on with one arm tied behind her back, and I'd put good money on her winning."

"I am King of England," said Harold loftily and with an unaccustomed pomposity brought about by his own fatigue and anger. "You'll be King of bugger all if you keep this up," Gyrth raged. "Yes, it's me saying it, your own brother. "I'm not some little toe rag you can bully into silence. This is my England too, you know." There was a momentary silence as they both stared at each other, breathing heavily. "Perhaps," said Aelfric from his corner of the room, "if you were both to sit and collect yourselves for a moment?" Aelfric had had just about enough of this, bringing out in him a strange and uncharacteristic statesmanlike air that was so out of keeping with his normal belligerent nature. "Harold," he said. "Gyrth has the right of it. Surprise worked well enough for you at Stamford Bridge. It will not work again. William knows full well that we are coming. He will be ready for us. You may be sure of it."

"Right enough," said Gyrth, grateful for his uncle's intervention and support. "We need to meet him when we are fully rested and with an overwhelming force. At London we must wait for the rest of the men from the north and for the men of the south east and the west. We must wait too for Edwin and Morcar." Harold snorted derisively. "Those two puppies? Fat lot of use they'll be. They couldn't organise a riot in a brothel, those two, or even plan one."

"Nevertheless," said Aelfric sternly, "we all need to rest, and to gather men and supplies." Gyrth broke in once more, adding fuel to the fire. "Instead of going in half arsed," he said. At that the whole argument opened up once more, just when Aelfric had hoped for a respite, a measure of peace and reconciliation. "Those vermin," Harold shouted, rising to his feet once more, "those vermin are loose and at large in our England, brother of mine. Not only that, but you will note that it is my lands they are trampling underfoot, not your lands. East Anglia is safe enough."

"Safe enough for the moment," retorted Gyrth, "but not for much longer if you insist upon this foolishness and throw everything away on the outcome of a fight provoked too soon. If Leofwyn were here, he'd back me entirely." Harold laughed out loud. "Leofwyn, ever the brains of the family. He always did make the right decisions." Aelfric was reproving. "Unfair, uncharitable," he said. "Enough now, let us sleep. For the love of God, we all need it."

Harold sought sleep, even if it were to bring on the old familiar nightmare, but sleep eluded him in that damp barn with most of the roof missing midway between Cambridge and Royston. Wulfstan, he needed desperately the kind words and wisdom, the solace and the blessing of the Bishop of Worcester, his second father. He wanted to see him once more, perhaps for the last time. How was that unruly boy of his doing under the patronage of the saintly old man? His mother. By now, surely, she would have heard the news, heard of Tostig's death. After Swein, Tostig had been her favourite and he resented this. The charming and feckless

Tostig had always been the favourite of most people. Her son's death was of his doing. How could he possibly go before her and find the words to explain? He had found Tostig lying dead and disfigured in a mound of strangers and foreigners. It was fratricide, pure and simple. Edith, his one and true love, she and the children. Where were they now? Could he summon them to London? His poor, mad sister, the other Edith, conversing daily with her dead husband in that claustrophobic little house in Winchester. Gyrth, with whom he had quarrelled so bitterly and to whom he owed so much. He felt bitterly ashamed of himself. Leofwyn, his amiable and large-hearted brother, whom he had so maligned a short time back. Wulfnoth, the other brother, rotting away in a castle keep in Normandy. Sleep would not come, and the long list of his sins of commission and omission continued to run through his mind.

He remembered now his time in Ireland. There in the little settlement of Tralee a poet had once told him the story of a blessed land to the west. Tir Nan Og? Something like that, he couldn't quite recall. It was to the west of that howling and wind swept coast, a land of reunions and happy endings. Could he not could put them all in a boat and sail them there? The dead. Could they come too? His sister, the maimed and mutilated Tostig, all the others he had loved in life and lost, reformed and reconstructed and loving. The childish fantasy drifted him off to sleep as he named the names in his head and his sleep was for once deep and undisturbed by nightmares.

In the midafternoon of October fifth, their fourth grueling day on the march, they entered at last into the familiar flat lands of Essex. London was just a few hours away and Harold was still trying to outdistance his personal demons. Not too far from here was the dreamy peace of the river Lea and his own endowment of the Abbey of the Holy Cross at Waltham. Perhaps, in the absence of Wulfstan, that would serve his needs. He decided upon a compromise. He glanced across at his stony faced and still angry brother. "Gyrth, he said, "Let there be peace between us." he said. "There have been harsh words said and for my part I am truly sorry for them. We have both spoken too hastily of late." Gyrth muttered inaudibly into his beard and continued to stare at the road ahead. "A week," announced Harold unexpectedly. "They have known of our coming for days now. I shall remain in London, as you suggest, for one week, rest our men and gather more people, and then we shall march." Gyrth acknowledged this overture of peace. "Agreed," he said. "It's glad I am that you've come to your senses, though I believe a week is scarce enough."

"A week," repeated Harold firmly. "Time enough, I hope, for the men of London, Kent and Sussex to gather. Time enough, also, I pray, for the men of the north to catch up and for the men of the west to come in. Who knows? Even Edwin and Morcar might pull their fingers out." Gyrth snorted, he very much doubted that, but, still, seven days respite was better than nothing. He would have time, at least, to rein Leofwyn and the others in and marshal and present their arguments to Harold with a united front. Harold, surely, could not go against an undivided council. Was that not the purpose of a Witangemot? To guide and discipline the King where and when guidance and discipline was required. Hatched already in Gyrth's practical and sensible mind was a scheme to keep Harold in London with the reserves whilst he himself took the army down south. If he came to grief in the attempt then at least there was a breathing space and a King still to govern, he would, he decided, work on this.

Harold paused before continuing. There was, he knew, a path still some miles ahead of them that led more or less directly to the Abbey at Waltham through the forest. "You and uncle Aelfric," he said, "take the men into London. I have no doubt but that Leofwyn will be waiting for you. Rest the men up at Blackheath. See that they are fed well. I shall join you at Westminster Hall some time tomorrow."

"Tomorrow?" exclaimed Gyrth. "And where in God's name do you think you are off to in the meantime?" He was alarmed, fearing some mad plan.

"To my Abbey at Waltham," answered Harold simply, "to worship there and to spend the night in vigil before the Holy Cross. By the time I arrive it will be the hour of Vespers. Believe me, Gyrth. This is something that I need to do. I shall take Leofgar and the rest of the boys with me."

They came at last to the parting of the ways, a familiar old bridle track snaking off east through the forest of Epping to Waltham. The main route of Ermine Street continued straight to London. The brothers reached across the saddles to grip hands. "Until tomorrow, Gyrth," said Harold. "Noon, or thereabouts. How you arrange it is your business, but I want an escort of fifty housecarls on this road here waiting for me by mid-morning tomorrow. I shall need some sort of show and escort." Gyrth, greatly concerned and more than halfway convinced that his brother was losing his grip, could only pray that Harold would find some kind of peace and perhaps some answer to his prayers at his beloved Abbey and before the Holy Cross. Perhaps he'd do himself and everyone else a favour and get a decent night's sleep, though he doubted it, with all this fanciful talk of vigils. For Gyrth, there were set times and days for reverence to the Almighty and he himself did not bother the Good Lord above unduly. He was sure that He had more than enough to concern Himself with as it was. He nodded, "I'll see to it all," he said. "They'll not like it overmuch, but the men you request will be waiting for you at the very next settlement along the road. I'll see that the rest are settled down at Blackheath, an admirable choice. I could wish you were coming in with me, but your mind is set, I see that." Harold nodded. "It is indeed, Gyrth. This is something I have to do. Please understand this. When I see you tomorrow, I shall want a clear picture of what has been happening. God speed you."

It was a muted and slightly mutinous brotherhood that trailed after Harold, cursing as they brushed back branches and brambles along the dark and narrow bridle path. It was a glorious autumn afternoon, with the leaves russet and orange and red and beginning to fall. Of those men of two years ago in Normandy, Adelbert of Southampton, never really of their number, had been the first to fall away, surrendered up to commerce and presumably plying his trade in and out of Southampton Reach. He was a world away from all that which the others had experienced since then. Harold's Danish kinsman, Bjorn, had been of their original number. He might have survived disease and fever and still might be living in some foetid and secured hole in the ground somewhere in Normandy. Caedmon, that gentle cleric who had stayed with Wulfnoth, had returned, haunted and scarred inside and out. In his compassion and guilt Harold had sent him away to the peace and tranquility of Waltham Abbey where now he served as Sacristan and personal secretary to the venerable Abbot, Harold's one time physician. It was to be hoped that he had found a peace of sorts. Ceofwyn of Cornwall, of course, had suffered a very public death at the hands of that solitary Norwegian on the planking of Stamford Bridge. Eadmar, the Gloucester iron master, had simply vanished on that same day and on that same battlefield, never to be seen again. It was as if he had been plucked from the face of the earth.

All of which left just the four of them, slapping at the gnats and midges and blaspheming at the raking bramble cuts. Willi was leaner and gaunter since the mad headlong dash north and appeared less given these days to boisterous practical jokes and impromptu songs. Stamford Bridge had proved to contain little of the romance of the epics of Brunanburgh or Maldon. He had been shocked to the core at the carnage, right enough, but even now the professional in him was beginning to mould and craft an epic of Stamford Bridge to rival all other epics. He hummed and fiddled with metre and rhythm and alliteration as he went. It was fair to say that Alfi had been unchanged by it all, for nobody really knew what went through the mind of the fey little man from the New Forest anyway. He had been seen to weep at Stamford Bridge as he roamed the battlefield afterwards and cutting the throats of injured horses. At some point during that day he had received a spectacular blow to the head and he still sported a bloodstained bandage that obscured one eye. He muttered and mumbled endearments to his horse, looking about with his one exposed expert eye.

Young Gareth, the Welsh hostage turned devoted follower, was a real worry to Harold. He had long promised himself that he would return the boy to his family in Rhuddlan, but events had intervened. Like all the others, he too displayed visible signs of the rigours of the past two weeks. It was as if his face had fallen in on its underlying bone structure, making his pale blue eyes enormous. "Do not send me back just yet," he had begged his lord at a point on the march south in his still very uncertain and sing song English. "Not yet awhile. We have, look you, the Normans for to see away first." Harold had laughed affectionately and ruffled his hair, but he still regretted the missed opportunity. He vowed to make it right.

Finally, there was the mysterious and taciturn Leofgar. He came last in the single file of horsemen and in a mood of apparent content. He seemed eternal and indestructible, the classic fighting man. He was older in years and wiser in the wicked ways of the world than the other three, though in fact few years separated them. As usual he was armed to the teeth, and with his beloved throwing knives festooned about him. He wore the fine body mail of a dead Norwegian Jarl, whose helmet of iron and leather and embossed decorations swung from his saddle. He had killed the man himself. Leofgar was an innocent wayfarer's worst nightmare, appearing like a fiend from the forest. He had had himself a fine and heroic time at Stamford Bridge. In the full sight of the army, he had avenged the death of Ceofwyn and had taken on the berserkers of the Vikings with equanimity. It had been he who had cut down the last standard bearer of the Land Waster and handed it to his King. Harold had rewarded the savage little Mercian with lands and a Manor up near Oswestry, thus conferring upon him the status of a thegn. Leofgar was thus content enough with his lot, and looking forward with enthusiasm to the next encounter with the men of Normandy.

The story of the foundation of the Abbey was linked in a curious way to the family of Aesegar, presently on his way south from York. The first church there had in fact been established by Aesegar's grandfather, a man known, and for all the wrong reasons, as Tofig the Proud. He had been one of the original cronies and fighting men of Cnut and deep in the King's confidence way back when the century was young. It had been at Tofig's own wedding feast when Cnut's son Harthacnut had gasped, clutched at his chest and dropped stone dead and face down into a giant venison pasty. To go with his increasingly guilty conscience, Tofig was awarded large lands and estates in Somerset and Essex and elsewhere and towards the end of his life he became much given to thoughtful and charitable acts and to the comfort of pious men. One night at a vigil, a vision of riches and treasure, both earthly and spiritual, came to one of these holy men and so powerful was this vision and his unshakeable belief in it that Tofig, to the great amazement of his neighbours, was sufficiently inspired to have one of his fields dug up near Yeovil in accordance with the vision. There, amidst the rotten timber and strewn rubble of the remains of an ancient church, they found a small cache of gold and silver, both coins and ornaments. With this, nestling within the remains of a leather bag, austere and undecorated, was a stone crucifix, a rood of uncertain age. A crudely carved Christ nailed to his cross stared back at Tofig with a fixed expression, an inscrutable and Byzantine gaze. At the time the find caused quite a stir owing to the strange nature of its discovery and the crucifix was of course held to be special. Awed and reverent, Tofig had it taken back to Waltham, his favourite place and handy for London when his morals slipped, and where he ordered a church to be built around it.

Shortly thereafter, strange things began to be reported. Local people praying before it, as people prayed to similar images throughout the land, began to report marvelous stories. There were those, it was said, who found themselves cured of all manner of physical and spiritual ailments, from warts to grief, from marsh opthalmia to chest pains. In very short order Waltham began to acquire the status of a shrine and a place of cure and the local Church and the population itself grew prosperous as the number of portents and manifestations increased and pilgrims and the money which they brought with them began to arrive in greater numbers.

And then, more than twenty years back, the Danes were out and Edward was in. Tofig was very much of the old order and Edward, keen to raise up the family of Godwin and to honour young Harold of East Anglia, as he then was, took Waltham and the neighbouring Manor of Nazeing away from Tofig and bestowed it upon the young Godwinson. Harold took a liking to the place and nurtured it. He spent a good deal of time there and at Nazeing but did not view Waltham with any of the especial reverence he was to develop in later years. Then, in a bitter and brilliantly conducted expedition against the Welsh, the hard-living years of campaigning finally caught up with him. He woke one morning, moved to stretch, and found that he couldn't. His spine had become a single fused column of unmovable stone and his legs were lifeless. He had to be conveyed on a litter out of the mountains and along the way every jolt was an agony. His father was dead and Edward ageing, childless and by now almost deranged by religious mania. This was no time for the first man in the land to be struck down with the rheum like some old ploughman.

Concerned at the news, Edward himself commissioned prayers and masses. More to the point, he loaned to Harold the expert services of Adelhard, his own German physician and a man of considerable distinction and reputation. Under Adelhard's implacable regime, Harold was purged and bled and starved in turn in an attempt to find a cure. He seemed destined, however, to remain a useless cripple for the rest of his days. Laid up at Nazeing, he commissioned pilgrims to petition the Lord at some of the more likely places, at Canterbury, Glastonbury, Bury St Edmunds and Walsingham. The Almighty appeared deaf to all requests until one night Harold dreamed of the Holy Rood and saw in his dream the humble little church at Waltham, just up the road from where he presently lay.

Harold had himself carried there and laid in the nave before the altar. He fasted and prayed all night and then, at some point towards the dawn, he felt himself strong enough to rise up from his pallet. He knelt before the cross, asking for forgiveness for all his many sins and for a cure and a return to strength. The stone Christ, now encased in pure silver set with gems, stared back at him sternly. In a voice that was not a voice, but rather words that went straight to Harold's mind, Christ reminded Harold of his many faults and sins and crimes and which had yet to be redressed. When Harold had returned from his Irish exile fifteen years back, he had ravaged the west in much the same manner as his brother had done in Wight and along the eastern coast just weeks ago. Make recompense now to those people, the land where first I was found, the stone Christ commanded him, and then perhaps I shall cure you. Confess your many sins and all might yet be well. Praise my name and you might ge granted peace."

In the early morning Harold walked, upright and rejoicing from the church. He walked past the vestibule and the porch festooned with the crutches and gifts of previous successful supplicants and immediately awarded from his purse of Wessex a huge donation of cash for the Shire of Somerset, to be used by the officials there for good acts and offices. His awaiting retainers and servants gaped and rejoiced. A miracle indeed! It was not, of course, only Somerset that benefitted. He commenced to shower endowments upon Waltham and granted the church additional land. Emulating his King at Westminster, he inaugurated a massive building programme to transform the humble little church. Six years back the new edifice was finally completed and consecrated. Edward himself, an habitual devotee and admirer of such occasions, was present. Even then Stigand was shunned from religious events such as this and old Cynesige of York, since then gathered to God, was cajoled down from the north to conduct the ceremony, magnificent in its celebration.

Warming to his theme, Harold went on to establish a seminary for secular priests and as a reward to Adelhard he appointed him as Dean. The new building gleamed with an application of new whitewash upon its freshly plastered walls and with the added artifice of gold and silver leaf and bright daubs of red, blue, green and yellow. The columns and the pillars were painted in bold stripes of red and black. Both the Abbey Scriptorium and the local school of embroidery came to enjoy a fast-growing reputation and the assembly of the Choir could hold its head up with pride and set itself against any other in the country.

Harold and his small following had not, of course, been expected and his sudden appearance from amongst the undergrowth sent the community into a positive flurry of panic and botched preparations. Old Adelhard was very frail now. Nearly blind and supported by two robust young novices, he greeted his King with both pleasure and concern, as did the still wraithlike Caedmon, hovering shyly on the fringes. Harold had calculated almost to the moment the hour of Vespers. "I have come to keep Vigil," he told them. "Any man who so chooses may remain with me. For myself, I shall pray and fast all night." Leofgar, Willi and Alfi made themselves scarce, finding duties with which to busy themselves. Harold thought no less of them for that, but the devoted Caedmon and Gareth stayed with him throughout his vigil. All night Harold knelt upon the flagstones before the miraculous Christ, drawing upon yet more reserves of stamina. He prayed for forgiveness for all his manifest sins, especially for the death of his brother Tostig and for his renunciation of his true love. He prayed also for poor Wulfnoth. Above all, he prayed for the necessary strength to meet the encounter that lay ahead of him. I shall make this Abbey mightier and more glorious still, he bargained with Christ, only let me prevail and bring a lasting peace to this land.

In turns, willingly or otherwise, priests and novices and probationers shared the vigil with their King and the sound of their mutterings and the constant clacking of rosary beads resounded off the stone walls. Towards the dawn, and with the shadows and the effect of dark and light fickle and capricious, an Essex man called Thurkill, a man of humble position in that community, a layman serving in the kitchens and who attended to the vegetable plot, looked up to the Rood in supplication. The hair rose up on the back of his neck and a sudden sweat started out on his forehead. No doubt of it. No doubt of it at all! The little Christ on his cross was nodding, nodding slowly in response to the King's prayers. The figure nodded once more and then his head seemed to sag down upon his chest once more, in his usual pose of death. Though he felt this to be a presentiment of doom rather than one of encouragement, Thurkill praised the Lord and rejoiced. His personal paternoster repeated again and again, went up to Heaven. When this vigil was finished, he would have a story to tell.

Harold rose without warning, genuflected once and left the Abbey and in search of a much-needed breakfast, men scuttling thankfully out after him. Within moments Thurkill had told his story to his especial friend, the herbalist's assistant, and to any others prepared to listen, as indeed they all were. By the time Harold and his men were fed and the horses were saddled, the story had gone the rounds and had reached the ear of old Adelhard himself. When Adelhard was conveyed over to Harold to make his farewells he was especially solicitous. He quivered with emotion and his near dead eyes were damp with tears. He made the sign of the cross over his King. "May the Good Lord keep you and protect you always, in this world and the next," he said.

Purged and cleansed by his vigil, Harold was affable and in high spirits. "And to you, my dear old friend," he said, patting the old man's shoulder. "God love you, but I'll be back before you know it, and I'll be after some of that excellent honey from your hives. The Good Lord knows, I've ploughed enough into this place." He grabbed Caedmon by his ears and hugged him vigorously. "Get some weight back on you, my boy," he said, "and look after the old fellow here for me." He mounted and kicked his horse into motion, leading his men back towards the track leading to Ermine Street and humming as he went.

After some time, and with their appointment with the housecarl escort just a short distance ahead, Willi, who followed next after him as they rode single file, ventured a comment. "They were in a bloody funny mood, when we left, that lot back there," he said. "What was all that about then, do you suppose?" Harold turned back and smiled at him fondly. "They are religious and God-fearing folk, Willi. Not like you and I. Things affect them in different ways. I saw nothing out of the ordinary." Harold was very tired, but the pain in his limbs, in response to prayers to God, had diminished and he had a sense of optimism he had not felt in many days. "It is up to the likes of us both, sinful and worldly as we are, to make the place safe enough for them to pray for us."

There were, as Harold had known there would be, boats to be had at the little Thames side settlement at Becton. He had used them before. The journey south to the river from Waltham and through the forest of Epping had been as swift as possible and conducted in near silence. All the noise and chatter arose from the escort of fifty men who fell in behind them when they reached Ermine Street. At some point on the journey Harold had changed his mind and at Becton he dismissed the incredulous fifty housecarls and told them to make their own way to Blackheath. They were fractious and as resentful as they dared to be. They had sacrificed the chance of being the first in the queue for rations at Blackheath in return for a glorious arrival at Westminster. Now, after an uncomfortable night, they were destined for Blackheath after all, and the sweepings of other men. Harold, though, was adamant. He was in no mood at present to make a public progress through London with all due and necessary ceremony and was content instead to view his capital from the river as he passed.

***

With his muted and uneasy companions, Harold sat himself in the sweeps of the little river barge and had himself conveyed upstream, staring out as the river looped and slowly narrowed past the small English and Danish settlements on either bank. Once, not so far back, the Thames had been the frontier. They sailed past the wharves and jetties and riverside tenements of London without attracting comment or attention and then ran the foaming and exhilarating whirlpool under the old London bridge. They arrived, unheeded and without ceremony, at Blackhorse ferry in the early afternoon. A reception committee had been left wrong footed on the Strand road between Westminster and London and the arrival of the King of England from a totally unexpected location threw everyone into confusion. Gyrth came racing back in a fine fury to face his brother waiting patiently on the quayside. "This way was quicker, and less bother," said Harold equably. With none of the precarious amity they had regained the previous day they walked together over to the precincts of the Palace, Gyrth still muttering at his brother's improvidence and lack of protocol and stealing sidelong glances to see how his brother was walking.

The Westminster residence itself was like an upturned ants' nest, with harassed servants and auxiliaries colliding and quarrelling with the groups of loafing onlookers now arriving in ever greater numbers. They clashed and squabbled in the narrow alleys and small open spaces, a confusion of noxious and foul-smelling mud, arguing men and handcarts. Gyrth was in the process, he explained, of attempting to provision the army of the north, now drifting into Blackheath in small and exhausted groups and contingents. At the same time he and Haakon were attempting also to organise and despatch the messengers going out to all points in the southeast and southwest. They passed the stables and the predictably crowded smithy, always a rallying point for warmth and gossip, on the way to the hall. The two brothers sliced through the respectfully parting crowds. "Been busy then, Gyrth?"

"Up since sparrow fart," said Gyrth, shoving an ostler aside. "The place is in a complete uproar. What with the

Hardraada dead in the north and the bastard very much alive in the south, people don't know whether to cheer or burst into tears. Nobody knows if it's Michael Mass or Maundy Thursday. A complete sod up and a shambles." Harold looked about him. "So I see," he said. They had reached the courtyard before the entrance to the hall. It was packed and seething with servants and resting housecarls. Sighting the brothers, the housecarls, many carrying wounds from Stamford Bridge, clambered to their feet and broke out in a rhythmic and baying greeting of acclaim. Harold acknowledged the greeting with a wave of the hand and they entered then into the dimness of the hall, Gyrth continuing to mutter his news as they moved forward to a welcoming fire blazing away in a hearth with a chimney of the new design. "Stigand is confined, Harold. The order was mine. He is over in the Bishop's Palace at Lambeth. Something came to light while we were away. He needs seeing to, I shall tell you later." Harold seated himself by the fire and called for drink. "Men are coming in all the time to Blackheath from the north," Gyrth continued. "They are for the most part in a complete state and will need a lot of resting. If you want to know ..."

"What you think?" interrupted Harold rudely. "I know what you think already, Gyrth. But we don't have the time." But Gyrth was remorseless, handing his brother a mug of strong mead. "The most of our men from Stamford are still on the road anywhere between here and Lincoln. It'll take days yet. Meanwhile we have a rabble of levies from the general fyrd arriving at all hours and making the place untidy. As they arrive I'm having them sent to Blackheath." Harold grunted absently," good, good." He sipped his hot, strong drink and stared into the fire. "Are you bloody listening to me at all?" demanded Gyrth. "No news as yet of Edwin and Morcar and the boats at Sandwich and Dover meantime are awaiting orders. You should know also that not three days since ten boatloads of Danes came sailing up the Thames, just like the old times, bold as brass and as damn your eyes as you like, calling us English puppies and runts and starting fights all over the place." Harold smiled, thinking of the panic even one boat load of visiting Danes could cause. He could just picture them carousing in the streets. "A gift from our good friend Sweyn?"

"Indeed so. They are fully paid and provisioned and ours for the duration. Two hundred mercenaries, to do with what you will. You can imagine their reaction to the news of the death of the Hardraada." Harold smiled again and nodded. "I can imagine," he said dryly. "Well I must visit them in all good time, and send thanks also to Sweyn. I imagine we can find appropriate gifts. Where have you put them all? I imagine the good people of London had a fit when they saw them."

Despite himself, the normally dour Gyrth actually grinned. "To be sure, they did. The Bishop had the sense to have them billeted out in Southwark, where I imagine they can seek out distant kin and patronise the brothels to their hearts' content. The good Bishop had the foresight also to send gifts and thanks to Sweyn on your behalf."

"He did well. And our other foreign guests?" Harold signalled for more drink. Gyrth spat into the fire, half afraid to inform his brother lest he set off south to fight them immediately. He was prepared to physically restrain his brother if necessary. Instead he delivered up a brief and informative summary, starting with the arrival of the invaders at the Pevensey flats, an estimate of their size and strength and ending with a report of their depredations as far as the southern reaches of the Andredsweald. Harold listened with a mounting horror to the news of the death and destruction brought to his own Kingdom and his own personal lands. Judging his moment, Gyrth concluded. "And our mother, Harold. She is upstairs waiting for us. She does know. But it is best if she heard it again from us and best if it were now."

In the intervening months since old Edward had breathed his last in this very room there had been few changes made to the Royal bedchamber. Harold himself, and mostly itinerant anyway, had always shunned the place and the bed had been occupied only by occasional visitors, too tired or too uncaring or perhaps even unknowing to ponder or brood on its last occupant. The gloomy and depressing tapestries of the agonies of Christ were still upon the walls, but the chests and Christmas gifts, the cupboard brimming with tawdry presents and the shelves of manuscripts had now gone, transferred to Winchester. There were a few stools, now occupied by three women busily sewing, some hastily stowed baggage and the bed itself, upon which, proud and erect, sat the dowager Gytha, Lady of Wessex. She had heard the voices below and the ascent of feet on the wooden steps and was thus composed and prepared. "Leave me," she said to her women. They rose and curtsied, first to her and then to the two men entering the room.

Gaunt and grey, still very striking, the old lady surveyed them as they edged in uneasily and towards her. They stood there, like two small boys detected in a crime, which, in her view, they had been. Her eyes were wide and expressionless, set about with the wrinkles of age and the dark patches beneath them denoting lack of sleep. "I'll hear it then," she said. Her voice was curt. "Mother," Gyrth began. "Are you then now head of this family?" she snapped. "I shall hear this from my oldest son, oldest of them living, that is."

Harold signalled to Gyrth to pull over two of the stools. They sat themselves and looked up at her nervously on her vantage point of the bed. "You will have heard," began Harold. "There was a fight." The old lady seemed blind, staring sightlessly into middle distance. Harold swallowed and continued. "Your son, our brother, he was a wolf's head.

You know this. He had been told, warned. Yet he returned to this land, bringing fire and death and destruction with him. He invited in the Norse, the Irish, the Scots, anyone he could think of. Men from Iceland, for God's sake. He came back to do mischief and harm, and in this he succeeded." There was still no reaction from the widow of Godwin and they were not sure if she was even listening any longer. "We found him, as you know, in the company of the Hardraada. A battle had already been fought and there was the blood of thousands of English on his hands."

"We went to him, pleaded with him," Gyrth took up the story. "We offered him lands and recompense, if only he would come away with us." This was not quite how Harold remembered the conversation going, but he decided to say nothing. "I will hear this from your brother, who is the oldest." The voice was distant and dreamy. Cowed, Gyrth retreated into silence, throwing a sympathetic glance at his brother. "There was, then, a battle," Harold said simply. "And Tostig died, as men do in battle. We took him to the Minster at York, Gyrth and I, and there he was buried before the altar with all Christian ceremony. There is now a chantry also for his immortal soul."

"The blood of the English on his hands," her voice was a whisper. "Was there any of his blood on yours?" The temptation to answer truthfully was great. Only when we picked him up, thought Harold to himself. Sensibly, he did not answer. Their mother shook herself vigorously then, as if emerging from a dream or dispelling an evil thought. It appeared she had returned to them. "So then, my beloved Tostig is dead. Little Tostig, the clever, charming one. He was such a beautiful little boy. Like an angel, he was. Dead, like his brother Swein and those babies I buried, dead like my beloved daughter. What chances do you give now for my poor little Wulfnoth over there in Normandy whom you failed to bring back? What chances do you give for yourselves and that great booby Leofwyn? Tell me that. Am I to lose five sons in a single year?" Distressingly, appallingly, a single tear coursed its way down from her left eye to gather on her lip. At the sight of it Harold and Gyrth were numb with grief, neither of them knowing what to say or do next. Besides this, the marshalling of armies and the fighting of a battle seemed easy enough. "A Christian burial, you say?"

"Yes," said Gyrth eagerly, "and masses in perpetuity for his soul." The old lady sniffed. There was a slightly sardonic and familiar sound to it which relaxed them somewhat. "You boys never knew my own father, of course. He was the son of pagans, proud Danish folk. If he were here now then he would say that Tostig is now feasting in Valhalla and getting up to all sorts with his brother Swein. Does the thought please you? Does it console you?" Neither knew what to say by way of an appropriate response. "If it pleases you, then so it does me," Harold managed finally, striking, what he hoped, was a conciliatory note. He was aware of renewed noises below. So too was Gyrth, who was beginning to fidget. "And your own father, Godwin. Do you know what he would ask?" she continued. "He would ask if his son's wounds were all to the front. Well? Were his wounds all to the front?"

The brothers exchanged a furtive glance, perhaps, through the Grace of God, not detected by their mother, as they recalled the obscene ruin that was the mangled carcass of their brother. Gytha suddenly slapped her knees in a brisk and decisive manner, causing Harold and Gyrth to start. "What an ill-omened family we are, to be sure." She declared. "And now the two of you and Leofwyn are off to fight the bastard. I have mourned, I am mourning and I shall continue to mourn. But now for some sensible and practical Danish advice. Delay. Do not fight this man just yet, though the provocation is great. Rest and gather your strength. Fight him only when you know beyond all reasonable doubt that you can crush him like an egg. They are chancy things, well matched fights. The people on my side of the family always knew that. That's how they beat the English in the first place." Inwardly, Gyrth rejoiced at this additional ally to his plans. Harold, for his part, was not at all pleased and by now, short though it had been, he had had enough of this very difficult encounter. He bowed his head. "Mother, if you can find it within you," he said, "then I ask you to bless me and Gyrth here."

Gytha nodded gravely, and with the ghost of a smile. "My sons, I love you both and in equal measure. Please do not bring me further grief. Bring me just yourselves and my silly Leofwyn back again, safe and well You have much to do and have spent too much time with me, so off with you now. My blessings upon you. I do not expect to see either of you again before you set off to settle matters with this Norman. I shall be with friends over at Kensington. Do not disturb yourselves with my arrangements, all is in hand. I pray to God, the Holy Mother and all the saints that you come back to me after." She placed her hand, in turn, on the head of her two sons. "And now go," she said, turning away from them.

CHAPTER NINE:

The Bell, the Book and the Candle

London & the Andredsweald: October 6th to

October 11th, 1066

As if absolved by confession and with their penance duly done, Harold and Gyrth returned to the hall below where a crowd of messengers was now gathering, drawn like bees to nectar at the news of the King's arrival. In order that his mother might make her own dignified and unobtrusive exit, he had them all led outdoors and away over to the garden cloisters at the side of the Abbey where once Aeldyth had told him she was expecting their child. It was a brisk, raw day and that open space was not an ideal location, but then these were stirring times. He and Gyrth pulled up a bench and had them all form an orderly queue to report their news and to make their requests in turn. Summoned by Gyrth, his uncle Aelfric and his nephew Haakon appeared shortly after. Three generations of the Godwin clan now sat in deliberation as the messengers waited in line to patter their news and to await their instructions in the cold October afternoon and with a hint of rain in the air. It had been not even an hour since Harold had arrived at the Horse Ferry crossing.

They should forget Devon and its fighting men, at least for the moment. The distance was too great for the militia of the shire to have any immediate role to play. They would send a message anyway for them to muster as near to the Dorset border as possible. Similar messages went out to the men of Somerset, Gloucestershire and Herefordshire. Devon was too far and across bad roads and there simply was not time enough. There would be time enough, perhaps, for the men of Bedfordshire and Berkshire, where messengers were known to have already arrived. They conferred and deliberated, hard at work to keep any note of tension or panic from their voices in front of all these messengers and the servants. "Let them come on to London as soon as they may," Harold decided. "They can be sent on down to us on the coast then." With the departure of the last of the messengers and the servants dismissed, they could at last make their true thoughts known, could speak with more freedom.

"By the living Christ," said Gyrth in exasperation, "why not wait for them here?" He was pulling a bay tree stem apart in his anger. "No time. There is no time. Let us turn to more local people," replied Harold. Aelfric rolled his eyes in his annoyance and exasperation. "Harold, the cupboard is bare in the midlands, and in Sussex too, come to that. You took them all north with you, and those that aren't bleached bones up there are still on the road south. The men of the north lie dead at Fulford Gate and at Stamford Bridge, or else they are scattered to the four winds and are God alone knows where." Harold nodded at the truth of it. "There remains," he said finally, "the Hertfordshire and Middlesex levies, the fyrds of Essex and Kent and the Londoners here. They have all been summoned."

"Why?" asked Gyrth angrily and speaking each word slowly, "will you not wait?" Harold glared at his brother with an ill suppressed anger. "Because, Gyrth, there is no time. That murderous bandit and his scumbag army, even as we speak, is burning and killing his way through the countryside. Because also the longer we leave things then the greater opportunity he has for further men to arrive and to roam abroad in open country and where we can't contain him and his horses. That, brother, is why."

"I say we wait," said Aelfric urgently, scratching in exasperation at an itch on his shaven tonsure. "I say we wait for the fyrds of the west and from the others to come down from the north." Haakon looked as if he wished to disagree but, being a very junior member of the clan, he kept his peace. "Another two weeks and we'd have twice the men we have now, fresh and rested," said Gyrth urgently. Harold's voice rose in anger. "Another two weeks and the bastard himself will be sitting right here in Westminster and planting his winter vegetables." Harold broke off as a late-comer was ushered over to them. The man went down on one knee, attempting and failing to grasp Harold's hand to kiss. "I come from the Lord Leofwyn," he announced in a flat monotone voice. "Do you now?" said Harold. "And where the bloody hell is he?"

"Over to Gravesend, Lord King, and awaiting your pleasure there. He has about him a gathering of the Essex men and he is calling up the people of Kent." Gyrth spoke hastily.

"I had much to tell you, Harold, this news amongst it." Harold appeared greatly cheered by the news. "Well, well, someone's doing something useful for a change, and bugger me if it isn't Leofwyn. Why Gravesend?" Aelfric was happy to elaborate. "The easiest way to the Normans and where they are is by way of Rochester and Maidstone," he said. "Going by the west route would take much longer."

"Off you go then," said Harold to the messenger, his decision made on the spot. "Give my brother my very best wishes and thanks. He is to continue to gather men and we shall travel to Rochester as soon as maybe." The messenger knuckled his brow and made himself scarce. Gyrth groaned in frustration. "And when is maybe?" he demanded. Harold smiled at him, some of the tension gone with the decision just made. "Within six days, brother. Six days, just as I promised you."

As had been the case in previous times of crisis, Harold seemed for the moment to have shed his fatigue and pain. He was in decisive mood. No later than the following Wednesday, five days hence, the militias of the nearest shires were to gather at Blackheath, to join there the men already assembled or still in the process of arriving. Further messages were sent before the cold and the damp finally caused them to rise and drove them indoors.

"Do you recall that single dead apple tree?" Harold asked Gyrth as they sat before a fire laid in the hall in Westminster Hall. The wood was damp and slow to catch and there was more smoke than fire. "No," said Gyrth, honestly and with a degree of suspicion. "What dead apple tree would that be then?" Harold stretched out his legs and placed his hands behind his head. "I pointed it out to you once, I can't remember how long back. It marks the boundaries of three different settlements. It is on a hill called Caldbeck. A road goes north there from Hastings, I know it well. The track meets the hill there and then divides." He indicated with his hands. "This way Lewes, that way Maidstone. Both ways, London. The Normans simply have to come along that road and I need to be there to stop them. It seems to be ordained. That is the way we must travel and that is where this fight will be."

Gyrth yawned and climbed to his feet. "I must be off back to Blackheath," he said. "It will be dark by the time I get there, but perhaps Aesegar has arrived by now. Harold, Before I go, for the love of God will you please see reason? If you do not wish to listen to me then listen to Aelfric, to your mother also, to all wise council." Aelfric, who seemed to tire easily these days, stirred in his corner at the mention of his name. He had, like an old dog, awoken at the mention of his name. "Wait up and gather strength," Gyrth urged him. "What can William do when he reaches the Andredsweald, save burn a few more villages here and there and string his army out on the march? Let him come to us here in London. Let him move against Winchester if he so wishes. Each day we wait we are stronger."

"And then he would be in open country," snapped Harold. "You forget, Gyrth, the orders have gone out. We shall be at that apple tree seven days from now. That is my bargain with you. Gyrth, Go to Blackheath by all means. Greet my men for me, but be back here by noon." Gyrth, still in ill humour and unhappy, rose and left the hall briskly, his heels resounding upon the boards. "I'm for bed myself," announced Aelfric. He drained his mug. "The way things are going round here who knows what the morrow may bring? The Holy Father himself might front up with a couple of pails of strong drink and perhaps the Devil himself, God save us, to sing and play upon the harp."

In fact what the morrow did bring was an embassy from the Duke of Normandy, something as unexpected and as unlikely as old Aelfric's personal predictions. The Embassy had come wreathed and garlanded all about with evergreens and branches of pine cut from the forest, eternal symbols of peace and parley. Making deliberately noisy and ostentatious progress through the Andredsweald and with much blowing of horns and other loud noises, they came with reversed lances and upturned shields and other gestures of pacific intent. The Embassy was finally intercepted on the approach road to Maidstone by men of the Shire Reeve of

Kent without violence on either side. Now here they were, the foreign delegation, at London Bridge, heavily escorted and with grim looking Englishmen hedging them all around.

Under heavy escort, they made their way down the old East Cheap and Cheapside and past the Church dedicated to Saint Paul and then past the Cross outside and then along the Thames Strand Way, with its scattered homes of the rich and the market gardens. Forewarned, Gyrth and Haakon had been called out to meet the Normans at the small settlement at Charing and then lead them on the short distance to Westminster and the precinct before the hall. There Harold awaited them with as much state as he had been able to muster in the brief time available. His tunic was of imported silk from Cathay, with mythical beasts sewn and embossed upon it. Jewels and amber glistened on his fingers, about his wrists and around his neck. The leathers of his belt and leggings had been whitened and brushed and in place of a Crown he wore a simple and thin band of Welsh gold about his head. Harold's naked sword was held aloft before him, gleaming and running with oil, by a giant East Anglian and the Red Dragon banner of Wessex flapped and snapped above his head in the strong breeze.

The embassy from the Duke of Normandy and aspirant to the Kingdom of England was composed of six Norman knights accompanied by their squires. Blue chinned and shaven headed, the knights looked about them with an undisguised and keen, if concerned, interest as a path was cleared for them through the hostile and curious London crowd. At their head rode William Malet, bearing with him his usual heavy load of mixed emotions. At his side, astride a large toothed mule of a dun grey colour and possessed of a vicious temper, was the monk Hugh Margot. It had been piously hoped that Malet would appeal to the better and the more reasonable side of Harold, as a friend of long standing and as godfather to Harold's own daughter. The monk

Margot, for his part, carried with him the deadly venom and anathema of the Holy Church. Both, empowered by William, came with terms to offer. Suggestions and compromises were included in the diplomatic portfolio, along with the naked threats. First the carrot and then the stick, a tried and tested policy of the Duke.

Gyrth was waiting at the head of a contingent of his East Anglians as the Normans came to the small settlement of Charing. They had been friends once, from the old days. As they raised their right hands in greeting, palm forward, each noted with shock how much the other had so suddenly aged. As they came close they nodded curtly to each other. "I am very grieved to see you here and in these circumstances," said Gyrth. Malet did not bother to extend his hand to the Godwinson. "And I also," he said, with regret and bitterness.

All the way from the north side of the London Bridge to Westminster, Malet had looked carefully and closely about him, taking in the mood of the sullen crowd gathered to observe his progress. He took also the opportunity to rehearse the Fecamp monk in his lines. In that monoglot crowd of oafish English, they were perfectly free to speak in French. As arranged, they would present their arguments and then their suggestions. They would begin with the barely tolerable and then move on, as conditions might dictate, to the wholly unacceptable. When all else failed, as they both individually knew it would, then Margot would produce and wield the ultimate weapon; the threat of the bell, the book and the candle. He would bring Anathema to Harold, and God's own curse on the country and to all those who might support and shield him, the ultimate sanction. "This only hastens the day, my Lord," said Margot, physically wincing at the jeers of the mob. From the inferior height of his mule he was obliged to crane his neck in order to look up at Malet. "This will bring the English on only the faster. They cannot be expected to agree to any of these terms, leastways their

King can't. And as for what I have about me, well, you can imagine the result."

"Monk," Malet snapped at him, "hold your tongue. You weary me. Our Lord Duke knows fully well what the reaction will be. He seeks to hasten improvident action. You will speak when spoken to, and not before. If all else fails then you may say your piece, and may God preserve us from the consequences."

Malet and the monk were separated from their entourage at the entrance to the hall and permitted to enter while their followers were left to cool their heels in an outhouse, surrounded by heavily armed Englishmen. Malet strode up the middle of the near deserted hall, his hobnailed boots crashing and scraping on the wooden flooring. Margot scuttled, crab like, beside him. Seated upon a handsomely carved chair, Harold stared at Malet without any apparent emotion as the unhappy Anglophile approached and bowed low. "Well now, William," he said to his former friend and godfather to one of his daughters, "I cannot say well met to you. I feel too that I know what brings you here. What is that creature that you have there beside you?" Nettled by this, Margot spoke up readily enough and displaying that he was not lacking in courage. "My name is Hugh Margot. I am a monk of Fecamp and once of Herstmonceaux, since taken from us."

"So," said Harold. "It can at least speak then. What do you want, William? What does your master want?" Malet looked Harold directly in the eye. "Peace," he said. "Peace and justice, and a resolution to all outstanding matters."

"Malet," said Gyrth from behind Harold's chair, "you are foresworn. There is devil a sign of peace and justice from the Pevensey levels all the way to the Weald. Your Normans have made it a wilderness." Irritably, Harold waved his brother down. "Let's have it then, William," he said wearily. "Get on with it and say what you are instructed to say." There was no invitation to sit or offer of refreshment of any kind.

Malet's carefully rehearsed statement took the length of five leisurely expressed paternosters to deliver. Harold, expressionless, heard him out in silence. His men around him, however, were more vocal, alternately hooting with derision or roaring with ironical laughter, which Harold made no attempt to curb. All of this came as no surprise to Malet, who could well imagine Leofwyn's reaction had he but been present. First he presented the utterly unacceptable, an immediate surrender of all lands and titles and a full obeisance to the Duke of Normandy, upon pain of death. Malet concluded that particular threat amid a perfect uproar of derision and outrage. "I'll take that as a refusal then, shall I?" said Malet as equably as he could under the circumstances. "Harold, I'll take the cell next to your own in whichever monastery the Duke may allot to us of his charity. Together we can practice our plain chants and work a vegetable patch." Gyrth hooted with uncustomary mirth. "Not in any establishment of mine," added Uncle Aelfric, "I have a reputation to consider."

Speaking patiently and above the uproar, Malet's next proposal was an intriguing one, and a little tempting. Harold's eyes narrowed at the thought. Personal combat, to the death, with the winner taking all. There followed a momentary silence into which the various sounds of the outside world filtered, and more than one man there debated inwardly whether their King, tired and ill and out of sorts and lately come from a savage battle and a breakneck journey, could possibly win such a contest. Of them all there only Harold, Haakon and Malet himself truly knew the personal danger presented by this Duke of Normandy, with his anger and his absolute determination and with the fighting skills honed since he was a boy. Harold finally broke the silence. "A ridiculous proposal, as well your Duke knows it to be. William, this country of England is not to be ventured like some prize to be won on the throw of the dice and I treat the suggestion with the contempt it deserves. When I come against your bastard Duke it shall be with all my men at my back, as he will have his." Malet nodded, it was not within his prerogative nor would it be wise for him to admit that he agreed. Instead he bowed once more. "I have something else that I am instructed is for your ears only," he said in his flawless Sussex accent. Harold waved his arms at the men around him in a shooing gesture and they dutifully backed off a few steps. "You too, monk," said Malet to Margot, remove yourself from earshot."

Malet walked forward a few paces to where Harold sat. Malet was a big man and he leaned down to speak softly in Harold's ear. "My Lord Duke says this," he murmured. "Take yourself north. North of the Humber has been suggested, but this can be further discussed. Take all of the north as far as the border with Alba for yourself and your brothers. What becomes of Morcar is of no concern to the Duke and he himself will take care of Edwin. Only, in return, make your obeisance and your apologies to his Grace the Duke as the rightful King of England that he is. You would be his right-hand man in council, his rod and his staff. You would be his 'Dux Anglorum,' as so he did appoint you in Normandy, his deputy to govern all of England in his absence. Upon his holy oath, the Duke swears this." Malet stared deep into Harold's eyes and there was, Harold could see, a deep and passionate longing in his expression for the Englishman to accept this opportunity of peace. "In this way may the honour of both you and he be satisfied and seen by all to be good." Malet stood upright again. In his low and quietened voice he concluded. "I beg of you to accept this offer, my Lord. I speak as one who valued your friendship and your trust and who made the vows over your own daughter, my beloved Godchild."

Harold leaned back slowly in his chair. It was the old offer of the 'Dux Anglorum' once again, with certain and more stringent modifications. It had been this very same proposal which, to all intents and purposes, he had agreed upon on that fateful day back in Normandy. To agree now, to send Malet and the strange little monk back south with his acceptance, would be to avoid a vicious and costly battle and the deaths and maiming of many good men. It would also cost also him his own self-esteem and the esteem that he hoped all others held him in. By these terms he would, of course, surrender up his own beloved Wessex, designated instead to maintain it in the future as a mere caretaker, a man now stripped of rank by a fall in fortune and surrender. What, then, of the whole of the south east and the west midlands? the lands of his brothers and of young Waltheof? What of the trust the men south of the Humber had in him and the immense sacrifices they had already made? What of their blood at Stamford and on the way back south? No, this was the temptation of the Prince of Lies. Never again would he be able to live with his conscience, nor look honest men in the face again. He had taken up this heavy burden of Kingship and the guarding of souls at the very birth of this momentous year. It had been a year that had, aside from all else, brought two bloody encounters, a new wife and the promise of an heir, a Haroldson to carry on the line.

Harold thus required only a heartbeat to consider his response. He would carry this burden for however long the mercy of Christ permitted and to whatever end it then took him. The recently slain of Stamford Bridge and the rotting corpses of Fulford Gate were owed a debt. By God and all his Saints in Heaven! He would honour it, There was no way on this earth that he would tolerate a pack of Normans, booted and mailed, with their feet under the table in manors and farmsteads that had once belonged to Englishmen and him reporting to them like some reeve with the corn yields. There was no way either that he would tolerate a crowd of rapacious Norman clerics, a tribe he particularly despised, making free with the ancient ways of the English church. He would gladly die rather than see Englishmen tilling the fields and bringing in the harvest in order to fill the bellies of foreigners. He would see the Duke of Normandy in Hell first. The man could not anyway be trusted to keep an agreement and he had seen for himself how the Duke dealt with all critics and opponents.

More practically, there came to him also a vision of northern halls filled and brimming with excitable and irate men fuelled with drink and bravado, baying at him, urging him into revolt against the foreign usurpers in the south. He could see the day when, in seeking to balance the interests and aspirations of the Normans in the south and his own English in the north, he would find himself with William to his front and a mob of irate and rebellious northerners in revolt at his back. Perhaps this is what the Duke really sought, to bring him low in this ignominious fashion rather than sacrifice the cream of his army in an open battle. It would be better by far for William to reduce and humble him by stages and then move to encompass his final end, perhaps in the manner of the poisoned glove of Conan of Brittany, than to risk all on the chancy and capricious cast and fall of a dice on a battlefield not of his choosing.

Malet had retreated a pace or two and was now regarding him anxiously. Harold leaned forward and beckoned to him. "No, Malet," he whispered. "No, and again no. I refuse all terms." As they had both truly known from the start, it would be all on the throw of a dice after all. "Did your noble and glorious Duke truly expect me to roll over on to my back to be tickled? Surely you, of all men, my former friend and neighbour, the man who made promises to God on behalf of my own daughter, would expect better of me" Harold raised his voice for the benefit of all those in the hall with him. "Tell your carrion eating Duke that he is nothing other than a brigand and a rapist. The man is a wolf's head here in

England, explain the term to him, should you need to, when next you meet. King to Duke, I defy him. By God, Malet, I will move against him and crush him. And then, when that is done, he may seek terms of me. If he yet lives."

"Then," said Malet bleakly, "let us hear what this monk has to say." On cue, Margot drew himself erect and began to intone in his faultless English. "I have privilege of clergy and the blessing of our Holy Father. On peril of his soul, let no man here touch me." He turned to Harold, staring him full in the face. "Harold, Earl of Wessex, false and self-proclaimed King of the English. Know by these words that you are outcast from the bosom of Mother Church and from all of her holy offices. Without due penitence and restitution you are surely damned for all eternity within the pit of Hell. So too are all those others who offer you aid and succour. Our Holy Father himself, successor to the blessed Peter, decrees this himself." In the ensuing shocked silence he added, "I have a document about me to that effect."

"Worm!" The single word actually emerged as a feral scream. Harold was off his chair, both his strong arms wrapped about the monk's throat in an instant. Before the horrified gaze of all, Margot gagged and turned blue as Harold's thumbs squeezed into his windpipe, lifting him into the air. The unfortunate cleric was allowed to fall to the floor, wheezing and gasping for breath. Without pausing, Harold kicked him heavily in the ribs and the stomach then the face and, finally, the groin. It was a blur of movement, a flurry, before Gyrth, now galvanised into action, leaped forward to pull him away. Margot scuttled out of range and to the shelter of Malet's broad back, gagging and wheezing and with blood pouring from both nostrils. Harold too was breathing heavily, gasping for breath, his complexion red and mottled. He reached for the chair and seated himself once more. It was one of the most distressing moments of Malet's already very crowded life. When Harold spoke again above the excited voices of the others his own voice was once more even and measured.

"It has been a wasted journey for you, William. Today and tonight you are confined, you and your men. Food and drink will be brought to you. Get you back to your master with my answer. I think it is simple and clear enough even for the most pig stupid of his followers to understand. Tell him I will meet with him shortly. And take that piece of offal with you before I feed him to my dogs. By God, monk or not, he is lucky to be alive. May you and I meet again in happier times."

***

There had been no other churchmen present save for the dubious ecclesiastical presence of uncle Aelfric, a man who liked to keep his beloved battle axe, with most unchristian runes engraved upon it, honed and shining and dripping with linseed oil, at that disastrous and ominous meeting within the hall. Neither had there been any gaping mouthed servants to carry idle chatter abroad. For the time being this knowledge of Harold's anathema was something shared only by those present of the Godwin clan and those others whom he had come to trust with his life. For a certainty, Gyrth now knew what would surely follow. "I will wait," said Harold with decisiveness, "a further five days. And that is it. No discussion. We have wasted time enough. By Christ, Gyrth, do not cross me further." He smashed his palm upon the arm of the chair and winced at the pain of it. "Sweet Jesus," Gyrth pleaded with him. "Wait a while, give it another week. Let me go down there in your place with Leofwyn's people. We could hurt them a little, here and there, hold them up for a while."

"Gyrth," said Harold. "The south is burning about our ears and our people lie dead in ditches while we wait. And while we wait, the bastard grows stronger. You were not there in Brittany, I was. The things I saw there. Believe me, when the bastard lets his dogs off the leash there is no thing, no act, that they will flinch from. There is also the fact that the more time we wait then the more time there is for that poisonous little monk's news to be allowed to take root and spread like a weed. I should have torn his tongue from his head. I still might. That news, as you well know, would be a disaster." He kept his brother's gaze. "Neither am I a man to send my own brother to do my work in my stead. I am King of England."

"You'll not catch him unawares," Aelfric pointed out. "Not as you did the Hardraada. He'll be there waiting for you." Harold, in his fury, appeared supremely unconcerned.

"Then may God allow me to be there waiting for him," he said, "and on ground of my own choosing. If they are allowed to get their horsemen out into open country then we are in deeper trouble than we are in now. I want him bottled up in that horrid little peninsular and starving by degrees until his men eat first their own horses and then their leather boots and then their own dung."

Both Aelfric and Gyrth sighed with resignation, exchanging despairing glances as they accepted this final and irreversible decision. There was none of the raw and strident acclaim here of the epic poems of the old Saxons, no beating and hammering of knife hilts on the mead hall and the desire to be at the throats of the enemy, just a dull and resigned resignation. "Then," said Gyrth as he reached for the ale, "we had better have the scribblers in and more messages sent, for there is much to do."

The work took them all of what remained of that morning and then the afternoon and then the sounding of the bell for Vespers. Harold would travel to Blackheath on the afternoon of Tuesday, just three days from now. There he would review and encourage the men still arriving and gathering. "Haakon," said Gyrth, "I want those Danes there as well. Keep them away from strong drink and women if you can. We don't want London going up in flames. See to it." His nephew nodded and made his departure. At a point in the mid afternoon a man came in from Blackheath. Aesegar had finally arrived from the north with the remainder of the mounted men and the first of the footmen. "About bloody time." said Harold. "Tell him I excuse his presence here tonight. Gyrth, by this time tomorrow, sooner for preference, I shall need a full reckoning of all those fit to travel on from Blackheath."

Horses, ponies, pack animals, always a problem. To move as swiftly as they intended, they would need as many fresh mounts as could be found. On the previous day Harold had summoned Willi and Alfi and deputised them with the task, armed with a large and intimidating group of men. When, finally, they delivered their report, both were grey and swaying with fatigue. Of all his personal companions, only Willi, his appointed poet and fool, could speak to him with any degree of frankness. "You'll have lost one or two friends here in London over the past two days," he observed laconically, "but there'll be at least three hundred of the creatures of one form or another on the morning we leave, mostly without saddles and very few of them of fine stock. There's none too much to feed them with neither." He chose not to mention the intensity of the hatred and the anger that he and his men had aroused amongst the Londoners as they scoured the stables and livery yards and transport businesses. It was not necessary for him to do so, Harold would be fully aware of this.

"Keep at it," Harold ordered. "It is not enough. Let them hate me for a month or so while I keep the roofs over their heads. Cast your nets wider into the countryside. You have two more days for the task. Take what men you need and do not report back to me. I shall see you at Blackheath, and, I trust, with better news than you are telling me now." Willi grinned. He pulled at his forelock ironically and swept the simple boy Alfi out of the chamber with him.

More precise orders went out to the fyrds of Kent and Sussex. The rendezvous was fixed, the landmark of the old apple tree at Telham hill for the following Friday evening. Despite the continuing bad weather, the ships at Deal and Sandwich were ordered out to sea and to patrol off Pevensey Bay and Hastings. Messages went to Crayford, Rochester and Maidstone. The King's army would rest there, or there-abouts, on the successive nights of their march. Let there be food and drink in sufficient quantity provided and waiting. If this was not in excess, then at least make it, for the love of God, appear to be sufficient.

"What about Leofwyn?" asked Gyrth in a momentary lull between messengers. Leofwyn, their amiable and feck-less younger brother. He had been excluded from the march north and they had heard that he was, by all accounts, jealous and resentful. "Tell him to carry on bringing men in," said Harold. "We shall meet him either at Rochester or at Maidstone or on the road between. He is also to gather horses and provisions, as much as he can. He may fight the Normans where he meets them, but not in force. He is not to provoke a battle." The bell for Vespers tolled out sonorously in the Abbey nearby. The light had all but gone. "I would dearly love to rest now," Harold admitted, "and I am also starving." He sighed deeply and stretched, lifting his head and bringing his shoulder blades together. His back ached like fury and there was a pain in his side. "Gyrth, you haven't told me about Stigand yet."

Gyrth related the sequence of events as best as he could understand them with an enthusiasm and relish but, as with all matters relating to the elderly prelate, his account was full of ambiguity and half of the facts had yet to be proven. Even before Edward's death and Harold's accession, both

Gyrth and Aesegar had made it their business to monitor and observe the various comings and goings to and from Stigand's borrowed apartments at the Palace of Lambeth across the river, hoping always to catch the old man out in some way and encompass his fall. There had always been rumours of one sort or another regarding Stigand over all the years. There had been reports, for example, of his complicity with the Aelfgarsons in the matter of the marriage of Harold to their sister. Then, of course, there had been Stigand's own very publicly delivered Papal Bull at Westminster. This had very effectively cast him out from the Communion and from the protection of Holy Church. The man had seemingly lived like an anchorite hermit ever since, though what he got up to in the privacy and isolation of his own rooms over the river was largely anyone's guess. Aesegar had insinuated a cook, a groom and a highly promiscuous serving girl with an additional talent for embroidery into Stigand's household, each wholly unaware of either the existence or the purposes of the other two, and he thus received regular reports, mostly trivial and inconsequential, from all three of them.

The Archbishop suffered from gout, increasing failure of sight and an appalling flatulence. He also clearly entertained unchristian and lustful thoughts regarding the serving girl. Then, even as Harold was rushing north to fight the Hardraada and his own brother, the groom had at last earned his salt by suborning and corrupting a messenger en route to Rouen and the Duke of Normandy himself with the help of the sure promise of a very large bag of silver. The document was thus intercepted, conveyed and placed into the hands of a gleeful Sheriff of London. The messenger, duly rewarded, made himself scarce.

The message was read with mounting glee and jubilation and its contents were relayed to Gyrth the very moment he himself arrived back at Westminster. Without any hesitation, Gyrth placed an even stricter confinement upon the titular Head of Christ's Shepherd of the people of the Holy and Apostolic Church in England with an immediate effect and until further notice. Harold nodded with satisfaction. "It must have been good," he said "Tell me everything."

Gyrth smiled with a deep satisfaction. "It is treason, brother, treason, pure and simple. "We have him bang to rights this time, and with his tits well and truly in the mangle." Harold laughed, "You look like a cat that's been at the cream. Do continue." Stated bluntly, in his letter, Stigand offered himself up to the full disposal of the Duke of Normandy as mediator between he and Harold, King of England. If his best Christian efforts at peace on behalf of all were to fail, and if it then pleased God to grant William a victory, then he prayed that, in appreciation of his good offices on this and on previous occasions, his Grace, the most Excellent Duke, would be duly appreciative and grant him honours and favours in keeping with his position. Further, it was to be sincerely hoped that his Grace the Duke would intercede with the Holy Father on his behalf and seek to reconfirm him once more in his position as Archbishop of Canterbury, removing all stains of the Anathema.

"Good offices on previous occasions," mused Harold thoughtfully. He ran his fingers through his thinning red and gold hair as was his habit when considering. "And I wonder what they were?" Gyrth shrugged, "we can't lay a finger on him, of course. We can, though, make life very difficult and unpleasant for our esteemed Archbishop."

"I think," said Harold judiciously, "that it would be for the best that the world at large does not hear that for the time being the chief churchman in England is being held in confinement." Gyrth was uncharacteristically urbane. "Quite so. In fact, it is Stigand's own suggestion that it be put around that he is indisposed owing to ill health and his advancing years, until such time as he is able to clear up this most unfortunate misunderstanding." The brothers enjoyed the moment together. "No pampering now, Gyrth," Harold chided him with humour. "Bread and beans and lentils and water. It'll do him a power of good." Gyrth considered this for a moment. "What if," he said speculatively, "his indisposition was to worsen and in fact prove fatal?" Harold considered for a moment. "It is a thought, Gyrth. It is a thought."

There was no such levity the following morning, however, when Harold despatched his child bride to Lincoln. It was an encounter he had been dreading. Aeldyth had been at Westminster all this time, waiting anxiously for news from the north. She was Queen of England and she carried the child of a King within her. As of yet, she displayed no outward appearance of her condition, but the word was out at the palace, of course, and she passed her days in a claustrophobic cocoon of over-indulgent and fretful women companions and servants.

Naturally, her slightest whim was acted upon, on the instant if possible, but she was not afforded any real independence of movement and was in fact a virtual prisoner. Then events began to overtake everyone. In the space of a few days, items of news of a spectacular nature crowded in on the palace with a numbing regularity. Whilst all there were still grappling with the contents of the previous despatch, another would then duly arrive. News of all this turmoil naturally found its way up to Aeldyth's rooms in time and anyway she also had people of her own operating on her behalf, her seemingly senile old Welsh servant for one. She would sit for hours at the common hearth in the servants' quarters for hours on end, mumbling to herself, generally ignored and absorbing everything. Aeldyth, a highly intelligent young woman, was then able to sort the wheat from the chaff at her leisure. She knew also when she was being deliberately lied to and when, for whatever reason, people elected to place a gloss on certain events. Thus then, the news of the impetuous battle and defeat at Gate Fulford and the humbling and flight of her unlovable brothers and their headlong rush to the west, just like their father before them. Then, while she and all others were digesting this particular item of information and after Harold had embarked on his epic march north, there came the latest annihilating news. The Normans were upon them, and all the coast between Hastings and Dover had gone up in smoke and flames.

Leofwyn had been on hand and had spent a few moments with her, in the midst of all the confusion and bustle. She had always had a soft spot for Leofwyn and she especially liked him for spending the time, though he had felt obliged. "Now don't you go worrying about your brothers," he had said consolingly. "I'm not, and I shan't," she had replied tartly. "They can go to Hell in a handcart for all I care." Leofwyn paused, puzzled for a moment, and then roared with appreciative laughter. "So, you don't like them either. I thought it was just me, and also just about everyone else." then he was gone, bawling for food and drink and a scribe. Soon after came the news of Stamford Bridge and, after that, the news that Harold was on the march south again.

And here was Harold himself now, pacing fretfully up and down before her in her bedchamber, looking desperately tired and with huge black rings beneath his eyes and, once, stumbling upon the loose rug. "There is no time to discuss this, Aeldyth," he said firmly. "You will be met at Lincoln by a man of mine, name of Maerlswyn, He sees to things for me in that Shire. He is a good man and I trust him with my life, and, consequently, your life. He'll keep you safe from all harm, his life and mine upon it."

"Safe from what?" she demanded angrily. Harold, to her eyes, was looking much older these days, looking haggard and drawn. He gave signs also, through occasional spasms and winces, that he was in physical pain. He did not answer her question and so she repeated it. "Safe from what?"

"I am going south to meet the bastard and to settle the account," he replied, "two days from now. I would leave today if I could." She kept her voice calm. "And you will win?" He nodded. "I will win." He snatched at her hands as she sat there, looming over her. "This is just for the present time, wife. Until matters are resolved and you and the child can return to me." He hoped that that would be the end of it. "Then why may I not remain here at Westminster?" She was fully aware that she was goading and angering him. Harold let go of her hands. "Very well then, Aeldyth. It is simply said, and you force me to say it. Let us imagine for a moment that the will of God dictates that I shall not beat the man. Let us imagine also for a moment that the bastard moves on London." He regarded her bleakly. "God deny and forbid that that should ever happen, but what a prize you would be to him! But you will not be here. You will be at Lincoln, safe, as I said. And from there, if it proves necessary, Maerlswyn will have you sent to my kinsman Sweyn in Denmark. It is all arranged."

"It is, is it?" She actually sneered at him. "What is agreed? Let me tell you what is agreed. A fast boat to Denmark and then a lifetime spent in exile. What if the child I bear you is a boy? What then? What of him? Girls count for nothing. A girl would be auctioned off to some dung encrusted lout just as I was, not once, but twice. First by my own father and then by my brothers, God bless and keep them."

Harold hooked a small stool over with his foot and then slumped heavily upon it. Surely, she had not said those words? Surely, he had not heard them? Dung encrusted lout? He placed his head in his hands and rubbed his eyes. "Go on," he said, his face obscured and his voice muffled. "And if it is a boy," Aeldyth was remorseless and relentless, "then like as not he will turn out like that miserable little runt Edgar. He will be a foreigner in a strange place and the target and the focus of ridiculous little conspiracies and plots for all of his years. You, of course, by your own reckoning will have long since been pushing up the daisies. And then, Harold, then some fine day perhaps he will come back to England to chance his luck and his life on some bloody idiotic venture to claim his inheritance, and that'll be the end of him. Just like Edward's brother Alfred at your father's hands. I, of course, will not feature in this tragedy in any real way. Doubtless I shall be embroidering away in some dismal little barn somewhere until I go daft in the head and too blind to see any more. Perhaps I'll enter a convent and have done with it." Wearily, Harold raised his head. "Are you quite finished?"

"By the living Christ, no I am not! I am Queen of England, thanks to you and to those dirt bag brothers of mine. I do so hope that they are both well and in the best of spirits. I carry within me a child who may perhaps become a future King of England in his turn. I am not to be put aside like some unwanted and inconvenient piece of furniture."

"In times of uncertainty it is a wise man who puts his most prized possessions where they can come to no harm." said Harold rather pompously and, in the circumstances, ill advisedly. Aeldyth positively screamed at him. "Don't you dare to patronise me. Do not call me a prized possession. Do not deceive yourself Harold. I am merely your prized Mercian heifer. I am merely your property in return for the support of my brothers. Now that the whole world knows that they are just piss and wind where does that leave you and me?" Harold looked up again from his hands, his face miserable and resigned. "It leaves us married, that's where it leaves us, and awaiting a happy event. With our backgrounds, with our families, our responsibilities, then love within a dynastic marriage such as ours may well be too much to hope for. I had thought and hoped and prayed it was coming to us, perhaps, in the short time that we have been together. God above knows, but I have sacrificed much."

Aeldyth sighed and sat back, her anger evaporating. And that, she thought with compassion, was God's own honest truth. He was very close to her and she leaned over and stroked his cheek, a gentle gesture that surprised them both. "True enough, my Lord," she said, "true enough. Now then, I have displayed my anger and stamped my pretty little foot. You know my thoughts. So, console me then. Convince me. This is just a precaution that you take? I happen to like being Queen of England. I hear bad things of Denmark and of all things Danish, the climate, the food, the conversation. I do not wish to be there, not for anything."

"There, my love," said Harold. "I have said it. You will return to me from Lincoln when I have settled things." He smiled at her in what he hoped was a conciliatory and encouraging way. "Until then, keep safe and keep well." He rose to leave, anxious to be off. She knew with all her wit and instinct how very hard he was finding all of this and that there was the constant thought of Edith the Swan neck and his children boiling away in his brain. God help us both, she thought bitterly as they embraced. God help him, and God help me if ever I find myself an unwelcome and unbidden guest surrounded by boorish and incomprehensible Danes. She held him tight and, despite herself, began to cry. "My beloved," she said. "Come home to me safe." Harold broke free and winked at her roguishly, a tragic and transparent gesture. "I shall," he said. "And with gifts too. Until that moment, fare you well." And then he was gone.

***

Just beyond where the last of the houses of the sparse development of Southwark on the south bank of the Thames finally gave way to open and slightly rising land, a space given over to market gardens and small allotments, Harold rode his gift grey a short way off the track and onto a small knoll in order to view, and be viewed by, his army as it made its way past. The first of them, his personal royal housecarls and those of Wessex, were passing him now. They raised their fists in salute and bawled his name. They rode four abreast along a road that was still well maintained, but which would degenerate very soon into mire and potholes with this mob of men and horses and carts passing over it.

The tail of the army and the rag tag crowd of hangers on and camp followers that invariably accompanied such a gathering were still only now passing under the old east gate of the city walls. All along Thames Street and the Eastcheap the crowds had been gathering since the night before, their numbers now swollen by enterprising market traders and apprentices and servants on unsanctioned holiday. The prevailing mood was one of righteous anger and a cautious optimism. Ever since the news of the landing at Pevensey and of the reported subsequent outrages there had been a general alarm throughout the city and many of the wealthier had already decamped to their country estates or to relatives in any direction but south, taking the more portable of their possessions with them. The majority had elected to stay, of course, not having the luxury of any other bolthole.

The news of Stamford Bridge, naturally, had been immensely cheering and here now was their King on his way to serve up the same dish to the foreigners in the south, or so they fervently prayed. Here and there, individuals broke into the ranks to greet a relative or a person recognised, to embrace or link arms, to press upon Harold's men hasty gifts of fresh baked bread and ale and cheeses and preserved meats. Many of the London apprentices, overcome by the occasion and by martial ardour, simply took their place in the column. Some clutched makeshift weapons they had hastily snatched up, hammers and staves and the like, even though they had no obligation to the London fyrd and were thus adding to the huge problems of the already overstretched and desperate commissariat. With their nail studded clubs and rusty and blunt axes, these enthusiastic apprentice boys from the docks, the weavers, the butcher boys from the Shambles of Smithfield, the ale makers and fullers, proposed to take on the finest the Duke of Normandy had to offer.

They simply, Harold reflected, had no idea of the possible effect upon them of concerted archery and crossbow fire delivered from a distance. They knew nothing of the fury and the power of a heavy horse trained to maim and kill, moving at speed and bearing a mailed man armed with lance and sword and experienced in the dark arts of killing since early manhood. Harold sighed as he viewed them, remembering his own people who had died at Stamford Bridge. He simply did not have the resources to send the men he wished to turn these foreign murderers back. He acknowledged their greetings, as a Warlord should and glanced back to London. As with all armies on the march, at the head all was pomp and ceremony and the brave fluttering of banners. At the tail it was all chaos and anarchy.

It had begun to rain again, an irritating and depressing grey drizzle that depressed the spirits and rusted the chain mail. London Bridge was crammed with men, those on foot now, the exhausted and traumatised survivors of the northern campaign mixed with the inexperienced and happy amateurs of the fyrdmen of the home shires of Middlesex and Hertfordshire and London. The further back one travelled along the column, the lesser the quality and the experience of the men and the state of their equipment. At the front of the column, however, some of the finest and toughest fighters in Europe were still riding past the knoll on fresh and rested mounts. They were proud and superb men, eager and armed to the teeth.

"This could take some time yet," said a much older looking Aesegar to Harold. "An hour, easily, probably more.

They'll be strung out on the march for miles." Aelfric passed them at that moment at the head of fifty mounted housecarls and a body of armed monks. He drew aside and approached them in the company of the Abbot of Peterborough, who had brought a similar contingent. "All is well now," said Harold sardonically. "Here comes the Church Militant." His uncle greeted him, wiping the rain from his face. "Fine day for it," he said. The two Abbots joined the group of men there, Gyrth and Aesegar and Haakon, Godric the Shire reeve of Berkshire, and Thurkill of Bedford. Waltheof was still absent, laid low by the severe and raging fever which had gripped him after his wound at Stamford Bridge.

Standing just behind Harold were his favoured men and companions. Willi and Alfi held aloft, limp in the rain, the unfurled banners of the Dragon of Wessex and the Fighting Man, that banner so lovingly created by the King's mother. The previous night both banners had been blessed by the Bishop of London in a very public ceremony, still blissfully unaware that in fact he blessed the banners of a man under anathema. Leofgar was there also, looking especially sardonic and villainous and keeping his own council. At his side was Caedmon, resuming once more his role of King's chaplain. He had appeared the previous night, having absconded from Waltham, and Harold had not had the heart to dismiss him. He owed Caedmon far too much and, besides, he had carried a very special message. Only young Gareth was missing. Harold had entrusted him with a particular task upon the completion of which he was to join Leofwyn and wait for his arrival.

Harold's response to the poisoned tongue of the monk Margot and the catastrophic information he carried with him was to put the dismissed Norman embassy into the charge of a group of Welsh speaking borderers, the idea being that as their command of English was almost non existent and that neither Malet nor Margot could be assumed to speak

Welsh, the poison of their message would remain mute. Thus they would travel, mutually incomprehensible one unto the other, all the way back to the waiting Duke of Normandy.

Harold paused on that small knoll until it was clear that only the flotsam and jetsam was now crossing the bridge. The boisterous contingent of Danish mercenaries passed by, singing their own rollicking songs and Haakon, their liaison officer and interpreter, peeled off to accompany them, raising his hand in salute and farewell. Harold cantered along the fields to the side of the line of march to take up his position at the head of his men on their journey to the scheduled overnight stop at Crayford. Only that morning he had received the terrible news from Lewes and there was a black rage in his heart that now quite overcame the fear and despair.

***

The previous evening, he had walked amongst the men at Blackheath as they camped out in the open. The harvest was in and the gathered army was well fed and seemed confident enough about the future. Everywhere he recognised and greeted familiar faces. His old gift for putting a name to a face, and often an accompanying anecdote or shared recollection, did not desert him here and those he thus greeted flushed with pride and pleasure. He recognised two men and gave his greetings, Storre and Oktel, both Danes from the far north. He remembered then that Oktel's wife had once put before him a fine and very welcome dish of braised lamb. He remembered the food, but not the background circumstances. He slapped the back of a man called Gebor and reminded him of the time he had had him fined for insubordination at the camp at Chester before they first went against the Welsh. The man grinned with pleasure, reminding him politely that, no, he was from Ely and not

Cambridge. The brothers Aeldryd and Osborn from Bristol were just fine, unlike their brother, who wasn't. He had died at Stamford Bridge and Harold shared his memory with them for a moment and praised his sacrifice. He had, he was reminded, once dandled the baby daughter of Ulf of Peterborough and given her a fine piece of black Whitby jet to play with. He remembered neither the man nor the incident, but he slapped his shoulder boisterously all the same and asked after his daughter. There were many such encounters that evening before he finally arrived back exhausted at his billet. It was the home of a local merchant adventurer, a man obviously doing well enough for himself, to judge by the fixtures and fittings.

There could be no rest yet, though they would all be up well before the dawn. A group of thegns were crowded into the single lower room awaiting him, anxious to greet and drink with their King. He indulged and humoured them before finally they were ushered out into the night by an impatient and irritable Gyrth. The leader of the Danish mercenaries, a squat barrel shaped man named Grimketl, proved less easy to remove. Haakon finally lured him away with the promise of a fine brothel he knew of over the way at the Shoreditch. Harold raised his eyebrows and sighed to himself as they left. That boy was so similar in so many ways to his father, Harold's dead elder brother. Aelfric and the Abbot of Peterborough, an ill-assorted pair if ever there was one, were off to pray at St Mary's All Hallows in the nearby village of Barking. Perhaps the King would honour God and the church by accompanying them? No, Harold had said, by now informed of the arrival of Caedmon. He would make his devotions with his personal chaplain.

Aesegar remained, armed with an inevitable list. Perhaps he had been born clutching a list. He was a private and self-contained man, utterly devoted to his task and with a strong and unshifting sense of duty. Looking at him now, Harold realised with a pang of guilt how little he actually knew of the man and how much he owed him. Aesegar spoke rarely and when he did it was always directly to the point. It was hard to imagine that in fact he had a house full of happy and exuberant children and a patient and pretty wife over in Bread Street. Persuading the man to sit and take a drink, Harold was conscious of how much he had come to rely upon him. In that frantic month of January Aesegar had been indispensable, scouring the streets and wharves of London for disaffected Normans and Flemings. While Harold was making his progress through the midlands and the north, Aesegar, keeping Leofwyn on a tight leash all the while, had been in virtual overall command in the south. He had ranged far and wide, executing the King's justice and maintaining his peace and making the time defying journey north ahead of Harold and had been at the Stamford Brook. He had led the battered army back here to the south and would have had very little opportunity to return to his turbulent, noisy and happy little overcrowded home. Spymaster, legislator and administrator, the dark and lanky Londoner with his diffident ways and nervous tic had been a tower of strength. "Aesegar," said Harold, "I have not been mindful of you."

"Lord?" Aesegar's tone was puzzled. Harold smiled, having reached a swift and impromptu decision. "I owe you much. Please accept my gratitude." Aesegar writhed with embarrassment and stared at his boots. He was a thegn already and the leading man in London and in all of Middlesex. "When all of this is over," said Harold, acting upon his impulse, "then half of the annual tithes and duties owing at Rotherhythe and Queenshythe will be yours and for your family in perpetuity. I shall have this drawn up and approved when time permits." Aesegar grunted, as if suddenly dealt a powerful blow to the stomach. Salt and fish, oil and leather and candle wax, ale and cloth and wine. This and much more was landed daily at the two wharves, and much duty exacted. Such a gift would multiply his present income many times over. An embarrassing silence fell over them both as Aesegar began to do sums in his head. "Now then," said Harold briskly and rubbed his hands. "What do you have for me?"

Six thousand fighting men, give or take, was what Aesegar had for him. Others were still arriving all the time from all over the country. He could only speculate as to what numbers Leofwyn and the levies of Kent and Sussex could bring to Telham Hill. Perhaps as many again? This was unlikely and anyway most of those gathered would be next to useless and woefully ill equipped. It would be a leaven of local thegns and their followers mixed into a thick porridge of local peasantry armed with bill-hooks and knives fastened to staves. They would, to be sure, make up the numbers, but they were likely to present more problems than solutions. These men would stand behind the shield wall, a stiffening of the defense, an advantage in advance and a total liability in retreat. Aesegar seemed to read Harold's thoughts. "We can assume perhaps two thousand good shield wall men," he said, "and we have those Danes gifted to us, of course." Only now, they both knew, would the thegns of the south west and the Welsh borders be setting about the raising of their own militias.

"There is one thing you need to know," said Aesegar. "There's many a battle won by bowmen. We have very few, they took a lot of casualties at Stamford Bridge. The Normans, though, will have many. It is essential we have more bowmen. I have a message also that Waltheof is now on the road south and raising more men in Huntingdon, I cannot give you numbers. There is no real news of the Aelfgarsons save that they are reported to be gathering their people at Derby."

Derby. That made sense, standing as it did on the cusp of Mercian and Northumbrian lands. Both knew also that

neither the willing Waltheof nor the unwilling Aelfgarsons
would arrive in time. "Lord? If I might say one thing?" Harold
nodded at him encouragingly. "Why will you not wait?" On
the instant, Aesegar regretted saying it. There it was, the
same question again. Harold considered his answer. "I have
my reasons, Aesegar. Go and rest now. Tomorrow you will
be the busiest of men. All those arriving within two days of
now are to follow on. Those arriving later than that are to
remain here in London until ordered otherwise by either
me or by someone bearing my writ. Is that understood?"
Aesegar bowed low. "Understood, my Lord." Harold dusted
his hands vigorously, as if the matter were settled. "Then off
with you now. My best wishes to your family and to their
future prosperity."

Which left Caedmon, who had clearly been waiting and
then almost immediately entered the low beamed single
room with deference and caution, fully expecting a rebuke.
Outside the men of Harold's personal gathering were still up
and active. A fire was bright and fierce in the yard and men
were roasting mutton over the flames on the points of water
drenched sticks. There was a festive atmosphere, with men
made especially loud and vocal by companionship, drink and
the occasion that had brought them all together. The voice
of Gyrth could be heard, ordering them to quieten down and
get some sleep. Harold smiled at his chaplain. "Well then,
Caedmon, my little absconder. And what brings you here?"

"You do, my Lord. You and my own responsibilities. I
am your man and will remain with you always, come what
may." He shifted his weight from foot to foot and scratched.

"Then you are most welcome. Will you hear my confession before I sleep?" Caedmon nodded. "It is my task and
privilege to serve," he said simply, "though you do have the
offices of a Bishop and two Abbots about you for that." Harold
smiled fondly, wearily, at the man. "They do not know what
you know. Neither were they with me in difficult times in

the past." Caedmon was clearly very ill at ease. "I am most honoured, but first I carry a message for you."

"From whom, Caedmon? Who would give you a message to give to me?" Caedmon hesitated. "It is from your handfast wife, my Lord, from the Lady Edith." Harold's heart skipped a beat. "Edith? You have seen her?" Caedmon shook his head. "No, my Lord. But a man of hers came to Waltham two days back and gave me this." Fishing about in his scrip, he pulled out a package of rolled vellum, still stitched and with a seal that Harold recognised instantly, the stamp of her ring upon the wax. "I am instructed to deliver this into your hand directly," said Caedmon. Tactfully he added, "and to read it to you unless you wish some other lettered man to do so. I am told that it is of a very personal nature." There was an awkward silence. The multiplicity of Harold's skills did not extend to a full and accurate reading of a document. It was so typical of the good sense and wisdom of the woman to entrust this to Caedmon. "Well then, you are my confessor and my old hearth companion," Harold finally said. "They are trusted and revered positions, the both of them. Sit yourself down and read it to me. I can think of no other better suited to do so."

Caedmon fumbled with the stitching and straightened the document out with a crackling sound. He held it up to the uncertain light of the fire and the candles flickering on the table beside it in order to see better. Harold, while he waited, imagined Edith dictating this message to an equally trusted scribe at her home and temporary refuge in the fenlands, with the youngest of the children roaming about underfoot. He hoped that the message would be short and light and uplifting. He was not to know, did not yet know or suspect that, in defiance of his instructions, she was even now on the road back to Bosham.

Caedmon cleared his throat and began, peering at the script written in the vernacular. There were, first, the usual and customary greetings and salutations, the place and the day. It had been written on the very morning that Harold had arrived at Waltham. The messenger had been swift indeed. Family news. The two oldest boys were still, respectively, at Norwich and Worcester. The Bishop Wulfstan sent his greetings and blessings. Harold's son, he reported, was well and happy but still, sad to say, lax in his duties and studies. Harold smiled to himself. He would have to take the boy away from there soon, perhaps send him to live with Waltheof. He would see to it upon his return. It had been arranged, Caedmon continued, for the oldest boy to come across from Norwich to stay. He had got himself into a bit of trouble, it seemed, a maidservant was expecting a child and he had not denied the allegation. Harold felt old then. Perhaps he was soon to be a grandfather, and his oldest son was old enough to stand in a shield wall. The other children were all well and thriving and missing their father.

There followed accounts of the successful learning of a particularly difficult psalm, an incident involving an experiment with poisonous berries in the kitchen, a fall in a midden and rides in the pasture on a patient little pony led by the equally patient Oswy. It all sounded like a rural idyll, and one that he was desperately anxious to share. Caedmon paused and frowned. Harold glanced at him. "There can't be that much more, Caedmon," he said. "Let's have it."

Caedmon read woodenly. "'Harold, my beloved. I love you with an intensity that I cannot put into words. I fear for you and I pray for you constantly. Do you recall we talked of exile? Of some place in Ireland where the grass is always green, and all men are scholars and poets? I would that you simply gave all of this up, that you turned your back on this country and that we went away, far from here and the troublesome Duke of Normandy.'"Caedmon glanced furtively across at Harold, who was himself staring blankly at the ceiling. He continued to read. "'But I know you will not. Come back to me safe, my heart. I pray to God, to the Blessed Virgin *and all the saints to keep you well.'"* Caedmon laid the document on the table. "That is it," he said gently. "It ends there." But Harold was not listening. His head now in his hands, he sobbed aloud with grief and loss. Caedmon was horrified, not knowing what to do or say. "My Lord," he whispered with compassion. Harold sniffed noisily and stood up. "No, no, Caedmon. I am fine enough. I am only glad that it was you and no other who read that to me." Caedmon bowed his head. "She loves you, my Lord, as do we all. Surely there is a solace in that?" Harold nodded in acknowledgement of this. "Some, Caedmon, some. Take my confession now and then leave me, I would sleep. It will be a long day tomorrow."

CHAPTER TEN:

Pacifying the South

Senlac Ridge: October 11th to

October 13th, 1066

They had been eleven days in England now and the army had grown fractious, bored and ever hungrier. The first few days, to be sure, had been exhilarating, days full of adventure and raiding, profitable and enjoyable days of theft and pillage. The years had seemed to shed like unwanted scales from Robert of Mortain, who hadn't enjoyed himself so much since the Brittany campaign. Odo was reported to have squirrelled away a tidy sum in hard cash and other valuables, judging from the activity around his encampment and tents of heavily laden and smug looking men. FitzOsbern, so the rumour went, had a beautiful English heiress hidden away somewhere and far from prying eyes. William very much doubted it and his beloved Fitz was vehement in denial. Quite how this could possibly have been achieved and then concealed in an armed camp brimming with thousands of curious men was not considered. William laughed and demurred when FitzOsbern invited him to search his camp and belongings.

And then there was nothing, for the best part of a week. Patrols went out and came in with monotonous regularity and each time they returned, on occasion leading riderless horses, they returned with less and less. By now the people of the surrounding countryside had simply melted away, flickering shadows in the thick forest of the Weald and where the Normans seldom ventured. From Rye to the east to Hailsham in the west, north to Bodiam and the start of the forest, William's men dominated the countryside. Between these three points, each with a garrison within a hastily constructed motte and bailey, they were busily employed in stripping the country down to its last elderly cow, ring worm riddled sheep and hayloft of wrinkled apples. The grain and pulses, the flour and the dried and salted meat was now doled out in ever less amounts as each day passed. They had not yet reached a crisis but, given another week of this, they soon would. Had William but known it, some sixty miles to the north Harold was being urged on all sides to delay. Here, on this bleak and dismal coast, on the other hand, William was being urged to hurry by the more bellicose of his advisers. True, there were those among the army who still muttered at the foolishness of the venture and who counselled evacuation before the arrival of an English blockade, Eustace of Boulogne for one, and FitzWimarc for another. William treated with them harshly, and in private. Still, the mood of the men was not good. They despised and feared this cramping peninsular between the waters of the Brede and Bulverhythe. It was a natural trap and they wanted to be out of there and in good open horse country where they could do what they were best at. The garrison at Bodiam reported back laconically on the fate of a missing archer, drawn by cupidity into the tree line. He had been found nailed to a tree at the forest's edge, and had been treated harshly before he died.

Within their temporary stronghold at Hastings, FitzOsbern, having taken the collective pulse, was delegated by the various leaders to question and push the Duke. If any man could get away with this then that man was surely FitzOsbern. Robert was too simple minded a man for such a task and Odo had ever kept his own council and ploughed his own solitary furrow.

Thus urged, FitzOsbern sought out the Duke and drew him aside. William heard him out in silence before replying. "He will come, Fitz, he will come," he said finally. "I know the man, and it will be soon. He does not have the virtue of patience, as I have. He acts upon the instant. I have seen it, as have you. When he does come then only then will he realise he should have waited."

"With all due respect, my Lord, that sentiment will not fill men's bellies or their purses or justify to them the reason for waiting. There is unease in the camp. They hate this place and the men feel like rats in a trap. In truth, this is not good fighting country for us."

It had begun to rain heavily. Men now gathered beneath it now for yet another gathering. A tarpaulin sheet had been secured to the inner wall of the wooden keep, kept taut by attached wooden stakes driven into the ground. The rain drummed and roared on the fabric and occasional spouts collected and fell to earth. The mud was ankle deep, rank and chilling. Beneath the pattering cover, William and those with him lunched off cold meat, bread and apples. The wine was provided by the Bishop of Coutances, who appeared to have an inexhaustible supply of it. Each day, apart from the old companions, William included a few of the other leaders to have lunch with him, an excellent tactic. On this occasion it was the volatile Aquitanian, Aimerie of Thouars, struggling as ever with the northern French speech, along with William de Warenne, Hugh of Montfort and Hugh de Grandesmil. All of the others were making as best shift as they could elsewhere. None of these men present could, in the language of the camp, be called 'rabbits.' They were all seasoned fire eating warriors, which was precisely why FitzOsbern had now engineered their presence on this occasion. Aimerie, an eccentric and a foreigner and thus allowed to behave extravagantly and speak as he saw fit, threw an apple core out into the mud and rain. "I say we move," he said in his musical, sing song voice. "FitzOsbern is right. Two days march from here is Dover or Canterbury, or Winchester even, anywhere, anywhere but this God forsaken hole. That will draw the English on, especially Winchester."

"Imagine the fun we could have in Winchester," Grandesmil mused dreamily. "We are running out of food," said de Warenne, striking a practical note. "The only serious threat of force lies to our north. East and west of here they are just a cowed and leaderless rabble." William decided to sound reasonable. "I am not interested in half-baked skirmishes with the local peasantry. I want one decisive battle, so too does the Earl of Wessex. And it will be hereabouts. You have my word on it."

"Fine by me," observed Robert of Mortain. "Why get blisters on your arse looking for a fight when if you did but wait long enough it comes looking for you?" William smiled. "Thank you, brother. That is precisely the point." Mortain beamed with pleasure, as he always did when receiving praise from William. FitzOsbern rolled his eyes with frustration. "What makes you so sure? And when will he come?"

"Any day now, Fitz. You may be sure of it. His pride will not permit him to wait much longer. Besides, these are his own lands we are so comprehensively laying to waste. The man is arrogant and proud. He is also full of confidence since he dealt with the Hardraada. He also thinks to trap us here. I know his mind. The quicker he comes then the easier he will be to beat. Mark my words. There is also, of course, the matter of Malet's visit to him, him and that monk. Any news of them yet?"

There was no news and so, with a sigh, FitzOsbern acknowledged defeat once more at the hands of a master. Tonight, once more, he and Odo between them would send their men out to the encampments and around the fires, armed with strong drink and encouraging words, staving off ever greater dissent with encouraging words for yet another night.

All will be well, the English will come, and we shall strike them down.

Malet, in fact, arrived back at Hastings at mid-morning the following day. All in all, he and his little retinue had had a truly punishing time of it over the past week. There had been that cold and cheerless night confined to a barn in Westminster with a grudging meal of stale bread, water and rancid bacon followed by three grueling days on the road in the company of their laconic and silent Welsh bodyguards. True enough, neither he nor the bruised monk had been able to communicate with them. At Maidstone they were obliged to run the gauntlet of the intensely hostile Kent militia. Stones had been thrown, and worse, and Thorald of le Bec had nearly had an eye put out by one.

Luckily for them, Leofwyn had been on hand to restore some semblance of order and for one night at least they had eaten and slept reasonably well. The journey beneath the dripping trees of the Weald had been a nightmare and had any loose packs of English decided to take matters into their own hands they would not have stood a chance and the Welshmen would have simply stood aside and watched. Just short of Bodiam they were turned loose and were obliged to run a further gauntlet through a screen of justifiably nervous Norman outposts. Of them all only Neel of Herve, a man who was fast rising in the Duke's council and estimation and who had volunteered for the task of bringing them safe home, could be said to have found the experience both interesting and enjoyable, but then the man had ever been a law unto himself.

William had Malet directly brought to him as soon as he received news of his arrival. Malet was ushered in, bow legged, blue jawed and ashen with fatigue from the whole experience. William adopted one of his favourite stances, legs astride, hands on hips and jaw jutting forward aggressively as Malet, the monk Margot and Herve entered his presence. "Have a good time?" he greeted them sourly. Irreverently, Herve grinned, which the Duke chose to ignore. "You look a sorry state, the three of you. I take it that you do not in fact bring me news of the abject apology of the Earl of Wessex, that he is not with you, barefoot, in sacking and with a halter about his neck?" Malet and Herve, of course, were well experienced in William's own particular brand of heavy sarcasm. Not so the monk, Margot, sporting a black eye and a badly gashed lip. "No, my Lord," he began. "In fact, when I began to speak he assaulted me."

"Speak when you are spoken to, toad," William snapped at him. Despite himself, Margot marvelled. "That is extraordinary. For his part, Harold called me a worm." William emitted a single bark of laughter. "Let's have it then Malet."

"Well then," said Malet. "It is easily said. You have a fight on your hands, and soon. Within days, if I'm any judge. It goes without saying that he rejected all of your arguments and demands, all of your offers, out of hand." William nodded sagely, "as I knew he would. Go on." At his side the little monk was bobbing and seething with anger and the need to speak. "He beat me," said Margot incautiously and with indignation. "Me, an emissary of the Holy Father. In his own hall, and me with the protection of Mother Church." William afforded the monk an icy stare. "I am not in the least bit surprised. I would have acted in no other way myself. I shall attend to you later. Remove yourself'"

"I felt dissent there," said Malet after the monk had gone, "that he and his brother, his family, were not in agreement. His family and all the others close to him want to wait, I am sure, until they can come against you in overwhelming force. Harold, though, there is a man who cannot wait to see the colour of your liver."

"Good, very good. It is as I wish it to be. Who else was there?" Malet shrugged, "there was his brother Gyrth, a dangerous and a capable man. There was that young sprig Haakon and Harold's uncle, the Abbot of Winchester, no real Churchman, him. Some earldormen and thegns, I knew a few. No sign of the Aelfgarsons or of Waltheof. His brother Leofwyn we encountered at the place they call Maidstone." William nodded, another item name to add to his expanding vocabulary of English place names. "I take it that you were not granted the honour of an inspection of his army?" Malet smiled. "Indeed not, your Grace. We were locked up for the night and then escorted straight back here, or rather to where the forest ends." William began to pace, his head bowed and his hands behind his back. "So, what can you tell me of his plans and preparations? Can you put a number to the size of his forces?"

"Quite a size, London," remarked Herve. "Not that we saw that much of it, from the London bridge to Westminster. They have an open space beyond the city wall to the east, a place they call Blackheath. It seemed to me that that is where his men are gathering. That, and our encounter with his brother at Maidstone, tells me that this is the route he will come by. The way to Westminster was full of armed men. They are angry and confident. I would put his force in London at between four and five thousand, with more besides coming in, and those we encountered in that forest on the way back, God help us all if we have to fight through that."

"He is awaiting reinforcements from the north and elsewhere," Malet added. "His brother Leofwyn had a good thousand men with him, many were housecarls, their first rank and finest fighters. All the way back through the forest we came across smaller groups of men making their way to some meeting point, twenty here, fifty there, all were moving south, not really fighting men, any of them."

"All on foot?" William demanded to know. "Saving their leaders, yes," continued Herve. "Three days and they'll be here is my best bet."

"And where is 'here,' exactly?" mused William. "I shall tell you. 'Here' is some six or seven miles to the north of us, that is where. "It is where the London roads cross and meet. Malet, you know where I mean. I want a screen of scouts out beyond that and on the Maidstone road. They can leave immediately and take the men at Bodiam with them. Give the job to de Tosny. He's always bellyaching that he's bored. I think also that we could do with a spot more provocation, just to make the point to the Earl of Wessex that we are not simply going to go away. I want him to hear that we seriously intend to move west, towards Winchester perhaps. That will throw his plans out a little. This place called Lewes, Malet. Tell me about it." He stepped back and regarded the man.

"Well, it is a tidy way from here, your Grace. There is a track of sorts that leads to it through a place called Polegate." Polegate, now a smouldering ruin of ash and charred timber and with dogs howling out from the gutted houses and gnawing at the rotting corpses. "Lewes is some twenty miles from here as the crow flies, longer, of course, along the track way. The going will be hard this time of year."

"Anybody left with fight in them in this place?" Malet considered. "I very much doubt it. The men of that place will now be mobilising and probably moving north to, what is the name of the place? Uckfield. "Yes, Uckfield. From there they would move along the southern fringe of the Weald to join up with their main force which, as Herve has said, is definitely moving on us from Maidstone." William nodded his satisfaction. "And," continued Malet, following the inescapable logic of the reasoning, "some thirty English miles beyond Lewes is Chichester, and Harold's most favourite home at Bosham, and where his family lives."

"Perfect," said William with a deep satisfaction, "just perfect. This is of course merely a feint. Harold might hope to catch us from behind. We are moving too far west than is really prudent. But, just for the sake of argument, if I were to unleash my gentle brother Robert, how long would it take for them to be aware in Lewes that he had come calling, and how long before they had news of this in Westminster?"

"A few hours of hard riding, perhaps six? As for this all getting back to the Earl of Wessex, that would depend upon whether he was still at Westminster or already on the march. Across the downs, as the English call them, and open country his chain of beacons would bring the news to London within a very short time. If he is on the march to the east then he would not hear until much later, depending upon the quality and speed of his messengers." William clapped his hands together. "It is now perhaps noon. My brother Robert is a good man for seeing in the dark. By God, by Vespers this evening they'll know all about him at Lewes."

William had no cause to doubt either the enthusiasm or the ability of his brother for such a task. No encumbrances, no infantry, just two hundred armoured knights in five separate groups of fifty men. By nightfall they had brought death and destruction to the small communities on the road between Polegate and Lewes and up onto the open downs beyond. It was the furthest west that the invaders had so far ranged, entering into areas where the locals had perhaps felt themselves safe for the time being. At Alciston they roasted the priest alive in his blazing church. At nearby Selmeston they drowned the priest there in the village pond, throwing stones at him to speed up the process. The little village of Glynde was next, though a knight who removed his helmet to wipe his brow was brained by an expertly thrown sling-shot coming out of the dark from an unseen assailant.

Beddington was best of all. Just about within sight of Lewes itself, the separate detachments met up and torched the large and prosperous village. A few appalled survivors fled the mile or so to Lewes with the news. At Beddington Robert called a halt and rested his men. He had had three fatalities and a number of men injured. There, encamped upon the high ground of the downs in order to afford him a better view, Robert watched a chain of beacon fires flare up into the night. From where he stood he could see five alight in quick succession, stretching far to the north east. Harold, if he were still in London, would have the message before the dawn, even if he did not know quite what it signi-fied, he would know that it came from Lewes and thus form his own conclusions. It had been a highly enjoyable day out, especially after all the recent inactivity. He gave orders for pickets and guards and a dawn departure. They would be back in time for lunch.

"Come now, a bit of effort please. You're not even trying." Neel of Herve was in the process of encouraging an itinerant priest, a native of the Anjou borderlands who had at some point attached himself to the expedition. In his time with the army the man had acquired a reputation for visions and the interpretation of dreams and portents and had as a consequence become quite well known. "If not a vision, then at least a promising dream," Herve wheedled. "Then my good friend Taillefer here can set it to music." By way of encouragement he pricked the priest gently on the neck with the point of his dagger.

"There was the time of the Comet, the hairy star. I was awoken by a cry," the priest began falteringly. "Done that one already," remarked Taillefer moodily. "God knows, they've heard it so often that there's now an alternative version with accompanying hand gestures. Think again." Since his encounter with the witch soon after his arrival in this rain sodden island and the foretelling of his own death, Taillefer had quite understandably become introspective and withdrawn. "Do you mind the time the Duke fell upon the sand?" asked the priest, struck by a sudden inspiration. "I saw that before even it had ever happened. His Grace fell and gripped the land with both his hands. I remember a voice came to me and..."

Exasperated, Herve slapped the man's face, hard. "No you weren't, and no it didn't. Clear off, you old fraud. Fat lot of use you've turned out to be." With gratitude the priest made himself scarce. "I shall report you to the Provosts" he shouted at a safe distance and Herve laughed derisively. The two men drank the sour wine of the flagon in a companionable silence. "I'm working on a new song," Taillefer announced at length. "The trouble is, I don't think I'll be around long enough to complete it." Herve, normally a man not much given to emotion, was moved. He counted Taillefer as that rare thing, a true friend. "Some presentiment, perhaps?" he asked.

Taillefer laughed. "You could say that. You do not enjoy the benefits of an education, you old Breton goat shagger. I was for the Church once. Did you know that? Until my brother got himself the lockjaw off a rusty nail and upped and died of it I was all set for the cloister. I was at the monks' school at Fecamp at the time. I slept through most of the lessons, but I do remember some of them. I woke up once and heard this story of an army. I don't know whose or when or even who they were fighting. Anyway," Taillefer sought to make himself more comfortable and took another pull at the jug. "Anyway, the leader of this army was told in a dream that he would prevail, but only when one beloved of him sacrificed himself, piling in alone against the front ranks of the enemy." Herve, a pragmatic hedonist and always a man for the moment, liked neither the tone nor the direction the conversation was taking. "You silly old sod," he said. "You're making me miserable now with all this talk. Tell you what. One of the Mainards has a woman with him that he hires out. What say we stroll over there? I'll treat you, it's on me." Taillefer smiled at him. "Might as well, I suppose," he said. "Then his Grace the good Bishop of Bayeux has paid me for the night again, to haunt the camp with encouraging songs and back slappings. I have a bit of time in hand."

***

He was coming, William knew it. He knew it with every logical thought and unfounded instinct. He knew the man, as he kept saying. Harold had lied on oath, on an impulse. He had rescued two foolish boys from a hideous death in shifting sands, on an impulse. Yes, he would come, acting on one impulse too many. It was close to dawn on the morning of Friday the thirteenth of October. William had barely slept, lying restless and awake on his pallet and listening to the sounds of the rain as facts and figures and logistics crowded out sleep. There was already a wood pigeon awake, cooing away incessantly on the roof. As on previous nights, he was in the downstairs room of a sequestered house in Hastings, its former occupant either dead or a refugee. He remembered when Hastings had been given over to the army. The man was most likely dead. He had left behind him few possessions to mark his life; some miserable sticks of furniture, a fine copper cauldron above the hearth, a woollen coverlet and some blankets. There was little else besides.

The boys, Drogo and Hugh, fidgeted and snored on a shared straw mat at the room's entrance. They were fine boys really and he would shield them from all that lay ahead, if he could. They were too young and unworthy as of yet for knighting. If the truth be known they were only middling good in their duties, for all the frequent beatings. But William loved and indulged them, for all his rough ways with them. True devotion was hard to come by. He was feared and respected and obeyed by all, but, he knew, he was loved by few who were among him now.

It had been his own towering energy and ambition that had brought them all to this place and to whatever lay beyond. He wanted this country, he wanted it badly, if only in revenge for the insult and the humiliation inflicted upon him that morning when the messenger had splashed ashore at Rouen and ruined his hunt for him back in January. He could, he knew, have outfaced that initial humiliation and outrage and still remain the unchallenged Duke of Normandy. A few weeks and perhaps the whole affair would have blown over. He could have expended his energies and those of his volatile and turbulent followers instead in sorting out affairs in Maine and Anjou, long overlooked, or else gone fishing in troubled French waters. There was plenty to do back home. He sighed, knowing that all men feel depressed and doubting at the cusp of the dawn and with no sleep at all. Well then, he would have Harold, and finish him. He would reward his men and quench the fire of their ambitions with lands and heiresses and wholly new and artificially created titles. He had gathered about him the finest army in Christendom, better by far than that rabble of the Hardraada or the stinking peasantry now facing him. Having already made a name for himself with generations yet to be born, he would further compound and strengthen it with the glory of his victory over the English. People would talk of him for hundreds of years to come.

He glanced across again at the FitzPons twins sleeping there in the half light. He had been younger than them, far younger, when he was orphaned, not knowing if the next day or night would be his last as he was hounded from one corner of the Duchy to the other. Fitz understood. He had been there and shared the times with him. His, he reflected not for the first time, had been a truly horrifying childhood. In fact it was fair to say he had had no childhood at all. This was why he was as he was, and no amount of good acts and endowments to the church and confessions and acts of faith could change this. He could change neither himself nor his vaulting ambitions. He would, he resolved, instead seek to live, in the future, more through his children, the girls, young Robert, his beloved eldest, and the baby they all called Rufus for his bright red hair. William swore, enough of this foolish wallowing. Today would be a busy one. Today he expected real news. He sat up and lowered his legs to the floor, reaching for his cloak to cover his nakedness. "That's quite enough of that," he said loudly to the boys. "Up, up, you useless pair." He nudged them fully awake with his foot. They squirmed and began to climb to their feet. "Hot water and my shaving things, one of you."

Yawning and bleary eyed, the boys stood. "Sleep well, did you?" he snarled at them. "Well, I am so glad. Get me young Beaumont here, quick as you like. And fetch me food." As if conjured by magic, Beaumont's son appeared at the doorway. He looked as if he had been up for hours, as indeed he had. Almost by default, he had become the Duke's chief warrant officer and aide de camp. "Ah, there you are, Beaumont," said William as Hugh and Drogo scuttled about and got in each other's way. "Let's all attend to nature and have a shave first and then I want the following men to attend me in one hour. Still raining, I see. We'll meet in the church." He reeled off the names and Beaumont muttered them to himself as an aid to memory. William had in fact named every significant leader in the host. This was to be a full gathering of all his principal men, his war council.

***

They made Crayford in excellent time, despite the state of the roads. By nightfall the last of the foot were joining their comrades in the meadows and orchards around the settlement, though such baggage as there was still far to the rear. There Harold learned that Lewes, though badly scared, still stood and that the marauders had apparently withdrawn to the east. He grunted his satisfaction. No matter, he was committed now, and on the march. That night, despite everything, he slept well.

The following morning, with the dawn, the army marched and passed Dartford near to the estuary of the Thames. A small contingent of fishermen and boys attached themselves to the rear of the column, now beginning to straggle, and turned due south. The rain was beginning to create difficulties to the condition of both the road and the men who marched along it. By the time they reached Gravesend, where Leofwyn was nowhere to be seen, it was well past noon and the army stretched back a good five miles from vanguard to rear. His brother, the locals had told him, had left the previous day, they would find him at Maidstone.

Harold knew this road almost as well as he knew the route over the downs from Guildford to Bosham. It wouldn't be fun, but he could be in Maidstone by well before nightfall. After a moment's thought he decided to press ahead with Gyrth, Aesegar and Haakon and a force of one hundred mounted housecarls, deputising his uncle to see to the line of march. "I shall be leaving Maidstone at dawn tomorrow," he told him bluntly. "Many of these men here will be marching through the night, I know. But I want an army behind me, not a rabble, when I move on in the morning. See to it as best you may." Aelfric pulled a sour face. "There had better be food there," he grumbled. "There was nothing at all back there in Crayford. We can't keep these men going indefinitely on a diet of war cries and psalms." Harold chided him. "God provides for all. Have you not always told me so?" Aelfric stared morosely at Harold's departing back as he and his escort rode up the track and into the gloom of the trees. "God helps them who help themselves," he muttered belatedly.

Harold splashed across the river just south of Rochester and drove his following along the track and past the little settlements with their ancient Kentish and newer Danish names. A few miles north of Maidstone the land rose and a clearance had been made upon this higher ground of Bluebell Hill. There, gathered on the hillside, Leofwyn and the men he had raised in Essex and Kent awaited him. As his brother bounded towards him enthusiastically, like some large affectionate puppy, Harold attempted to calculate the numbers gathered there in that chanting and gesticulating crowd, he rather thought about two thousand or so. Perhaps less.

Leofwyn, red faced and beaming and with his standard of the Boar held beside him, would have brought his own house-carls, some fifty well trained and hardened men, all of them mounted. There would also be those thegns of Essex and Kent with their own followings, well armed but inexperienced. Say, for the sake of argument, another two hundred men or so. The rest would be general fyrd. They could not be faulted for enthusiasm and determination, but they were a rabble, none-theless. More staves and billhooks. Harold sighed to himself. Well, it could not be helped. He mourned once more all those dead of Fulford Gate and Stamford Bridge, experienced men who could truly change things.

It took some time to calm Leofwyn down after the joy of the reunion and the excitement of the encounter. "Well, brother, it's glad I am to see you, and Gyrth there. Haakon, you young rascal! Not dead of women yet then?" Haakon beamed, proud of the notoriety of his many love affairs. Harold smiled fondly at his brother, a man denied the glories of the north. He had done well enough here.

Leofwyn was now peering back over Harold's shoulder at the track beyond. He too was doing his own calculations. He looked anxious. "Rest easy," said Harold. "The army comes on behind. Perhaps as many as six thousand. Can you count as far as that?"

"Not even if I took my boots off and counted my toes," said Leofwyn and laughed uproariously. "And what do you have for me here, Leofwyn?" His brother turned and looked behind him. "My own personal following," he said. "And as many of the men of Essex who could reach me in time. There are people here from Romford and Basildon and from as far north as Chelmsford. The men of Kent are still coming in. We got your message and we'll be met at that place of yours by more levies from Kent and Sussex, but here," he waved expansively, "we have eight thegns and their men, and the people of Chatham and Gillingham."

"How many, Leofwyn?" asked Gyrth gently, "and how many true shield wall men?" Leofwyn waved his arm once more, looking exasperated. "How the bloody hell should I know?" he demanded. "I haven't counted them yet." And there in a nutshell and as Gyrth and Harold exchanged glances, was their brother, revealed in all his strengths and weaknesses.

***

Waltheof of Huntingdon, following the old road, arrived at the London Bishopsgate at nightfall on a blown horse suffering from saddle sores. Waltheof's leg wound was heavily bandaged and still oozed blood and pus. He also had a spectacularly high fever and was made slightly deranged by it. Two devoted men, playmates of his none too distant childhood, rode to either side of him, lest he should topple from the saddle. It had been an unbelievably swift journey from the north and Waltheof's personal leech, a Jew of

Lincoln called Mordecai, was gratified at his own skill in not only keeping the Earl alive, but also up and moving. This boy, the last surviving son of the formidable Siward, had pushed himself to the limit. The walls of the city swam and shimmered before his burning eyes and he wished simply to sink to the ground and sleep for a week. Perhaps that would remove the fatigue and the pain of the leg and the blinding headaches. Whenever he closed his eyes all he saw was purple and red and sparking white flashes of bright fever light.

Behind him, equally exhausted and starving, came a personal following of some three hundred men. They had deviated off the main road south just below Tadcaster, knowing as they did that the way, the obvious route to the south, would have long since been swept clean of all food and provisions. Thus they did well enough for themselves with food and fresh mounts on this longer journey. Rejoining the main London road, they passed straggling groups of walking fyrdmen plodding doggedly towards London and they urged them on as they passed.

Waltheof half walked and was half carried to a nearby inn just within the walls and there presently, in the absence of Aesegar, the deputy shire Reeve of London was brought to him. The Jew of Lincoln, Mordecai, fussed and fretted over the Earl's wound while the London official delivered up his news. The King had left that morning, leaving instructions as to the meeting place and a number of guides. Waltheof winced as his leg was dressed with fresh bandages. "Cobwebs," said the Jew enigmatically. "Cobwebs would be good. Still, no matter. Do you have moss upon the tiles here?" Everyone present continued to look baffled. "Food and drink for my men, for the love of God," Waltheof commanded, "and provision for the horses. The men shall rest where they are outside the walls for the night. We leave again in the morning." The physician opened his mouth to protest and then decided upon silence as the best policy. He was fascinated and intrigued to see how far this man could go. He had grown fond of this stupid, oafish goy, but nonetheless he longed deeply for the sunlit arcades and courts of his native Cordoba, where patients did what they were told and all the medicines and herbs and poultices of his profession were present in abundance.

"But one day of rest at least, surely?" the Deputy Shire Reeve protested, not that it was within his interests to accommodate and feed a force of three hundred ravenous men and beasts. "Our Lord King, by all accounts, scarcely paused, "said Waltheof. "Why then should I? A bowl, if you please. I am about to throw up."

***

Far away to the north, at Derby, the Aelfgarsons were locked once more in strident disagreement while their respective armies, or what remained of them, sullenly licked their wounds and sought to bolster their injured pride. The brothers' angry and upraised voices travelled beyond the hall and into the courtyard where the servants and housecarls of both brothers listened in an enthralled silence. Mercifully, their voices did not reach as far as the encampments of the select and general fyrds of Mercia and Northumbria, some two thousand disaffected men. Rumour and gossip, however, of this incessant bickering between the brothers was already common knowledge.

"You snivelling little shitehead," Edwin was now yelling at Morcar. "You delay now and you are lost." Outside in the courtyard a Northumbrian thegn raised an eyebrow at this and looked enquiringly over at Aelswyn, a thegn of Mercia. Since the disappearance of Edwin's right hand man at Gate Fulford, Aelswyn had managed to engineer himself into a senior position. He smiled now conspiratorially at the Northumbrian and waved both his hands down gently, once, twice. It was a conciliatory gesture, one of peace, and he winked. "Let these two infants have a good old shout at each other and sort themselves out" was the clear meaning of the gesture. "No need for the likes of you and I to fall out over it." The Northumbrian understood, nodded and relaxed, throwing a warning glance at his own followers. Dear God, but wasn't everyone and his dog sick to death of the Aelfgarsons?

"So just shut your face and give your arse a chance for the moment," Edwin snarled. "Just listen to me." Too late, he became conscious of how far sound could travel on a still evening such as this and he lowered his voice. "Harold took our sister in return for the support of the men of Mercia and Northumbria. Can you remember as far back as that? After Fulford and after Stamford, especially after Fulford, he is of the opinion that our support is not worth a nun's fart. This being so, and if he is granted victory against the Norman bastard, then what use has he for you or I if we don't lift a finger to help now? He can set our sister aside, put her in some convent or something for the rest of her days and strip us of our Earldoms. He wouldn't think twice, believe me. Waltheof will take your place in Northumbria quite happily and do not fool yourself that you will be sadly missed. I know how things are there. As for my Mercia, who knows? Perhaps absorbed into Wessex? My best guess is that he'd divide it up between Gyrth and that nephew of his."

It was a long speech, and he was not at all sure how much of it Morcar had absorbed. Edwin was still incandescent with rage. He put his hands on his hips and screwed his nose up. "I say we should wait and see," he said in a whining and lisping parody of his brother's voice. "You make me sick."

Morcar, sullen and equally angry, was crouched on a stool and staring at the floor boards. "And so we should, wait, that is. I still think so." His eye was still bruised and purple from the single injury he had carried away from Gate Fulford. "Wait for what?" Edwin hissed. "We leave for the south tomorrow, and with you tied to your horse if that is what it takes. If we do not put in an appearance to assist the Godwinsons and they then beat the Normans without us then, let me tell you, it is all up with the House of Aelfgar. Do you really fancy Scotland or Wales or, God forbid, Ireland? The very best we could hope for would be Flanders. Do you fancy being an exile for the rest of your life? Well, would that give you pleasure?"

"No," mumbled Morcar, defeated. "Why don't you leave me alone? I'm not well." Edwin rolled his eyes in exasperation. "And if this Norman Duke wins? What then? Do you fancy your chances with him?"

"We would be safe enough here in the north," said Morcar, defiance again in his voice. "We could treat with him for terms."

"Dear God. Do you truly believe that?" Edwin's voice rose in pitch once more. "You have the brains and the backbone of a sheep. We leave for London tomorrow, the pair of us. And that is an end to it." The argument flared and crackled for a short while longer until, in a fury, Edwin slapped his brother across the face twice. Morcar yelped and Edwin hurled himself onto his straw mattress. "You had better get some sleep," he said. "You are going to need it." Outside the thegn of Northumbria and Aelwyn heaved sighs of relief and exchanged a further glance. Both were relatively elderly men, the one a former servant of the uncompromising and straightforward Siward and the other of the charming and feckless Alfgar, men both now long since in their graves. They had known how to do things differently and these two elderly servants, both out of their time, mourned their passing.

***

The town of Hastings, where no man was now permitted to loot or destroy buildings in search of firewood, lay in a narrow valley running down to the harbour and set between the two towering cliffs. On the higher of these the Duke's team of builders, masons and carpenters had been hard at work for over a week on the construction of a fortified position. Already a ditch had been dug and a mound raised within it from the spoil. Upon this the beginnings had been made of a circular wall of raw undressed flint and stone laboriously quarried from nearby. Piles of timber lay piled up, stacked neatly. Wooden pegs and iron nails had been carefully collected and stockpiled on the strict instructions of William's thrifty master builder.

It had still been dark when William climbed up the track in a fine drizzle to survey the progress of the work, his jaw red and smarting from the pumice of his shave. He turned on his heel and made his way back down to the town. He had been expecting the drowsy and sullen awakenings of the encampments, bored sentries, the occasional rousted out and resentful servant on some errand. Instead he encountered quite a crowd staring out beyond the harbour with its nestling, nudging invasion barges and to the open sea beyond. He followed the direction of their eyes and gestures as he pushed his way through the gathering crowd.

Out there, beyond the harbour and beyond reach of harm, he saw other vessels. He cursed and began to count. Where his boats were plodding mules, donkeys, these newcomers were sleek greyhounds. Slim and streamlined, they lay in station, bows facing the harbour. There were a score of them. With their slender shapes and flitting oars, backing water occasionally to maintain their station, they looked for all the world like the insect water boatmen of some Normandy pond. Beyond these, displaying their flanks and with raised shields over the sides, were another ten, progressing gracefully from east to west. A blockade, by God!

They were trapped within the harbour. William stamped his foot in anger. "Do I see you skulking there, Martin?" He had spotted the Flemish pilot in the crowd of men. Martin detached himself from the others and cautiously approached the Duke, fully expecting the flare up of the famous Ducal rage.

William glared down at him, rocking on his heels and arms behind his back like a master of men at arms. "Well?" he demanded. "I would not set too much store by it, your Grace," said the master mariner. "They'll be out of Sandwich and Dover, sailing with the wind behind them. It is a show, a display, nothing more. They'll not be able to stay there like that for long. Season, time and tide will force them off soon enough. That, and lack of food and water. Maybe a day or two, and then they'll be obliged to move off, my word on it."

So then, thought William to himself. A show of strength and intent. Harold had indeed served notice that he was coming. He himself did not understand the sea, but he knew that the Earl of Wessex did. William, perversely, felt encouraged. "You hear that, you lot?" he demanded of the glum faced and anxious looking little knot of noblemen standing close by. "Spread the word to that effect around the camp. This is mere display, the shallow gestures of a dunghill cock. But it does mean that the English will be upon us soon. The waiting is over."

***

The central aisle of the small and cramped Church of Saints Mary and Martha was dominated by another of William's beloved sand trays. Four planks of wood formed the edge of the rectangular shape. Malet, Margot and FitzWimarc had spent a happy few hours, reminiscent of the play of childhood, the previous evening in creating in rough the shore line, the two rivers and the trackway heading north to the convergence of roads at the higher ground of Caldbeck Hill. They had bickered amiably as they heaped mounds of damp earth to denote high ground and placed lengths of blue ribbon to indicate the rivers. They picked out the intended route with a line of rusty chain links from a discarded hauberk and placed pebbles here and there to indicate villages and hamlets. They had, the three of them, enjoyed the task immensely and at last stood back to view their efforts with an unconcealed pride. This, more or less, was the land as a bird would see it, flying over.

William had a travelling foldstool brought for him, as had the venerable William de Warenne. Like the Hardraada, William had discovered that meetings and assemblies proved to be shorter and more productive if men were obliged to stand and so no seating arrangements had been made. What seating there had been in the church, the pews and stools, had long since gone up in flames. As he entered the church, men hard on his heels, quite a crowd was already gathered. Not all were present. De Tosny, de Laisle and Geoffrey FitzRotrou were away with the pickets to the north. Humphrey de Tilleul still ploughed his lonely furrow over at the toy castle in Pevensey and both Tustin FitzRollo and Roger FitzTurold were guarding the roads to east and west. William walked through the parting throng and seated himself at the head of the sand tray. There were the two Bishops, Odo and the Bishop of Coutances. His other brother Robert, jaded and liverish, looked as if he had had a hard and enjoyable night of it somewhere. FitzOsbern, saturnine and sardonic as ever, hovered at his elbow, inwardly predicting William's opening sentence.

Mutual despair and desperation had thrown Eustace of Boulogne and young Enguerrand of Poitou together in a conspiratorial corner. Looking at them, William frowned. He would have to do something about those two. Some of the old faithful, Hugh de Montfort, Hugh de Grandesmil, Walter

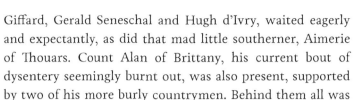

Giffard, Gerald Seneschal and Hugh d'Ivry, waited eagerly
and expectantly, as did that mad little southerner, Aimerie
of Thouars. Count Alan of Brittany, his current bout of
dysentery seemingly burnt out, was also present, supported
by two of his more burly countrymen. Behind them all was
a crowd of the lesser nobility, more were craning their necks
at the Church porch.

"Gentlemen, I shall be brief," said William, and
FitzOsbern smiled to himself in secret satisfaction at the
accuracy of his prediction. "Well, now. We arrive at the
heart of the matter. You will all of you have seen the English
out there beyond the harbour. There is now no going back
from this place. Their army I expect tomorrow, or perhaps
the day after." William carried a stick, and with it he indicated the line of chain mail links leading to the heaped earth
of Caldbeck Hill in the sand pit before him. "Between this
point and where we now stand are some eight English miles.
I have had men walk it and ride it slowly at the pace of a
wagon. When the time comes, of course, we shall make this
distance very quickly. We shall make the journey in less than
three hours. If we do not then heads shall roll. I do not speak
lightly." He paused for a while to allow the threat to sink in,
some there were not the sharpest blades on the cutler's stall.

"The most of us here will be in the vanguard with our
cavalry. My Lord of Thouars, you shall be second to move,
with the contingent of the French and Flemish horse. My
Lord Count Alan, you shall be first with your Bretons and
the others." This reference to 'the others' was in fact a
polite euphemism for the flotsam and jetsam of the landless
knights. The Bretons were held in a general contempt and
the men of Thuringia and the other German speakers were
a lawless rabble of mercenary and dispossessed younger sons
drawn to the enterprise from the Empire. Added to this,
there were equally unpredictable and independently minded
young adventurers from Italy and Spain, a sprinkling of

Hungarians and a man who spoke very rarely but said he was Irish from a place called Tralee.

Count Alan winced, no man there envied him his task. "I wish you well of it," said William cordially. "You can begin by getting them to camp down with your Bretons this evening. I shall be most displeased to hear of any disturbances or unpleasantness. Now then, to continue. The knights of Normandy shall come next, to take up the central position on the battlefield I shall describe to you presently. Infantry and archers next, my Lords FitzErneis and FitzRollo with their followings shall lead them. My Lords Warenne and de Tosny will take up the rear. De Tilleul will remain at Pevensey until further notice and Richard FitzGilbert and Ralf of Tancarville will remain here at Hastings with their men. They have been informed."

Briefly, he acquainted them with the contents of the sand pit, pointing out the major features and the land upon which the battle would be fought. He indicated the positions that each separate section of the army was to occupy and how they would deploy. "Mark it well, my Lords. Mark it well." William glanced around, searching for any visible signs of dissent.

The unspoken thought was shared by all there. "What if we lose? What about those English boats? What about a mob of vengeful and rampaging English at our backs?"

William never embarked upon such a statement of intent without careful thought and consideration, and a review of possible objections. "That is it, my Lords. As I say, I expect news very shortly, perhaps tomorrow. All of you see to your people, inform and prepare them, put some fire into them. I want everything in order. I do not wish to ask twice and I do not expect to be bothered with any minor details. If anything occurs to you or needs to be dealt with, then I refer you to FitzOsbern here or to our Seneschal, Gerald. The Bishops of Bayeux and Coutances will celebrate Mass at the time of Vespers and I want your chaplains to do likewise with your men. The day's rations will be delivered at the harbour side this morning, same as usual, and the men will receive a double ration of wine, bread and meat. Tell them to be sensible with this, as I cannot guarantee them a meal tomorrow. That is all."

The noblemen began to troop out in a lively buzz of conversation, their day already mapped out for them in a busy round of activities that would keep them on the move until past nightfall. FitzOsbern, last to leave, hovered in the porch beneath the crudely carved tympanium and its vivid images of hell and destruction. "Well, go on then," said William irritably. "Ask the question everyone wanted to ask but no one did."

"Very well then, and by your leave. What if we lose?" William smiled at him. "Then we are in deep, deep trouble Fitz. If we lose then it will be because a third of our men will be casualties, dead, or as good as. Those that live will come racing back here and to the boats. If the boats have not been burnt then there will still be the English out there somewhere beyond the harbour. They would have any of us who attempted to leave for breakfast. The English in front of us, on the other hand, will either rush us at Hastings or simply sit down and watch us starve to death. In any event, you may be absolutely sure that it will be the end of us all."

It was a sobering thought. "I think that answers your question adequately enough," continued William. "If, on the other hand, we do lose but remain as a cohesive whole and in a position of strength, then the English might just choose to treat with us, as they did with the Danes in times past." He uttered his characteristic bark like laugh. "They might even pay us to go away. If I survive this battle, Fitz, and if we lose, then what chances do you give me of surviving even a year if ever I get back to Normandy? If, that is, I am permitted to leave at all."

FitzOsbern shrugged, "Just thought I'd ask, that's all."

William leaned his broad shoulders against the rough flint and masonry of the wall. "That is why we shall not, must not, cannot lose. What I have just described is a picture of what every man, unless he is a complete cretin, has seen in his mind's eye. There are those, of course, who lack either imagination or fear. I envy them, truly I do. For my brother Odo and for Coutances there is benefit of clergy, something even the English understand. For all others, yourself included, defeat is a bleak prospect and with no niceties such as the payment of ransom."

William slapped the wall a few times. "So then. I do not like to venture everything on a single throw of the dice, but here I am obliged to make an exception. I wonder how long those boats out there really can stay like that? It is a wise man who makes plans for an uncertain future, Fitz. Only a fool or a dreamer makes plans founded upon an imagined future success." They left it at that, each going his separate way and towards a very busy and eventful day.

***

It had been hard work to rouse the men at Maidstone. There were several reports of men simply dying of exhaustion in the night, whilst others were not so exhausted that they had been unable to rouse themselves in the dark hours and slip away back to their homes. The Godwinsons and their uncle and nephew and the dependable Aesegar roamed the fields and pastures cajoling, bullying and rousting the men out and awake and into some semblance of an order of march whilst those housecarls that were still mounted saw to their beasts. There were empty and growling stomachs, gripped with cramps, and the constant exhortations and blessings of chaplains as the army moved off once more into the forest and with the cold rain of the previous night dripping from the eaves of the trees and down the back of their necks. Attempts at rousing songs faltered and died away and they had about them little of the jollity they had displayed as they marched across London bridge. Well beyond nightfall the previous evening, Aelfric had shepherded in the last of the footmen and those who had caught up with them from London. These had been the hardest men of all to assemble that morning.

By noon, trudging through the dense and intimidating forest, they had got only as far as the village of Staplehurst and the line of march was once more strung out for miles. There was now no food to be had beyond that which the more prudent of the men had conserved in their wallets and packs. In the van, the elite followers of the King and the Earls were bearing up well, grim and determined and occasionally bursting into snatches of song. At the rear Aesegar, who had not slept the previous night, and his equally exhausted provosts were resorting to heavy blows with sticks upon the labouring backs of men and were obliged from time to time to go chasing off into the trees after absconders, occasionally they were successful, most often not. The rain and the darkness of the forest cast a depressing shadow over every man there. Some slept as they marched, occasionally falling beneath the stumbling feet of those following.

The thegns of Staplehurst and Hawkhurst with their combined following of forty men and a crowd of excited villagers awaited the army with what they had fondly imagined to be a veritable feast of bread and meat, cheese and ale. The provisions scarcely went beyond the first ranks of the housecarls and the villagers scattered before the hoots of derision and shouts of anger of the rest of the army as it passed by the empty tables set out there. Shortly after, they crossed the Kent ditch and into Sussex and more open country. It was midafternoon. There was a moment of excitement as they flushed out the lonely and nervous outpost of ten Norman knights and their followers at Bodiam, their first sight of the enemy being their fast retreating backs. The Normans would be back at Hastings with the news before nightfall.

Leofwyn, for his part, was in party mood, as if on the way to a wedding feast. He twirled his battle axe on its short leather thong and bawled out songs either of a military or amorous nature, encouraging others to join in. The youngest of the three brothers there, he had not been in the raiding parties of the Godwin clan during their period of exile fifteen years before. True, he had seen the devastation after Northampton, but he had not been with Harold and Tostig in Wales and he had not experienced the horrors of the two recent battles in the north. His experience of violent and sudden death, of spilled entrails and brains and the slack jaws and staring eyes of butchered men was strictly limited. As a consequence, he was like a child in anticipation of a long overdue treat. Even his young nephew Haakon had seen more during his Norman boyhood and, more recently, in the north.

Harold and Gyrth, more experienced and worldly wise, were not inclined to disabuse him. Leofwyn was, after all, good for morale and his enthusiasm buoyant and uplifting. Gyrth, a thoughtful, prudent and provident man who ever prided himself on thinking ahead, was angry with both of his brothers. He was angered by Lefowyn's unthinking high spirits and with Harold for this headlong leap into the unknown. By now his every last argument had gone stale. Most immediately, what were the men to eat or drink? There had been nothing for them since the very little that had been available the previous morning. They could not exist on fresh air and puddles of rain water and for a fact he knew that no provision had been made for them at the meeting place of the dead apple tree. The men would arrive there by stages through a landscape laid waste by the invaders and then be required to fight a battle. On his occasional canters back down the line of march to confer with Aesegar he had seen men gathering acorns, horse chestnuts and beech mast, attempting to pound them into a pulp to eat as they marched. They would be stomach griped before long.

Gareth the Welsh boy approached the brothers, holding out smoke cured bacon and stale bread. "There are men back there," said Gyrth grimly, "who have not eaten in two days. How can I eat when they cannot?" Harold stretched painfully in his saddle. "This food will only provide for three," he observed, "and so it might as well be us."

"Fair point, agreed," said Leofwyn, leaning across to snatch at the food. "How much further can these men be driven without food in their bellies?" demanded Gyrth. Harold bit hungrily into the bacon. "They are driven, as are we all, by the need awaiting us. These are extraordinary times, Gyrth. We can seek rest and the bounty of the harvest when we have seen to things here."

"There is food in the wagons," added Leofwyn. "There is some food in the wagons," Gyrth corrected him, "and not enough. Besides, those wagons are miles behind. For all we know they haven't even reached Maidstone yet."

"Haakon," commanded Harold. "Back to Aesegar with you. Tell him to send fifty men on horses back to the wagons and to collect as much food as possible. They are to distribute this to the men, beginning with those in the rear that they first encounter on their way back. They may also commandeer pack horses." It was a concession, and Gyrth was thankful for small mercies.

It was shortly after this that they began to come across the first of the bodies. They lay sprawled and slumped in ditches and in fields along the way, men, women and children alike. Some had most obviously been lying there for some time. English dead in English ditches, a growl of anger arose from the men each time they encountered them. Harold's face was set and angry as he gazed upon a woman and two children, their bodies already gnawed upon by wild animals. "Do you see now why I hurry, brother?" he said to Gyrth. "By God, they will suffer for this in their turn."

Harold's Brittany veterans rode in a huddle slightly behind their King and provider. Leofgar and Alfi appeared quite unmoved by this first evidence of the Normans, but the other three were struck with the same emotions as their master. "Remember Brittany?" Leofgar asked them. "We were all there. We have seen this all before. Breton or English, a body is a body." Willi nodded his agreement. "True enough," he said. "Remember what you all saw there," continued Leofgar. "You can only do this kind of damage if you are quick and mobile and have plenty of space to move around in. Remember how exposed a horseman is on his own? Or even a small group? Let's see them try to do this against a good old-fashioned shield wall, and with men swinging steel at them." This remark seemed to console Willi and Gareth, though it was hard to see if it had left any impression on simple minded Alfi. Caedmon continued to offer up prayers to God in his head as he passed each body in turn. Willi thought for a while and then raised his voice in a shout, invoking the one insult guaranteed to drive the Duke of Normandy into an unreasoning fury. Soon his cry was taken up by the men around and behind him and went rolling and booming back along the length of the army. "Out tanner, out tanner, out, out, out!"

***

The single chapel bell of the Church at Hastings began to ring out. Men, puzzled, paused in their work and looked up at the sky. Too early for Vespers, surely. The bell continued to toll and the men of William's host began to gather together in larger groups. Messengers came amongst them from the Duke himself from the primitive castle on the high ground. The English had come at last! They had been seen and were on the road south leading to them. Before matters could get out of hand and ill conceived rumours be allowed to fuel the flames, their individual Lords arrived, ordering them to finish off what they were doing and then return to their lines, encouraged by blows and curses. Up within the emerging castle, where men were now redoubling their efforts with the construction work, William was receiving the latest intelligence reports from FitzWimarc and de Tosny, both of whom had arrived in person with the news.

"It is as you said it would be," said FitzWimarc, "though it is clear that this is only the vanguard. They are well past Bodiam now and with my own eyes I saw the Dragon of Wessex and the Fighting Man. With them was the Blue Boar of Kent and the Ship of East Anglia. His brothers are with him."

"All three of them," said William with satisfaction. "Good, very good."

"Smaller groups of men have also been seen," added de Tosny. "Footmen, moving in from the east and the west. They'll most likely be Sussex men. His main army is still on the road behind him."

"Back you both go then," said William. "I want you and your men on this Telham Hill. Keep good watch for me and I want to be informed immediately of any new activity or any new arrivals. Do nothing to provoke them. You may withdraw if they advance upon you, though I doubt that they will. We shall join you there in the morning. Enjoy the rest of your day."

Mass was celebrated at the appointed hour, both Bishops gorgeous in their robes and vestments. Below these costumes both were armoured and at Odo's side his great iron mace slapped at his thigh as he moved. Being a man of the church, he was forbidden to shed blood with a naked edge. The Holy Banner of the Pope was taken in solemn procession through the camp, the men kneeling and crossing themselves as it passed by in a cloud of incense. The chaplains were also busy, roaming the ranks, hands raised in benediction and blessing. The road beyond Hastings was reinforced with excited and nervous men and the English boats with their silent crews and fighting men still lay off just outside the harbour entrance. "Get them all settled down as early as possible," William ordered his commanders. "An early curfew for them. They are going to need all the sleep they can get."

***

It was dusk when the Godwinsons rode up to the single stricken apple tree on top of Caldbeck Hill, riding out of Duniford wood and up the incline of the highest land for miles around. All around them were smaller hills set with woodland. Crows and rooks, seeking rest, were wheeling and cawing above the trees, unable to settle for the noise of the arriving army. They rose in their scores and made off to safer and quieter places far from their familiar roosting places. The men awaiting the Godwinsons on top of the hill, some four hundred of them, were men of Kent and Sussex. They were congregated around that single tree, beating their fists upon their shields of lime wood and raising their voices in a paean of praise and welcome. Harold raised his arm to them in reply and had his standards thrust into the ground. It was still light enough to look out upon the land to the south, all the way across to Telham Hill and Black Horse Hill. On the morrow the bastard would appear between these two points. The track before them dipped first down and then ascended a long and narrow spine of land running east to west, perhaps a half mile away from where they now stood.

"And that, my brothers," said Harold, pointing, "is Senlac ridge. We shall form our shield wall there. Gyrth, I want two hundred trusted men on it right away." It was evident that Harold did in fact know the country around here very well indeed, evident also that he had picked his position in advance and with care. "Go with them before the light fails completely and see for yourself how the land lies."

Gyrth left, calling for men amongst his East Anglians. Harold knew that Gyrth would find the sight from the other side of the ridge, its south side, to be very gratifying. There the land dipped again, not dramatically, but enough to slow up the enemy horsemen nicely as they advanced across a sodden water meadow and marshlands bisected by small tributary streams and dotted about by ponds of unknown depth. This battlefield would be of the choosing of the English, and to their advantage. It would be very hard for them to be outflanked. Still, a momentary doubt, the ridge seemed to be less in length than he remembered or had hoped for. Harold frowned to himself. It would be very crowded up there. Did he have too many men? He laughed to himself at this foolish notion, he should be so lucky. He turned now, to greet the enthusiastic local thegns in appropriate fashion and to address other matters. No sleep yet for him awhile, but then he did not feel especially tired anymore.

Neither, some miles away, did the FitzPons boys. They had been ordered away and out from under the feet of the scurrying, intent and absorbed leaders and the only place of safety seemed to be upon their straw mattress in the home of the presumably deceased Hastings merchant. They sat huddled together, listening to the noise and chaos outside. "Will we be permitted to be there?" asked Drogo. "We are the Duke's men," said Hugh, always the more assertive of the two. "We shall be required to hold his horses, to carry his weapons and to attend to him and to his needs as required. We shall not be left here. We are necessary." He was stropping a vicious looking dagger on a pebble, managing in his zeal to take the edge off it. "Well, that's fine then, I suppose," said Drogo doubtfully. There was a slight pause. "Hugh, are you afraid? Afraid of tomorrow?" His brother sneered at him, rather unconvincingly. "Not me, no. You are no kin of mine if you are. Did you not see the Pope's Holy Banner? We all saw it, we are blessed by that, we are." He punched Drogo very hard on the shoulder. "Just say your prayers and go to sleep, for God's sake."

"Our mother," said Drogo piously, "would not care to hear you say such harsh words to me." Hugh snorted derisively. "Away with you," he said, simply and uncharitably, but presently the boys raised up their treble voices together in the chanting of the Lord's Prayer.

As more of the English began to gather in the darkness on the hill they came dragging and carrying picket fences, fallen wood and wood freshly cut to make fires which they would tend throughout the night, beacon points guiding weary men to the meeting place of the dead apple tree in the small hours. Here and there was some food, though precious little of it. In their scouring of the countryside the Normans had been very thorough. There was, as always, more to drink. Amongst the fyrdmen the accents of London and the south eastern counties mingled with those of the far west and the Welsh borders and East Anglia. Here and there, occasionally, could be heard Northumbrian and Mercian voices raised in song or dispute. The Godwinsons, as was their duty, spread themselves around, taking care to be seen by as many men as possible. Through whatever agency, Leofwyn had men with him carrying sacks of now stale loaves. The food did not go very far, but it was most welcome. The brothers took care to welcome each bone tired contingent and direct them as they came in. A moon, near full, had risen, bathing the landscape beyond the illumination of the campfires in a general, dim glow.

The Godwinsons finally reconvened once more beneath the tree. It was approaching midnight. Someone, somewhere, had miraculously procured a sheep or had conveyed it, safe, all the way from London, carried on the shoulders of men. A sheep would not have survived the attention of the Normans. The old creature had been slaughtered and the smell of roasting mutton drifted over to them from a group of Kentish men. From a completely different direction the Essex men were giving tongue once more to their own version of the song of Malden. Malden, after all, had been an Essex affair and its hero an Essex man. Voices began to be raised in protest from other groups nearby. Did they not know the hour? It was time for sleeping, let them sing tomorrow night, if they could. They could shove the Epic of Malden up their arses. The brothers grinned at one another and Haakon was sent over to keep the peace.

Amongst that large gathering of men, perhaps nearly eight thousand of them now, there was an intimate and precious period of time for the Godwinsons. In the flickering light of their own fire, Leofwyn fiddled with wax and cloth and a small square of chain mail links sewn on to a square of kidskin. He cradled his battle axe between his knees and alternately honed and scraped and polished the steel. Already the curving two foot edge of the blade was razor sharp. "The urine of a mare in foal. Best thing, they say, for the forging of a sword and the honing of an edge," he said to no one in particular. Gyrth laughed his rare laugh. "Aesegar," he called to the man as he crouched about his own tasks in the shadows, "any mares in foal?" Aesegar raised his shoulders and eyebrows in mock apology, interrupted in his personal devotions. "Old wives' tale," said Gyrth as he cradled his chain mail shirt on his lap and fiddled amongst the links in search of gaps and weaknesses like a mother searching the scalp of her child for nits. It was an absorbing task, he found comfort in it.

Gyrth appeared to have cheered up somewhat since his earlier visit to the ridge to the south. From there, the light had been just good enough to survey the land and to see its potential. Across the dip in the land between, he had seen the fires of the Norman pickets camped out on Telham Hill just across the way there. He had noted the obvious advantages of the position and had measured his way across the ridge way from end to end, from where it dipped to both sides in a mixture of thick scrub and waterlogged bog to its central hog's back, all well and good. It was a fine place for a shield wall, if that was what was needed. God above, but the space was truly narrow and confined, a thought that had similarly struck Harold. In the half light, half dark, Gyrth's gaunt and weary features very much resembled Harold's. Men glancing over marvelled at the fact. He was shorter and burlier, with more of the ginger than the gold to his hair and beard, but none could fail to recognise him as the King's brother.

Harold himself sat with the thoughts racing through his head, struggling with the mixed emotions of fear and doubt, elation and relief. The final fight would be tomorrow. It would be a fight, too, to make that of Malden, the telling of which still drifted over in snatches, resemble a brawl at a country market. It would be hard, harder than the fight at the bridge at Stamford, where they had come running down like wolves upon the unprepared north men. Over there these were iron men on iron horses they were facing now, men who knew they were here. He shuddered at the memory of Brittany. But they had the ridge, and a shield wall of fearless fighting men. The Normans had never faced that in their lives. Should he have waited, as Gyrth and all others had urged? Waited until the strength of his force was irresistible? He remembered the threats of that monk at Westminster as he denounced him, remembered too all those sprawled bodies on the way to this place. It was too late now, with the army hunkering down beside him. It was too late for anything but to fight in the morning and to give it all over to the judgement of God, that God whose current Apostle on earth had declared him outcast and excommunicate. His thoughts would have continued along this theological path had not Gyrth, mercifully, intervened.

"Well", he said, still fiddling with the mail shirt. "It's a fine enough place to arrange to meet someone, so it is. And it is perfectly clear that the only way out for him is through and over us." Harold gave a start. "Yes, yes it is," he agreed. Leofwyn spat onto the edge of his axe blade and rubbed away contentedly, humming to himself. "So there is no more thought, then, of carrying on to the coast and catching him there?" Harold stared at the haze of light rising above the ridge opposite, caused by the Norman fires beyond. "He knows that we are here, right enough," he said. "There is no surprise to be had. This is no Stamford Bridge. No, we hold him there on that ridge in the morning. We hold him all day if that is what it takes. We fight on the defensive until the rest of our people come up to join us." He snapped some dead wood to shorter lengths and threw it on to the fire, piece by piece. "We hold him here," he repeated, "or we hold him nowhere. We cannot be forever racing up and down the length and breadth of the country fighting battles. We need an end to all this. There is more to being a King than running about bawling and screaming and waving an axe, at least I hope there is."

Ten short months. That was all that he had had. All those plans he had entertained! He had hoped to bring an honourable peace to the Welsh, to mend fences with the Scots. There were his plans and his projects for the development of trade out of Bristol and the west, proper iron foundries, controlled and regulated, in the Forest of Dean. He had hoped to reform the coinage and to establish new mints. Deal and Dover and Sandwich would be transformed into the finest shipyards in Christendom. Moots and Councils to attend, writs and charters to issue, his people to cherish and nurture, a firmer grip of the north. Perhaps a visit to the Emperor and a return to Rome. Above all, moments of tranquillity and pleasure with his family. Instead of all of this, he had spent day after day in the saddle, stamping out fires and shoring up leaky dams. He had been forced into a marriage he had not sought and had spent a vast amount of money out of the Royal Treasury and his own coffers in preparing for and waging war. He had disrupted the lives of thousands of men, brought death to his own brother. He had, God forgive him, broken the heart of his own mother.

Perhaps, in that moment, Gyrth sensed all of this in some way. "Harold," he said gently. "Tomorrow let me lead, I beg you. Return to London and rally the others. Dig the Aelfgarsons out. Draw a line across the Thames. We all need you and we cannot spare you. If things go badly in the morning, then you are still our King of the English." Harold leaned across and grabbed Gyrth's shoulder. The time for argument and harsh words was over, they both knew it. "If I did that, Gyrth," he said, "then I could look no other man in the face ever again." Gyrth nodded his acceptance and bowed his head in sadness. "Don't know what you are both so exercised about," said Leofwyn. "It's in the bag, I tell you." He snapped his fingers and his man Osketl came forward with a blanket. "I'm for some shut eye. God bless and save us all."

"Amen to that," said uncle Aelfric. "And also the good will of the blessed Saint Calixtus, whose day this is." He stood up and raised his hand in benediction over them all, a rare gesture of piety, before moving off and away to where his contingent of housecarls and monks lay already stretched out nearby. "And who was this Calixtus, when he was at home?" Leofwyn called after him. Aelfric shrugged. "I don't rightly know. I daresay some Greek or some such. But God's blessing on us, all the same."

CHAPTER ELEVEN :

The Feast of Saint Calixtus

Senlac Ridge: October 14th, 1066

Harold was nudged out of a fitful half sleep by Leofwyn. It had been a half sleep crowded with inconsequential, chaotic and vivid images. Woken suddenly and abruptly, the visions in his mind were still very real. The horse blanket he had slept under was heavy and damp with the dew, he ached.

"Not yet dawn," said Leofwyn. "A very good morning to you, brother. You need to know that a local man has just come in. The bastard is already on the march." Harold groaned and stretched and sat upright. "Then we have an hour or so," he said. "You and Gyrth see to it. I want our men up on that ridge, quick as you like. Get them moving. I want no fuss and no messing about. You both know your positions." Leofwyn nodded, indeed he did. It had been dinned into both he and Gyrth the previous night. On the hog's back of the ridge and in the front rank would stand Harold's own housecarls and those men of experience of the select fyrd of all the shires represented there; the well-armed and eager aristocracy of the thegns and their followers. A special place had been reserved also for the rowdy Danish mercenaries on loan from Sweyn Estrithson. Behind them, in that crowded and confined space, would stand the less experienced and less well-equipped men of London and the home counties and the rag bag of men from other places and any further reinforcements coming up behind. This would be the finest shield wall ever to gather in England, a bristling mass of determined men standing eight ranks deep. And to either side, as the ridge dipped into marsh and streams and scrub, would stand Leofwyn and his men of Kent and Essex to the west and Gyrth with his East Anglians, veterans also of Stamford Bridge, to the east, two Godwinson hinges of the door of the English, greased and gleaming and ready.

"I want them all in position by first light," Harold said. Men were moving now amongst the mass of huddled bodies, kicking them awake. Some had arrived barely two hours back. Gyrth was already on his way back to the ridge, accompanied by Aelfric. Aesegar had been there all night, supervising a contingent of men industriously damming up the Aspen brook to the east. At first light they would gleefully release the built-up flow of water downhill to the treacherous ground over which the Normans would have to pass. Group by group, the men on Caldbeck Hill picked up their weapons or their farm implements and began to make the half mile journey to the ridge along the track which led up to it. They greeted their King cheerfully enough as they passed.

The sun came up, a thin and watery October light barely filtering through the oppressive grey cloud cover. It was cold. The rooks and crows, disturbed once more, were up and wheeling above them. Harold's personal housecarls had roused themselves and were now standing behind him. Here, now, was Willi, holding a pair of slightly charred barley cakes and a measure of mead. Harold smiled his thanks.

Caedmon, a lean, spindly and dun coloured figure, stood beside Willi. His clerical scrip containing his battered and beloved book of devotions and a ragged scrap of purple, his ecclesiastical scarf, was clutched tight to his sparrow chest. Harold sighed and nodded at him before kneeling. It was time to commune with God. The purple scrap of material about his neck, Caedmon took Harold's frugal breakfast and muttered in Latin, blessing it. He broke a piece off one of the barley cakes and placed it in Harold's mouth, giving him then a sip of mead to drink. The mead warmed him as it flowed down his throat. "Take this," Caedmon murmured in the vernacular to his excommunicant King, "this is my body and my blood." One by one, the others of the companions, even the profane Leofgar, knelt and received the Sacrament. Last of all, Caedmon administered it to himself. All over the camp and amongst the now moving men, itinerant monks, hedge priests and chaplains were performing similar offices, mostly with just sedge grass and brackish water in place of the bread and wine, there being no bread and wine to be had. Harold crossed himself and rose to his feet. "My God," he said to himself and to his Maker, "this will be a busy day. If I should forget you, then please do you not forget me."

***

The men of the Breton division took to the road first, as had been previously agreed. They were roused and assembled and then led onto the five-mile march along the trackway through the devastated and barren wetlands leading to Senlac ridge. Ahead of them there rode an advance guard of picked men led by William Malet, who was thus the first man to link up with the extremely nervous small contingent who had been left to watch the north from their isolated position on Telham Hill. Malet's task upon arrival at the battlefield was to lead his column of men and those upon the hill and with the whole Breton contingent to an appointed place on the flank and to ensure that they stayed there, instead of setting off on individual vainglorious and ill-fated forays against the English.

No room for futile heroics for Malet!

To label all these men now setting out from Hastings with the title of Breton was of course a convenience and it hid a multitude of sins. To be sure, the archers of the first column, their bowstrings prudently nestling in their caps or in their tunics against the threat of damp, were indeed men of that rugged and mysterious land bounded by marsh and the wide Atlantic. So too were the bulk of the footmen in their mail or half mail, their assorted weapons at the shoulder and their round shields upon their backs. Within their ranks there now marched also disgruntled and disaffected knights. Deprived for whatever reason of their mounts since they had arrived at Pevensey, they each harboured a deep anger and humiliation to be seen thus labouring amongst an alien rabble.

Those other knights within the Breton force that were blessed with horses were presently without armour and leading their mounts amidst this mob of uncouth and savage men. The Bretons, as all others in the army agreed, if they agreed only upon one thing, were a tribe of savage and half tamed barbarians. The whole pack of them, with their alien language, their bizarre habits and the multiplicity of their uncanonical saints. They were quite beyond the pale. Within their ranks, and a source of almost constant trouble since the days of those first encampments in Normandy, were all those others from all over Christendom insufficient in number as to justify a separate contingent. These were the polyglot landless adventurers, the third and fourth and fifth sons of impoverished aristocrats. There was nothing for these men at home and they had been attracted to the enterprise from far and wide by a sense of adventure and the promise of easy gain and riches.

Alongside the purebred Breton Knights were Spaniards from Aragon and Castile and the County of Barcelona, dark and Moorish looking men with a fondness for knife play. There were the loud and intimidating German speakers from the lands of the Empire. They were big, blonde and argumentative men, proud and very swift to take offence. They came from Thuringia and Saxony and Swabia and from lands beyond, where they spoke their German as a second language. Sensible men gave them a wide berth, as they did also with the equally obstreperous Italian and Sicilian Normans. They were men whose fathers and grandfathers had been exiled or else forced out of Normandy by William's own father and grandfather. This whole mongrel tribe of men were fractious and divided and already seeking quarrels, even as they lined up and prepared to move out. They had been a constant headache to the much put upon Count Alan Fergant of Brittany, into whose keeping they had been entrusted. Fergant had now, in fact, already washed his hands of the whole task of disciplining them and this unenviable task had devolved upon FitzWimarc, himself half Breton by blood. It had been he, despite his protests, who had been assigned the task of liaising between Count Alan and the Norman and the French divisions and of translating the needs of the Duke to them as these occurred and arose. William watched them contemptuously and with no charitable thoughts as the notional Breton column moved off. The greater the number of casualties inflicted upon them by those English up there on that ridge, he reflected, then the less trouble afterwards and, of course, the more land and titles there would be left to reward his own more reliable Normans.

This much derided first contingent made its way past where William and his party sat their mounts, saluting and roaring at him as they went. William noted their passage with the occasional Ducal wave of a mailed hand. He gave the last of them what he judged sufficient space before signaling Aimerie of Thouars, Eustace of Boulogne and Enguerrand of Poitou to set off at the head of the French and the Flemings. This, at least, was a slightly more homogenous gathering.

When they arrived at the point between Telham hill and Black Horse hill the French contingent had been ordered to file off to the east and to take up their position before the ridge there. There were more of them than the Bretons. They were certainly more encouraging in their appearance and at least technically spoke the same language, though the Northerners amongst them had yet to understand one buzzing and whirring word in five that was uttered by Aimerie's own Aquitanians and Provencals, whilst for their part, the Southerners thought that the men of the north sounded like men speaking with mud and sand in their mouths. Their supposed unity was in fact only skin deep., the slightest of scratches and a yawning chasm would appear.

The archers and the foot and dismounted knights came first, then the mounted knights and their own retinues of foot, from Poitou and Boulogne, the Ille de France, the little buffer states of Le Marche and Maine and Blois, from Anjou. From Count Baldwin, that most expert and accomplished of all fence sitters, had come an especially impressive contingent of Flemish knights. They bred the best war horses in the world in Flanders, and these big, phlegmatic men of the lowlands had the best of these. The horses were huge and ponderous beasts, sixteen hands and more at the shoulder. They were massive fighting animals, a weapon of rolling and rippling muscle and sinew, trained since they were young colts to charge into obstacles and to kill and maim with their hooves. When they charged as one then the ground shook and thundered. These giant creatures, and the horses of the Normans, made most of the mounts in the Breton contingent look like spavined nags and fit only for soup and glue in comparison. The Flemish were of course fully aware of this fact and justly proud and boastful as they led their horses past the Duke.

Aimerie of Thouars, their titular commander, was beside himself with excitement and the glories of the moment and the promises of the day. The lands and riches he took after today, he had decided, would go to his second son, whom he loved and favoured much. The eldest son, for whom he did not greatly care and who now rode beside him, could shift for himself, earn his own lands, were he to live to sunset, it was all one and the same to him. His third son was already making his steady and inexorable progress up through the ranks of the church and a Bishopric beckoned. Back home on his languid and sun-drenched estates, the yellow and purple fields, the vineyards full of fat black grapes, the buzzing of angry wasps and the vast expanses of olive trees and orchards, he had a fourth son. The child was an imbecile who twitched uncontrollably and slobbered and had a club foot and was not capable of two connected thoughts. The boy was nonetheless his wife's most favoured son. He would be cosseted and looked after for the rest of his days, unless he outlived his mother. Thereafter his future would be uncertain. As for his numerous tribe of daughters, they would without a doubt and in their own time make good and profitable marriages amongst the local aristocracy. Thus, it was that Aimerie of Thouars, a small man with vast ambitions, fortified by a confession of sins and a shriving, along with a large measure of excellent apple brandy, rode to the battlefield in the very best of high spirits.

William's two reluctant half hostages rode together, twinned in misfortune. Eustace of Boulogne, a man with his own agenda and dynastic aspirations, continued to seethe and bubble with inward rage. The young heir of Poitou, there to keep his own father, the obnoxious poison dwarf Guy, in line, had also learnt early in life to keep his own emotions and ambitions to himself. In the event both of them looked spry and martial enough, but William's eyes narrowed at the sight of them conferring together. He neither liked nor trusted either of them, which was precisely why no less a person than William FitzOsbern and Robert Beaumont's son Roger rode with them, engaged upon a task much the same as had fallen to FitzWimarc.

FitzOsbern raised a hand in salutation to his old childhood friend as he passed, and William returned the gesture. He recalled the previous evening's conversation. "Fitz," he had said then, "if anything unfortunate or, God forbid, tragic happens to either of those two tomorrow then I want you to understand that you are not to blame yourself." FitzOsbern had raised a sardonic eyebrow at this but did not seek any further elaboration on this oblique invitation of assassination. Should one or both of them not be breathing on the morrow, then this would make life less problematic, would certainly solve a whole host of problems back home.

Back in Hastings, amongst the narrow alleys and all the way along the main thoroughfare leading north, there was the usual anarchy amongst the men of the baggage train. Mean and rickety little carts had been seized and gathered together since the arrival of the invaders at Pevensey. These heavily overburdened vehicles would now follow the army to the battlefield, carrying food and supplies, including dozens of sheaves of arrows and crossbow bolts. The disorder had finally caused the provosts to come amongst them with raised voices and sticks, but there was no such evident disorder amongst the final column, the fighting men of the Duchy of Normandy, the most cohesive and disciplined of all of the army. All told, they represented about one third of the Duke's entire fighting force of eight thousand men. The bowmen and the foot, as they waited for the order to move off, roared out profane ditties and then, ragged at first but then in glorious unity, the old song of Roland, the doomed paladin of the Emperor Charlemagne and the battle of Roncesvalles.

Some way back in the column of mounted knights, Herve sought to raise the spirits of Taillefer. Herve was in fine form. He had had a very spirited half an hour the night before with the Mainard's woman and had also done very well at the dice afterwards, comprehensively fleecing a trio of dull-witted Bretons. He was now looking forward to the day immensely. "Well then, Taillefer," he asked as the sound of the singing drifted back to them. "You're the expert. What do you think?" Taillefer inclined his head to listen. "Keen and eager enough," he said after a few moments, "but flat, hopelessly flat. It might serve to impress the English, but then I am also told that they have fine singers amongst them." Around his neck, secured by drawstrings, was a linen bag containing his precious harp. While Herve had spent what was possibly his last night on earth committing at least three major sins, the minstrel knight had waxed and anointed and rubbed at the precious thing, declining to draw his fingers across the cat gut strings in the certain knowledge that this would inevitably draw an unwanted crowd.

Exasperated with him, Herve leaned across and poked him. "Take pleasure in the moment, why don't you? The face on you this morning is fit to curdle milk. Mind you, my old mother, God rest her soul, used to say that if you can't think of anything good to say, then it is best to say nothing."

Herve's horse, a fine and spirited bay and as excited as he, barged at Taillefer's horse with its shoulder and attempted to take a bite at it. Herve turned it away and slapped it hard on the muzzle. Taillefer paused in an attempt to imagine an infant Herve at a loving mother's knee and then gave up. Even a man as imaginative as he could not conjure up such an image. No, Herve had sprung into the world as he was now, vital, fully grown and irredeemably steeped in villainy.

William also appreciated the sentiment and the effort that lay behind the singing of his own Norman people, if not the singing itself. He had ever been tone deaf and completely indifferent to the very different harmonic beauties created by both a Church Choir and of men gathered around campfires and on the eve of battle. His mount staled, and he rose in his stirrups to assist its efforts. He had conserved this particular war horse for this moment, riding only hacks and mares up to now. The horse was a giant creature. It was as black as the pit, as black as his gift to Harold, and all glistening haunches and stamping feet. It rolled its eyes wickedly and attempted to bite any other horse that came within reach. A gift from the King of Castille, it had crippled two stable boys and inflicted damage on any number of others on what must surely have been an eventful journey over the Pyrenees and through France to Rouen. The other horsemen around the Duke thus kept a respectful distance. The two Bishops, Geoffrey of Coutances and Odo of Bayeux, were nearest to the Duke. There was little semblance to the man of God about Odo on this particular cold October morning. His giant mace, a fearsome weapon of iron and studded with nails, swung at his side. His two favourite squires, that type of handsome, upright and well moulded young man that the Bishop especially favoured, stood close by, to either shoulder of his horse, carrying between them his helmet, chain mail, kite shield and personal banner.

Two men had volunteered gladly to carry the banners of the Duke and the Holy Father. Tostain of Bec held the shaft of the fragile looking guidiron of the Papal Banner. In his ham like fist it looked like a child's toy. Tostain was a very big man and not given to immoderate displays of emotion. It was thus impossible to fathom by the expression on his face if he was moved by or indifferent to this most especial honour. He was without a doubt a good man to have at your side in a fight. At Varaville, William had seen him hack down four of Anjou's finest, one by one. Roger of Bigod, on the other hand, was an easier man to understand and rub along with. He held the Leopard of Normandy, skilfully executed in gold on a backdrop of white linen. With the wind behind it, as it was not at the moment, the flag was a proud and glorious four feet square. At present it drooped and hung mournfully upon its staff. As Gytha, Harold's mother, had brought into being the Fighting Man for her son, so too had the Lady Matilda's no less skilful sewing women created this banner. "You drop that thing, Roger, and I'll have you digging latrine pits for a week," said William in one of his rare and lumbering excursions into wit. Roger of Bigod, a very amiable man, grinned by way of reply.

Naturally, Robert Mortain was also close by to his brother. He leaned across the withers of his horse, hawked productively and spat. He looked up at the slowly lightening sky. "Sun up soon," he observed. "It is a good day for it, probably no rain." Rain, the nightmare of both bowman and horseman alike. Involuntarily, William fingered the talisman around his neck. Secured by metal clasps and hanging from the twine were some of the more inconsequential bones of Rasyphus and Ravennus, two very minor figures in an already heavily overcrowded calendar of saints. What made these two Saints significant, obscurely martyred for their faith in an equally obscure location and at a likewise obscure time, was that it had been upon their bones, upon their mortal remains, that Harold had sworn that perjured oath back in Normandy.

"No," William agreed, "no sign of rain." With rain they would lose all possible advantage to their being big men on big horses. From his scouts and his own observations, William knew already how little the land favoured them and how much it favoured the English standing there above them on their defensive line. "Then may God be praised and thanked," observed Odo piously. Robert by far a simpler man than his brother and his half-brother was content. "If that means no rain, then by all means," he replied and crossed himself.

A short way to the rear, in their mail and standing by their horses, the leading men of the Duchy, the representatives of the major families, were gathered together. Some shriven, others not, fed or unfed, they stood there, blue chinned, shaven headed and hollow eyed. Between them, they were the embodiment of William's power. Should things go badly wrong today then they might support him against his eager enemies back home. Equally, they might well prove to be so many serpents clutched to his bosom, ready to bite and revolt. He cast his cynical eye over them with his usual mixed emotions. DeLisle, FitzRotrou, de Grandesmil, Giffard, Gerald Seneschal, D'Ivry and all of the rest. Some of them he quite liked and respected. What a struggle it had all been, these past ten months, at Rouen and Lillebonne and elsewhere, to bring them all together to this one place. Now, with an English fleet blocking off all thought or chance of retreat, they were committed. They were here now through a blend of cupidity and ambition and naked threat and there could be no turning back. As his glance raked across and over them they gathered themselves and raised a slightly half hearted war cry, the fighting shout of Normandy. "Dex Vult!" they yelled in unison, "Dex Ai!"

"I certainly hope so," said William to himself. "I certainly do hope so." He caught a sudden movement out of the corner of his eye. The FitzPons boys, laden down with William's armour and equipment, were attempting to hide behind the backs of the men. William looked down upon the two of them sternly as they scuttled out of reach of William's bad tempered and over strung horse. "As for you two," he said, "you can come as far as the end of the march and then no further. Then it's back to the rear with the pair of you, and may the Lord save my soul for being a sentimental man."

"Your Grace, my Lord," said Hugh. He was emboldened and uplifted by the glory and the solemnity of the moment, the marching and singing men, the stamping horses and the proud banners. "We are your men, my brother and I, your servants. We have been raised for this, and trained." Robert of Mortain chuckled indulgently at them. "Trained to this, my arse," he said. "You haven't been trained even to scratch and think at the same time properly. Now, my young puppies, you just listen to your lovely old uncle Robert and do what you are bloody well told. You couldn't fight your way out of a leaking wineskin, the pair of you. And what are we meant to do when some hairy great Englishman starts carving bits out of you with his axe?"

By now William was anxious to be off. The last of the French and the Flemings were some way up the road by now. "My Lord of Mortain has the right of it," he said. "I have seen too many good fighting men killed in protecting or rescuing some amateur enthusiast off on an adventure. You will do as you are bidden." He kicked his gift horse of Spain in the ribs and the men of Normandy at last set off along the beaten and churned path and out of Hastings, singing and chanting as they went. The wagon train, some semblance of order established, prepared to follow on. Out beyond the harbour, the English boats still rocked at deep anchor. Those men that William had left behind at Hastings, the mariners, the non-combatants and the half resentful and half glad garrison of three hundred footmen and a sprinkling of knights, settled down uneasily to see what the day might bring.

***

For the second time that morning Gyrth, accompanied by Aelfric, paced the Senlac ridge, this time moving from east to west and towards the position his own East Anglians had been assigned to occupy. Aesegar, called away from his damming and digging, accompanied them as, moodily, Gyrth walked and counted out the thousand or so paces and stared across occasionally to Telham Hill, rising like an island out of a sea of mist. The journey from east to west, from the dip of the land into brush and scrub and bog, along the spine of the ridge and to this decline in the ground here had taken him perhaps a quarter of an hour. He was experiencing a mounting sense of unease. At one and the same time his brother was both right and wrong. If ever there was a place to stop the invaders from breaking out into open country from the bottleneck of their peninsular then this was it. He looked down at the low lying and sodden ground beneath him and the deceptively gentle slope leading up to the ridge with satisfaction. That would slow the bastards up, and no mistake. The flanks were favourable too. They would have trouble working around that broken ground. Against that, though, was the undeniable fact that the space they held was too confined, too cramped.

"Too narrow," said Gyrth. "How in the name of God can a man be expected to swing his weapon? What do we have with us? Eight thousand men, nine thousand? Put them in line here and you couldn't swing a cat, let alone a battle axe." He turned on his heel and strode across the ridge. It took him just twenty strides before the land started to dip again towards the north where the English army was now on the move. "If he has any sense," said Gyrth, mostly to himself, "he'll keep the most of them back here and out of harm's way until they are needed." There was little point in recriminations, nor in going back over old arguments with his brother once again. Here they were and here was where they would hold the line.

He could see the track snaking up towards where he now stood, raised in places and skirting the marsh. Behind it, just out of sight beyond the woods, were the two routes to London itself. Men were beginning to arrive on the ridge in greater numbers now, filing out along the ridge and jostling for space, chivvied and bullied by the men set above them. The common men of the fyrd stood aside respectfully and deferentially as the swaggering and confident royal house-carls and those of Wessex and the south pushed through to form the front rank. The morning was cold and they stamped their feet and blew on their hands. Great gouts of vapour emerged from their mouths and noses in the cold dawn. They laid their kite shields and weapons on the ground before them as they assisted each other with the leather and laces of their chain mail shirts. "They'll most likely have to stand side on," observed Aesegar, a note of doubt in his voice, "or else spread out more. At least they are close packed for a cavalry attack. They'll have to be pretty handy with their shields though. Lined up like that they are God's own gift to a bowman." Gyrth nodded irritably. He had seen that for himself. "They'll be fine enough, but what about that lot back there?"

He was referring, of course, to the men and boys of the general fyrd, now beginning to come up behind the front lines, blithe and excited like a crowd at a fair. They carried with them swords and spears, axes and farm implements, these men of the shires summoned away from the bean feasts following the harvest. Unlike only a few of the brag-ging and dangerous looking housecarls of the front rank, now fast becoming the front two ranks, they had no experi-ence at all of fighting. They had never been required to stand up to a determined enemy before, let alone one as daunting as the Normans now beginning to appear out of the mist like silent ghosts on the lower ground beneath them. They could hear nothing of them, for the wind, rising now, blew towards them. For every sword or axe among them there were ten billhooks or scythes or knives lashed with twine to staves. There was scarcely a shield or a helmet or a leather jacket to be seen. They looked brave and resolute enough at the moment, but God help them against a rain of arrows or a massed charge by men in mail on heavy horses. Already the front two ranks of the professionals were turning back to them, shoving and snarling at them to move back and keep their distance.

Sweyn's Danish mercenaries arrived on the ridge in a mass, a rowdy, swaggering and utterly self-assured gathering of some two hundred men. Taller and heavier than the English and heavily armed and armoured, they thrust and barged their way into the front rank at the centre, causing the line of English to ripple to either side to accommodate their arrival. They began to swing their immense battle axes experimentally, vicious and finely-honed half-moons of the best Swedish steel two feet across on long hafts of elm and ash. Haakon, their appointed liaison officer, was there with them. They had come to grow fond of the boy and laughed good naturedly at the errors of his Danish as he pleaded for patience and tolerance from them. Gyrth swore colourfully. "This," he said, "is turning into a right shambles. Where in God's name is Harold?" The English had begun to chant. "Why are we waiting? Why are we waiting?" they intoned in a mock plaintive way. They were making sheep like bleating noises.

"Enough is enough," said Gyrth. "I shall go fetch him myself. See if you can't get a bit of order up here." Aesegar pointed to the west. Some four hundred paces off, the Kent and Wessex housecarls were forming line along the dip in the ground. "I see Leofwyn over there," he said. "There is his banner. Who is looking after your East Anglians?"

"At this moment," said Gyrth bitterly, "no one."

***

At the highest point on Telham Hill, de Tosny looked across at this sudden eruption of men appearing like specters out of the mist on the ridge opposite. He had never seen the like of this before. Hitherto his military experience had been confined to raids and counter raids in and out of Anjou and Maine and Brittany, relatively low-key affairs involving at most perhaps a few hundred men and not all at the same time. Here instead were men in their thousands, the grim and fearsome men of this northern isle. "Holy Mother of God," he breathed. He would have crossed himself at the sight but for the fact that the men surrounding him might think the less of him for it. He had his reputation to think of. "That'll be the English then," said his lieutenant, a deeply unimpressionable man, somewhat redundantly. "I rather imagine it would be," said de Tosny drily. He hadn't chosen the man for his quick wits but rather for his dependability. "Post someone back to his Grace the Duke immediately. Tell him the English stand before us and are blocking our path."

They stood and watched as the English coalesced from a seething swirl of figures into a dense and compact line of men, their alien shouts and cries carrying over to them. After what seemed a very long time Malet himself rode up the hill to where they stood, taking in the scene at a glance. "It is as I would have done," he commented. "He could have done no differently." Emerging from the narrow gap between the Telham and Black Horse hills, the first of the Breton column was filtering out into the valley below them and moving out to their left, provoking a roaring jeer of derision from the English. The bowmen and the foot scurried to form line ahead of the knights. It was now fully daylight, two hours since they had left Hastings. They had made good time, but now they stumbled and lurched across the treacherous and uneven ground, to the accompaniment of the banging shields and chants of the English.

By the time Harold arrived to stand by his brother at the very centre of the ridge the first of the French and the Flemings were also appearing in the gap between the two hills opposite. They moved in relatively good order to their right until they began to encounter the widening shallow lake of water caused by the release of the water that normally flowed into the Brede to the east. The Normans had yet to arrive and the gap between the French and the Bretons was enticingly wide, an open invitation to attack. It was only with difficulty that Harold had forced his way to the front. The ridge and the trackway running along it was now dense and seething with men. He found his two brothers, his uncle and nephew and Aesegar gathered together and watching the scene unfolding below. "Now would be a good time," Leofwyn greeted him excitedly. "Look at them down there, milling around like old tarts at a wedding." He indicated the gap between the two wings of the army. Harold considered, it was indeed a temptation, though now more men were appearing to fill the ground. It was the first of the Norman foot.

"Now listen to me very carefully, Leofwyn," said Harold slowly and precisely. "Listen to me, all of you. Whatever the provocation, whatever the temptation, there is to be no breaking of the ranks. No one leaves this place unless I say so. Is that absolutely clear? This is not Stamford Bridge. This is a different kettle of fish altogether. This time we wait for them to come to us. All we have to do is to hold on. It is all very simple. We hold the high ground and we protect the road out of here. They can go nowhere unless they go over and through us. The longer we hold them here on this high ground then the more men there are coming up from behind to support us. If we hold the bastard for the day then he is truly beaten and we'll all enjoy a good bonfire of his boats tomorrow. This is my only order to you all. Hold the line." Aesegar coughed deferentially. "We are, my Lord, too confined here. There is not enough space for all to stand in the line. Already we have had reports that men are turning back, saying that there is no room and that we have people enough here already."

Harold lost his temper at that, a temper that had become increasingly frayed over the past few weeks. "God's blood! Then stop them. Hold them back on the road behind, cowards that they are." He smacked his forehead with a cupped hand in exasperation. "Not cowards, brother," Gyrth replied. "They are merely judging by the evidence of their own eyes. What they see here is a mighty army. They see more people than they have ever seen gathered together in one place in all their lives. They can surely be forgiven for thinking as they do. Let us at least extend our flanks."

"Very well then, Gyrth, within reason," said Harold. "You and Leofwyn shall be responsible for that. Have those still coming up or attempting to return draw up behind your people." He looked behind him at the ridge, noisy and boiling with excited men. The army was now ranged in ranks eight deep, and with more arriving. A few paces away from them the left flank of the Danes had finally lost patience and fist fights had broken out. "See to that, Haakon, will you?" The young man hurried off to attempt to restore order. "Haakon, Haakon, Haakon," the Danes chanted as a greeting, a mixture of mockery and affection.

Harold gazed, deep in thought, at the latest of the arrivals opposite and below. So he had come at last, that grim and brooding and powerful man who had held him in his power two years back. The reunion they had both known would happen was about to occur. He could now see clearly the fluttering large golden leopard and the much smaller and fragile looking banner beside it. This must be the much-vaunted insignia of the Holy Father. The menace and power of it was out of all proportion to its meagre size. A knot of horsemen surrounded the banners and even at this range he could make out the man clearly, a man last seen waving at him from a Normandy quayside.

***

William reined in and sucked his teeth as he came into the valley and had his first view of the English drawn up against him. Even he, with all his experience of the numerous pitched battles that he had fought in his crowded lifetime, had never seen such a sight. Even the fearless Robert looked slightly taken aback. "Now there is something," he said, "the like of which I've not seen before. They look something fierce, don't they just." At the appearance of the Norman banners that vast crowd of men up on the ridge again erupted with shouts and cries. An alien chant came booming down to them, raising the shaven hair on the backs of their necks. It was the same chant that Willi had raised the day before. "Out tanner, out tanner, out, out, out!" Here was Malet now, galloping over to him through the lines of the Norman archers and footmen as they took up station in the centre ground. He reined in and saluted his Duke.

"Well, Malet?" said William. Malet feared to tell him what those English up there were chanting. It was the old and unforgiveable insult. Once the men of besieged Alencon had shouted much the same from the town walls at the Duke's army below, the same insult referring to William's illegitimacy and the trade of his mother's father. He had stormed into Alencon and those men who had survived the capture and subsequent sack had either had their hands and feet hacked off or their eyes put out. Honesty, decided Malet, was the best policy, and might serve best. "It is a reference, your Grace," he began cautiously, "to the profession practiced by your mother's father." Robert hooted merrily at this indelicate reference to their mutually shared grandfather. William's face grew dark with anger. "Such wit," he said at length and then, mildly, surprisingly, "well now. Sticks and stones may break my bones, but names can never hurt me.

Let us see if they can still be as humorous once I have torn the tongues out from their heads. How many would you say are up there?"

Malet was gladdened by this change of subject, pausing to think as the first of the Norman horsemen made their way past to take up position. "Their best men, their housecarls are to the front. Behind them are their fyrdmen, common, ordinary folk, yokels and town guttersnipes. No discipline or experience or weapons to speak of, but handy enough up close. Who might still be behind them I do not know, but I would say there are about nine or ten thousand of them. Look there straight ahead of us." He pointed at the two English banners in the centre. He recognised the Red Dragon of Wessex and also this new design of the Fighting Man with his brandished club and suggestive loincloth. Everywhere in the Duke's army this emblem had already drawn comment. "That is Harold himself up there," said Malet. "We know his two brothers are with him. They'll take the flanks. Watch out for the East Anglians, they are known to be fearsome fighters. Harold knows that we would wish to draw him to us," continued Malet with absolute certainty. "You may be sure that his orders are for them to stand where they are." What Malet did not say William already knew for himself. If he did not break that chanting and abusive army by nightfall, then he was truly lost. With a beaten army and an enemy fleet at his back he could only, should he survive, sue for an ignominious surrender. Should he then be permitted to return to Normandy then he did not give a stinking fish for his chances. He was interrupted in his thoughts by the arrival in quick succession of FitzWimarc from the Breton lines and Beaumont from the French. Both sections of the army were now drawn up and as ready as they would ever be for the fight. His own central division of Normans were now just about in position, having filled the gap between the two flanks. William stood in his stirrups in order to see better. Compared to the compact gathering on the ridge, his own lines of foot and horse looked frail. They looked thin and flimsy. In stark comparison to the English, no cries or shouts came from their lines.

William thanked the harassed looking Fitzwimarc and young Beaumont, who was fairly seething with excitement. "Get you back to your places then, and God's fortune on you both. You will be informed when I wish the foot to move forward. The horse shall be held back for the time being." He turned now to his brothers and the Bishop of Coutances. "Well then," he said briskly. "Time's getting on. If he won't come to us then needs must we shall go to him." He hooked his leg over the high saddle and jumped to the ground. He held his arms out before him as Hugh FitzPons approached with his hauberk. There was a moment of grunting and fiddling before Hugh stood back in dismay, his face ashen. "It's on back to front," said Robert helpfully. "It's a beating for you at the end of the day, my boy." William cursed and struggled out of the thing. Omens, why was he forever beset with omens? Falling on the sand and shingle at Pevensey had been bad enough, and now this. Where before FitzOsbern had been on hand with a helpful remark it was now Odo who intervened, his handsome face creased in amusement. "It is indeed a world turned round about," he observed in his habitual smooth and urbane way. "You come here this morning a Duke and by God's Grace you shall this evening be a King." They all nodded in appreciation at the well-chosen words and as the humiliated Hugh made good the damage. So, then, the ill-omened moment passed in a little flurry of good humoured chuckles.

All along the line of Knights their squires and valets were performing similar services. They secured and laced hauberks, adjusted buckles and straps and pulled the chain mail coverings over the heads of their masters. Once back in the saddle, the knights settled their pointed helmets with their nasal protectors onto their heads. They loosened the swords in their scabbards and swung their decorated kite shields to the front, placing their left arms through the twin brackets and clutching them close. They offered protection of sorts on their left from the eyes to mid shin. Some knights, more individually minded, carried right-handed maces or vicious looking spiked balls attached by a chain to a short haft of elm. Others, in the English and Danish manner, carried axes. They were then handed up their javelins. For the most part they would hurl these at the enemy over arm whilst at the same time attempting to settle and control their excited and over bred horses, a task that required considerable training and practice. There were those, faddish and foppish, who favoured the relatively new practice of charging with the javelin couched under the right armpit.

In their mail and with their helmets set they all at once became uniform and anonymous, dark hair, red hair, blonde hair, disappearing under the metal cones. Any distinction to be made between them now came only from the designs that some among them displayed upon their shields, ill executed and amateur affairs of griffons and eagles, stars, chevrons and bars. Here and there was a unicorn or a salamander, a bear, a hog, a prancing horse. There was also variety to be found in the fighting destriers they rode, stallions and geldings. There were greys and blacks, duns and bays, all equally irritable and nervous and causing considerable difficulty to many of their riders. To each knight worth his salt there were three or four servants. Their immediate task done, these men then hurried off with their own weapons to join the lines of infantry ahead.

A half hour passed as the Duke's army addressed its ranks and the Lords of Normandy, France, Flanders and Brittany rode amongst them, bawling instructions. Amongst the Breton contingent an especial disorder still prevailed. Alan Fergant chose not to intervene personally. They were here, weren't they? What more was required of him?

Bringing order to the ranks was a task, surely, for lesser men. He had done his bit. All that remained now for him was to lead them into battle, a fight that he very naturally prayed he would survive. All was not well back home in his beloved Brittany. The successor of Conan, he of the poisoned gauntlet, he would need to return as soon as possible after he had secured his rights and titles in this England. His own Breton aristocracy were not men to be trusted. He had no love of or trust in the Duke of Normandy. He would not be yet cold in his grave, he knew with an utter conviction, before Normans would come swarming across his borders to subdue and seize.

The troubles within his own command on this particular morning were for the greater part caused by the non-Breton knights he had reluctantly and resentfully taken responsibility for. There were perhaps four hundred of them in this division and they were already fighting and scuffling amongst themselves now, seemingly oblivious to the fact that there was a large and highly intimidating army facing them not five hundred yards distant. A German had, for some reason, clashed violently with a Barcelona knight. They were actually at each other's throats and rolling on the muddy, sodden ground, urged on by all in their immediate vicinity. The argument, whatever or whoever had started it, was occasioning great interest and the promise of money was actually being placed on the outcome. The clever money seemed to favour the German. FitzWimarc arrived at last to pull them apart. "For the love of God," he bawled at them in a language that neither understood, "leave off. Your enemy is to the front of you." The German spat out a tooth and wiped his mouth and the Spaniard grinned at him wickedly. "See you later, pig's offal," he said.

Affairs were far more decorous amongst the French and the Flemings. "We wait for the signal," FitzOsbern said yet again to Eustace, the sprig of Ponthieu, and to Aimerie of

Thouars. "We do not move until such time. All along our front the bowmen and the arbelists are to soften them up a touch and then we send in the foot. Let's see how the English like that. Keep the horse tight together. We'll direct them at that copse over there and see if they can't work upwards from the side." He indicated a point ahead of them slightly to their right and occupied now by Gyrth's East Anglians. Eustace, in fact a personally courageous man, was anxious to be off. "But when?" he demanded. "Soon, soon," said FitzOsbern soothingly, as if placating a child denied a treat. He was also wondering how best he might encompass this man's death whilst avoiding any possible personal blame and a long-standing blood feud. FitzOsbern knew a thing or two about blood feuds.

From the lines of the English the booming and the chanting continued unabated. Here and there, individuals left the shelter of the shield wall, capering down the slope for a few paces, making obscene gestures and revealing their buttocks to the enemy below. The thegns and the heads of the contingents of housecarls of the King and the Earls patrolled the front, ensuring that this habit did not become general. The Danes had now begun to direct their derisive sheep noises at their English neighbours. The King of Denmark's loaned men had at least come well provisioned and flasks of strong aqua vitae were now being passed from hand to hand. The theology and subject matter of their own heartily bawled songs would have scandalised any passing English churchman capable of understanding. Abbot Aelfric was in fact standing close by with his own housecarls and monks. He had grown up alongside Danes and knew every nuance of their language. He was also wise and well versed in the wicked ways of the world. He smiled to himself and turned to his black cowled men. Their first calling may have been to God, but they looked determined enough at the moment. "I think a Psalm might well be in order," he said.

CHAPTER TWELVE:

Senlac

Senlac Ridge: October 14th, 1066

Time now for the final throw of the dice. William looked around him and ahead of him, he breathed in deeply and took the decision to make the opening move. "Well, best to get started, I suppose, before we all die of old age." It was a curiously flat and simple statement with which to set such a momentous act in motion. "God keep you in His care, my Lords." He settled his helmet down over his shaven head. "Right way around this time, brother," said Robert. "The strip of metal to the front to cover the nose, that's the way to tell." He laughed uproariously at his own wit.

A trio of horsemen cantered out of the group, like birds startled from a covert, on their way to give the order to the three separate divisions. The bowmen of the very front ranks were under the direction of trusted and experienced sergents, no self-respecting aristocrat would ever dream of leading them. The bowmen were to advance, with the rest of the foot coming up behind them in support. Within their ranks were keen eyed experts, specialists in calculating wind, trajectory and range. At about one hundred and fifty paces they would halt and let fly. The English, they had been told, had precious few bowmen of their own and they would be safe enough at that range from the slingshots and the hand thrown objects of the baying mob before them. It was optimum range, and uphill at that, but it would serve at least to set things in motion. Unless, of course, the English came racing down the hill to meet them, in which case they would be dead men, caught between the English and the mounted knights who would ride over them without compunction. They moved off across the capricious and sodden ground that sucked at their ankles and at this the English shouts and jeers rose in volume. Already the vagaries of the ground were beginning to tell and they arrived at their appointed distance in scraps and ragged groups.

Arrows and the occasional crossbow bolt began to flicker up the slope, making a vicious whickering noise as they went. For the most part, and shooting up hill, it was an ineffectual beginning to things. Most of the missiles fell short and, mockingly, the English of the front rank danced around as much as they were able in that confined space and competed to collect arrows on their shields. There was the occasional lucky shot as an arrow passed over the heads of the housecarls to whir into the ranks of the unprotected fyrdmen behind. Here and there they began to take casualties. Not too far from where Harold stood an arrow fell directly upon the crown of a hapless Hertfordshire man. He dropped like a stone in a pond, unprotesting and as dead as mutton.

Naturally enough, the men of his own village were around him, aghast at this sudden taking of life, and him the best pig breeder in the district. Whatever would his wife say? And she expecting her fourth! This early death was a novelty to them and they made much of it. They had all seen death before, of course, an elderly relative, an infant child, a man struck down by a blow to his heart as he laboured in the fields. This, though, was new to them. By now Gyrth and Leofwyn had left to take up their own places before their men on the flanks. Harold's farewell to them had been studiously casual. On one thing only had he been formal. Hold the line. No breaking away, just hold the line. Do not move forward.

Aesegar was with him. "They'll not do too much harm at that range," he observed, "and they would not dare to come closer without support." Harold pointed at the slow-moving lines of the advancing infantry. "And that," he said, "is what is coming up now." The footmen were finding the going even more difficult than the bowmen and, unlike the archers, they were required to actually close with those screaming banshees lining the ridge up there. They did not find this an enviable prospect and were already finding it heavy work, using their spears and javelins as aids to walking. The bowmen ducked back and took up position behind them. The English urged these unwelcome invaders on until they were within throwing range and then met them with a shower of sticks and stones. One of the Danes, invoking his pagan past, advanced down the slope and threw his spear deliberately over the heads of the front rank of Norman foot. It was not designed to kill but to serve notice. Odin, God of battles, owns you now. His comrades shouted their approval as the man returned to the ranks. Here and there some of them turned their backs and exposed their buttocks to the enemy once more. Thus far they were finding it all immense fun.

"And what is this now?" Harold asked, pointing again. "A messenger? Well, it's a bit late for that I would have thought." A single horseman had separated himself from the Norman cavalry in the centre and ridden to the foot of the rise. Everyone, from William downwards, assumed that he was a messenger off with some instruction to either the Bretons or the French, but now the horseman, and in no particular hurry about it, was riding his horse directly up the slope, barging the archers and footmen out of the way as he went. He appeared to be chanting, for it could be seen that his mouth was opening and closing. Those nearest him and sufficiently knowledgeable recognised he was chanting the song of Roland, the doomed champion of Charlemagne. His shield strapped to his back, he guided his horse using just his knees. In his left hand he clutched a javelin and in the other he was actually juggling with his sword, catching it dexterously each time it fell and throwing it up into the air again. "That's Taillefer," said William, recognising the man. "In God's name, what does he think he is doing?" Robert shook his head. "Nothing that will do him any good," he replied. The two armies watched, stunned, as, some twenty paces off from the shield wall, Taillefer spurred his horse into a canter. Ten paces off he hurled his javelin. The first of the housecarls was down, the blade deep in his throat. In retaliation throwing axes came hurtling out of the ranks, cutting into both man and horse and bringing them down. Men came down from the wall and hacked and stamped the strange minstrel knight to death. "And what was all that about, do you suppose?" asked Robert, utterly mystified, but the only man who could have told him was dead.

This very public death of Taillefer seemed to embolden the Norman footmen, arriving piecemeal and unsupported and now right up to and against the English shields. The French and the Bretons had yet to arrive in any appreciable numbers and the Normans, with the steeper climb, were already winded. The English stood sideways on to them, their axes rising and falling upon their heads. Fyrdmen, anxious too to be at the enemy, pushed from the back, causing the line to buckle in places. Frustrated at the cramped space, individual English began to break from the line in order to be able to swing their axes more freely.

The Norman crossbow bolts made a vicious whirring and thumping noise as they travelled to and then found their targets, hurling men backwards with the speed and weight of the bolts. Slow to load and cumbersome, they were deadly at this range, travelling with ease through the wood and hide of shields to pierce the chain mail behind them. On more than one occasion the weapon had actually been banned by Papal decree and there was absolutely no mercy on God's earth for a trapped and cornered arbelist. Where arrows as often as not wounded or caused inconvenience to mailed men, these iron bolts invariably meant death if they found their target. Haakon was screaming and ranting along the Danish line in the centre, pushing men back. A crossbow bolt missed him by a hair's breadth, killing the man standing next to him and showering him with blood and brains and splintered bones. A score or so of English came running downhill at a tangent towards an equal number of bowmen and arbelists seeking to send in a concerted volley. They fell upon them and killed them almost to the last man. "Back, back," the thegns were yelling. Grudgingly, the English returned to the crest of the ridge and pushed their way back into the line. They gathered arrows and snapped them as they went to prevent their being used against them a second time. There were so few English bowmen they could possibly hand them to.

The French and Flemings were only now arriving at the English shield wall and were experiencing the same savage mauling as their Norman comrades to their left. Over on the other side of the ridge, the Bretons and their greater numbers of knights on foot were having a more even affair of it on the less steep ground and had already opened up gaps amongst the Kent and Essex men to reach the men of the common fyrd beyond. Despite his relative inexperience, Leofwyn was fighting like a demon, clearing a path before him and his immediate companions. At some point his cheek had been cut open and he had picked up a stab wound in the fleshy part of his thigh. "Out, out, out," he yelled. A dark, wiry little man attempted to slip in under his guard and Leofwyn crushed the man's skull with his axe like an egg. Others scuttled out of his way and went in search of easier adversaries. He turned to the Earldorman of Basildon standing beside him. "Hot work, but we have them now," he roared. But the man wasn't listening. He was on his knees, his face a mask of blood and making an animal like whimpering noise deep in his throat. There was no time for Leofwyn either to assist or sympathise. He turned away. "One more push, boys," he yelled, "One more." He paused to exchange blows with a giant flaxen haired German knight. The man's teeth were bared in a feral grin and a tuneless dirge was emerging from his mouth. After a few moments of useless parrying they both gave up and moved away from each other, the German knight hewing down an imprudent and over-confident farm labourer before backing off and away down hill and in search of the protection and comfort of others.

The movement seemed to be becoming general and more flights of arrows now flickered overhead as the bowmen were provided with targets not obscured by their own comrades. Now they were definitely running. Many had discarded their weapons and were exposing their backs to a volley of throwing axes, spears and stones dug from the Sussex earth and gathered in heaps the night before.

The English line boiled and erupted into a noisy head-long charge in pursuit, the fyrd following after and gleefully ransacking the dead and wounded for any valuables and picking up discarded weapons as they went. In the centre, even as the Norman attack petered out and men returned to their lines in good order below. Harold became aware of the commotion to his right. He swore vigorously, it was his worst fear realised. Craning his neck as he stood on a small mound on the ridge he could see only too clearly. He screamed with rage and despair. "Alfi, Leofgar, off to my brother now. Tell him he is to hold his line, for God's sake." The two men turned to carry out his instruction, but in that confined space they could make no headway at all through the mass of men and so the command went undelivered.

Leofwyn's housecarls at last came to their senses. Bunched up and with shields held before them, they made their way back after cutting down some of the slower of the Bretons. The men of the fyrd, though, were unstoppable, or at least they believed themselves to be. The Breton flank was a rout, a fleeing rabble pursued by less than half of their numbers. It had all happened very quickly and William's response was equally swift. If the rest of the English chose to follow after, and with that huge gaping hole in their flank, then they were in serious trouble indeed. The Normans and the French were still retiring in reasonable order. The only way, though, for Alan Fergant and his horsemen to be at the English would be to ride over their own infantry. The Norman knights were drawn up in ranks six deep. William loosened his sword in its scabbard. "Rear three ranks, wheel to your left," he shouted. "We shall take them in flank." The exultant English streaming down from the ridge seemed utterly impervious to any possible danger right up to the moment that big men on big horses came smashing into them from the side. They did not stand a chance, those fyrdmen of Kent and Essex. They were ridden down and trampled, skewered, clubbed, slashed and poleaxed. The struggle was over in moments and the ground lay clogged with English dead and wounded. Few made it back to the safety of the ridge, though about one hundred of the fyrdmen made it to the comparative safety of a small hillock rising out of the valley, panting and their chests heaving, before they in turn were cut down by a number of determined cavalry charges.

Here and there a few horses with empty saddles wandered, snatching at the rough sedge grass and bog myrtle.

William returned to the centre, flushed and breathing heavily. He had killed and killed again; it was a good feeling. He had not personally taken another man's life since Brittany. It was a good feeling, a lesser number of Englishmen to worry about. Blood dripped down his sword and onto his arm. "They'll not be doing that again in a hurry," said Robert, joining him. "More the pity if that is so," replied William. His breath was short and laboured. "But I have a feeling that they will."

Count Alan and his captains, it could be seen, were attempting belatedly to restore order to their mauled and demoralised front ranks. Bowmen all along the line were out hunting for spent arrows and the footmen were leaning heavily upon their spear shafts and seeking to catch their breath. Up against the English wall, like some tidal wrack, there lay a thick line of bodies. Perhaps a half hour had passed since the very first arrows had been loosed against the English and it was time now for both sides to pause and to take stock. The English were out amongst the fallen men, stabbing the wounded enemy and taking their mail and weapons, struggling at the leather straps with chilled fingers and snatching food from the wallets of the fallen, which they crammed into their mouths. Here and there came cries of triumph above those of the wounded as coin was discovered. Amongst the thick mound of English dead lying where the Norman horsemen had caught them there was nothing worth taking. On both sides there arose bitter arguments and recriminations. Caked in blood and moving stiffly, Leofwyn left affairs to his chief man Osketil and made his way with considerable difficulty through the mass of men to Harold's side.

Harold was near apoplectic with rage and passion at the sight of his brother. Ignoring Leofwyn's obvious wounds to his shoulder and face and leg, he jabbed him viciously in the chest. "And what, in the name of all that's Holy, do you think you were playing at?" he demanded. Leofwyn removed his helmet. Sweat had plastered his hair to his scalp. He shrugged, "There was simply no stopping them," he replied. "Not even you could have stopped them. They thought that they had them cold and perhaps, if the whole line had come on, we could have finished things." The flowing blood from his cheek wound had begun to congeal, he felt weak and he ached all over. Harold looked over at the dead of Kent and Essex, his brother's men. In a more conciliatory tone he said, "For the last time of telling. Our defence, our victory, lies with us standing firm and making them come to us. There will be no more breaking ranks and running at them. Do you understand me, do you hear what I am saying?"

"And have us stand there and let them shoot us full of holes?" Like most men there, it was Leofwyn's first experience of arrow and crossbow bolt fire. "Then you may attack. But you do not pursue. Is that clear?" replied Harold. "Leofric, you can see now, can't you, what horsemen in open ground can do? Your people didn't stand a chance against them."

Back amongst his own Normans once more, William was equally scathing. The hapless recipient of his anger was Robert FitzWimarc, who had made his apologetic way over to the Duke, his horse stepping delicately around the bodies. "Tell my Lord Alan that I have pulled his chestnuts out of the fire for him this once. Tell him that I do not propose to do so a second time. When next we move we do so together and in the fashion of the professional men that we are, not like some drunken rabble at a wedding feast. Tell him that. You have my permission to be as rude as you like."

Robert Beaumont had arrived from the other flank with news and requests for orders. To he at least, William was moderately civil. "A rather poor showing, Robert, do you not think? Upon my oath, that's a fine old shiner you've got

there. Been in the wars, have you?" Robert was as painstakingly honest as his father. "No, your Grace. A man hit me
in the eye with his shield. It was an accident, and he apologised" William laughed at him, not unkindly. "Well, so long
as it wasn't some nasty rude Englishman, that's good enough
then. I trust that my Lords of Ponthieu and Boulogne are
well, that they have not met with any mishaps?" Beaumont
shook his head, slightly puzzled at the question. "They are
well and have taken no hurt your Grace and thank you for
asking. They are, though, most keen to be at them up there,
and want to know when." William assured him. "Soon
enough, but we do need a certain amount of time to organise things here, and to get our illustrious Breton friends
back in line." Odo leaned across to mutter in William's ear.
"The Count of Boulogne does have a point there, brother.
The longer we delay then the better it is for the English." It
was hard, sometimes, to credit that the Bishop of Bayeux
was not yet thirty. "I know, I know," said William testily.
"We have both hurt each other a little. The next time things
will be different."

There was no prospect of food or any other provisions for the English, just a constant trickle of arriving
men, exhausted and famished. As they appeared out of the
woods and laboured up the track to the ridge Aesegar and
his men directed them to the depleted ranks of Leofwyn's
command and where Leofwyn himself, in a towering rage
and muttering imprecations, had just arrived after his very
public argument with Harold. The English, after the fighting
of that first hour, were baffled by the lull that had now settled
over the battlefield. Gyrth, undamaged and grim, paid a brief
visit to Harold, not wishing to be separated from his East
Anglians for too long for fear that the enemy should come
at them up that greasy and treacherous slope once more.
It had taken him some time to shoulder his way through

the crowd. "That was a lesson for us all back there," Harold greeted him. "We stand where we are."

"Agreed," said Gyrth, "but it's devilish hard to hold them when their blood is up. Praise God, but we didn't take too much harm amongst our people. Are you going to stand here at the back all day like a boil on the arse, or do you propose to do any fighting yourself?" The remark was intended, in Gyrth's own fashion, to be humorous and Harold, knowing his brother as well as he knew any man, took it in the right spirit. "Boils can burst, you know. And when they do it is not very pleasant." He would have said more but Gyrth interrupted him, pointing. "Would you credit it?" he exclaimed. "I do believe that they are sitting down for breakfast!"

Sure enough, the first of the carts had come up from Hastings. Any illusions on the part of the wagon men that their task was now over were swiftly dispelled when they found themselves bustled with blows and curses into the ranks of the infantry. There were fresh sheaves of arrows and bundles of crossbow bolts, more spears, sacks of bread and boiled meat, cheese and raw onions, fresh water and the thin acid wine they had all been drinking for weeks. Up on the ridge, the starving English could see the horsemen being handed food and drink in the saddle. Food was also coming forward to the footmen. The English, anxious to be at the enemy below once more, could scarcely believe their eyes. After their apparent earlier success, they were all for going down and helping themselves to the food they coveted. Harold himself paced the length of the shield wall, letting himself be seen. "There'll be plenty for all soon enough," he told his men. "Just hold the line. Hold the line."

***

This pause, the delay, could not go on for long. De Lisle, always one of William's most ardent followers, called across to him. "Your Grace, let us be at them again." William threw aside a lump of highly suspect mutton. "Very well then," he agreed. "Only this time we'll do it my way." Thus far, his Spanish mount had behaved admirably, he patted its neck, making sounds of praise as it pawed curiously at a corpse at its forefeet. "Footmen in close support and all three contingents arriving at the same time if you please. The knights are to come on as well. If it fails the first, the second, the third time, then we'll keep on at it until we do succeed."

There was no longer any joy or elation to be found in this second assault upon the ridge. William's army surged up the now greasy slope. They struggled and hacked and heaved at the crowded and screaming English line and then withdrew sullenly to lick their wounds and regroup. There was, as William had surmised, a first and then a second move forward, urged on by their bawling leaders, but the English wall still held, immoveable. It was a revelation to the angered and frustrated Duke as he looked up the slope, watching the enemy axes rise and fall rhythmically and remorselessly upon the heads of his men. A determined line of heavily armed men on foot was not something that he had ever come across before. In all of his experience footmen, when faced with cavalry, were meant to scatter and run like hares. This was, clearly, a lesson to be learned and noted for the future. Trained since early boyhood in the skills of combat, his mounted knights were fighting as individuals, each seeking to take on an individual opponent. But here, in this fight, there were no individual opponents or the opportunity for any public glory or individual satisfaction in personal combat. Instead there stood an anonymous and roaring wall of men striking out in a vicious fury. Here and there individual knights went crashing through the shield wall through sheer force and weight of horse and armour, killing and wounding as they went, only to be absorbed into the dense crowd beyond and brought down. In this way

Roger FitzTurold rode straight into a pack of housecarls, striking out left and right with his sword and taking blows upon his splintering shield. A fyrdman with a knife slipped in from behind and neatly hamstrung his horse. Kicking free of his stirrups, FitzTurold leaped clear. With certain doom before him and screaming the war cry of his ancestors, he caught the first man to stand against him. It happened to be the Shire Reeve Aesegar. Two handed, he brought his sword down onto Aesegar's collar bone and cut deep into his body before one of Aesegar's followers stepped up and brought his axe down on the Norman's skull. The leader of the men of London and Middlesex, moaning and bleeding profusely, was carried to the rear through the jostling men. It seemed very unlikely now that he would ever reap the benefits of Harold's generous rewards. Aesegar was deposited on the reverse slope of the ridge, left there amongst the growing numbers of dead and dying.

It was at this time that William lost the first of three horses that day, the homicidal and much-loved black stallion from Seville. With Robert and Bigod at either knee and with more horsemen jostling behind, he found himself caught up in the general movement and crashing into the section of the line held by the Danes. The wall buckled slightly at the impact and the Danes went dodging away as the horse lashed out, front hooves flailing. William stood in the stir-rups, screaming for support. Bawling and grinning through the thick undergrowth of their beards, the Danes were now coming right back at them. Robert flung his lance over arm and rode right side on to his brother, beating down on the kite shields beneath him. On William's left Bigod did likewise as wild eyed and screaming men leaped up at him, seeking to snatch the Golden Leopard from his grasp. Seeing the Duke in difficulties, a mixture of his men, Knights and foot, struggled forward to reach him. The horse shud-dered, suddenly and violently, and then sank to its knees, a throwing axe deeply embedded in its unprotected chest. William leaped clear, still swinging his sword to make space for himself. "Deux Veult," he yelled, "Deux Ai." There was a film of blood, obscuring his vision.

A first and then a second man fell back before the vicious sweeping arc of his sword. others moved back out of respect for the still flailing forefeet of the iron shod horse as it screamed out the last of its breath. A rumour began to percolate back through the ranks of his uncertain men, wavering there at the edge of those swinging swords and axes. "The Duke is down. The Duke is dead." To the rear, men began to turn and slip back down the slope. A mounted knight of Avranches whom William vaguely recognised was now beside him. "Off that horse," he commanded. Without pausing to think, the man freed his feet from the stirrups, jumped down and helped the Duke into the saddle before turning to meet the Danes and his own almost immediate death. William cantered along the line of battle, ducking stones and spears as he went. He took off his helmet and pulled back his chain mail cowl, showing his reddened and maddened face to his people. From the ranks of the Danes above came the derisive chant they had picked up from the English. "Out, tanner. Out, tanner. Out, out, out."

Bigod had come back down the ridge and was now back with him, brandishing the Ducal Leopard and his brothers were back at his side. William's passage, weaving through the uncertain and wavering men, brought the desired effect. They halted and cheered, attempting to dress their ranks once more. It was on the Breton wing, and not for the first time, where the greatest danger presented itself. There Count Alan's severely mauled command was on the edge of breaking and falling back as the Kent and Essex housecarls hooted derisively at them and banged upon their shields. There it came again, the booming cry of "out, out, out." Count Alan was shrieking hoarsely and ineffectually in Celtic Breton and

French at the ragged and tattered collection of men under his ostensible command and it looked as if at any moment the English might resolve themselves once more into a vengeful surge down the slope. William took a moment to glance around him as he wiped the sweat and blood from his eyes. The Norman centre and the French right was withdrawing again and in reasonably good order and the English facing them there seemed apparently content enough to watch them go. Time was on their side and Gyrth's supervision and control of them was firm. But here, once again, the less disciplined right wing of the English did indeed come bounding and leaping down the slope, housecarls mixed with fyrdmen.

The knights of the Norman centre had formed up once more, save for those now lying on the ridge or still fighting their own doomed individual battles surrounded by enraged Englishmen. It was to be hoped that the men of the French had done the same, but in the chaotic moments of the last attack William had had no news from there. He noted the running men away to his left. "It is there that we shall have them," he commented to Odo and Robert, "there on the flanks. If we can work around them then their centre cannot hold." This battle was taking too long, longer than he had expected or any other battle he had personally experienced. He looked up at the grey and overcast sky. There was no real clue there to determine the hour. Certainly, though, it must be approaching mid afternoon. This had to be finished, and finished quickly.

Turning around in the ill-fitting saddle of the hapless Avranches Knight, William spotted the seemingly indestructible Neel of Herve in the ranks of horsemen assembled behind him. William beckoned him over. "Away now to my Lord of Boulogne," he commanded. "Tell him he is to maintain his attack on the men to his front, whatever the cost." Herve knuckled his forehead and spurred his horse. Ahead the Normans were still backing away sullenly, in sufficient strength and order to deter any counter attack. Amongst the Bretons, though, it was still clearly a hopeless mess and showing every sign of getting yet further out of hand. Robert of Mortain had already anticipated William's most likely order in the circumstances. He was off at a tangent and with a force of perhaps one hundred knights, pounding across the littered front to strike once again at the exposed English flank.

Leofwyn, mindful of his brother's earlier bitter rebuke, was meantime hard at work marshalling and manhandling his people back up the slope and into line. They were returning at last, gleeful at this latest success and not too mindful of or insulted by the Earl's colourful and vituperative language. The veins starting out from his face and neck, Lefowyn screamed and yelled at them as they trotted past. "Have you such poor memories that you do not remember what happened last time?" he demanded of one such group of men. They did not appear to be listening. Instead they gaped over his shoulder and then began to run. Leofwyn became suddenly conscious of a thudding and pounding above the general noise behind him, of the sound also of metal jingling against metal and of alien shouts. He began to turn but, before he could do so, he felt a sudden painful blow in the small of his back that made him gasp. Not even the best of chain mail shirts could have resisted the force of that blow. There was a blur of grey and brown away to his right and he was sent flying. The sudden and violent pain took his breath away and before he fell to his knees he looked down in puzzlement. There, emerging from his chest, was a spear point and a good six inches of wooden haft. The man who had inflicted Leofwyn's death wound rode on, whooping as he went, followed by a number of other riders, all of whom trampled him into the mud as they rode over him in their hurry to be at the English. There was no time for last thoughts, just a sickening blow, a piercing pain and a blinding light.

As before, it was the fyrdmen who suffered the most, falling helpless beneath the flailing hooves and swinging steel. Robert, returning to William's side, was his usual overwhelmingly cheerful self. "That's the way to serve them," he announced. "Lure them down and then carve them up. Those Bretons, did they but know it, did us a service."

***

From his vantage point on the ridge Harold noted the growing danger. Knowing nothing of his brother's death, he despatched Leofgar and Alfi over to the right flank with the repeated order to stand fast. "Elsewise he'll lose this battle for us for sure," he called after them. He regretted the remark on the instant and touched the wooden hasp of his axe for luck. The two men set off, racing along the less crowded rear of the line and leaping over the dead and wounded lying there. They arrived finally to find the very extreme end of the English line turning in on itself at a right angle. Gaps had now appeared in the wall and mounted men were riding through them. The enemy foot was close up behind and arrows were now falling like a steady rain upon the unprotected fyrdmen.

There was no sign of Leofwyn. Leofgar recognised a Middlesex thegn standing there, as if in a daze, blood pouring from a scalp wound. "Get back along that ridge and bring men down here," Leofgar barked at him. "There are men standing idle up there." Leofgar was of the King's personal bodyguard and so not be argued with. The thegn wiped the blood from his eyes and set off at a dogtrot in search of fresh men.

Immediately between Leofgar and Alfi and the swirling fight, the many dead and dying and the wounded each seeking the sanctuary of their own lines a handsome bay horse lay on its side, rolling in an attempt to rise and screaming in pain. One of its front legs was clearly broken and the sight of this proved too much for the Hampshire boy. Alfi drew his knife and, heedless of the fighting all around him, set off to cut the horse's throat. Neel of Herve, just arrived back from his mission to the French, noted this new isolated target with pleasure and spurred his horse.

Horrified, Leofgar saw the danger. He cupped his hands and shouted. Alfi looked up, turned and ran. Herve was already upon him. As he drew level with Alfi he swung his sword in a vicious scything movement. The blade cut into the boy just above the waist. Had he not been wearing mail he would have been cut almost clean in two, but it was a mortal death wound nonetheless. Herve wheeled his horse and followed up with a second blow which cut deep into Alfi's neck, partly severing his head. Leofgar screamed again in his anguish and launched himself in a flying leap at the Norman, momentarily distracted by the task of removing his blade from Alfi's body. Herve was taken completely by surprise and the two men fell rolling into the mud. Leofgar had dropped his axe and Herve's sword had been knocked out of reach.

The two men panted and swore at each other in their separate languages, climbed to their feet and circled each other at the crouch. In background and outlook these two, did they but know it, were very similar to one another, with many a shared philosophy. They were also quite without fear of the other. To each man his opponent was merely a problem to be solved. Leofgar pulled one of his knives from his belt, thin bladed and with a slightly curving blade. He grinned mirthlessly at Herve who, backing off, tripped over Alfi and fell. Leofgar was on him in an instant. Herve had suffered wounds before, but not the like of the knife thrust into his side. As he gasped and arched with the pain of it

Leofgar slashed twice at his face. The knife had a custom-
ised serrated edge. By averting his head just in time, Herve
instead of having his throat cut from ear to ear received a
raking cut that lay his face open from temple to chin. The
second slash, also a hurried one, scooped his eye out from
its socket and spread it like a jelly down his blood covered
cheek. Leofgar did not have the time for more. Their little
duel, short lived as it had been, had attracted the attention
of others, now urging their horses towards him. Leofgar
realised that he was alone now in that space among the dead
and dying. He kicked the badly wounded Herve hard in the
groin for good measure. "Goodbye Alfi," he said. "My regards
to the others. I shall see you all there soon."

Neither the English nor the Normans could sustain a
fight of this ferocity and the casualties that it brought with
it for much longer. The sun, what could be seen of it, was
already dipping away to the west. The ranks of the English
along the ridge, formerly eight, were now reduced to five
and many of the fyrdmen, in hastily taken up armour and
with new weapons, were now standing in the front two
ranks. Harold moved amongst them, punching their shoulders and screaming hoarse encouragement. "If we hold
them, boys, then we have them. We must hold them till the
dark. Hold them until the dark and this fight is ours." The
enemy infantry continued to roil up like waves. Blows were
exchanged and they withdrew. In each pause there came
further showers of arrows that brought yet more casualties.
Many of the fyrdmen had now equipped themselves with
the weapons and helmets and shields of dead housecarls,
the straps and harnesses ripped and loose and the axes and
swords uncertain in their hands. The enemy horse now
seemed to be concentrating on the gentler slopes to either
side. Harold wondered how his brothers were faring and
he worried over the fact that Leofgar and Alfi had not yet
returned to his side. Now, disturbingly, the enemy seemed

to be to three sides of him. He looked along the front of his line, still firm and yelling defiance.

Near to him a body was being passed over the heads of the men. As it was being carried back to the rear, he recognised the burden the men were supporting. It was his nephew Haakon. The boy was still alive, but clearly not for very much longer. His face was grey, and his chest heaved and laboured. Harold hurried over to him as he was being lowered gently to the ground. Harold groaned with despair and grief. "Well then, my nephew," he asked. "How goes it with you?" With difficulty Haakon turned up his head to look at him. "Not so good, Uncle, if the truth be told. I think it is all up with me. God's Love, though, but aren't those Danes the boys for a fight?" He smiled the old mischievous smile that Harold had come to know so well and then he started suddenly, his head came up and he died without another word.

The Danes were indeed the boys for a fight. Their numbers had now been reduced by over half, but the enemy dead lay thickest before their ranks than anywhere along the line. William's horse, taken from the Avranches man, was badly blown and now, from where he sat on his third horse of the day, the enemy looked as if they were peering over a boundary wall of dead. The sight of that mound of men and the defiant giants standing and gesticulating behind it decided him, that and the failing light. He looked around him once more for trusted men to ride to the flanks. There seemed to be precious few of them around, not men that he could immediately spare anyway. Where the hell was FitzWimarc when he needed him? In fact, FitzWimarc, the extravagant and exuberant adventurer, the one-time patron of the best brothels in Southwark, was lying face down and stone dead in a pool of water, trapped and drowned beneath an equally dead horse. In the event Bigod was prevailed upon to surrender up his banner and to ride over to the Count of

Boulogne and Aimerie of Thouars. Robert de Vitot, miraculously unwounded and provided with a fresh mount, was sent off to the hard-pressed Bretons. Their orders were the same. Be at great pains, he told them to impress the need to keep up the pressure on the flanks, to force the English back, to keep attacking and, with the archers there, to give them no rest.

When Bigod finally found Eustace of Boulogne and FitzOsbern they were already engaged upon the task, as indeed they had been since the morning. "Keep at it? Keep at it?" screamed Eustace when Bigod had delivered his message. "What the hell does his Grace think we've been doing all bloody day? We're not picking flowers here. Lord God Almighty! They are murdering us up there. How about if his Grace the good Duke comes over here to take a look for himself?" Eustace was incandescent with fury as he incautiously pushed his helmet back on his head and ran the back of his hand across his heavily sweating brow. Bigod, a literal man, would have been perfectly happy to relay this message back, word for word. "What the Count means," said FitzOsbern with care, "what the Count is saying, is that we have the matter in hand, as much as we are presently able. I am grieved to inform his Grace that the noble and gallant Aimerie is dead. We shall continue to press forward and trust that our Breton friends over there will do likewise."

De Vitot was unable to deliver his identical message to Count Alan. The Count lay unconscious and bleeding as servants attempted to revive him, splashing murky water over his unresponsive face and head. De Vitot seized the initiative for himself, sending as many mounted knights to the centre as seemed practical and prudent and directing the Breton foot and archers against the now crumbling lines of the Kent and Essex men. He went forward again once too often, in the brawl at the front of the English line he killed and killed again until he received an axe blow to his unprotected neck and shoulder that it would take six long weeks for him to die from.

The sounds of the fighting to either side travelled clearly to Harold, standing there on the highest point of the ridge with his bodyguard and standards around him. He stared below him, beyond the heaps of dead at two well-ordered lines of the enemy, with bowmen and arbelists ahead of them, though much reduced in their numbers. Compared to the continuing roar of the English and the constant shout of "Out tanner, out tanner, out, out, out," the noise coming from them was muted. As he stared down, he noted the reinforcements of horsemen now massing and concentrating on either flank. He swore vividly. There had to be near on a thousand of them down there. On this shorter front directly in front of him almost the same number, or so it seemed, had gathered behind the archers and foot. They looked irresistible and they were clearly coming straight for the middle of the English shield wall. His nephew was dead, and he had had the news that his own uncle and his dependable Aesegar were likely to die of their wounds. He had no time to grieve, that he would do later.

From the decimated ranks of the men of Kent and Essex, Leofgar had finally got a message across to his King. The man knelt at Harold's feet, his chest heaving and labouring like a bellows. Leofgar, he told him, was presently obliged to stay where he was in order to see to matters. He did this in the absence of any other notable thegn or earldorman. "And my brother, then. He is dead?" The messenger nodded, gulping for breath and staring at his feet. Harold lifted his head to the darkening sky and howled at the news. It was an eerie cry of guilt and rage and anguish that rose into the air above all other sounds and had men turning around to stare.

Leofwyn, the family buffoon, the ever-amiable butt of every family joke. Leofwyn his brother, short on tact and judgement, a great-hearted man, a lover of life to the full. Harold looked once more at the dark mass of men gathering at the foot of the ridge. He burned with anger and the need for revenge. In all of this day he had yet to strike a single blow and the light was failing fast. The Abbot of Peterborough had stood in the front rank all that long day, swapping blows and killing and not taking a single hurt. He knew exactly and precisely what was passing through Harold's mind at that moment. "Your place is here," he told his King sternly as he leant upon the haft of his axe and struggling for breath. There was no attempt at any formal address or the proper forms normally required, he had known Harold since he was a boy. "You brought these people here and to this. Now take the consequences," is what he wanted to say, but didn't. Instead, he said, simply, "We may grieve for your brother and all of the others when this is done and finished."

Under Gyrth's meticulous and well-ordered command, the men of the English right fell back like a door on a hinge in order to prevent the enemy from outflanking them and coming down upon them in their rear. There were now just three ranks of men, mostly of the fyrd, stretching for about one hundred paces or so. There was a mad scramble for any discarded shields as, unmolested, the French and Flemish bowmen loosed their arrows against them once more. There was no defence against the iron crossbow bolts when they struck. The East Anglians were now becoming intermingled with the Londoners and the Middlesex fyrd as their line contracted. "God willing, we shall hold them," Gyrth told his companion, a man called Breme. Sent by Harold for news, Breme had been specifically instructed not to speak of the death of Leofwyn. "They are trying to flank you here," Breme said unnecessarily and pointed out a mixed force of about two hundred bowmen and foot labouring across the flooded stream to their right. "They'll have a hard time of it," said Gyrth, attempting to bind a strip of linen over a gash on his left forearm. He couldn't even remember when he had taken the wound. "Here, let me," offered Breme. He tied the linen strip tightly in place and immediately the strip turned crimson. "Maybe they will have a hard time of it," he continued. "But what you need to know is that the bastard has brought together as many of his men on horses as he can gather in the one place and he is now going straight for the centre of things. They could cut you off from the King. Can you shorten your line and make it deeper?"

Gyrth thought back to that morning, it seemed like weeks ago, when the main concern had been too many English in the ranks. "If I do that," he said, "then these people we face over here will work around behind us and my brother will have spears and arrows and God knows what coming at him from behind. He needs to know that. You have seen what he has not. Go back and tell him." Breme was never able to. On his way back to Harold an arrow, falling at the end of its arc, caught him in the nape of the neck and killed him outright.

***

"A task for you," said William to de Tosny, who happened to be on hand. "Tell whoever it is who commands those bowmen ahead, I assume someone does, that I will have them loose their arrows at the vertical. I want them falling directly on their heads. Let us see if the English can fight one handed and with shields over their heads. Let's see what that does." To d'Ivry he said, "clear those foot out of the way. Ride over them if necessary. There they are neither use nor ornament. Send them to right and left to support the flanks. We shall do this with horsemen and archers." The much-abused foot were all of them more tired than they had ever been in their lives before. They had moved up and down that slope all day, for more than six hours now. They had been trading blows with that implacable shield wall since early morning and their limbs felt like lead. They had taken horrific casualties, by far the highest of any separate part of either army, to little effect and with no thanks whatsoever. It required no massive strain on their imaginations to surmise what their fate would be if night fell and the English still held out. They were equally aware of the concentrated mass of horsemen gathering behind them, men who would ride them down without a second thought. When the order came, they moved to either wing with alacrity, parting like a curtain to escape the men and horses coming up behind them and the bowmen and arbelists moved up.

Behind them there came three lines of horsemen. There were perhaps five hundred of them, riding over a front so narrow that they rode knee to knee. The horses were covered in blood up to their fetlocks and most of the horsemen, equally grimy and muddy, carried at least one wound. Perhaps now, they sensed, they were at the end of things. The feeling was good and gave them new confidence and heart as they prepared for yet another assault.

New horn blasts from either flank summoned the footmen in once more against the now much weakened English wings. With admirable timing a fresh shower of arrows flew upwards, this time almost vertically. In the rear ranks of the English, men were falling in their dozens now, struck by the barbs and unable to fight back. The cries and moans of the injured and the dying seemed to rise in pitch and intensity. Harold screamed "shields up" just in time as the arrows fell. Caedmon, unarmoured and without shield, was unlucky. He yelped as an arrow, its flight nearly spent, struck him on the shoulder. "To me, little one," murmured Harold and hauled him under the protection of his own shield. Willi also crouched there. "I daresay this will hurt somewhat" he said and grinned. Without ceremony he pulled the arrow from Caedmon's shoulder. He knelt and ripped a strip of linen from the tunic of a dead man at his feet and handed it to Caedmon to staunch the flow of blood. The cleric yelped once more, "It is only a scratch, Caedmon," he chided him. From somewhere Willi had thieved a leather flask of aqua vitae, perhaps from a dead Dane. He poured some of the drink down Caedmon's throat and the cleric gagged and spluttered. "There, that'll put hairs on your chest," Willi encouraged him. He would have said more but at that moment a double horn blast signaled the movement forward of the knights below.

The enemy bowmen scuttled swiftly to either side as the horsemen approached like a grey tide. Harold and the Abbot of Peterborough moved along the greatly diminished ranks, shoving fyrdmen into the shield wall. "Here they come again," shouted Harold. "Stand fast." He encouraged them in the war cry once more, "out, out, out." The horsemen were now twenty paces off, moving their tired horses into a protesting canter, when Harold took his own place in the shield wall at last. The ground seemed to tremble beneath his feet and at this close distance he could smell the sweat and blood and leather and of horses rising up from the oncoming enemy like a miasma. It came back to him then, and with a piercing clarity. That old recurring nightmare, the screams, the rushing sound and the sudden darkness. This was it. This was the end of all things. There would be an end of it all here. He had just time enough to shout across to Willi. "Just like Brunanburgh, like Maldon, yes?" Willi saluted him with a mock gravity. "Bigger and better," he shouted back. And then the horses were upon them. It was death pounding and drumming towards them, big men on big horses. They had held them off all day when they had come as individuals or in small groups. Now they were coming for them in their hundreds, slate grey men, only their eyes showing between shield rim and helmet and this time with their spears couched underarm. Trained for this, the horses barged into the line and broke it immediately in half a dozen places, each gap exploited by five or six riders before closing up once more. The rest of that front line of horsemen surged up against the wall, hurling their spears and raining down blows with sword and axe and mace.

A knight, a tall man anonymous in his mail and his features hidden by his helmet and nasal guard, was coming straight for Harold. Perhaps he had decided that this was the oath breaking King, an opportunity for everlasting fame and glory. Harold stepped neatly to the side and the knight went ploughing into the ranks behind, trampling men underfoot. Harold swung up at him backhanded, cutting deep into his spine. The man shrieked and fell as Harold turned to face his next adversary. He had killed at last. In the throng of the English it was all but impossible for them to raise their weapons, even in defence. The knights of that first rank lost perhaps twenty of their men in those first few moments as the rest cut themselves out again and back down the slope. This time, in their fury, the English of the centre did break ranks to pursue them, until called back by Harold and those thegns that still lived. They arrived back just in time for another hail of arrows to fall upon their unprotected backs and heads. Once more Harold held his shield above his head as arrows thudded into it, he felt their impact. He screamed desperately again for the line to close up and hold, though he was by now hoarse and his throat was burning for a drink.

Just below the English centre William and Odo came together for a brief moment. Both were panting heavily from their exertions. It was hard to talk above the din and their excited horses danced and bucked as the brothers struggled to control them. Odo was wide eyed and spoke as if drunk. "This is the way it is to be done, brother," he gasped. "I have not seen the like of it, they are real fighters." At some stage he had received a wound to his upper thigh, someone had strapped a wad of a torn tunic upon it and it seemed to no longer bleed. He was paying it no heed now, swinging his stained mace on its short leather strap in an enthusiastic and most unecclesiastical manner. "By Christ," he yelled, "We shall break them yet." Old, white haired Warenne, much too old for this type of activity was at the head of the next line. It was heartening to see him unscathed and William waved him on furiously as once more the bowmen scuttled out of harm's way. "Next line forward and into them," William yelled. "It will be dusk soon, and then it will all be up with us then."

The Kent and Essex men had had enough and nothing that Leofgar could say or do gave them pause. Those that remained of the fyrd began streaming north to the supposed protection of the woods behind and Leofgar was left with perhaps a score or two of housecarls, many of them badly wounded. Harold's flank had all but ceased to exist. They continued to trade blows with the bone-tired Breton foot and won each encounter easily. Leofgar killed four men in quick succession, darting and weaving and selecting his blows with a professional precision. There was no especial passion or anger, just a job of work professionally carried out. These boys from the apple orchards and the marshes of Brittany were no match for a royal housecarl in a rare old rage and who had learned more dirty tricks in close order fighting than they had had hot dinners. Here too, now, the arrows were beginning to come thick and fast. When these finally ceased there was the inevitable enemy coming up on them once more. This time they were also appearing from behind. As Leofgar turned to rejoin his king a large wedge of horsemen came thundering up the slope and cutting him off. He quickly took the scene in. The wiry little Mercian had never in his life been on the receiving end of a lost fight but here, beyond a doubt, the day was lost, and with it his future. He had seen a lot of dead heroes that day and he elected instead to live on to fight again on a more propitious day and on a more propitious field. He remembered the road in from the north, perhaps they would rally at the crossroads there. He led perhaps ten unwounded men off the field and in that direction, moving at a ground consuming trot. The Bretons, panting and struggling for breath, were only too happy to let them go.

Having no trust at all in the young heir of Ponthieu at his side, FitzOsbern over before the still defiant East Anglians on the other flank instead sent him back to the Duke with the message. Perhaps the young pest would get on the wrong end of a weapon on his way over there. The enemy ahead of him were weakening, their numbers thinning, and the horsemen were now beginning to get around their side and behind them. He calculated that they had considerably less than an hour of full daylight or half-light in which to conclude things. There had been absolutely no opportunity in that busy and crowded day for him to do anything whatsoever by way of bringing the careers of either Boulogne or Poitou to a sad and premature end. He had been busy enough and his left arm, now dangling uselessly at his side and causing him immense and ceaseless pain, was clearly broken. He and Count Eustace watched as a score of knights led by Beaumont went crashing into the very edge of the English flank and sent it spinning. They wheeled back and away and a party of Flemish archers and arbelists immediately moved in to loose at the English remnants at close range. All that day Count Eustace had been beside himself with excitement and full of fierce and coura- geous acts. FitzOsbern, who rarely misjudged the strengths and weaknesses of a man, had wholly underestimated the Count. He had had him marked down as a feasting hall brag- gart, but Eustace had proved him wrong. He had been in the thick of the fighting all through that terrifing day and had taken no serious hurt. "Look," said Eustace, pointing. "They are moving off to their right. They know they have to shorten their line." Here, with bogs, a treacherous slope, undergrowth and with exposed and foot entangling tree roots, it was dangerous country for horses in a failing light. FitzOsbern, wincing, tried to restrain him, but the Count was off once more with twenty horsemen at his back.

Gyrth was standing in brief conference with Godric, a thegn of Lowestoft, and reviewing the fast deteriorating situation when the tip of a crossbow bolt appeared just above the bridge of the man's nose like a third eye, his head seemed to explode in a shower of blood and bone. The arrows were falling upon them in ever greater amounts now and the rear ranks of the fyrd were shouting out panicked warnings as small squads of horsemen began to appear behind them for the first time. Gyrth swore violently and bitterly. "I hope that my brothers are holding them better than we are," he remarked to no one in particular. He wondered briefly if Aelfgifu his wife had given birth to the latest child yet back home in Norwich, it was certainly due. He knew now in his bones then that he would not be walking away from this place. Left here, they would be cut off and isolated, easy prey for those bestial grey men on their giant horses. Already he had lost well over a third of his men. They lay stretched out in thick piles at his feet, promiscuously entwined with the dead of France and Flanders. "Move to your right," he bawled. "To your right. Close up on the centre. No running, no panic, faces to the enemy." He took a swift drink of just about the last of his honey mead and began his dangerous journey back to his brother, walking backwards and with kite shield raised.

***

William de Warenne's one hundred knights rode with William and his brothers and another forty mounted men into the English shield wall even as the arrows were still falling. The carnage of this new attack was even greater, with the war horses trampling over a wall of dead and wounded to be at the enemy. The Danes were down to a dozen men, still jeering and hooting. Grimm and Ulfketil, both of Aarlsborg and companions to King Sweyn himself, were the acknowledged leaders of the men remaining. Both were skilled and hardened veterans of the unending war against the Hardraada. Both were well into their forties and accustomed more to shipboard fighting. Perhaps, in this cramped space, there was little difference. Coming straight for them was Odo and his little band of devoted 'tirones,' especially chosen boys handpicked for their fine blood lines and their even finer looks. "That fat one on the chestnut there," said Ulfketil, pointing out Odo. "His head would make a fine trophy on the wall above the fireplace back home, wouldn't it just?" Grimm nodded in agreement. "It would indeed, but who is going to hang it up there for you, you old bastard?" Ulfketil had little time for further comment for the horsemen were nearly upon them. They had both grown up together, since they were young boys serving out a difficult and punishing apprenticeship in the old garrison at Jutland and learning the wicked ways of the world the hard way. They were in their last fight; they both knew this. "I pray to both the White Christ and to Odin," said Ulfketil. "Whatever, wherever, whoever, I hope that Heaven and Valhalla are much the same thing." Grimm smiled at him and turned to the surviving Danes. "Let's not wait for them. Let's go do them." The last of the Danish Vikings went screaming down the slope, roaring defiance and swinging their axes. They met their opponents head on, a most unexpected tactic, and had most of Odo's favoured boys out of their saddles before reinforcements from de Tosny and Guy Seneschal rode over and finally finished the business.

***

This was the end, the end of things. The stark, bitter truth of it weighed Harold down with despair like an additional

weight as he fought his way back to where his two standards still flew. The line was broken again, perhaps this time
beyond repair. Already he could see it curving in on itself
and forcing men down onto the reverse slope and where the
opportunity to break and run was now too great to resist.
The housecarls were now fighting in small knots of men.
Now, at least, they had room to swing their weapons. The
old Abbot of Peterborough was down at last, attempting to
crawl away from the trampling horses and the probing spear
points. With Willi and the Welsh boy Gareth at his back,
Harold lashed out at the horsemen converging on him, for
he was now a visible and clearly identifiable target. The down
swinging blow of Hugh de Grandesmil, that ambitious and
cautious man who had defied William at Rouen and again at
Lillebonne, was designed for him and him alone. He saw it
coming only at the last moment. A dark figure flickered in
front of him.

The little cleric, Caedmon had appeared, seemingly from
nowhere, holding up the stave of a broken spear to parry the
blow. The sword passed effortlessly through the wood and
deep into Caedmon's head as, from another direction, a second
knight transfixed him with his own spear. William's chaplain,
his conscience and on occasion his salve, dropped to the ground,
his eyes staring up sightlessly at the darkening sky. Willi swung
his axe at de Grandesmil's horse, striking it in the neck with
an immense force and killing it. The Norman fell heavily to the
ground, rolling to avoid the axe as it came heavily down once
more to bury itself in the earth. De Grandesmil clambered to
his feet and ducked away out of range. Willi and Harold had
just enough time to exchange a glance. They both knew now
that this was a lost cause. There was no fear at all in Willi's face,
just an all-consuming pity and compassion for his King.

Forgotten, ignored, unbidden, the FitzPons twins rode
on ownerless horses in the wake of de Warenne's line of
cavalry, their Duke in sight of them just ahead. Hugh

clutched a spear and Drogo a sword. It was much too big for him and he regretted the choice. All day they had watched the fight from a range that had divorced them from the brutal realities of close quarter fighting, the sprays of blood and the maiming wounds. True, they could hear everything, and they had seen the corpses and watched as wounded men of quality were carried back to the rear. They had gazed wide eyed at all of this. But that was not the same thing at all as riding in defense of their Lord. This had of course been Hugh's idea, though they both ran the risk of being beaten soundly for it afterwards. The reality of it all was far removed from the bragging stories and the legends and songs they had absorbed since infancy. There were men ahead of them who would kill them if they could. Robert of Mortain, fighting desperately, punching a man in the face who came leaping for his reins, saw them at last out of the corner of his eye and cursed. He wheeled his horse around just as the horn sounded another retire. The horsemen, in a body, wheeled and came thundering back down the slope once more with Englishmen racing after them. At that very moment Hugh's nervous horse tripped and threw him. He was on his hands and knees as the knights rode over him, breaking his bones and knocking him senseless. He was still lying there as a pursuing Bedford fyrdman paused to cut his throat.

***

Gyrth was ducking and weaving his way through the shambles of the English left flank. What few remained of his veterans of Stamford Bridge followed after in a tight group, shields held high against the arrows. There was open space between him now and where the standards still flew, but even as he made for this it was suddenly filled with yet more horsemen. He could just make out his brother, standing there on that slightly raised ground. "No going through that lot," he shouted at his men. "Fall back to the apple tree, back to the apple tree. Watch your backs."

Odo, consumed with grief and a black rage at the massacre of so many of his fine and lovely boys, noted the hurrying figure, now momentarily separated from his comrades. Gyrth, slightly shorter, slightly less golden in colour, was so much like the older brother that Odo had known in Normandy two years ago in appearance that the Bishop naturally took him for the king himself. Here then was revenge, and advancement too. He kicked his horse into a canter once more and set off after the figure. He bore down upon him, swinging his mace by its short leather strap. Powerless to intervene, Harold glimpsed his brother and the horseman on the same converging course. Gyrth was thirty paces off and still shouting, but Harold could not hear the words. "Fall back, let's hold them there," was what Gyrth was actually yelling. The men on the knoll appeared to be waving at him and shouting back. "You silly buggers," thought Gyrth to himself as he ran on, leaping over the bodies. "Don't you see how it is?" At that point the fighting Bishop of Bayeux finally caught up with him, reined in his excited horse and brought the full weight of his mace down upon Gyrth's neck in one lethal rabbit punch. The Earl of East Anglia fell like a dropped sack of flour and the Bishop of Bayeux wheeled, exultant, as the trumpets signalled the retire once more. He had killed the King! His reputation and position was made.

Harold witnessed it all as once more the horsemen retreated like a wave from the shingle. "Wulfnoth," he said. "Only my Wulfnoth left to me now." Gyrth was gone, the best of all his friends and advisors. He pulled the helmet from his head and ran his fingers through his thinning hair. "I am responsible for all of this," he thought. "This is all my doing, my fault. I should have listened to him. That should be me lying there dead instead." As the arrows began to fall once more he looked up and saw now that the light had failed and that it was truly dusk.

He heard again the rushing noise of his dream, very loud, and then he reeled from a massive blow and a sudden, fiery pain. He was knocked clean off his feet and he fell heavily onto his rump. He could not see and, not understanding why, he moved his head quizzically to the side. The movement caused him to scream with the agony of it. "Sweet Jesus." He heard a voice but did not recognise it. "The King is down." His hands, groping at his face, encountered a wooden shaft. His searching hands knocked it and doubled the intensity of his pain. He was blind. "Hold still, my Lord, hold still." The voice was urgent, gentle and imploring as he sat there supported on his arms and his head held back. He felt another hand exploring tentatively at his face as gently as possible at the wound. In the background he could hear a voice screaming. Was that him making that noise? No, he recognised the voice of Gareth, his Welsh boy. The voice was insistent and full of fear and pain. Abruptly, the voice ceased with a single gasp.

"It is bad," said another voice, "as bad as can be." The arrow, falling nearly vertically, had struck at an angle just above his right eye. Blood and eye tissue was now dripping down his cheek. He had never known an agony such as this. "They are coming back," another unidentified voice yelled. The next voice, however, familiar and reassuring, was Willi's. "Just hold still there my Lord, and we'll have you away from here presently. For the moment we are just a touch busy." The loss of his sight seemed to have given his sense of hearing an immense surge of power as he lay there, dazed and traumatised with loss of blood. He could hear everything, all of it, so very clearly. What he heard, and he knew this for an absolute certainty, was a thundering, it was the sound of his own approaching doom.

***

The fyrd was away now, broken and streaming towards the shelter of the woods. The knights went hallooing boisterously after them, like men at the hunt. The housecarls of the King, of two Earls and two Abbots, those that still lived, chose to fight where they stood. They were no longer a unified wall, but disparate and separate huddles of men, raging against the odds. The Dragon of Wessex and the Fighting Man still acted like a lure, attracting also in greater numbers the attention of the enemy horsemen. A whole crowd of these arrived almost simultaneously. Eustace of Boulogne and his eldest son came trampling over the dead, so too did Walter Giffard, Hugh de Montfort and Hugh of Ponthieu. Perhaps twenty housecarls now surrounded their stricken King. One by one they went down beneath the trampling horses in the most vicious and close up fighting of the day as, loyal to their oaths and traditions, they fought to the death. They had eaten of the Lord's salt and drunk his drink. Their feet had been beneath his board times enough, they had been feasted and rewarded. Their obligations to this contract were clear enough to them. A giant of a man, a Hampshire thegn called Brand, cut down two of his tormentors and wounded a third before falling beneath the flailing hooves. Another, Thurkhill, managed to behead a horse with one final swing of his axe. Had he survived this feat then it would have kept him in drink for the rest of his life. Knights were plucked from their saddles, knifed or kicked senseless, but more were arriving all the time. They thrust with their spears and cut down with their swords. All this Harold could hear with an absolute clarity as he lay there, the screams and the shouts, the thudding of the horses and the sharp and dull sounds of iron on iron and iron on flesh. The hooves of the horses churned the ground to mud.

Willibrod, Willi, Harald's beloved clown and poet, was amongst the last to fall, defending his ring giver to the end before three men fell upon him with a rain of blows that extinguished his bright spark forever. Harold was unaware of his passing.

The last act was played out. Hugh of Ponthieu was first through to him. His horse dancing, he thrust his spear deep into Harold's chest. A moment later Eustace of Boulogne arrived. Leaning down over the stricken man, with one angry sweep of his sword he dealt a savage blow to Harold's head. There was now a mob of men jostling each other ill humouredly in order to get in a further blow or stab at the body.

***

It was unfortunate for Walter Giffard that William himself arrived at that point to see him, dismounted and hacking at the corpse's crotch with his knife. William roared with anger at the sight and rode the man down, spinning him around. "Vermin, filth," he spat at Giffard in particular and all of those others there in general. He struck Giffard a few blows with the flat of his sword. "You are exiled, disgraced. If ever I see you again then I shall kill you." Baffled, resentful and cold with fear, Giffard scrambled away and out of sight. The others too moved off in search of those few remaining English still fighting on the ridge. William looked down with regret at the maimed, mangled and headless body at his feet. Once he had liked and respected this man. He would have made him his 'Dux Anglorum,' married his own daughter to him, held him in honour for all of his days, or so he believed at that moment. That perjured oath had changed all of that and brought them both here to this place of destruction. It came to him then, the realisation that he was now King of England, King of England by right of conquest and through the intercession of the Holy Father in Rome. He felt for the bones of Rasyphus and Ravennus in the doeskin wallet at his side so that he could kiss them. The wallet and the bones had gone. In fact he had lost the wallet some hours previously, but the ever attentive Hugh FitzPons had seen it fall and had placed it in his own purse for safekeeping. The dubious relics would never be found and prayed over now, thrown aside in anger and disgust by a beaten Englishman.

The Earl Waltheof, still in a raging fever, had forced the pace further, driving his men of Huntingdon and Cambridgeshire and Northamptonshire relentlessly through the Andredsweald. Perhaps a third of them were mounted. The rest came running after in a dog trot. By now many had fallen far behind on that two-day march and he had with him now perhaps only three hundred men, probably less. He himself, riding up and down the line, had covered twice the distance of any other man there, urging them forward as they ran. They had reached Maidstone the previous night long after dark and were off again before dawn. It was late afternoon by the time they passed through Tonbridge and on to where the trees began to thin. It was there that they encountered the first of the fugitives from Senlac. Waltheof, at the head of his men, reined in, puzzled. Those first few arriving men actually ran to either side of his column. They kept going, not pausing to answer the shouts and enquiries of either the Earl or his followers. These haunted and exhausted looking people, a rabble, were unarmed and by their dress and appearance were of the general fyrd. Waltheof frowned and had the next group of men to arrive forcibly held. They crouched, panting, with hands on knees and heads down like cornered prey. It proved necessary to rough them up a little before any coherent information could be had from them. They spoke in the accents of London and Kent, of Hertfordshire and Essex and Middlesex. There had been a fight, a terrible fight that had gone on since sun up. Such a terrible slaughter there had been. They were beaten men and the enemy were right behind them, breathing down their necks. They could say nothing of what had befallen the King and his brothers.

In those few moments, as the panicked men related their garbled versions of events, Waltheof realised the sickening reality of it all. It was finished and to no purpose, those preparations for war all that summer, that heroic race to York and the dreadful fight that awaited them there, the race back and to this place here. It had all counted for nothing. They had lost and nothing would ever be the same again. Waltheof felt truly lost and alone. There was no man here he could talk to or confide in. He was just twenty years old and nothing in his short life had prepared him for this. His one constant thought since leaving London had been to get his people to the King and to stand in line beside him once more. Now that he had arrived, here was the worst of all possible news. He saw no other possible alternative than to stand fast and see what happened next. The full weight of the responsibility for all those disconsolate men bunched up around him bore down upon his young shoulders.

Their stories told, Waltheof let the fugitives from Senlac go, disappearing into the lengthening shadows of the Sussex Weald. His own men he ordered to move forward once more, and to halt all others fleeing from the battle and bring them along with them. In this they were only partly successful, most they encountered running back ducked and weaved away into the undergrowth at the sight of them. Within half an hour and in failing light they found themselves astride the track and above a narrow but deep ravine hidden by undergrowth, bushes and brambles that descended sharply on both sides. "Here," Waltheof announced, "is as good a place as any. We shall wait here for whoever comes, be he friend or enemy." He deployed his small force of men along that narrow front, cajoling and threatening by turns and settled himself down wearily upon the damp bracken to await upon events.

The victors now held the track way and the road to London was open. Those foot men of the three divisions still capable of moving first encountered large numbers of wounded and injured English piled up on the reverse of the slope. They moved among them busily with their knives. There was no quarter here, as they knew, equally, there would have been none for them had things turned out differently. By some chance, the badly wounded Aesegar was spared. Perhaps it was the relative finery of his costume that saved him and he was set aside with a few others for future use, overlooked by camp followers indifferent to his wounds. Next, moving down the slope, they encountered the horse lines. These creatures were a far different type to the quality and mettle of the horses of Normandy, France and the Low Countries. They were ponies for the most part, hungry but well rested. Dismounted knights and men at arms haggled and poked among them well into the darkness.

It was Count Eustace, who had spent an exhilarating day, who appointed himself to head the flying column north to break the English up still further before the onset of full darkness. A stream of knights, riding four abreast and about a hundred in number, clattered and chinked after him, cutting down all of those English unfortunate enough to be in their path. FitzOsbern, his arm now hurriedly strapped and in a sling, was reunited once more with his friend and Duke. Both men were grey with fatigue. William, cautiously and uncharacteristically, leaned across the withers of his horse to embrace him. "Well then, Fitz," he said. "Good to see you still in the land of the living. You are still alive, I take it? By the Grace of God, the day is ours."

"I have never seen the like," said FitzOsbern sombrely as he looked out over the stricken battlefield, the mounds and heaps of men and the figures prowling around in search of loot and the wounded. "Varaville, Val et Dunes, Mont St Michel. They were nothing to this. I pray to God I never see such a sight again." Even Robert of Mortain was impressed into a shocked silence, though Odo continued to rage. He had lost so many of his fine boys and now, it transpired, he had not in fact killed the King. "There are still more to kill here," he snapped, "and more after that. These English are vermin and must be treated as such." Poor, poor St Ser, he was such a fine and promising boy, and Thibault too. Thibault, who had had such a touch with the massaging after a hard day in the saddle. "To be sure," said William placatingly, absently. "To be sure." He too was in deep awe of all that he saw about him. "But soon we may rest. For the time being I'm off to see what Count Eustace is up to. Anyone up for that?"

The pursuing Normans and those men of Waltheof's who had not yet flitted off into the night came upon each other in the all but complete dark, though they had heard each other sometime before. The sound of the Normans' approach would have been impossible to miss, and this provoked a loud yell of anger from the English. At the head of the column, Count Eustace made out in the gloom a seemingly fresh line of English some fifty paces off. He couldn't assess their number, but the adrenalin of success and victory was still pumping through him and the men behind. They were victorious, unstoppable. The English, knowing full well what lay at their feet directly below them, watched incredulously as some forty horsemen rode straight at them and then into the nothingness of the ravine. More, unable to stop, followed after, a tumbling mob of screaming men and horses down the steep slope. The rest of the column pulled up in time and watched impotently as the English came skidding and sliding down the opposite slope. They made short work of all the dazed and injured lying there, killing every last one of them.

Count Eustace had managed through some outstanding stroke of fortune to avoid the carnage. He raged and blustered on the southern slope as he attempted to get his men to wheel to either side. A large rock, an exceptionally lucky or otherwise skilful throw, struck him hard between the

shoulder blades and he fell from his horse, blood pouring
from his nose and mouth. He was the last of that day's casu-
alties amongst the high aristocracy of the army. Waltheof
called his men, summoning them like dogs to heel. The
English clambered back up the bank and into line once more.
It had been a victory of sorts, but there was nothing else to
be done here. A forced night march would take them back to
Maidstone and a chance to rally other men as they went. The
Normans would not pursue them now, not until daybreak.
Perhaps they would all gather their strength again at the
London Bridge. Perhaps Edwin and Morcar had arrived by
now. If they couldn't hold them at the Thames then perhaps,
they could in the Midlands, in the north, the Welsh borders
or in the fenlands of the east. Whatever, wherever, he
would fight on. Waltheof knew in his heart that none of
the Godwinsons had survived that battle. He would act for
the young Aetheling until the boy was old enough and wise
enough to stand on his own two feet.

William, notified of the disaster at the ravine, arrived
to see for himself. He watched as Count Eustace was carried
past on an improvised stretcher of a horse blanket and two
spears and surrounded by a cluster of his men, attempting
in vain to hide his disappointment at the Count's survival.
Enguerrand, the Count's son, was there. William made vague
and polite enquiries as he watched this political gadfly taken
away. Enguerrand was only eighteen, torn between grief and
fear for his father and the very attractive and enticing prospect of becoming the next Count of Boulogne. "Men who
know of such matters, your Grace," he said to the Duke,
"tell me that my father shall live." William contrived to look
relieved. "Well, that's fine then. Very good, excellent news,"
he muttered.

The silhouettes of the enemy opposite were disappearing
from view, leaving just the outline of a solitary figure on a
horse. Though William did not know it, he was looking at
the Earl of Huntingdon. At last this figure too turned and

disappeared, swallowed up into the night. "Do we work around and pursue, your Grace?" it was the old and dependable de Warenne who asked the question. "No," William replied. "No, we do not. Enough has been done this day. We rest now and in the morning, we return to Hastings. We can address matters from there on." Had he ever in his life been this tired before? Had there ever in his life been such a day as this? He removed his helmet and massaged his aching temples, running his hand across his balding scalp. He shook his head vigorously. There would be time enough for the luxury of reflection later. "Pickets, Warenne. I want a line of men you can trust with your life along here to keep watch throughout the night. Also, along the ridge back there, and a guard on the English horse lines. Their biggest problem will be in keeping awake. See that they do." He permitted someone to lead his horse back in the darkness and through the stiffening mounds of dead.

In his absence his old campaign tent had been erected on level ground beneath the ridge. This would doubtless have been FitzOsbern's doing, broken arm notwithstanding. Inside was a straw mattress with neatly folded blankets, the cruciform stand for his armour and his foldstool. Outside, men were in the process of lighting a fire with flints and straw and kindling. Placed upon an empty upturned barrel was cold meat, cheese, bread and a flask of wine. He realised he was starving. The shafts of the two banners that had been carried into battle had been thrust into the ground. The banners hung limply. Lying beneath them were the banners of the Red Dragon and the Fighting Man, torn and soiled and muddy. His brothers were waiting for him, along with FitzOsbern and a few others. He dismounted, looking around for the FitzPons boys to attend him, to help with the intricacies of his laces and buckles.

Robert, it seemed, did have a sensitive side to him after all. He had guessed what William was thinking and was likely to say next. "Hugh FitzPons is dead, William," he said, "and his brother is in no fit state to serve." Tears came to William's eyes. His brothers and all those there watched in amazement as the iron Duke of Normandy wept openly. William cursed himself for the weakness. One small death out of so many, yet he wept for it. He gathered himself. "My Lords, your forgiveness, I beg of you. It has been a very long day. I thank you all. Later, when he is judged ready, have Drogo brought to me. I would talk to him." De Tosny limped forward. "If my Lord, your Grace, would permit me the honour." Gently he began to work at the various straps and buckles. Robert, divested of his mail, came forward with the foldstool and carefully, and with a surprising gentleness, caused his brother to sit.

The fire was alight. More food and drink and men arrived. They were cautious and muted at first in the presence of the Duke. Presently, warmed and fed and glad to be alive, they began to compare experiences of that awesome day. Tentatively, they began to relax and celebrate. Emerging from shock, they fell to bragging and laughing, as men do in such circumstances. More tents were pitched and further fires lit. Soon there were scores of them, twinkling and crackling in the night as men returned from the woods beyond the ridge with fresh firewood. They called across to each other, good natured abuse or else enquiries for news of missing comrades. Running like a constant stream through all of this came the constant moan and murmur of injured and dying men, punctuated by occasional screams. William was hunched forward, clutching a mug of wine, no dilution of water this time, and staring into the fire. He seemed oblivious to all around him and he was last left alone to his own thoughts. FitzOsbern, recognising the old signs of the familiar black dog of depression gripping the Duke once more, suggested sleep. William shook him off irritably. Sleep would come soon enough. He continued to gaze into the fire, as if the sight of it would provide him with the answers to the questions presently roaring through his head, or if not then at least grant him peace.

CHAPTER THIRTEEN :
Full Circle

England and Normandy: October to

December, 1066

In the chill and in the first grey light of the dawn William was up and stalking his way along the bitterly fought and hard-won ridge of Senlac. It was a difficult task. He lurched and jumped over the mounds of bodies. Marble white and disfigured, many stripped naked by looters, they were daubed with blood that had turned to the colour of mud. Occasionally he missed his footing, stumbling over the pallid and stiffened figures, their eyes often wide and staring and with the occasional arm or leg lifted to the sky as if in protest and accusation. Heads without bodies, bodies without heads, the distended bellies of once prized and cosseted war horses. No battlefield was pretty, especially upon the following day and when the looters and despoilers had been hard at work. Here it was as if every battlefield he had ever seen had been combined into one.

The dead, there were so many of them. They lay in their hundreds in all directions. They lay north down the incline and away towards the Malfosse, as that fateful ravine would now come to be known. They were heaped and scattered here upon the ridge like tide wrack and south down the slope to his original position of the previous day. They lay in mounds or lines or in small groups, according to the particular nature of the fighting that had laid them low.

William massaged the throbbing ache in his temples and tried to spit out the acid, foul taste from his mouth. He was surrounded by more dead than he had ever seen in all of his far from gentle career. The human carrion crow had gone now, those mutilators of ring fingers and breakers of unprotesting legs and arms. Instead, now, the feathered variety were arriving with the first light, alighting on the bodies and beginning to peck and pull experimentally. One such hopped quite near him and then onto the entwined bodies of a Sussex thegn and a Mainard knight. It pulled and then held something he could not nor did not wish to identify in its beak. He threw a clod of earth at it and it rose heavily, protesting angrily, into the air. "I never knew it could be like this," he said to himself wonderingly.

He tripped over a body and would have fallen but for the fact that his brother Robert, massive and reassuringly alive, appeared at his side and grabbed him by the elbow. "Mind how you go there," said Robert genially. The dead, so many of them. "Care for a spot of breakfast?" his brother asked him, and the bile rose once more in William's throat. He felt he would be haunted by this scene forever. He could remember very little now of those last hours between the final collapse of the English and the sweet, merciful and dreamless sleep that came after. Who was alive? Who was dead? He struggled to remember now, making a mental inventory of men he could remember seeing still standing and breathing the night before as now he shrugged off the offer of breakfast.

In this place, in all of this, there was nowhere he could be alone. The victors of the battle were stirring, were up and about. Fires were being rekindled and men spoke boisterously, their breath emerging as gouts of steam. Nearby a group of archers were frying livers, kidneys and hearts taken from dead horses, the best meal they had had in over a week. Those with small carefully hoarded wallets of salt were especially popular. They laughed and joked callously, ecstatic at being alive amongst all that carnage. He could scarcely blame them.

William drew a deep breath. This would simply not do. "Some kidneys would be good," he said to Robert, who grinned at him. Robert himself lacked sufficient imagination to be overwhelmed by the sight of Senlac. He too rejoiced at being able to breathe in and out and in again and, besides, he was already attempting to reckon and calculate what would be coming to him after yesterday's work. Close by, some of his more senior surviving nobles looked on anxiously and they relaxed somewhat to hear him speak at last. A single hand, still clutching a broken axe stave, lay at the Duke's feet. William, struggling not to vomit, kicked it away from him.

"Let their dead bury their dead." Such was William's command that morning after the battle. "We shall see to our own." News had come early from Hastings. By what alchemy or agency nobody knew, but the English of the blockading ships had somehow come to hear the news and had gone in the night. The small nervous garrison of Normans there awoke to the sight of gratifyingly clear water. Hundreds of idle men were thus freed up and marched to attend to the putrefying mess on and before and behind the ridge. They arrived at mid-morning and with spades and picks and mattocks commenced to dig a wide and deep ditch in the yielding boggy soil beneath the blood-soaked high ground. In the course of the day the ditch became ten feet wide and ten feet deep, running like a ribbon below the base of the ridge. Into this they tumbled all the bodies that were palpably or probably Norman or French or Breton, or at least were obviously not English. The English were left to lie where they had fallen.

FitzOsbern and others were ready with the tally sticks by mid afternoon. By a rough reckoning one man in three of the Duke's army had died the previous day or else had been so wounded that he would follow on shortly. The calculation was arrived at by a tally of the nobles still standing and the assumption that those missing had lost one third of their men. It was a rough and ready equation, but it would suffice for the moment and in the days that followed it proved to be a fairly accurate assessment. The greatest amongst William's followers could now be named. William asked God's grace and forgiveness for an impious and ungrateful thought, but too many of his own troublesome aristocracy had survived for his own liking. He would have preferred to negotiate with and reward their more malleable and impressionable heirs. Gerelmus de Penileus, Roger FitzTurold, both dead. At Judgement Day the angels would have a real task of piecing together once more the body of Robert FitzErneis, caught up in a tangle of English and Danes. Perhaps the body of Taillefer, the first of their casualties, had been recovered and interred. What to make of that strange and unnecessary death? Taillefer's friend Neel of Herve, lying close to death himself, had other things on his mind. Judging by his wounds, it was unlikely that Robert de Vitot would live. Regrettably, it would appear that Eustace of Boulogne would. That was indeed a pity, as his demise would have provided the solution to a number of pressing problems. FitzWimarc lay where he had fallen, trapped and drowned beneath the body of his horse, a corpse as yet undiscovered. The irascible and excitable little southerner, Aimerie of Thouars, was mourned and buried by his own devoted and heartbroken men, all of him save his head, which they could not find. At least Count Alan Fergant, leader of the Breton contingent, still had his head upon his shoulders, but he had yet to recover his wits. He lay upon a muddy blanket, alternately silent and raving. Young FitzPons had been stamped and trampled to a jelly and his throat cut in the last few moments. Drogo, his twin, was inconsolable and part out of his mind with the grief and shock. That previous night William had gathered the boy up and enfolded him in a bear hug, squeezing and rocking him, murmuring in his ear. It had helped for a little time and then he had him sent back with an escort down the track to the coast.

Here now was FitzOsbern, drawn and haggard, his arm in a sling. "We hurt them more than they hurt us," he observed laconically. "Just look at them all. They stretch out further than the eye can see." This was true. The English had brought perhaps nine thousand men to the ridge at Senlac and now half of them lay dead in the churned-up mud. William glared at him. "Giffard," he said. "Walter Giffard. He is dishonoured and exiled," he was remembering now those last few desperate moments around the English standards and as the dusk fell. "I do not wish to see that man ever again. I am sure that there is a place in Italy or in Spain for a man of his talents." FitzOsbern nodded slightly, "it is already done." He paused; it was a characteristic FitzOsbern pause that William knew from experience meant something else was due to follow. "Well? Out with it, Fitz. I want to be in Hastings by nightfall."

"It concerns the body of the Earl of Wessex," said FitzOsbern, "and which appears to have been mislaid. Malet has a person with him who says that his death can be proven beyond all doubt, however badly hacked about though it was," He added, "this person, so Malet tells me, wishes also to ransom the body with its own weight in gold." William raised his eyebrows. "Does he indeed? I feel I should meet this man." FitzOsbern fiddled with his sling. "The fact is, William, that it is a woman. She says her name is Edith and is known as 'the swan neck' for her complexion. In the English manner she is the hand fast wife of Harold and the mother of his children."

***

Malet, of course, knew Edith Swan Neck more than passing well. They had, after all, been guests at one another's homes often enough in the past and had encountered one another on many occasions besides. It had been by pure chance that he had been ordered out as part of a patrol on to the Lewes road and when they intercepted a small group of riders laden down with the evergreen emblems of peace and parley. In the midst of a small and nervous English escort there was Edith, as pale and as proud as ever. Malet grasped the reins of her horse and led her aside and away from his unpredictable command. He was staggered and horrified by her sudden appearance here. "Lady," he said, "you have come from Bosham, I suppose. Whatever possessed you to come to this place?" He was quite at a loss as to what to do or say next. "I had my reasons," Edith replied in a measured way. "There has been a battle, I know, and England is lost. If there is worse news yet than this then tell me now, and quickly." Malet, that gentle Anglophile and most reluctant of warriors, bowed his head in his grief for her. "Then, Madam, know that your husband is dead, his brothers too. We think also his uncle and nephew." Edith swayed in the saddle and he reached out to steady her. "It is as I feared and knew," she said at last, her eyes unseeing. "Take me to him." Malet's men were beginning to get restless and looking askance at the English escort. "Madam," Malet pleaded, "it is a battlefield. It is a sight that not even men should have to look upon. I never wish to see such a thing again. It is full too of angry men still seeking vengeance. I beg of you, turn back, and have prayers said for his immortal soul at a place of safety." He truly feared for her safety amongst that group of unknown men.

"Nonetheless," Edith replied firmly, "I shall go on. I shall not be turned back. Malet, if ever you loved my husband and held me in respect then take me to him. I shall recognise him sure enough by secret signs, no matter how rudely he has been treated. I wish also to have him buried in honour and in the fashion of a true Christian man."

With Malet and a few of his trusted men for company and escort, Edith came at last to the battlefield, passing through the heaps of dead and the curious onlookers, her face without expression, she began to search the ridge. She peered closely at the bodies and even had some turned over on to their backs for her. Her gaze was unflinching. In this way she at last found the bodies of Willi and Gareth, broken and maimed and naked. Nearby was the equally mutilated body of the gentle cleric Caedmon. She tried to close his staring eyes, but these had fixed, and she could not. She muttered prayers and made the sign of the Cross over the three of them as, entranced, William Malet and his followers observed at a distance. Edith's logic was cool and clear enough. Where they lay then so too, somewhere close, she would find Harold. The next body she recognised was that of Gyrth. Like the Bishop of Bayeux the previous day, she thought at first that she had at last found Harold. She wondered where Leofwyn was, and Haakon and the Abbot of Winchester.

Nothing, even there in that place, prepared her for the shock when at last she did find her beloved. His face and half of his head had gone. His left leg was missing and someone had been at work on his groin with a knife. Like the others, the body was naked. There, in the crook of the right arm, was a familiar scar that once she used to trace with her fingers. All down the outside of the leg that remained were other scars, the tell-tale wounds of a horseman, and across the chest the mark of a mishandled knife thrust in the Welsh marches many years ago. No Ireland for them now. There would be no Tir Nan Og and a life of blissful ease with green fields and fat cattle and the songs and stories of learned men. She offered up a brief prayer and wept. Then she climbed wearily to her feet and beckoned.

***

No, no, and again no. William, confronting Malet, was absolutely firm. No, the body would not be ransomed and released. Not even for all the gold in Rome and Constantinople together. The body was his by right of conquest and at his disposal alone. Malet had come to him as he sat upon his foldstool before his tent, pleading and closer to defiance than he had ever been in all of his good-natured life. William heard him out and said, "Malet, you are a brave and honourable man. You have lost much, and you have followed me faithfully where many have not. I owe you a number of debts. This, then, I shall grant you. Let the Earl of Wessex, as was, be taken to the cliff side at Hastings. You may bury him there. Raise him a cairn if such is your wish. He can guard the coast in death as he did in life. But I shall have no services or the pattering of churchmen over him. My final word on it." He waved Malet away and turned away to address other matters, for a whole queue of men had formed behind him with their own pleas, requests and demands. He dealt with all of them brusquely for he was anxious to be off. He had had two fine horses killed under him the previous day and when he did finally return to Hastings it was on a far poorer and blown mount, its previous owner presumably now lying somewhere under the rich autumnal loam.

Late as it was, Edith also made the journey to Hastings, riding at the head of a small file of mounted and walking men. Out of his own purse Malet had paid ten footloose mercenary knights for the task of accompanying them, augmented with trinkets and other items he had variously come by after the battle. In their midst four Englishmen, one of them the devoted Oswy, carried the mortal remains of Harold, last King of the English, bundled up in a blood-stained horse blanket. It was a heavy and awkward burden for the five miles or so of the journey. There was plenty of traffic going up and down the track in both directions. What this group of men carried was obviously a body and they attracted a certain amount of comment and specula-tion as they passed. The presence of Malet's intimidating and extremely unpleasant looking mercenaries served to discourage any further interest or speculation.

All that chill night Edith kept her vigil on the cliff edge with her four men and the body of Harold. She stared out to sea, not noticing when Oswy crept over to place a cloak about her shoulders. In the meantime, and after a deal of searching, Malet had finally tracked down the monk Hugh Margot to where he had been sleeping peacefully in a barn. Malet hauled the man up and hurled him back against one of the wooden walls, his knife at the monk's throat. "I won't, you know," said Margot bravely enough in response to Malet's demand. "Oh yes you will," replied Malet. "No one will miss you, not in the least. No one will give you a moment's thought. You'll just be another one of the dead." He rammed the palm of his hand into the monk's windpipe until his face mottled and his eyes bulged. Margot could see the truth of this, as he fought for breath. Malet released his hold. "And there is this in it for you as well," he said, jingling a small bag of coin. "And if you so much as breathe a word about this afterwards then you are a dead man. I swear this to you by all that I hold sacred."

So it was that on the following dawn a grave was dug on the cliff and the mangled remains of Harold, the last King of the English, was laid gently within it. They piled the earth upon him and raised a cairn of stones and flints and lumps of chalk while Margot, suitably robed, intoned the Office of the Dead. When it was at last over, Malet turned to Edith. "What now?" he asked. "Where will you go?" Edith the Swan Neck, the indomitable wife of Harold, was utterly composed. "We talked of Ireland once or twice, he and I," she replied. "I will take the children there. There is no place in England for me now and no place in England where my children will be safe. Farewell, Malet. Perhaps I should thank you, I don't know." She sighed. "Well, it is a long enough journey to Bristol." Oswy and his three companions awaited with the horses. Malet watched them for a while as they set off for the Southampton road. Edith did not turn around to offer farewell and, with an aching heart, he turned back to his own many neglected tasks and duties, attempting to lose himself in the itemising and prioritising of them.

Late on the night of the battle a solitary Englishman, avoiding the town of Hastings itself, went scrambling like a mountain goat down an obscure cliff path and waded out into the chilling sea. The boats had lights at their mastheads and he swam to the nearest with his burden of news and was then conveyed by boat to Eadric the Steersman. The grieving Eadric wept bitter tears and then. taking advantage of a favourable wind and with sails and oars led the boats off east. He paused at Romsey and again at Dover before setting out once more for the estuary of the Thames. The news of the disaster arrived by land and sea at London and Westminster two days after the battle. The city was paralysed by shock and a flood of rumours. The Normans were a morning's ride away, went one report, and the better heeled began to trudge west and north and away to the supposed safety of Middlesex and Hertfordshire. Others kept their heads and a scratch militia of old men and apprentices were forced out of their homes and workshops, herded together and threatened and cajoled to the London Bridge by Aesegar's own Deputy.

Those who had survived the battle fled in all directions, making their way to their respective homes as best they could and spreading the story of Senlac as they went. In this way, the survivors of Aelfric's contingent of loyal monks set off for Winchester, bearing their gravely wounded Abbot with them. The monks of Peterborough, those that remained, travelled in a body to London. They paused briefly there, where Stigand, his agile mind racing away within the dome of his bald and shining head, and the timorous Bishop of London brought them gifts of food and money and interviewed them before they resumed their journey on the Cambridge road. Only Waltheof and his following, some two hundred of his Huntingdon men and gathered up refugees, arrived back at London with any form of cohesion and order.

Through his own messengers, Stigand had been just about the first to receive the news, a canny and cynical old man with forty years of active and turbulent political life behind him. Once more he bullied and cajoled the ineffectual Bishop of London into action and they gathered together to conduct a Requiem Mass in the Chapel at the Lambeth Palace. Stigand, still technically under house arrest, then prevailed upon the Bishop to send a party of armed men to secure and escort the person of Edgar Aetheling over at Westminster to old Edward's country retreat at Bridford near Oxford. The Bishop, old and beset with panic and indecision, allowed Stigand to exert full authority in all things. Stigand, a good fifteen years older than the Bishop, hid his contempt for him with soothing words and apt biblical texts. "What are we to do?" the Bishop bleated at regular intervals. Utterly fearless, and a schemer to the end, Stigand knew precisely what he intended to do and set in motion two wholly separate plans of action. He turned his attention first to the conquering foreigner who had destroyed forever the power of the House of Godwin, a family that had hedged him about all of his life, sometimes working in fairly amiable concert and at other times in active emnity, as the various shifts of the political wind had dictated.

Within his possession Stigand had a tame Norman chaplain, a protégé reserved and hidden like a bottle of good wine laid down for a special occasion. Neither Gyrth nor Aesegar, the latter now lying mortally wounded in a leaking boat shed in Hastings, had known of this man's existence and neither had they dared to lay a finger on the Archbishop's personal fortune, which was considerable. Stigand dipped now into one of the chests in his borrowed apartments and picked out a quantity of coin and hack silver. There were any number of unemployed English and Danes loafing about in the streets and on the quaysides of the port of London and he had sufficient numbers hired to ensure the safety of his Norman on an embassy to the Duke. They would be sufficient protection against the predators and bandits that such times would invariably conjure up to plague the roads. He ensured also that they would be sufficiently weak in number as to present any threat to the victors of Hastings. Accompanied by these and the banner of the Prelate of Canterbury, garlanded with green for peace, the Chaplain set off in search of the Duke on the Maidstone road. In all things and at all times, so the message ran, had the Archbishop of Canterbury, mindful like the good shepherd of Holy writ, sought peace and reconciliation.

Now, at this most difficult and uncertain of times, his message told the Duke, it fell to him to bring peace and reconciliation to this troubled land. He would spare no effort in attempting to do so, should the Lord God preserve him for the task. In the interests of both speed and harmony, all replies should be addressed to the care of the Bishop of London, presently to be found at Lambeth. He recommended secrecy in this and suggested that perhaps FitzWimarc or

Malet should be entrusted with the task, FitzWimarc for preference. What, Stigand now pondered, to do with that firebrand Waltheof, recently arrived in London, and with the troublesome Aelfgarsons and with the young Aetheling? Stigand sat, chin resting on the steeple of his clasped hands, and considered.

***

The army was ill, stricken with that sickness that comes upon large groups of men with a poor diet and suspect water and confined within a small space. The battlefield had been left to its unburied dead and its ghosts and they had returned to Hastings, carrying with them the wounded and the maimed. There this act of God, this curse, fell upon them, striking the stomachs and the bowels of the men. Scores died from it and had a fresh force of English in sufficient numbers fallen upon them then the victorious army at Hastings would have been powerless to resist. No less a man than the Duke himself was likewise struck down by the illness that drove him, shivering and sweating, to void his bowels in the common open latrines in the company of the least of his men.

Now, less than a week later, William was over the worst of it and back on the road again. He led a swift and unopposed descent upon Winchester and an especial example was made of Harold's beloved Bosham. It burned in the wake of the army and Harold's Manor was gutted and despoiled. The little Church of Saint Christopher with its leaking roof was spared. Winchester, a prize well worth having, submitted and at a single stroke the Treasury of England and all of Harold's own personal fortunes fell into the Duke's hands. William toured the treasure house, fingering the furs and the coin, the ingots of silver and the piled-up collections of jewelry and precious stones, as Harold had done in his turn. He was satisfied and then called next upon Edward's strange

widow. Edith received him in her freezing cold hall in front
of the empty fireplace. It was an eerie confrontation. She
was preparing to depart for a new life of permanent contemplation in a Convent and William was only too happy to let
her go, with a rich purse into the bargain. She fixed William
with an owl like and disconcerting stare. "Edward instructs
me to send you his greetings and his congratulations," she
said. "Body of God," Robert of Mortain, who had also been
present, remarked afterwards, "but the old bitch must have
good hearing."

Now William turned his attention to the east. Retracing
their steps in a wide arc, the army burned Romney and Rye
to the ground and those that they found there they massa-
cred. Proud and independent Dover, the cause of so much
previous friction, submitted. So too did Canterbury, the
ancient home of English Christianity. There the leading men
appeared before the Duke barefoot and in shifts of sackcloth,
offering a symbolic key up to him in the saddle. Conscious
of his immortal soul, he left them in peace after exacting a
heavy fine. The army, now in better health and spirits, set off
at last on the road to London itself.

'Brothers in Christ,' wrote Stigand to Ealdred of York and
Wulfstan of Worcester, 'by this I would have you know that not
three days since, our gracious Lord, the King Harold, was struck down
with his brothers and all of his army in battle against the Duke of
Normandy at a place near to Hastings. May God in His mercy rest
the souls of all who fell there. Our precious Aetheling Edgar, may God
protect and preserve him, is now travelling to the royal Manor at
Bridford. There he instructs and I request that you do likewise to meet
us without delay so that we might meet in council and discuss what
best is to be done now. Hasten, and may the good God see you on your
way, both now and in the difficult times to come.'

Stigand watched impassively as the signed document
was sanded and rolled and sealed and embossed with his own
ring of office. The Bishop of London continued to fret and to

rock backwards and forwards in a corner of the room, now an almost forgotten figure. A similar message had gone out to the Aelfgarsons, it being the unenviable task of five separate couriers to attempt to track them down, as no person quite knew where they might possibly be. Stigand had had a very busy time of it of late. In effect he had made himself the Regent of England and had been obliged to turn his attentions to many things. It was a moment of power that had been denied to him for many years and it had endowed him with a burst of energy that belied his years. Not since the good old days of Emma, Edward's mother, had he enjoyed such freedom of action.

The Manor of Bridford, where news of the rebellion at York had first reached Harold and where that first catastrophic argument with Tostig had occurred, had been one of Edward's favourite retreats. It was well appointed and capable of accommodating large numbers of people at short notice. It was also a comfortable and admirable little bolt hole and enjoyed an equally admirable and equivocal location. From there a man might flee in any direction. In Stigand's case this might be either Bristol or Norwich. In both seaports he had excellent contacts and unimpeachable financial resources. He was, after all, a Dane raised in Norwich. If the worst came to the worst, then he could end his days in Denmark. He knew, of course, for a certainty that Rome would never welcome him, the best he could hope for, should he survive the long journey, would be incarceration in a monastery for the rest of his days. By courier he summoned leaderless and uncertain men to gather together in that one place and where he could exercise his considerable will over them. He feared only Wulfstan for his honesty and Waltheof for his belligerence. If the Aetheling were to be acclaimed and anointed King then he knew he would not be permitted, uncanonical and censured as he was, to conduct the service. That old fool Ealdred would be only too happy to oblige and thus be held accountable. He would emerge safe yet. Safe, and smelling of flowers, the peace broker of England.

A hooded and furtive figure appeared in a farmyard near Twyford where the few remaining monks and housecarls of the Abbot of Winchester were resting, roasting their faces in the fire, whilst at the same time their backs froze. "Winchester is crawling with Normans," he announced. "The Treasury is seized, and Edward's widow Edith has submitted." Winchester, the ancient capital of both Wessex and of England, was gone. On his stretcher, lying beyond the light of the fire, Aelfric stirred at the news. "This is the end of all things," he muttered. Attempting to clear his throat he discovered that his mouth was full of blood, he was choking. He coughed feebly once and, unheard, by any, he died.

***

William made an example of Maidstone. The people there had had the temerity to resist and one of his patrols had been cut up on the road leading in. It was a feckless act of bravado and bound to lead to reprisals. He viewed the naked bodies of the patrol, flung into a ditch like discarded waste. "Burn the place," he commanded, "and kill them all, all of them. Destroy everything."

Finding himself obliged to deal with him face to face, Stigand found Waltheof of Huntingdon a far different proposition by far to all those he had up to now addressed by letter. Covered in mud and stained with the blood of many men, Waltheof was in no mood for conciliation or delay. He was hungry and depressed and the wound he had received at Stamford Bridge pained him. Even he was aware of how much he smelt. Though very young, he had been involved in the doings of the Godwin clan long enough to be able to detect a Stigand plot at a hundred paces. "You did what?" he demanded in outrage. "The Council decreed that the Aelfgarsons should go instead to Oxford," Stigand repeated. Waltheof's handsome face was contorted with bitterness and rage. "Council? What Council? I see no Council. The men of Mercia and Northumbria need to be here in London, to hold the bastard at the line of the Thames. We can beat him yet. But you, your Grace, have seen fit to allow to happen what Harold died trying to prevent. You have made his death and the deaths of all others meaningless."

Stigand sighed expansively and spread his arms. "Their deaths are a waste, whatever happens. At Oxford at least we shall have time to draw breath and consider. Please calm yourself, my Lord. Do you propose to fight the Duke all on your own?" Waltheof glared at him, murder in his eyes. "I cannot, and you know it," he said bitterly. "Well then," Stigand said, "rest up for a while. Attend to your wounds. Call in your Jew to see to them, I am informed that he is most learned and skilled, it is clear that you are in some discomfort. Perhaps a bath? I can arrange it."

The old lady, the indefatigable Gytha, widow and mother of five dead sons, moved westwards to the town of Exeter, a place within her gift. On the way, at the old Roman Aqua Sulis, she met up finally, as arranged, with Edith the Swan Neck. Edith had all of her children with her, including the two oldest boys. The battle was now nearly two weeks into the past and the boys had travelled with speed to join her from Norwich and Worcester. It was a large gathering in the deserted and eerie ruins of the Roman spa and the sound of flowing water, with a combined retinue of nearly a hundred armed men attending upon them.

The two women, both overcome by tears, embraced whilst the younger boys chattered and skylarked. Respectful and dutiful, the two girls and the older boys waited in turn to greet their grandmother. The boys were proud and prickly, and sufficiently old enough to know their value as hostages and prisoners of the Duke. Free and unbound, they were a natural focal point of any further resistance.

Edith and Gytha drew apart and regarded each other. "Do not tell me that my sons received Christian burial," said Gytha. "I have always prized your honesty above all your many other virtues." Edith smiled at the old lady. "I cannot speak for your sons Gyrth or Leofwyn. As for Harold, I saw him buried myself, with a Priest and a Mass. "She shrugged, "well, a sort of Priest and a sort of Mass. Your son Harold, our beloved, lies on the cliff face at Hastings. When the time is right, we can have him moved, perhaps to Bosham or Waltham." Gytha shook her head. "Do not deceive yourself, my girl. The time will never be right, never again. This is a new age and you are right to be leaving for Ireland." Edith chose her words carefully. "My mother," she said. "I carry his last child."

Gytha, descendant of the Danish royal bloodline and the matriarch of the now defunct Godwinsons, was silent for a while as she allowed this information to sink in. She held Edith close to her once more and squeezed her as tightly as her frail strength would allow and while both women wept. Presently Gytha sniffed and stood back. "You and that Mercian girl. I attach no blame to her and I wish her no ill will, only happiness, though I feel in my heart she shall never find it. Well, those are two grandchildren I shall never see in this life. Edith, neither of them will ever be safe in this country and we would be fools to ourselves to think otherwise. The sooner you are gone and with good sea water between you and this country then the better it will be."

They rested and feasted, after a fashion, by the springs and the unsettling and disconcerting and tumbled down buildings with their Roman ghosts. Gytha told her grandchildren stories of their dead father, provoking in turn both tears and laughter. They slept in the open by the banked-up fires and parted the next morning with a brief farewell, as if they planned to meet again in the next few days. Both women knew they would never see the other again.

The first of Stigand's exhausted messengers, in the company of a clerk hastening from Bishop Wulfstan's chancellory at Worcester, finally tracked down the elusive Aelfgarsons on the road out of Shrewsbury and as they moved south east down old Watling Street and into the teeth of an English October rainstorm. They had left the town not two hours since. Their men, a combined force of close on to one thousand men, the survivors of Fulford Gate and hastily summoned levies, tramped disconsolately, desperately hungry, through the mud and mire and potholes of the old Roman road. Edwin and Morcar took shelter in a barn as they absorbed the news of the fall of England. The King was dead and his army destroyed and scattered. All of the treasure of Winchester was lost and the victorious Normans were nearer to London than they, and in far greater numbers. Stigand had been at great pains to point out the strength of the Duke's army. Both Stigand's man and the Worcester clerk urged caution before they were ushered out and into the driving rain. The brothers looked at each other, two discredited Earls with very little indeed to bring to the bargaining table beyond the suspect strength of their men presently marching past and the equally suspect loyalties of their respective Earldoms. Their chief bargaining counter, their sister Aeldyth, was now as useful to them as tits on a bull, as Edwin colourfully put it.

"We'd be better off back up north," said Morcar reflectively. "In Chester or York. We'd have a few weeks, maybe months even, to work things out. We could either build up our strength or else negotiate with the man. I say we turn back." As usual, Edwin was made of sterner stuff. "We go on," he said firmly. "Oxford is on the way, whatever. No hardship there. And if we are not at Oxford then we have no voice in this Council."

Morcar punched the wooden beam he leant against in his frustration and winced at the pain of it. "What Council?" he demanded, unwittingly echoing Waltheof. "A handful of old churchmen, that brat of an Aetheling and Waltheof. My God," he said, bringing to mind the tangled strands of fifty years of blood feud in Northumbria, "I wish he'd died there." Edwin nodded, "I'm sure you do," he said. "It would have made life a whole lot easier for you if he had. But he didn't. When it comes to council talk then my position within Mercia is far stronger than is your own in Northumbria. I at least don't have Gospatric or Copsig to worry about. Copsig, you do remember him, don't you? If you know what's good for you then you'll come to Oxford." And, as ever, Morcar finally agreed.

***

Martin, the Fleming, was a master mariner of exceptional skill and knowledge and with an ability bordering on genius. William had ever had the knack of drawing such men into his employ. Less than a week after the battle the news he returned to Normandy with was reverberating up and down the quays and wharves and the streets and alleys of Rouen. The bells of all the churches and of the near completed Cathedral gave noisy tongue and the entire city turned out in celebration. Graciously, and with a typical understanding of the public mood, the Regent Duchess Matilda ordered barrels of the year's new wine, thin and acid, to be issued to the populace. Carts rolled noisily over the cobbles to the main square. The raucous and ecstatic sounds of celebration carried clearly to the main hall of the castle where Matilda now sat next to her proud young son Robert. Lanfranc, aesthetic and abstracted and fiddling with his beads, was present, along with Montgomery and Beaumont, the other two Regents of Normandy. Respectfully skirting the walls was a crowd of stay at home noblemen and city dignitaries, attracted to the castle by the newly arrived news, the commotion and by summons. Beaumont's eyes were still red and inflamed. Ridden with gout, he had been called from his sick bed to be told that his son Roger was alive and well. His beloved boy had conducted himself with great honour and bravery. The talented and frenetic Montgomery was, as usual, more than slightly drunk. Lanfranc, occupying a peripheral position as was ever his habit, was considering if this might not be an appropriate time to raise once more the subject of his English protégé Wulfnoth Godwinson, presently languishing in hardship in the cold, dark and dank of the keep several floors below them.

No man ever refused a command or a request of Matilda. In all the time that William had been away there had not been the faintest brimstone whiff of intrigue, treachery or revolt. The entire Duchy and the lands beyond had been on the very best behaviour and waiting for news. Had they been in receipt of bad news then even now they would be preparing for domestic revolt and foreign invasion. Matilda sat calmly upon the raised dais, a figure so tiny and doll like that men standing before her seat on its raised dais still towered over her. She had ever known how to use her size as a strength. "A message to my dear father, the Count of Flanders," she ordered, "though doubtless he knows already. He has always had his own ways and means."

It was Friday evening, six days after the battle. Technically it was a day of dried fish and no strong drink, though that had gone by the board following the arrival of William Warenne, neatly and safely deposited at the quayside by the excellent Martin. The story of Senlac would now be racing through the lands of eastern Normandy, from mouth to mouth and as fast as the fastest horse could travel. But what of the south and the west? The news, it would be seen to, would be proclaimed after Mass in the churches and open spaces of Jumieges, Lisieux and Evreux this coming Sunday. The other large towns of Caen and Bayeux, Avranches and Mortain would hear it soon after. "I tire of Rouen," Matilda announced brightly. "We shall have us a little outing, I think. Yes, I believe it would do me good." Out of her direct view, Montgomery rolled his eyes and moaned to himself. It was as he had both feared and expected and he knew who would be drawing the short straw when it came to making all the necessary arrangements.

"My Lord Beaumont," said Matilda, and in confirmation of Montgomery's thoughts, "In deference to your years and taking into account your present indisposition, you shall remain here. It is time, though, that the future King of England be seen by his people." She leaned across and ruffled Robert's hair. The boy shivered in a mixture of embarrassment and excitement. Surely that was him his mother was talking about! Would they let him wear mail as a treat and carry a sword? Surely they would. He would choose the grey to ride upon. He looked good upon it, he knew, and did not appear to be as diminutive as, in truth, he was.

Montgomery's excellent skills of prediction continued to function, unimpaired by the quantity of strong drink he had taken on board, as Matilda described the elliptical route. She would go spinning like a fierce little comet through the Duchy, scattering coin and largesse as she went. First the short distance to Evreux, then the long road west to Mortain and then Avranches. North to Bayeux, all through a thronging and joyous countryside. Next east, to her beloved Caen and a visit to her daughter in the Convent there. Lisieux and Jumieges, and back to Rouen once more. "Monday, my Lord Montgomery. We leave on Monday. We shall now, with proper escort, permit ourselves to be seen by the people of Rouen." She stood up and swept out, ushering Robert and the beautiful child Agatha before her. "Does this mean," Agatha was heard to ask of her mother, "that I shan't be marrying that Englishman?"

***

William and his brothers and FitzOsbern rested their horses on the high ground above the suburb of Southwark and the London Bridge. Predictably enough, it was, of course, raining. Had they but known it as they shivered there beneath their cloaks and woollen caps, this was the very place that Harold too had paused to watch his army cross the river. Below them lay the ribbon development of the Southwark, the broad rolling river and the bridge itself. They could see clearly the city of London set within its ramshackle walls and the marshes to the east and north and then the high land beyond. Even more clearly, they could see at both ends of the bridge a large and swirling mass of men that appeared alarmingly reminiscent of that noisy and intimidating shield wall at Senlac. Had they been any closer then they would have worried less. "A rabble," remarked Robert, not for the first time. "A swept-up collection of wharf-side rats, greybeards and serving boys. I say we go down there and sort them out." William ignored him and stared down at the scene. Robert turned his horse aside, muttering to himself in his anger and frustration. "How many, Fitz? How many would you say?" asked William. FitzOsbern squinted through the rain. "It's a rabble right enough, but it's a big rabble for all that. Three thousand? And then with all of the city to fight through after that." Odo agreed. "We didn't go through that battle back there in order to get carved up piecemeal down alleyways. We need London, to be sure. But there are other ways of belling this particular cat. It'll fall into our laps soon enough and easily enough if we continue to wear them down."

At their backs there came a force of perhaps four thousand toiling, cursing men, plodding along up to their ankles in the churned-up mud of the track. The insistent and chilling rain fell upon them to drip down their shoulders and backs and rusting the chain mail that would have to be scoured and scraped and polished at the end of the day. Many of these cursing and wholly disaffected men were the walking wounded of Hastings or else still suffering the effects of the disastrous dysentery epidemic shortly after. The remainder of his army, cripples and convalescents, servants and a leavening of fit and experienced men, were scattered in isolated camps and fortified positions between here and the coast. William knew, his brothers and commanders knew, that a fresh English army would scatter them all like chaff. A wrong decision here and the whole expedition, the whole grand plan, would fall apart and end in farce and tragedy. Until the spring tides there would be no fresh men crossing over the Sleeve. For the space of half of a year they would have to conserve and preserve their forces, like a miser counting out coins. William nodded, Fitz and Odo were right, as so often they were. He sighed and slapped his gauntleted hands together. "Very well then. But they shall know at least that we have at least visited, by God!" He indicated the suburb below him. "Have all of that burned to the ground. Robert. See to it. But I will not have you involving yourself in any unnecessary brawling. Is that clear? Until next we visit, I want London to have something to remember us by. We shall follow the river on this side to the west and cross over where it narrows." Malet's frequent lessons in elementary English geography were clearly bearing fruit. "By Christ, I shall make the people in our line of march know we have been there."

***

Of all of those now gathered together at the hunting lodge at Bridford only young Edgar Aetheling appeared to possess no real or firmly held opinions of his own. Last of the ancient Saxon bloodline of Cerdic, young Edgar fretted and fidgeted and chewed his nails whilst all around him talks went on and over his head regarding his acclamation and coronation, or perhaps even the postponing of it. Exasperated and irritated, the adults at last banished him from the discussions, leaving him free to roam happily about the estate, teasing the livestock and splashing in puddles. He threw stones at the ducks whilst his future was discussed. "He's not all there, is he? Not the full shilling," remarked Morcar to Edwin during a pause in the meeting. "What that boy needs," replied Edwin, "is the loving care and tutelage of two good uncles." Morcar's jaw dropped, thinking of their sister. "You cannot be serious?" he said. By way of reply Edwin smiled his annoying lazy smile.

Archbishop Ealdred of York, the weight of his years heavily upon him, arrived at last and was eased out of his saddle by solicitous acolytes. Not too far off the Duke of Normandy's men burnt and killed and looted their way through the once prosperous lands of Hampshire. In a moment such as this, the elderly prelate's good humour and lack of imagination was perhaps a strength and an asset. Ealdred's intellectual shortcomings and misplaced affability certainly suited Stigand's purposes at this moment as he greeted him with ostentatious affection and issued instructions for his comfort to his scuttling minions.

Ealdred, the man who had crowned and anointed Harold, could most certainly be prevailed upon and persuaded to agree to the opinions of a stronger and more intelligent man, If Ealdred was a puppet or a cipher then Wulfstan of Worcester most certainly was not. In one thing, though, did the Bishop of Worcester and Stigand agree upon profoundly. At all costs and in every way the integrity and the independence and the continuity of the Church of the English must be maintained, though both did hold this view for different reasons. The curing of souls had never been especially high on Stigand's own particular agenda.

In their lifetimes, both men had experienced the rule of three foreign Kings, all of them Danes. Cnut had had the wisdom and statecraft not to interfere unduly with the doings of the Church and neither Harthcnut nor Harald the Harefoot had been around long enough to do any lasting harm. As for Edward, that other foreigner, he had lavished love and riches upon the Church. This Norman Duke, on the other hand, he would be a different proposition altogether. In Council Ealdred, when prodded, concurred. If they must now seek peace with this man, then the interests of the Church must be promised and guaranteed and upheld in return for their support. It did not occur to any of the three highest Churchmen in the land that, if faced with opposition, the Duke would, and with the full support of Rome, simply call in Lanfranc and his team of expert advisers, men with the love of Christ in their hearts and ice in their veins, to carry out whole scale root and branch reforms.

These three very old and very tired men sat together and rubbed their hands in front of a comforting brazier of charcoal in a small chamber off the main room of the hunting lodge. They indulged themselves in a little wine and melted cheese on toasted bread, believing that they possessed the means to secure the continued well-being of their flocks. They all agreed that such a pact with the Norman would of course involve a formal submission at the earliest possible opportunity and the surrendering up of the Aetheling. Young Edgar, meanwhile, was blissfully unaware of all this as he continued to lob stones at the ducks on the lake with an increasing accuracy. Elsewhere, both Edwin and Morcar had arrived at full agreement at last. Their decision, they had decided, would be to keep themselves to themselves. The rulers of Mercia and Northumbria had arrived at the view that they could treat and coexist with these Normans and that life could go on and only get better. Some minor concessions might well prove necessary and they planned towards this.

Only young Waltheof of Huntingdon argued passionately for further resistance. Still in immense pain and weakened from his wound and the ague that accompanied it, consumed also by an anger and bitterness and the sense of a loyalty betrayed, he limped and patrolled the Lodge and its environs like a gaunt shadow. He pursued and ambushed other members of the Council, urging resistance to the end and, stepping outside into the invigorating autumn air, all other members of the council checked first to see if the coast was clear.

"It will be November soon," said Edwin as the three of them paced a ploughed field already hardened and rimed with frost. "The bastard has not enough men to come after us in the north, not with a weakened army and lacking provisions and local knowledge. If he wants peace and quiet and a chance to grow strong in the south, then he will need us." To grow strong in the south! These two were fools, Waltheof reflected. He had never liked them. They were both fools and knaves at one and the same time. Faced with the twists and convolutions of the families of Bernicia and Deira over the past seventy years or so, the promiscuous mixing of Norwegians, Danes and English, the third wives and the second husbands, the ambitions and plots of cousins and in laws, even as practiced and enthusiastic a genealogist as Odo would have thrown up his hands in defeat. Added to this, of course, was a protracted blood feud that had brought death by murder to the principal men of every generation. Waltheof was the inheritor of all of this and also, he felt, the rightful heir to Northumbria. He had been a child when Tostig had come into the Earldom. That Morcar had in turn replaced Tostig was, of course, a deep rooted source of anger and a passionate grievance to him, it was the patrimony of his own father and his heroic pagan death. "Huntingdon is a damn sight further south than either Chester or York," he pointed out with bitterness. "We should fight him now or fight him in the spring."

Edwin sneered unpleasantly. "We simply cannot fight him now and, in the spring, more men will cross over the sea. I say we submit now and sue for peace, have him confirm us in our lands and titles. He can either fight us, which he would, or have us rule the north for him. It is within his interests." Again that fatal flaw, the belief that they were somehow indispensable. "And have us roll over like puppies to have our bellies scratched?" demanded Waltheof. "And what when all changes and it is within his interests to move north against you?"

"Let us," said Edwin, "worry about that if the situation arises."

***

At Wallingford the army of the Duke found an old wooden bridge across the now far narrower Thames. Unopposed, they crossed over it and into Berkshire. They camped for the night and, lest the people of Berkshire be under any illusion that they were in any way exempt, they spent the next two days in raids and in the collection of provisions from the farms and barns and granaries almost all the way to Reading. They were joined at Wallingford by reinforcements up from Hastings and Pevensey. Amongst them, and sufficiently recovered from his wounds, was Neel of Herve. His former good looks were quite gone. He had lost his left eye and his front teeth, and a livid scar stretched from the left side of his mouth to his temple, giving the appearance of a permanent and vertical grin. For his pains and for his service the Duke would award him lands and a rich estate in Middlesex along the banks of the river Brent. It was good fertile land, with plenty of serfs, a mill, a weir and fish pools and the benefices of four parishes. In time he would take a local heiress for a wife and breed a large family of Anglo Bretons. He would become the scourge of the district, all that was worst in the change of regime, and to the end of his days the people would make the sign to avert the evil eye whenever they came in sight of him, taking care that he would not notice.

On their third day at Wallingford English emissaries appeared at the camp, cautiously like unbidden guests, and were taken to the Duke. With Malet providing the translation, they delivered their message. "Nearly all our eggs in the one basket," said Odo with great satisfaction as the names were given. "Very convenient. But no mention of the Earls of Mercia and Northumbria. I find that disturbing." William listened to the message impassively, his heart soaring and jubilant. They were suing for peace and submission, by God! Edwin and Morcar could wait. He would catch up with those two puppies soon enough. The longer they delayed then the worse they made their case. "No," said William when the message was delivered. "I shall not come to them cap in hand like some mendicant. They shall come to me. This is how things are now."

The English council had thought of this eventuality in advance. Malet listened, head to one side. The man had a very broad local accent which he found difficult to follow. "Then let this meeting be at a place called Berkhampstead, three days from now," he translated. "They will come to you there and you can meet them in appropriate state. I know this place, your Grace, I have stayed there in the past. It is about twelve English miles east from here as the crow flies and about thirty miles from London. There is a thegn's Manor there and a large ancient burial mound. It is perfect for an assembly." William was not a man to offer public displays of emotion. "Berkhampstead it is, then," he said.

***

Leofgar was holed up in Lowestoft for the winter, waiting for the spring sailings. The little fishing village was an absolute pig of a place to the well-travelled housecarl, but then he hadn't come for either the scenery or for the night life. After the fight and after the Malfosse, where he had found himself swept up by a flood of fleeing men, he had fallen in with Waltheof's Huntingdon men as they made their way back in good order to London. Waltheof had recognised him in the ranks and sought him out as they marched, extracting from him the story of the battle and of Harold's last moments.

"No," said Leofgar in answer to a question, "I shall not go back to Mercia. I shall not serve that arse wipe Edwin neither. My only Lord is dead, and I, "he said with bitterness," should be dead too." He remembered their time together in Brittany two years before, when he had been the first of all Harold's men and high in the estimate of the Earl of Wessex. He remembered Harold telling him of the fear and hatred that the Normans had invoked in Italy and stories of Mikklegard, the fabulous Constantinople, into whose lands the Normans were also encroaching. He had noted it at the time. They were like ravening wolves, the whole cursed pack of them. "I am leaving England forever, my Lord Waltheof. I am getting out of this island. I mean to fight the Normans. Fighting is what I am best at," said the man who had so nearly done for Neel of Herve.

"There will be opportunity enough of that here in England," had said the then still optimistic Waltheof as they trudged through the fallen leaves of the Andredsweald. Leofgar regarded the youth sadly and with a degree of affection. The world may have been turned upside down, but it was still not his place to tell Waltheof that such resistance was doomed and that he also wanted to be on the winning side of a fight and not a member of some hole in a corner band of half starved brigands. With an absolute certainty he knew that the Normans were here to stay. No, he would go to this Mikklegard and enlist with the Emperor's Varangian Guard. He would fight the Normans for the Emperor, and for good pay and rewards.

Gyrth had left a wife and a crowd of noisy children back home in Norwich and Leofgar agreed, reluctantly, to convey the news on his way to the coast. No man likes to be the bearer of bad tidings. At London Waltheof supplied him with a horse and with money. Three days later at Norwich, Gyrth's widow, prostrate with grief, still remembered to instruct her steward to give the little Mercian another large bag of coin for his services. Leofgar had killed again and again at Senlac. He had always been the greatest of the fighting men beneath the banner of Harold's Fighting Man. Even if his methods were somewhat unorthodox, it was the result that counted. He had killed two knights, probably a third, and in a lull in the fighting had helped himself to their possessions. Now, with the purse of an Earl and the purse of the widow of an Earl, he was richer than he had ever been in his life. Harold had made him a thegn after the fight at Stamford Bridge, but he would never reap the benefits of that now.

He had a small and flea infested room above a tavern and, with his stories of his colourful past, rarely had to pay for his supper, not yet at least, not until men began to avoid him as a freeloading bore. Already there were reports of tentative Norman patrols probing east and north. Perhaps a boat would sail before the spring. The first opportunity that presented itself and he would be off. Men sailed to Hamburg and Frisia from these parts, Denmark also. He spent much of his time on the shore, staring out at the rolling iron grey sea.

***

In a locked and secure cellar in the vaults of the donjon at Rouen, Wulfnoth found it all but impossible to keep track of the passage of the days. There was a certain regularity to the arrival of food and the removal of night soil, but this varied quite considerably at times and often he would not know if it were morning or afternoon. Only the nights were certain. Occasionally, if he strained to listen, he could hear bells proclaiming the Office of the hour and, with his liturgical experience he would know if they rang for Vespers or Terce or if it were the Angelus bell. By the same means, he was usually also able to identify a Sunday. It was much colder now too, the year had obviously marched on into the late autumn. One morning, without warning, men arrived with fresh straw and horse blankets.

Bjorn, his obscure Danish kinsman and companion in captivity, had begun slowly to go mad. Wulfnoth calculated that this would have been around about May. Bjorn had been displaying distressing signs of his deteriorating wits for far longer than that. It was only to be expected that confined men would pace the floor and occasionally scream with anger in between long and brooding silences. Now Wulfnoth, his own nerves on edge, feared for his life at the hands of this man who now refused utterly to speak in English. At night he forced himself to keep awake, waiting for Bjorn, grimy, red eyed and soiled, to fall asleep first. When, at last, Bjorn took to attacking his gaolers whenever they appeared, they too recognised the nature of the problem and removed Wulfnoth's fears and restored to him the opportunity of a decent night's sleep by the simple expedient of having Bjorn chained to a wall. There was now just enough space for Wulfnoth to exercise without coming within reach. Once or twice, unwittingly, he had strayed too near and Bjorn had gone for him, raking at his eyes. He implored him constantly in Danish to come close and scratch his back for him, in a cunning and wheedling voice. He would come to no harm at his hands.

Instead Wulfnoth sang hymns to the poor man and recited psalms. He told him all the stories of the lives of the

Saints that he could recall from his happy cloistered days in an attempt to prevent himself from going mad and Bjorn from going madder. Just a few days after William sailed off in pursuit of his denied destiny Wulfnoth received an unseasonal and most unexpected visitor. Lanfranc had defied the Duke once or twice in the past and, in this instance, was prepared to do so again. He had hoped to appear to his beloved English protégé rather as the Angel who released Saint Peter. When the massive door swung open, however, Lanfranc went grey and was sent gagging and reeling by the stench. The gaolers were made of sterner stuff. "Morning, your Lordships," one of them sang out cheerfully, "I trust you both slept well?" Bjorn swore and then howled, receiving a hefty kick in the ribs for his pains. "Good morning," said Wulfnoth politely, for he had always been instructed that good manners cost nothing. "You," the gaoler said to him, "You are out of here. Look lively and say goodbye to your nice little Viking friend here." Wulfnoth, blinded by the light, had failed to see Lanfranc, presently chilling his sweating forehead against the wall outside and still struggling for breath. He was certain he was going to his death. "Goodbye Bjorn," he said, "and may the good God above bless and preserve you." Bjorn was unmoved by the sentiment and snarled at him, his breath like the tomb. "Piss off," he said in Danish. Wulfnoth sighed, resigning himself to the garrotte or the axe or the knife that was surely awaiting him. Instead, in tears, there was old Lanfranc. "Oh my son," he sobbed. "Just look at the state of you." His voice was muffled by the cloth that he was clutching tight against his mouth and nose. "May God forgive us for this." In all that hell of the past nine months Wulfnoth had managed to retain his sweetness and good nature. "But of course he will," he replied, slightly puzzled by the statement, but speaking with absolute confidence.

For the next twenty years of his life, despite William's occasional grumbling, the last of the Godwinsons was content enough. His room in another part of the donjon, was considerably more airy and let in more light. He could now hear the bells clearly and distinguish night from day. He was allowed books and writing materials and a small brazier and wood in especially cold weather. Lanfranc visited when he could to hear his confession, though in truth Wulfnoth had precious little to confess. Occasionally he deputised and clerics of his visited instead to ask after Wulfnoth's progress with his writings. Lanfranc had given him a bogus commission to write up a history of Saint Jerome and other doctors of the Church to keep him occupied and, on his own initiative, Wulfnoth also embarked upon a lengthy and savage critique of the Pelagian heresy, refuting it in full and with learned asides before his eyesight, ruined by flickering candlelight and strain, finally failed him completely. Then he made up hymns in his head instead as he too became progressively deranged. The food had improved immensely, but he was never permitted to leave the room.

***

Like Leofgar, Maerlswyn, Harold's devoted and attentive deputy in the north, was also awaiting a favourable wind and tide. Aeldyth, he had discovered very early on, was a highly difficult and problematic guest and a great responsibility. She was also very trying on the nerves. The news had come on to him at Lincoln from Gyrth's bereaved family at Norwich and his subsequent encounter with the dead King's pregnant child bride had left him bruised and shaken to the core. Aeldyth had first railed at the world in general and then at him in particular, as if all of this was entirely his fault and responsibility. Aeldyth, her now prominent stomach cupped and cradled by her hands, had wept and rocked back and forth. This, Maerlswyn reflected, was only to be expected, he himself was also gripped with grief and fear for the future. In time, did he but know it, he too would join the swelling ranks of dispossessed and forgotten Englishmen. At this particular moment, unaware of his future slavery, he reflected merely that this was the way of women at such times and he had had some prior experience of the vagaries and eccentricities of pregnant women. He was, though, thoroughly sick of acting as nursemaid. Only by chance had he been at Lincoln when the message came and now a whole host of responsibilities crowded about him. Technically he was now Regent for the Aetheling, but he had received no summons to attend at Bridford from Stigand. The last person Stigand would have wanted there was so firm a supporter of the Godwin clan as that stalwart from the old days.

While he coughed and fidgeted uneasily and Blodwyn, the old Welsh servant Aeldyth took everywhere with her, fussed about, Aeldyth surveyed her bleak future once more. If this Duke of Normandy ever caught up with her then a Convent for the rest of her life was the very best she could expect. Most likely, she thought, she would experience a brief but fatal illness. As for the child she carried, the legitimate child of a defeated and dead King, it didn't bear thinking of. She dried her eyes. "What now?" she demanded of Maerlswyn, "what provision have you made for this?" It was a reasonable question. "The same as those made by my Lord, your husband," he replied. "The south is closed to us and, if I know the families of Northumbria, which I most certainly do, then the whole of the north will soon be in turmoil. There is always the protection of your brothers, but I do not know where they are."

Aeldyth snapped at him. "Forget them. They are not an option and not worth the trouble of thinking of." She sighed deeply, thinking of that time when she and Harold had travelled from York to London. She had been almost happy then. "Then it is Denmark, I suppose." Maerlswyn bowed deferentially. "That was my Lord's instruction to me, should events turn out in the way that they have. For the time being you are safe enough here in Lincoln, but we need to stay near the coast, against such time as a boat can be arranged." Please God, but may that be soon, he thought to himself. "If the situation changes then there are a number of places along the coast where you will be perfectly safe. My people will see to it, they are good people that you can trust with your life and who will accompany you. I, though, must leave for York immediately. There is much to be seen to." He bowed once more to his Queen and made a hasty and thankful exit, glad to be away from there.

Aeldyth walked to the doorway of the hall and looked out into the open space before the Minster there. This news was not yet general knowledge and outside people bustled about their business. The two housecarls standing guard at the door straightened, their features stern and blank. Would Denmark be so very different to the scene facing her? Doubtless it would be colder and wetter. She disliked Danes. She had encountered so many of them in her life and it seemed to her that all of them been oafish and drunken and truculent. She had growing within her now a little Aetheling. Two generations of Aethelings had lived in exile in this place called Hungary. Doubtless, for the third time in her young life, she would be married off to someone or other. It was a chilling and depressing prospect. She would be a petitioner and a supplicant at a foreign court, there on sufferance and tolerated only in the hope that some day some political or procreational use might be made of her. She would sit well below the salt and be by turns ignored, snubbed or condescended to. She, a Queen of England! "I curse the day that I was born," she said aloud on an impulse and in the fluent Welsh she had learned from her first husband. "If my Lady would care to return inside," said one of the housecarls, a stolid Lincolnshire man and not possessing the gift of tongues. "I fear that out here in full view we are attracting attention."

Aeldyth smiled sweetly at the man, the natural smile summoned up without effort and which had never failed to disarm and disable. The housecarl flushed visibly under the effect and stared at his boots. "I shall attract attention for as long as I am able," she said. She was, undeniably, a very beautiful woman. She was sick of England, sick of this kin and dynasty obsessed little island. It was, she assumed and hoped, a little island and with a far wider and more promising world beckoning to her beyond. Besides, England was turning out to be downright dangerous. Perhaps exile was indeed preferable. Perhaps there waited, even in wet and gloomy Denmark, a rich and handsome and well set up young nobleman who would care for her and pamper her to the end of her days. "Well then, young Harold," she said, again in Welsh and to her stomach, "or whatever you are. Time is getting on and there is a lot to be doing."

***

There had been a falling out at Bridford, in fact a very serious one, between the churchmen and the Aelfgarsons. Edwin, with the enthusiastic support of his brother, had changed his mind completely, leaving poor Waltheof completely wrong footed and Stigand and the others dumbfounded. Perhaps it had been the well meaning and conciliatory Ealdred who had precipitated the argument, with all his talk of the unsettled north and ill founded rumours of Danish invasion and raids from Scotland. He gossiped like an old woman of the doings of the house of Bernicia, Waltheof's kin and of how the whole of Cumbria was going to the dogs. Copsig, that faithful old lieutenant of Tostig, was reported to be back, and raising men in the dales and the wolds. All of this was more than enough for Morcar, anxious as he was to be as far away from the wrath of the Duke of Normandy as possible and back home in Northumbria and seeing to the protection of his own interests.

But it was Stigand, unwittingly chancing his luck too far and once too often, who had finally alienated Edwin, the driving force of the Aelfgarsons. "Now let me see if I have this right," Edwin said with a deep sarcasm and turning to the Archbishop as they sat at the board. "We make our submission and swear our fealty and then we offer ourselves up as hostages for the good behaviour of Mercia and Northumbria." The expression on his face as he looked at Stigand was deliberately and annoyingly enquiring. Never mind Morcar's own problems with the men of Bernicia, the Scots and the Danes. He could well imagine what the troublesome Welsh in the west and those mongrel breeds to the north in Cumbria would make of such an opportunity. Then there were the Irish Vikings of the Isle of Man and of Dublin also to consider. In his mind's eye he saw Chester and Hereford in flames and wild red-haired men roaming the streets with axes and firebrands and yelling in Norse, just as they might have done in York had it not been for the intervention of Harold.

Stigand beamed at him condescendingly, fully aware of the youth's animosity. "Quite so. You have it correct. Quite correct, my Lord Earl. You have an understanding of things quite beyond your very few years" Take note, little infant, he thought to himself. I have been at this game for far longer than you. I can yet bring you down. Stigand idly turned a wrinkled autumn pear in his hand. "And I am sure too, as I must trust in my own salvation, that in the fullness of time the Duke will confirm you in all your lands and titles."

Wisely, Bishop Wulfstan, whose own diocese lay in Mercia, kept out of the conversation and Ealdred was insufficiently quick witted to make any contribution. "In the fullness of time?" Edwin retorted, his face blazing in anger.

"Your Grace, I do not think so. I have to tell you that when I meet with this Duke then it will be with a display of strength behind me. I shall not come to this man on my knees and in supplication. I am no enemy of the Duke of Normandy and I look forward to the moment when we shall meet as friends." Beside him, his brother Morcar, aware that a row was brewing, kept his face down and began carving into the table with his knife. Old Ealdred of York was beginning to look puzzled, he had once more lost the thread of things, and Wulfstan sighed deeply. "This is surely the end of all things," he thought to himself. "If it not be a sin, then may our Lord God please take me away from all this." Resignedly, he leaned forward in his chair, prepared to intervene when necessary.

"Your Grace, I would consider it a favour if you were to tell the Duke of Normandy of my thoughts and wishes, should you meet with him before I have that great honour. Please also convey to him that I and my brother will work for him and with him, for he has proven himself to be a better man than Harold Godwinson. My brother and I shall hold the north for him. Tell him we shall guard it against all comers." Suddenly and abruptly Edwin thumped the table, causing Stigand to start and wince. "But tell him also that I am still the Earl of Mercia and no man's supplicant."

This was precisely the same form of ill-judged bravado that had led directly to the disaster of Fulford Gate. "You made the same promise to Harold," said Waltheof bitterly. Edwin turned upon him. "Harold is dead, and God helps them who help themselves." Stigand's vision of a single peace agreement and with him as its acknowledged architect lay in ruins. "You delay the hour, Edwin. That is all," he warned him. "Either in the next few weeks or the next few months, the Duke of Normandy will hold you to account for this. I beg of you to stay, and to come with us to meet him."

"No," said Edwin firmly, "neither me nor my brother." Morcar, only half comprehending the discussion but perceiving that his brother had made a telling point, grinned in triumph and for a moment it seemed as if Waltheof would lean across and strike one or the other of them. "And what of me?" he demanded. "What of you?" Edwin replied, unmoved. "You are the Earl of Huntingdon, a man who has already resisted the Duke. Unlike me and my brother, you do need to make your peace, I grant you that. We, on the other hand, are two men of authority that he may deal with in peace. So, look to your own future," he finished contemptuously. "Now, if you will excuse us, my brother and I have much to do. We leave tomorrow."

There was a long pause after they had left, broken finally by Wulfstan. "Peace, my brother," he said gently to Stigand, and with no trace of irony or criticism. "At least the Church of the English remains undivided. Let us all at least be thankful for that."

***

"Here they come now," said Roger Beaumont quite unnecessarily, pointing over to the east. A cavalcade of English riders with a Norman escort had appeared on the bemired path below them. For once on this God forsaken island it wasn't raining, at least not yet anyway. For the purposes of the occasion, though, William had been fully prepared to conduct the entire ceremony in the open and in the streaming rain.

The ancient barrow of Berkhampstead, level upon its crown, was wide enough to take William's campaign pavilion, repeatedly packed and unpacked and erected and packed once more and each time to the accompaniment of low muttered oaths. Set about it were a number of other tents, those of the chiefs of his followers. There was space enough also for men to ascend the slope and to then kneel before a handsome carved chair of bog oak acquired in Winchester on which the Duke would seat himself. In deference to the elderly prelates that were expected and as a rare mark of diplomacy, matting had been provided for them to kneel upon and folding stools on which they could then seat themselves once proper obeisance had been observed. The golden leopard of Normandy and the delicate papal banner flew jauntily in the breeze behind the chair. Not so the dragon of Wessex and the Fighting Man. Of a purpose, these, now soiled and torn, had been left lying conspicuously upon the ground before the Duke's handsome chair.

The manor of Berkhampstead and all of its outbuildings behind the mound had been appropriated and beyond them the much battered but victorious army had set itself down with as much comfort as was possible. In an English October and with the poor means at their disposal, the men were fractious and irritable. All the way back through devastated Berkshire and Hampshire, along the coastal path to Hastings and Pevensey, William had left small garrisons of men to police and terrorise their allotted districts and to cow the already traumatised local populations. There were men also at Maidstone, Canterbury, Dover and Romney. He had with him here a force of perhaps four thousand discontented men. They were all of them turned out and paraded for the occasion, armed and armoured for full effect. FitzOsbern, who had a gift of his own for stage management, had arranged it so that the English would be obliged to travel up a corridor of these grim faced and dangerous looking men in order to then dismount and clamber up the greasy slope of the barrow to kneel at the feet of the Duke.

This ascent would not be easy and would certainly not lend them any dignity. "I want nothing to be too easy for them," William had instructed. "They are beaten men and the representatives of a beaten country. Once they have submitted and humbled themselves and sworn their public oath then shall I raise them up." He was addressing his assembled aristocratic survivors that previous night. "They will then go surety for a peaceful entry into London." First, then, the humiliation of surrender and then the feasting upon local mutton, beef and pork now being prepared in the kitchens over at the manor. These English would then be his honoured guests, but also hostages for the good behaviour of the beaten English. He would make this very clear to them and then ship them over to Normandy in the spring to gawp and be gawped at. In separate ways he would appease them, whilst at the same time rewarding his own followers who had survived with lands and honours.

William wished that Lanfranc was here with him to deal with the churchmen. Pious as he was, he had never been truly at ease in the company of men of God and this delegation now arriving was of an unknown quality. He was, though, looking forward to the occasion immensely and to meeting this man Stigand at last. For the moment he must seek not to completely alienate any of them, for the moment they were needed. In time he could turn over church affairs to Lanfranc and to a papal nuncio. For now he required their services at his forthcoming coronation, particularly Ealdred of York, the man who had crowned Harold. That would be a very nice touch indeed.

He knew also of the importance of Wulfstan. In the past, it had transpired, the Bishop of Worcester and Lanfranc had been occasional correspondents, communicating on various matters pertaining to the universal Church and swapping Latin tags and acrostics, for which they shared a fondness, as a pleasurable diversion from business. From what he had learned from Malet, the Bishop was extremely influential and held to be something of a Saint within his own diocese. More than any other, Wulfstan held the key to church unity at this difficult time and his influence along the length and breadth of the Welsh border was considerable. William had had a lengthy meeting with Malet the night before. In his diffident and self-conscious way Malet had fidgeted throughout it. On one issue, however, he was very firm. "Of them all, your Grace, honour the Bishop of Worcester. You need his support and with all respect I suggest you do not presume upon the privileges of the English church for the moment." He waited for the inevitable explosion of anger. It did not come. Instead William looked reflective. Malet had not given him bad advice yet. "He is also," Malet continued, "a good man, much loved and revered. Where he goes, others will follow."

What, also, to do with the Earl of Huntingdon? He too was of this embassy. William understood him to be a very young man, and therefore both headstrong and quick to take offence, but also impressionable and perhaps easy to flatter. He did not know then that it was Waltheof, if not the actual architect, who had brought about the disaster of the Malfosse. William had heard a great deal recently of the troubles and difficulties of the north. He knew too that for the time being he could not in safety travel there. Perhaps this young Northumbrian with his truncated little Earldom might be the man for him there until such time as he could be replaced. Well, he would have to see.

As the English approached and began to ride down the long line of the Duke's gathered army, Malet was still rehearsing them in their lines and behaviour, muttering urgently to them. To the rear was a rag tag collection of local thegns, a brace of Abbots, three earldormen of the home shires and some of the more prominent London citizens, including Aesegar's deputy. They would all have to take their chance and copy the manners and gestures of their betters. Wulfstan was polite and attentive, as was his way. Stigand was expressionless and Ealdred positively beamed with good will. Inwardly Stigand was raging. He was now possessed of the strong and abiding feeling that things would not now turn out as he had hoped and that little good would come of this meeting.

All of his most recent messages to the Duke had gone unanswered. Waltheof, riding erect and with dignity and ignoring the hostile wall of Normans to either side of him, was all icy dignity and rigid pride. A short distance behind him rode the justifiably nervous representatives of Northumbria and Mercia, the two brothers being absent. Those bastards, Waltheof said to himself, he would settle accounts with them yet, unless the Duke of Normandy got to them first. He had good old-fashioned Northumbrian plans for those two that his pagan ancestors would have approved of. He would personally carve out the blood eagle on their scabrous backs. Young Edgar Aetheling, the ultimate Norman prize, rode beside him. He was excited and waved to the Normans now hedging him about, believing, clearly, they were there in his honour. Gifts, there would surely be gifts! He wanted a war horse instead of this placid little gelding he presently rode, something with fire and spirit. He wanted armour and weapons and a banner to wave, more besides. It was very good of this Duke, he reflected, to pay homage to him in this way with this meeting.

The Bishop of Worcester and William Malet rode side by side. "I fully understand," Wulfstan was saying to Malet in his musical tones. "We approach and then we kneel. I believe that this is the common practice on such occasions. I believe also I have the formulae correct. We speak it, and you translate. Then we are bidden to rise and await his Grace's pleasure." Malet was eager for there to be no unfortunate misunderstandings regarding protocol. "Just so," he replied. "His Grace is a stern and fearsome man, but he is loving and forgiving when it is appropriate to be so." Wulfstan smiled sadly at Malet. The man was trying so hard to reconcile the irreconcilable. Since the battle, Wulfstan had heard a great deal of the supposed love and forgiveness of William, Duke of Normandy. He remembered also, vividly, Harold's own account of the campaign in Brittany. "Malet," he said. "We are just about there and out of this forest of hard faced men. Time soon for me to climb up that slope there ahead of us and then fall to my ancient and creaking knees. I know you for a man with a good heart. I ask you now to remember this one thing. I seek peace and reconciliation for this poor and abused country. I shall make every effort to achieve this and I pray to Almighty God for the necessary strength and purpose." The Bishop leaned across and seized Malet's wrist in a surprisingly strong grip. "But know this. I shall be like a rock in defence of the Church of this land and the people it protects."

"His Grace is mindful of this," Malet replied. Gently he removed the Bishop's hand from his gauntlet. "It is merely that he is very firm on the strict observance of proper protocol, especially with so many looking on. Any breach of this might bring on an unfortunate anger." Wulfstan subjected Malet to a humorous stare, obliging the other man to look away. "To be sure," he said placidly. "Then it behoves us all, whatever language we may speak, to make this public event both decorous and harmonious. How things may then turn out after that is within the jurisdiction of our Lord above and it is not our place to question." Malet, an intelligent and thoughtful man, found the remark cryptic and not one that really permitted any appropriate response. He had no time to ponder further anyway as they were now at the base of the mound. They dismounted under the curious scrutiny of thousands of men. At the foot of the rise ushers awaited them, their expressions solicitous and polite.

The English delegation carefully negotiated its way up the difficult slope, slipping here and there, and to the seated and awaiting Duke. One by one they knelt, placed their hands within his and took their oath, the short English utterance "I become your man." Malet performed the introductions and the translation as the Duke spoke to each one in turn. Then, one by one, William raised them up and thus made them his own.

***

Christmas Day, one year to the day since Harold had come here. The Christ child was born once more, his birth celebrated in the echoing chamber of the Abbey of Westminster. Old Edward had been justifiably proud of his choristers. They had been begged, borrowed and frankly kidnapped from Abbeys and Minsters the length and breadth of England and beyond. They were certainly doing his memory proud now. "Gloria in Excelsis Deo" resounded and reverberated off the stone walls as men, their armour hidden by surcoats and cloaks, stamped their feet and blew on their fingers against the numbing cold. There had been midnight Mass, of course, and the dawn devotions and all the other necessary observances. It would culminate now in the coronation of a second King of England in the space of precisely one year.

In defiance of the bitter chill William, by the grace of God Duke of Normandy, knelt at the High Altar. He was barefoot and in breeches and a loose shirt. The favoured men of the assembled front ranks marvelled at the sight, never seen before and never to be seen again, of their Duke as a humble supplicant. ArchBishop Ealdred of York, surrounded by a flock of acolytes and an aromatic cloud of incense, approached to conduct those same rites of Coronation and anointing that he had conducted on this very spot just one very eventful year before. Other clerics stood nearby, assembled in their finery to lend further gravity to the occasion.

Wulfstan and Stigand were there too. Stigand, his expression blank, raged inwardly at this, the second occasion he had been denied the officiating rites of a King of England. Wulfstan's face, equally, contained no emotion. Each had his own memories of this momentous year and his own provisional agenda for the future. Ealdred, a far simpler person than either of them, ploughed and bumbled his way amiably through the ceremony and at last the crown of England, the simple band of gold, was settled upon William's head. William, by the grace of God, Duke of Normandy and King of England. The holy oil of anointment dripped down his impassive face and gathered at the creases and folds of his eyes, nose and mouth as the congregation roared out its acclamation and joy. The kiss of peace was exchanged between the leading churchmen, running along their line. Ealdred to Odo, gorgeous in his robes. Odo turned to the Bishop of Coutances and Coutances, with an ill suppressed expression of distaste to Stigand who relayed the greeting on to Wulfstan. If any words were exchanged then they were not heard above the Anthem that now rang out from the choristers and the continuing yells from the main body of the Abbey.

Those gathered there as witnesses numbered perhaps five hundred men, a majority of the Duke's men and a scattering of English. All of William's barony as could be spared were present, rubbing shoulders with those English who had submitted in the same way as their fathers and grandfathers had once submitted to another foreign King. The shouts of 'Gloria,' 'Dex Veult' and, more cautiously, the English 'Wassail' mingled and spread beyond the Abbey to the large crowd outside in the Minster precincts.

The sound carried outside and to the ears of a very nervous and inexperienced young knight who had been rather injudiciously appointed duty officer responsible for crowd control for that day. To him the noise came as one of disturbance and anarchy rather than of celebration. At the western porch and with fifty horsemen and two hundred men at arms at his disposal, he panicked. Before him the English crowd seemed to boil up and surge, a dun and brown and grey mob on the very edge of violence. To the young man, promoted beyond his means and abilities and experience, the threat was tangible as the crowd of people before him too began to shout and stamp their feet. A fear that he had not felt all day at Senlac gripped him. "Right then," he shouted. "That is it. That is enough." His sword rasped out of his scabbard and, without waiting to see if he was followed, he kicked his horse into a trot and rode it straight at the mob.

The confines of the Abbey precinct were small and packed with people. Suddenly, huge iron men on giant horses were riding into them and swinging their weapons. The chances to duck and weave and dart up the narrow alley-ways between the wooden and thatched roofed buildings were limited. The people, defenceless, cowered, their arms held above their heads in vain as the blows rained down upon them and the horses knocked them to the ground. The horses ploughed through and straight after came the footmen, stumbling over those already fallen, hacking and jabbing with their spears. Within a very short period of time dozens of figures lay upon the muddy and half frozen ground, either stilled forever or else writhing in pain. The brazier of an enterprising vendor of roasted chestnuts was overturned. Burning embers alighted upon some bales of straw stacked foolishly against the timber frame of an open barn recently treated with pine resin against the damp. The fire caught and the building went up in flames, sending further sparks and embers to catch amongst the thatch of the surrounding buildings. By the time the new King of England was robed and invested with all pomp and ceremony FitzOsbern and a few others, alerted by the sudden commotion outside, had rushed in alarm from the Abbey.

A sizeable section of Westminster seemed to be now in flames and, to his horror, FitzOsbern observed enthusi-astic knights and their followers scything down people in the square or else chasing them up alleys. "Oh dear God Almighty," moaned FitzOsbern, recognising an omen when he saw one. "Whoever is responsible for this, I'll have his balls on a skewer. Find me the man who caused this."

The first of the celebrants now also reached the porch, expecting with confidence the acclaim of the crowd. There they saw instead a scene of chaos and confusion reminiscent of their old raiding days. The smoke was thick and ashes and live embers fell upon them. Norman knights and men at arms with hangdog expressions were being whipped and cuffed into line and bodies lay everywhere like discarded refuse. The crowd of spectators had retreated to the ditch of the Tyburn brook. They were hooting and jeering now and hurling sticks and cobblestones and anything else that came to hand. FitzOsbern was prominently on view in the midst of all this. Injured arm or not, he appeared to be attempting to strangle a young knight who was putting up no resistance whatsoever. He slapped the hapless youth twice across the face with his mailed glove.

William himself now stalked the aisle, preceded by Gerald Seneschal holding aloft a naked sword and de Tosny and FitzWarren carrying the two banners of Normandy and the Holy Father. The choristers continued to sing praises. William frowned at the hold up caused by the mass of men blocking his exit, the displeasure clear upon his face. He wished to greet his new people. Odo, reeking of incense and perfume, came to whisper in his ear. "My apologies, brother. There has been a slight complication, a small disturbance only."

"Complication? Disturbance? Clear the way there. I am coming through." Irritably, William barged and shouldered his way through and out into the open air. Back in January Harold had stood on this very spot. Then a bird passing overhead had paid its own particular tribute to him and his brother had laughed and told him that it brought him good luck. Now, on this Christmas Day, two different brothers stood there. Smoke drifted into William's eyes, causing him to blink as he surveyed the scene before him. He winced as a hot ember settled upon his cheek. Hurriedly, he brushed it aside. Behind him the choir sang on, a beautiful and unearthly sound. Before him there rose up the moans and cries of injured and dying people, the crackling of timber and thatch, the crying of children and the defiance of the mob.

"Is this how it is to be?" William asked of Odo. His voice was high pitched and anguished. "Is this now what we have to face for the rest of our lives?" And to this Odo, who in the normal course of things had an answer to everything and everyone, could find nothing to say.

EPILOGUE:

The fortunes of those who survived that momentous and fateful year were a combination of tragedy and triumph, mostly tragedy.

Edgar the Aetheling outlived nearly all of them. He remained an insignificant cipher, a dilettante and a burden upon the good favour of royal and aristocratic households to the end of his days, though he did prove to be of occasional political use to certain of the well-placed schemers of the time. It suited him to marry his sister off to Malcolm Canmore and thus the line of the ancient royal Saxon House of Cerdic entered into the line of the Kings of Scotland. He flirted with intrigue, revolt and rebellion and, by turns, was both an honoured guest and an undesired and unpopular political refugee in exile in a variety of foreign courts. He finally died on the Normandy estates granted to him by King Henry, a person not yet born in the year of Hastings. With his death there came to a final end the five-hundred-year line of Cerdic, the conqueror of Wessex and the descendant of the god Odin.

Gytha, wife of Godwin and mother of all those ill-fated sons, disappeared from historical record after a brief but spirited defense of Exeter. It is to be hoped that Edith the 'swan neck' found some form of peace and happiness in Ireland, but this is not known. For a while, the two oldest Godwinsons, sailing out of Ireland, made a thorough nuisance of themselves in senseless freebooting raids and acts of unashamed piracy. These always failed to properly coincide with the periodic revolts that broke out amongst the Welsh borderers, the men of the north and of the west and the people of the eastern Danelaw. They were, in the final analysis, a brief irrelevance, much as William would dearly have loved to have had them in his possession, and in due course they too disappeared from history without trace. So too did Harold's wife Aeldyth of Mercia, that tragic bargaining counter and carrying within her womb the now defunct support of Mercia and Northumbria. Perhaps she made it to Denmark and then to Hungary beyond. The fate of her brothers, on the other hand, is documented.

Forced to be made aware at last of inescapable facts, the two brothers Edwin and Morcar finally submitted to William in January 1067. They were then swept off to Normandy in the spring of that year along with all the other significant English political survivors in the ambiguous dual role of guest and hostage. As with most people, William clearly never grew fond of them. For those years remaining to them they too, like Edgar, flirted with rebellion. In 1071, frustrated at the continuing lack of favour shown to them by King William, they were prominent players in the great revolt of the north. Morcar finally submitted, spending the rest of William's own life in miserable solitary confinement until being pardoned and released. He died very shortly afterwards.

With an ever decreasing band of followers Edwin, who had never lacked personal courage, flitted from hiding place to hiding place until, exasperated with him and his vanity and his constant demands upon a fast vanishing loyalty belonging to an earlier age, his own people cut off his head and had it conveyed in a canvas bag to the King, at whose feet it was deposited unceremoniously one night during a feast.

Even the loyal and uncomplaining Copsig had his own brief moment of glory. Baffled by the complexities of the dynastic feuds and vendettas of the northern families and at a loss of how best to deal with them, William experimented by having the man actually made Earl of the ancient territories of a much-reduced Bernicia in 1067. It was a brief and inauspicious rule and was over really before it had begun. The experiment ended in Copsig being burnt to death in his own hall, consumed in a fierce and roaring fire lit exuberantly by a small group of his numerous enemies.

Old Ealdred died in 1069, thus happily avoiding the inevitable purges of the Church of the English which followed shortly afterwards. The saintly Wulfstan survived all of this, unassailable through his rare blend of consummate statecraft, cunning and innate goodness. The old schemer and plotter Stigand was not so fortunate. The old man finally died in 1072, deposed, discredited and broken, chained to a wall and forgotten in a dank Norman cellar.

William had raised the young Earl Waltheof of Huntingdon up on that mound at Berkhampstead. William made a favourite of Waltheof, keeping him by him and in the hope that this young man would be a bridge in the years to come between the English and their Norman masters. Honours and estates in both England and Normandy followed. In the early days, before all the many small and great acts of disobedience and revolts that finally and irrevocably estranged William from his new English subjects forever, he had hoped that those of the English high aristocracy who he permitted to remain would support him and make his path all the smoother. Thus, Waltheof retained his precarious Earldom and was William's brightest burning English star. As such the Earl received a pardon for his own role in the great northern rebellion of 1069 and was even married off to William's own niece Judith. It was Waltheof's tragedy that he was pardoned for something he did and condemned for something he did not. Now Earl of Bernicia, he was implicated in a foolish conspiracy in 1075. He had made plenty of enemies in his short life and now they all united to encompass his total ruin. Not even the combined pleadings of Lanfranc and Wulfstan could prevail and William finally gave the order to execute him. Skilled women were employed to sew his head back onto his neck again after his death. When they finally came to bury him, so it was said, his body was complete and uncorrupt. There was not a mark upon him of violence or of the rotting of flesh. In life Waltheof had sought always to be a warrior. In death, the man whose father had leapt from the walls of York invoking Odin, achieved an unofficial cult status of saint and martyr, with miracles attributed to him.

The troubled and tormented Edith, daughter of Godwin and widow of Edward, remained locked within her own maddened mind, a recluse living in the past and making alarming predictions for the future. She died in 1075 and William gave the order for her to be reunited with her husband beneath the flagstones of Westminster Abbey.

William knew that he could not go back on the promises made to his supporters. He was as good as his word and there were certain among the more favoured of his men who lacked for nothing to the very end of their days. William Warenne, for example lived on for a further twenty-two years before dying in the defence of that wilful and troubled red haired child of William's, his youngest boy, William 'Rufus.'

Roger of Montgomery outlived Warenne by six years, dying peacefully in his bed surrounded by mourning relatives, one of the richest men in England. Roger Bigod lived even longer, becoming a virtual monarch in East Anglia and tyrannising the former subjects of Gyrth and Waltheof. For all of the leading survivors there came lands and riches taken from the dead of Hastings. Eustace of Boulogne was rewarded but was lured into rebellion against his King by the men of Kent, offering him the crown that he himself had always considered to be rightfully his. Imprisonment and exile followed, as it did to so many of William's followers who sought more than he himself felt them entitled to. William Malet was returned his former lands in Sussex and in Mercia by a grateful Duke. Five years later his horse kicked him the head whilst being shoed. He lingered on for a few years after that, confused and rambling and incapable of doing anything for himself or of recognising members of his own family.

Few men rose higher than William FitzOsbern, William's faithful childhood friend. With William's first return back to Normandy, FitzOsbern and Odo were left as joint Viceroys in England. Together they launched the first of the terrible 'pacifications' of the English, in the south west and along the Welsh marches, in the East Anglian Fens and north of the river Trent. FitzOsbern was made Earl of Hereford and more besides, acquiring lands and titles in great quantities. When William returned to England with his wife, his son Robert, Montgomery and Beaumont and all the cowed and intimidated English hostages, FitzOsbern sailed to Normandy to take up his duties as Regent there. Ever mindful of his continental obligations, William appointed FitzOsbern also as Regent of Flanders after old Baldwin died and as protector of Baldwin's young heir Arnulf against the predatory ambitions of his enemies. In 1071 FitzOsbern was ambushed and this loyal and skilful warrior politician was pulled from his horse and bludgeoned to death in a ditch by hired mercenaries.

The master statesman Lanfranc died in 1089 at the ripe old age of 79, Archbishop of Canterbury and the leading figure over the wholescale dismantling and reform of the Church of the English. He had made sure to leave the machinery of power in good working order and in good hands when finally he died and was buried at Canterbury.

Robert of Mortain had ever been a loyal brother and supporter and he was thus rewarded by William, becoming one of the richest men in England. For as long as William lived Robert remained loyal but, like so many others, he then backed the wrong side in the struggle between the sons of William in the disturbances and civil war of 1088. Exiled to his Norman estates, he died soon after.

Odo, the commissioner of the Bayeux Tapestry, was as dissimilar a man to his brother Robert as possible. Odo maintained his rare political skills and gifts of manipulation almost to the end. In addition to all his clerical titles and positions he was made also Earl of Kent. In 1082 William and his own son Robert finally fell out violently over the division of the spoils of the new Norman Empire and Odo threw in his lot with his nephew whilst at the same time attempting to bribe his way onto the Pontiff's throne. To break openly with his brother in this way proved to be a rare slip and extremely foolish and so for the rest of William's life Odo remained a prisoner confined in the keep at Rouen, disgraced and impoverished. When William finally died his son Rufus restored his uncle to his former estates. Odo was soon in revolt once more, however, and was banished to his estates at Bayeux. He then took the Crusader's Cross at the Council of Clermont in 1095 and joined the First Crusade. He never made it to Jerusalem and the Holy Land, dying instead of a fever in Norman Palermo in Sicily. He was, as a contemporary wrote of him, "a man more given to worldly affairs than spiritual contemplation."

Twenty-one years of life remained to William after the carnage of Senlac. These years were, predictably, difficult and busy and spent mostly in the consolidation and spirited defence of his gains and the ruthless crushing of an unremitting series of revolts and rebellions that convinced him finally that England would not ever be governed by an amiable and consenting council of Normans and English. A firm ruling hand was clearly required and by the time of the devastation of the North his course was set. The writer Orderic Vitalis, usually an ardent admirer of William, wrote thus of an expedition to the north in the years 1069 and 1070:

'My narrative has frequently had occasion to praise William, but for this act which condemned the innocent and the guilty alike to die by slow starvation I cannot commend him. For when I think of innocent children, young men in the prime of their life, and hoary greybeards alike perishing of hunger, I am so moved to pity that I would rather lament the griefs and sufferings of the wretched people than make a vain attempt to flatter the perpetrator of such infamy. Moreover, I declare that assuredly such brutal slaughter cannot remain unpunished. For the Almighty Judge watches over high and low alike; he will weigh the deeds of all men in a fair balance, and as a just avenger will punish wrongdoing.'

William died in the Priory of Saint Gervase just outside Rouen at dawn on September 9th, 1087. six weeks of constant pain after the destruction of the city of Mantes, where the ailing King, grossly corpulent and diabetic, was thrown against the pommel of his saddle by his horse, which had trodden on a red hot ember and had reared up violently, seemingly causing a massive and fatal rupture of the kidney. In the six weeks remaining to him he showered endowments upon the Church in Normandy and England. There was money in abundance for restitution and for the hearing of masses in perpetuity for his immortal soul to the Minsters and Abbeys and parish churches in England, a general amnesty was declared. Those who remained faithful stayed at his deathbed. His beloved son William, called the Rufus, he had sent to England to secure the country for himself. Robert, the oldest boy and from whom he was estranged, stayed away. To Robert, passed over, went the Duchy of Normandy. His second son, Henry, rising eighteen, was also absent. He had been endowed no land but received instead a payment of five thousand pounds in hard cash. In his final moments William prayed to the Virgin for forgiveness. He commended himself to God and then he died. His audience then promptly scattered in haste and in all directions to look to their own respective futures. William's body was left alone. Sometime later servants and common men entered the Chapter House and ransacked the corpse. They stripped the stiffening fingers of rings and tipped the body of the former King of England and Duke of Normandy to the floor, where it lay until the following morning.

A local landowner, a humble knight called Herluin, at last appeared to restore order and some seemliness, hanging a few suspected looters on the spot. Out of his own purse he paid a local butcher and his apprentices to carry out the most cursory and bungled of embalming, ripping open the rotting stomach of the corpse and piling coils of his blue and grey intestines into buckets. They poured bags of salt into the cavern of his stomach and sewed the body up once more. They hacked and sawed into the skull and spooned out the brains, pouring more salt in there as well.

Wrapped in blankets, so the story goes, William's body was placed in a barge and transported to his beloved creation of Caen. There it was laid on a bier before the High Altar as a sarcophagus was acquired and a pit was hastily dug. Scarcely had the official Vigil for the dead begun, and with an assembly of reluctant churchmen again rounded up, when a large fire broke out nearby, predictably enough in a baker's shop. At this everyone scattered once more.

The interrupted funeral mass was finally resumed, and the sarcophagus lowered into the pit, ready to receive the mortal remains of William Duke of Normandy and King of England. There came loud and bitter complaining from the back of the Church, the voice of a citizen of Caen. The land taken for the burial belonged to him, the land upon which this Abbey stood had been seized unlawfully from his own father. Encouraged by a highly partisan crowd of supporters, he demanded compensation before he would permit this man to be buried in the very ground he had stolen. Those knights that were present were too few in number to restore order. A sum of money for compensation was found to pay the owner of the land.

William's swollen and stiffened body was then removed from the bier to be placed in the stone coffin. Unfortunately, the coffin was too small and too narrow and could not contain its intended new occupant. In desperation, the attendants attempted to force the body in. The amateur embalmers of Rouen had been paid too little and had worked with even less expertise. The poorly stitched body of William burst open and the stench of corruption rose up in the confined space. All then fled from the open grave in their anxiety to escape the burning city of Caen, and the body remained unburied.

The End

Bibliography

Aitchison, Nicholas Boyter., Aitchison, Nick. *Macbeth: man and myth*. United Kingdom: Sutton, 1999.

Ashley, Maurice. *Life and Times of William I*. United States: Welcome Rain Publishers, 1999.

Barclay, C.N. *Battle 1066*. D. Van Norstrand Company, Inc., 1966.

Barlow, Frank. *Edward the Confessor*. United Kingdom: Yale University Press, 2011.

Barlow, Frank. *The Godwins: The Rise and Fall of a Noble Dynasty*. United Kingdom: Taylor & Francis, 2013.

Bates, David. *William the Conqueror*. United States: Yale Uinversity Press, 2016.

Bennett, Matthew. *Campaigns of the Norman Conquest*. United Kingdom: Taylor & Francis, 2014.

Bland, A. E. *The Normans in England: 1066-1154* (Classic Reprint). United States: 1kg Limited, 2019.

Bradbury, Jim. *The Battle of Hastings: The Fall of the Anglo-Saxons and the Rise of the Normans*. United States: Pegasus Books, 2021.

Brechin, David, *The Conqueror's London: Discovering London 2*.

Bridgeford, Andrew. *1066: The Hidden History in the Bayeux Tapestry*. New York: Walker & Company, 2006.

Brondsted, Johannes. *The Vikings*. N.p.: n.p., 1965.

Brooke, Christopher N. L. *The Saxon and Norman Kings*. United Kingdom: Wiley, 2001.

Brown, R. Allen. *The Normans and the Norman Conquest*. United Kingdom: Boydell Press, 1994.

Campbell, James. *The Anglo-Saxon State*. United Kingdom: Bloomsbury Academic, 2000.

Crouch, David. *The Normans: The History of a Dynasty*. United

Kingdom: Bloomsbury Academic, 2006.

Danziger, Danny., Lacey, Robert. *The Year 1000: What Life was Like at the Turn of the First Millennium: an Englishman's World*. United Kingdom: Abacus, 2000.

Davis, Ralph Henry Carless, Davis, The Late R H C. *The Normans and their myth*. London: Thames & Hudson, 1976.

Denny, Norman, and Josephine Filmer-Sankey. *The Bayeux Tapestry: The Story of the Norman Conquest: 1066*. New York: Atheneum, 1966.

Douglas, David C. *William the Conqueror: The Norman Impact Upon England*. United States: University of California Press, 1964.

Douglas, David Charles. *The Norman Achievement, 1050-1100*. Berkeley: University of California Press, 1969.

Finberg, H. P. R.. *The Formation of England, 550-1042*. United Kingdom: Paladin, 1976.

Fisher, D. J. V. *The Anglo-Saxon Age C.400-1042*. United Kingdom: Taylor & Francis, 2014.

Fletcher, Richard A. *Who's who in Roman Britain and Anglo-Saxon England: 55 BC-AD 1066*. United States: Stackpole Books, 2002.

Fletcher, Richard. *Bloodfeud: Murder and Revenge in Anglo-Saxon England*. United Kingdom: Oxford University Press, 2003.

Foote, P.G. and Wilson, D.M. *The Viking Achievement*. London: Sidgwick & Jackson.

Gravett, Christopher. *The History of Castles*. United Kingdom: Globe Pequot Press, 2007.

Green, John Richard. *The Making of England*. United Kingdom: Macmillan, 1885.

Higham, N. J. *The Norman Conquest*. United Kingdom: Sutton Pub., 1998.

Higham, Nick. *The Death of Anglo-Saxon England*. United Kingdom: Sutton Pub., 1997.

Hill, Paul. *The Road to Hastings: The Politics of Power in Anglo-Saxon England*. Spain: Tempus, 2005.

Howarth, David. *1066: The Year of the Conquest*. United

Kingdom: Penguin, 2002.

Hunter Blair, Peter. *An Introduction to Anglo-Saxon England*. Spain: Cambridge University Press, 2003.

Jones, Charles. *Fulford: The Forgotten Battle of 1066*. United Kingdom: History Press, 2007.

Jones, Gwyn. *A History of the Vikings*. United Kingdom: Oxford University Press, 2001.

Lawson, M. K. *The Battle of Hastings, 1066*. United Kingdom: History Press Limited, 2007.

Lloyd, Alan. *The Year of the Conqueror*. United Kingdom: Longmans, 1966.

Loyn, H.R. *Anglo Saxon England and the Norman Conquest*. United Kingdom: Taylor & Francis, 2014.

Loyn, Henry and Sorrell, Alan. *Norman Britain*. Lutterworth Press.

Mason, Emma, Shoemaker, Robert Brink. *The house of Godwine : the history of a dynasty. United Kingdom*: Bloomsbury Academic, 2004.

McLynn, Frank. *1066: The Year of the Three Battles*. United Kingdom: Random House, 2011.

Nicolle, David. Gravett, Christopher. *The Normans: Warrior Knights and Their Castles*. United Kingdom: Bloomsbury USA, 2007.

Patterson, Benton Rain. *Harold and William: The Battle for England 1064-1066*. United Kingdom: History Press Limited, 2002.

Reeves, M.E. *The Norman Conquest*. 1959.

Rex, Peter. *The Last English King: The Life of Harold II*. United Kingdom: History Press, 2008.

Rowley, Trevor. *The Norman Heritage, 1066-1200*. United Kingdom: Paladin, 1984.

Savage, Anne [trans.]. *The Anglo-Saxon Chronicle*. London: 1968.

Sayles, G.O. *The Medieval Foundations of England*. United Kingdom: Taylor & Francis, 2019.

Stenton, Frank Merry. *Anglo-Saxon England*. United Kingdom: OUP Oxford, 2001.

The Anglo-Saxon Chronicle: Translated with an Introduction by G.N. Garmonsway. United Kingdom: n.p., 1953.

Sturluson, Snorri. Trans. Magnus Magnusson and Hermann Palsson. *King Harald's Saga*. New York: Dorset Press, 1986.

The Bayeux Tapestry: The Complete Tapestry in Color. United Kingdom: Thames & Hudson, 2004.

The Oxford Illustrated History of the Vikings. United Kingdom: Oxford University Press, 2001.

Walker, Ian W. Harold. *The Last Anglo-Saxon King*. United Kingdom: History Press, 2011.

Whitelock, Dorothy. *The Norman Conquest, Its Setting and Impact: A Book Commemorating the Ninth Centenary of the Battle of Hastings*. United Kingdom: Scribner, 1966.

Williams, Anne and Martin, G.H., eds, *Domesday Book: A Complete Translation, Somerset*: Alecto Historical editions, 1992.

Wilson, David Mackenzie. *The Vikings and Their Origins: Scandinavia in the First Millennium*. United Kingdom: Thames and Hudson, 1972.

Wise, Terence. *1066: Year of Destiny*. Osprey, 1979.

Wood, Michael. *Domesday: A Search for the Roots of England*. United Kingdom: BBC Books, 1999.

Woolf, Alex. *Anglo-Saxon and Viking Britain*. United Kingdom: Franklin Watts, 2006.

Wright, Peter Poyntz. *The Battle of Hastings*. United Kingdom: Russell, 1986.

About the Author

Julian de la Motte was born in London. He graduated in Medieval History and Theology from SDUC Lampeter, University of Wales, and gained a postgraduate qualification in Medieval Art from the University of York. After spending three years in Italy as an English teacher he returned to the U.K. and worked as a teacher, teacher trainer, materials writer and specialist in Cross Cultural Training before becoming a Director of Foreign Language training to the U.K. corporate sector. This was followed by a career in International Sales and Marketing, involving extensive overseas business travel. *Senlac* is his first novel.

About the Publisher

The Sager Group was founded in 1984. In 2012 it was chartered as a multimedia content brand, with the intent of empowering those who create art—an umbrella beneath which makers can pursue, and profit from, their craft directly, without gatekeepers. TSG publishes books; ministers to artists and provides modest grants; and produces documentary, feature, and commercial films. By harnessing the means of production, The Sager Group helps artists help themselves. For more information, please see TheSagerGroup.net.

More Books from The Sager Group

Chains of Nobility: Brotherhood of the Mamluks (Book 1)

A Lion's Share: Brotherhood of the Mamluks (Book 2)

The Swamp: Deceit and Corruption in the CIA
An Elizabeth Petrov Thriller (Book 1)

The Living and the Dead

Three Days in Gettysburg

Vetville: True Stories of the U.S. Marines

Straight Fish: A Correctional Officer's Story

Miss Havilland: A Novel

The Orphan's Daughter: A Novel

Lifeboat No. 8: Surviving the Titanic

THE SAGER GROUP

Artifex Te Adiuva

Printed in Great Britain
by Amazon